What people are saying about

Leave It to Chance

"Leave It to Chance *is a delightful read, full of enough ups and downs to keep readers cheering for the characters and hoping for a happy ending. Watch for more great novels from Sherri Sand.*"

—LAURAINE SNELLING, BEST-SELLING AUTHOR OF *BREAKING FREE* AND THE RED RIVER OF THE NORTH SERIES

"*A delightful new voice in Christian fiction. Sherri Sand creates an artful balance of inner struggle and tenderness, warmth and whimsy.*"

—SHARON HINCK, AUTHOR OF *RENOVATING BECKY MILLER* AND *SYMPHONY OF SECRETS*

"*Sherri Sand's characters are likeable, engaging, and approachable. She has crafted a tender, romantic tale about learning to let go of fear and latch on to the love of God.*"

—SUSAN MEISSNER, AUTHOR OF *A WINDOW TO THE WORLD* AND *BLUE HEART BLESSED*

"Leave It to Chance *is a heartwarming story about a mom who has to confront her greatest fear for the sake of her kids. Congrats to Sherri Sand for an inspiring debut!*"

—MELANIE DOBSON, AUTHOR OF *TOGETHER FOR GOOD, GOING FOR BROKE,* AND *THE BLACK CLOISTER*

"A heartwarming story about a single mother trying to make it on her own against all odds. Leave It to Chance *is an excellent debut novel. The characters are so real and so well developed I felt I knew them. Sherri Sand has a way of reaching out and touching the reader's heart. Look for more from this very talented writer."*

—BARBARA WARREN, AUTHOR OF THE GATHERING STORM

"Sherri Sand writes from the heart. Her characters are ones you feel you might even know. Likable single-mother Sierra faces fears that every parent can relate to, and her spiritual journey is coupled with hope, romance, and reconciliation. This is a thoroughly enjoyable debut."

—ERIC WILSON, AUTHOR OF A SHRED OF TRUTH AND
FACING THE GIANTS

"Leave It to Chance *is a story of renewal, romance, humor, and hope. Readers will enjoy Sherri Sand's colorful characters as Sierra and her children learn to deal with their heartaches and reach for their dreams— aided by a wily old horse with a few secrets of his own."*

—KACY BARNETT-GRAMCKOW,
AUTHOR OF THE GENESIS TRILOGY

"Leave It to Chance *has it all—love and second chances wrapped in grace."*

—LINDA WINDSOR, AUTHOR OF FOR PETE'S SAKE AND
WEDDING BELL BLUES

LEAVE IT TO
Chance

❧ A NOVEL ❧

SHERRI
SAND

David C Cook®
transforming lives together

LEAVE IT TO CHANCE
Published by David C. Cook
4050 Lee Vance View
Colorado Springs, CO 80918 U.S.A.

David C. Cook Distribution Canada
55 Woodslee Avenue, Paris, Ontario, Canada N3L 3E5

David C. Cook U.K., Kingsway Communications
Eastbourne, East Sussex BN23 6NT, England

David C. Cook and the graphic circle C logo
are registered trademarks of Cook Communications Ministries.

This story is a work of fiction. All characters and events are the product of the author's
imagination. Any resemblance to any person, living or dead, is coincidental.

LCCN 2008922245
ISBN 978-1-4347-9988-3

Published in association with WordServe Literary Agency
10152 Knoll Circle, Highlands Ranch, CO 80130

The Team: Susan Tjaden, Traci DePree, Jaci Schneider, Karen Athen
Cover Design: Brand Navigation
Interior Design: The DesignWorks Group

Printed in the United States of America
First Edition 2008

1 2 3 4 5 6 7 8 9 10

022608

For Mat, who never doubted the Giver or the gift

And to my father-in-law, Art Sand,
the Sid dear to my heart

In memory of Loren Ellis Herbert (1919–2007),
who left behind a legacy of love

Thank You

To the precious jewels of my prayer team: Laura Hicks, Lorene Smith, Amanda Hvass, Jill Purcell, Brenda Leighter, Becky Edwards, Diana Thatcher, Linda Frizzell, Tammy Dorsing, Kimberly McConnell, and Stacy Skrip. This book is a direct result of their prayers and faithfulness.

Special thanks to my agent, Greg Johnson of WordServe Literary, for his belief in me.

Heartfelt appreciation goes to Susan Tjaden, who is an amazing editor to work with. All authors should be so fortunate. Her skill, friendship, and lively sense of humor made tailoring this book a complete joy.

Without the editing skills of Traci DePree, this book would not be what it is. She found the diamond buried deep beneath a mountain of coal. Thank you!

The whole team at David C. Cook who made this book possible. Thank you all!

Many thanks go to Lisa Thornburg, Wanda Dyson, Miralee Ferrell, and Traci DePree for their horse expertise.

Thanks to Master Gardener, Susan Fields, my dear aunt who loaned me her green thumb and gave wonderful advice on plant life. Any errors are my own.

Thank you to Marissa Korthuis and Debbie Korthuis for the excellent 4-H help. I couldn't have done it without you two! Any errors are my own.

Thank you to John Thornburg for helping me understand how a police officer would handle a missing-child call.

Thank you to Claudia Womack for her unemployment benefits expertise. Any fudging of the facts is my own.

Special thanks to Sharon Hinck for paving the way and holding my hand.

Much appreciation to the women of my two critique groups: Sharon Hinck, Katherine Scott Jones, Jenna Reedy, Karen Kennedy, Miralee Ferrell, Kimberly Johnson, and Teresa Morgan.

A special thanks goes to my pastors, Sean and Tan McCartin, for their love and commitment to see me fall more deeply in love with Jesus.

Thanks to my parents, Bill and Lorene Smith, and Vincent and Dolly Gwillim, for believing in me and molding me into the person I've become.

And especially to my beloved husband, who has been excited every step of the way. You are my dearest treasure and best friend. And to my precious children, Tristan, Logan, Brielle, and Kaden. You've made my life complete.

Chapter 1

"A horse? Mom, what am I going to do with a horse?" Just what she and the kids did *not* need. Sierra Montgomery sagged back against her old kitchen counter, where afternoon sunlight dappled the white metal cabinets across from her. She pressed the phone tight against her ear, hoping she'd heard wrong, as her four-year-old son, Trevor, ate grapes at the kitchen table.

"Miss Libby wanted you to have it. I'd think you'd be delighted, what with the kids and all. You remember Sally, Miss Libby's daughter? Well, she just called and said it was all laid out in the will. None of their family could figure out who Sierra Lassiter Montgomery was until Sally remembered me from her mom's church. So she called and sure enough, you were my daughter." Sierra's mom *tsked* into the phone. "Well, you know how Sally is."

Sierra hadn't the foggiest how Sally was, or even *who* she was. She barely remembered Miss Libby from her Sunday school class eons ago.

"She acted pleased that her mother gave you the horse, but I could tell she was miffed. Though what Sally Owens would do with a horse, I'd like to know." Her mom's voice was tight and controlled as if they were discussing how to deal with black spot on her Old English roses.

"But I don't want a horse. You, of all people, should know that after what happened when—" How could her mom even suggest she get a horse? Painful pictures of her childhood friend Molly floated through her mind.

"Honey, accidents like that don't happen more than once in a lifetime. Besides, Miss Libby wouldn't have owned a crazy horse."

Sierra stared out the window where the school bus would soon release her most precious treasures. Her mom never had understood the resounding impact that summer day had made in her life.

"You really need to think of the kids and how much fun they'd have. It's not like you'd ever be able to afford to buy them one."

Sierra wished she were having this conversation with Elise rather than her mother. Her best friend would understand the danger she feared in horses, and in her humorous way come up with a sensible plan that would include *not* keeping the animal.

Her mom, on the other hand, lived life as if she were on one of those moving conveyors at the airport that people can step on to rest their feet yet keep moving toward their destination. As long as everyone kept traveling forward, she could ignore the emotional baggage dragging behind.

"I don't understand why Miss Libby would give the horse to *me*."

"You know how my bingo club visited the Somerset rest home every week? Well, Miss Libby's been there for years and she always did comment on how horse crazy you were when she taught your Sunday school class."

"Mom, that was a phase I went through when I was ten and found *National Velvet* and *Black Beauty* at the library. I haven't seen Miss Libby since middle school."

"Obviously you were special to Miss Libby. I'd think you might be a little more grateful."

Deep breath, Sierra told herself. "I am grateful." An errant grape rolled next to her toe. Trevor's blond head was bent, intent on arranging the fruit like green soldiers around the edge of his plate. Sierra tossed the grape into the sink and considered how to respond to her mom. She was a dear, but sometimes the woman was like dry kindling on a hot day, and one little spark…. "I'm just not sure that owning a horse would be a wise move at this point in our lives."

The front door slammed and Sierra felt the walls shudder with the thud. The 3:00 p.m. stampede through the house meant it was time to get off the phone and determine how to get rid of a horse before the kids found out about it.

Her mom sighed. "It's too bad Sally won't keep the horse at her place for you, but she said her husband wants the horse gone. He wants to fill the pasture with sheep."

Sheep? A kitchen chair scraped over the linoleum as Trevor scooted back from the table and dashed for the living room. "Mommy's got a horse! Mommy's got a horse!" *Wonderful. Little ears, big mouth.*

Braden and Emory shot into the kitchen, bright eyes dancing in tandem. Their words tangled together in fevered excitement despite the fact that she was on the phone.

"Where is it?" Braden's eleven-year-old grin split his face, and his dark hair was rumpled and sweat streaked, likely from a fevered game of basketball during last recess.

She held a hand up to still the questions as her mom went on about the sheep that Sally's husband probably did *not* need.

"We have a horse?" Nine-year-old Emory, her blonde hair still neat in its purple headband, fluttered in front of her mom, delight and hope blooming on her face.

Despite the fear of horses building deep in Sierra's gut, her children's excitement was a little contagious. She wished Miss Libby had willed her a cat.

Sierra ran her hand down Emory's soft cheek and whispered. "I'll be off the phone in a minute, sweetie."

"Can we ride it?" Em looked at her with elated eyes.

Braden tossed his backpack on the table. "Where are we going to keep it?"

The kids circled her, jabbering with excited questions. Sierra rubbed her forehead with the tips of her fingers. "I gotta go, Mom. I've got to break some cowboy hearts."

The kids clamored around her, Braden taking the lead with an arm draped across her shoulder. When had he gotten so big? "Do we have a horse, Mom?" He asked the question with a lopsided grin, a foreshadow of the adolescence that had been peeking through lately. The preteen in him didn't truly believe they had a horse—he was old enough to realize the odds—but little-boy eagerness clung to his smile.

"That would be yes and a no."

"What? Mom!" he complained.

"I was given a horse, but we're not going to keep him."

Braden's arm slid off her shoulder, a scowl replacing his smile. "Why not?"

"Someone gave you a horse?" Emory ignored her brother's attitude and flashed her most persuasive grin. "Can we keep him? Please!"

Sierra smoothed her hand over the silky hair and leaned close to her daughter's face as Emory went on. "I think we should get four horses so we each have one. We could go trail riding. Cameron's mom has horses, and they go riding all the time as a family."

"We're not a *family* anymore," Braden cut in. "We stopped being a family when mom divorced dad."

A shard of pain drove into Sierra's gut. She hadn't had time to brace for that one. Braden's anger at the divorce had been building like an old steam engine lately.

"That's not fair!" Outrage darkened Emory's features. "It's not Mom's fault!"

Sarcasm colored Braden's voice. "Oh, so it's all Dad's fault?"

Sierra saw the confusion that swept over her daughter's face. She was fiercely loyal to both parents and didn't know how to defend them against each other.

Sierra spoke in a firm tone. "Braden, that's enough!"

He scowled at her again. "Whatever."

Sierra held his gaze until he glanced away.

"Guys, we're not going to play the blame game. We have plenty to be thankful for, and that's what is important."

Braden's attitude kept pouring it on. "Boy, and we have so much. Spaghetti for dinner every other night."

"So what, *Braden-Maden!*" Emory made a face and stuck her tongue out at him.

"No more fighting or you two can go to your rooms." Her kids were not perfect, but they used to like each other. Something had changed. Her gut said it was her ex-husband, Michael, but what if she was falling into the whole "blame the dad" thing herself? What if she was really the problem? Two weeks without a job had added stress and worry. Had she stopped hugging them as often in between scouring the want ads and trying to manage a home and bills?

"Mom?" There was a quaver in Trevor's soft voice.

"Yes, honey?" Sierra gave him a gentle smile.

"Can we keep the horse?"

Emory's blue gaze darted to meet hers, a plea in them. Braden sat with his arms crossed over his chest, but his ears had pricked up.

Sierra looked at them, wanting them to understand and knowing they wouldn't. "None of us know how to handle or care for a horse, so it wouldn't be safe to keep him."

Emory's face lit up. "Cameron's mom could teach us."

"Honey, it's not that simple. We can't afford an animal that big. He probably eats as much in groceries as we do, and it would be very expensive to rent a place for him to live."

"I could mow yards." Anger at his sister forgotten, Braden turned a hopeful face to her. "We could help out."

Emory jumped onto the working bandwagon. "Yeah. I could do laundry or something for the neighbors."

Braden drilled his sister a look that said *idiot idea* but didn't say anything.

Trevor bounced in his chair, eager to be a part of keeping the horse. "I could wash cars."

"Those are great ideas, but they won't bring in quite enough, especially since it's getting too cold to mow lawns or wash cars."

"You just don't want to keep the horse, Mom," Braden said. "I get it. End of story."

"Honey, I'd love for you to have a horse, but when I was young I had a friend—"

Emory spoke in a helpful tone. "We know. Grandma told us about the accident."

They knew? Wasn't the story hers to share? "When did Grandma tell you?"

Braden's voice took on a breezy air. "I don't know. A while ago. Come on, Mom. We're not going to do something dumb like your friend did."

Defensiveness rose inside. "She didn't do anything *dumb*. It was the horse that—"

"So because something bad happened to one person, your kids can never do anything fun for the rest of their lives."

Sierra gave him a look. "Or you learn from your mistakes and help your kids to do the same."

Braden rolled his eyes at her.

Worry drew lines across her daughter's forehead. "Are you going to sell him?"

"Yes, Em. So we're not going to discuss this anymore. You and Braden have homework to do." At the chorus of groans she held her hands up. "Okay, I guess I'll have to eat Grandma's apple pie all by myself."

Braden grabbed his backpack and slowly dragged it across the floor toward the stairs, annoyance in his voice. "We're going." Emory trotted past him up the stairs.

Trevor remained behind, one arm wrapped around her thigh. "I don't have any homework."

She squatted and pulled him in for a hug. "Nope, you sure don't, bud."

He leaned back. "Do I get a horse?"

Sierra distracted him by inching her fingers up his ribs. "What, Trev?"

He tried to talk around his giggles. "Do I get—Mom!" Her fingers found the tickle spots under his arms and he laughed, his eyes squinted shut and mouth opened wide. She found all his giggle spots, then turned on *Sesame Street* as the second distraction. Good old Bert and Ernie.

Now what? She had roughly forty-five minutes to figure out how she was going to get rid of a horse and not be a complete zero in her kids' eyes.

She eyed the phone and made her next move. Five minutes later a white Mazda whipped into her driveway. Sierra hurried out the front door waving her arms to stop Elise before she could start her ritual honking for the kids.

Wide eyed, her platinum blonde friend stared, one long plum-colored nail hovering above the "ooga" horn on the dash. "What?"

"I don't want the kids to know you're here."

Wicked delight spread across her perfectly made-up face. Light plum shadow matched her nails. Tomorrow, both eye shadow and nails could be green. "Let me guess! Mr. Pellum asked you out!"

"Nooooo!" Mr. Pellum was a teacher Sierra and Elise had had a crush on in seventh grade.

"Ummm … you robbed a bank and need me to watch the kids while you fly to Tahiti?"

Sierra gave her a mock-serious look. "Done?"

Elise tilted her head. "Can I get out of the car?"

Sierra glanced toward the house. All was still silent. "Yes, you may."

Deadpan, Elise nodded and opened the door. "Then I'm done for now." Her plump body, swathed in a creamy suit with a purple scarf draped across one shoulder, rose gracefully from the small two-seater.

Sierra closed the door for her, then leaned against it. Elise had a way of removing the extraneous and reducing a problem down to the bare essentials. "Elise, I'm in a predicament."

"Hon, I've been trying to tell you that for years."

Sierra shook her head. "I don't think you could have seen this one coming even with your crystal ball."

Elise gave her the *spinster teacher* look through narrowed eyes. "I don't think I like the implications of that."

Sierra held her hands out. "You are the queen of mind-reading, according to my children."

Elise chuckled. "It's a good thing I was just headed out for a latte break when you called. Now what's the big emergency?" She owned a high-end clothing store for plus-sized women in downtown Eugene.

"A horse."

Elise glanced around as if one or two might be lurking behind a tree.

"A herd of them or just one?"

"One. Full-sized. Living and breathing."

"I believe I'm missing some pieces here. Is it moving in with you? Holding one of the children hostage? What?"

Sierra breathed out a slight chuckle and tucked a stray hair behind her ear. "You're not going to believe this, but I inherited it."

Her friend's eyes grew wide, emphasizing the lushly mascaraed lashes. "Like someone died and gave you their horse?"

Sierra nodded, raising her brows. "And the kids want to keep him."

Furrows emerged across Elise's forehead. "Who is the idiot that told them about the horse?"

Sierra tilted her head with a look that only best friends could give each other.

Elise's perfectly painted lips smirked. "Moving along, then. Why don't you keep it? The kids would love it. Heaven knows they deserve it." She clapped her hands together. "Oh, oh! They could get into 4-H, and Braden could learn to barrel race. That kid would think he'd won the jackpot. Emory and Trevor could get a pig or some of those show roosters."

Sierra let the idea machine wind down. "I don't think so."

"Angora rabbits?"

"No farm animals."

Elise's mouth perked into humorous pout. "Sierra, you're such a spoilsport. Those kids need a pet."

"A hamster is a pet. A horse is not."

Diva Elise took the stage, hands on her ample hips. "Don't tell me you didn't want a horse growing up. Remember, I was the one who had to sit and watch *National Velvet* with you time ad nauseam. You've said yourself that Braden needs something to take his mind off the problems he's having at school and with his dad."

Guilt, a wheelbarrow load of it, dumped on Sierra. "You are supposed to be helping me, Elise, not making it worse. I want to get rid of this horse and ..." her eyes dodged away from her friend, "... you know."

"Mmm-hmm. And still look like Super Mom in your children's eyes."

Sierra nodded, but couldn't find the nerve to say *yes*.

"Sierra Montgomery, those children have been to heck and back in the last couple years and you're willing to deny them the pleasure of owning their own *free* horse because ... because of what?"

Sierra stared at the ground for a moment, feeling a tangle of emotions rise within. She let her eyes rest on Elise's and said quietly, "Fear? Terror? Hysteria?"

A look of puzzlement, then understanding settled on Elise's face, smoothing away the annoyance. "Molly."

Sierra nodded. "I won't put my children in that kind of danger."

Elise leaned forward and grabbed Sierra's hands, holding them tight. "Oh, hon. That was a long time ago. Don't let your life be ruled by the what-ifs. There's a lot of living left to do. And your kids need to see you taking life by storm, taking chances, not hiding in the shadows."

"That's easy for you to say. You were voted most likely to parachute off the Empire State Building."

Elise gave her a cheeky grin, both dimples winking at her. "We could do it tandem!"

"If you see me jump off the Empire State Building you'll know my lobotomy was successful, because there is no way in this lifetime you'll catch this body leaving good sense behind!" Sierra heard the words come from her own mouth and stared at her friend in wonder. "Oh, my gosh. That was so my mom."

"It was bound to happen, hon."

Was she serious? "You think I'm turning into her?" Sierra brought a hand to her throat and quickly dropped it. How many times had she seen her mom use the same gesture?

Elise laughed. "You need to stop fretting and just *live*. We all turn out like our mothers in some respect."

"All except you. You're nothing like Vivian."

"Other than the drinking, smoking, and carousing, I'm exactly like her."

Sierra lifted a brow. Her mom had rarely let her go to Elise's house when they were growing up—and for good reason.

Elise struck a pose like a fashion model. "Okay, I'm the anti-Vivian." She gave Sierra a soft smile. "All funnin' aside, I really think you should keep the horse."

"I'm not keeping the horse. And even if I wanted to, I couldn't." Sierra took a settling breath and stared at the tree over Elise's shoulder.

"Michael still hasn't paid?"

Elise knew more about her finances than her mom did. "He paid, but the check bounced again. So now he's two months behind in child support."

"Have you heard if Pollan's is rehiring?"

"They're not." Jarrett's, the local grocery store where she worked for the three years since the divorce had been recently bought out by Pollan's. They had laid off the majority of the checkers with the possibility of rehiring some.

Elise cringed as if she was bracing herself for a blow. "And the unemployment fiasco?"

Sierra shut her eyes. "Mr. Jarrett did not pay into our unemployment insurance, so there is no benefit for us to draw from. Yes, it was illegal, and yes he will pay, but it may take months, if not years, for various lawyers and judges to beat it out of him." She gave Elise a tired smile. "That's the version minus all the legalese."

"So the layoffs are final, no unemployment bennies, and you're out of a job."

"Momentarily. The résumé has been dusted off and polished." She gave a wry grin.

"I wish I could hire you at Deluxe Couture, but I promised Nora full-time work. And besides, your cute little buns would drive my clientele away."

Sierra waved a hand over her jeans and sweatshirt. "Your clientele would outshine me any day."

"You sell yourself far too short." Elise glanced at the hefty rhinestone-encrusted watch on her wrist. "Anything else I can do for you? Help the kids with their homework? Babysit while you sweep some tall, dark, handsome man off his feet?"

Sierra laughed. "And where is this dream man going to come from?"

Elise gave a breezy wave of her hand and opened the car door. "Oh, he'll turn up. You're too cute to stay single. I actually have someone in mind. Pavo Marcello. He's a new sales rep from one of my favorite lines. I'll see if he's free Friday night. You aren't doing anything, are you?"

"Hold on!" Sierra stepped in front of the car door to keep her friend from leaving. "First, I'm not looking. Second, given my history, I'm not the best judge of character. I've already struck out once in the man department." She pointed to her face with both index fingers. "Not anxious to try again. Third, you just told me I'm turning into my mom, which makes me definitely not dating material."

A twist of Elise's lips signaled a thought. "You know, now that I think about it, I believe he has a boyfriend." She shook her head and lowered herself into the car. "We'll keep looking. I'm sure Sir Knight will turn up."

Sierra shut the car door and grinned down at her friend. "And what about finding *your* knight?"

Elise gave her a bright smile. "Mr. Pellum is already taken. You really need to find a way to keep that horse; it'll be your first noble sacrifice."

"First?"

The little car backed up, and Elise spoke over the windshield. "The others don't count."

Sierra stared at the retreating car. There was no way she was keeping that horse.

After dinner, Sierra crept into Braden's room. He sat on the bed intent on the Game Boy in his lap, the tinny sound of hard rock bleeding out of his earphones. She waved a hand and he glanced up. She waited and with a look of preteen exasperation he finally pulled the headphones to his shoulders.

"What, Mom?"

"I just wanted to say good night."

"Good night." His hands started to readjust the music back into position.

"I looked at your homework."

"You got into my backpack? Isn't that like against the law or something? You're always telling us not to get into *your* stuff."

She crossed her arms. Frustration and worry gnawed at her. "You lied to me about doing your assignment. Why, honey?"

He ignored her and started playing his Game Boy.

She took one step and snatched the game from his hands.

"Hey!"

"I want some respect when I talk to you, Braden."

His chin sank toward his chest, his gaze fixed on his bed, his voice low. "I didn't want to do it."

She sat next to him, her voice soft. "Is it too hard?"

He shrugged. "It gives me a headache when I work on it."

"Braden, if you need help, I'd be happy to work with you after school."

He stared at his knees and picked at a loose string of cotton on his pajama bottoms.

"I got a phone call from Mrs. Hamison today."

His body came alert, though he didn't look at her.

"She said you're flunking most of your subjects, and she hasn't seen any homework from you since school started a month ago."

He glanced up, his jaw belligerent, but with fear in his eyes.

"What's going on? I know school isn't easy, but you've never given up before."

"Middle school's harder."

She wanted to touch him, to brush the hair off his forehead and snuggle him close the way she used to when he was small. Back when a hug and a treat shared over the kitchen table was enough to bring the sparkle back to her son. "She thinks we should have your vision tested."

"Why?"

"She's noticed some things in class and thinks it might be helpful."

He shrugged again. "Can I have my game back?"

"You lied to me, son. Again."

"*Sor*-ry."

"You break trust every time you choose to be dishonest. Is that what you want?"

His voice was sullen and he stared at his comforter. "No."

She touched his leg. "What's bothering you, honey?"

"I dunno. Can I have my game back?"

She stood up. There was a time for talking and this obviously wasn't it. "You can have it tomorrow."

But would tomorrow be any different?

Chapter 2

After kissing Emory and Trevor good night, Sierra wandered back downstairs for a glass of water before getting ready for bed. She was glad for the quiet. She set the empty glass on the counter when the phone rang.

"Hello?"

"So how'd it go? Were they thrilled?"

"Elise, I'm not keeping the horse."

A patient sigh sounded through the line. "I wish you could just let go and let God."

"Elise …" Her friend made it sound like she could just sashay into some grand dance with God.

"I know, I know. Not a topic for friendly discussion."

Sierra stayed firm. "Not if you want to *remain* friends."

"I just wish you and God would get back on speaking terms."

"It's not a simple matter of speaking to Him; it's about trust. You know, a God who showed that He cared through hard times would've come in handy."

"Okay, so moving along."

Sierra smiled.

"So what'd you tell the kids?"

"Before or after they got into a fight about whose fault the divorce was?"

"Oh, hon, it has been a day!" A significant pause. "Will you ever tell them why he left?"

"No, you know that." Sierra sank into a kitchen chair. "Braden has gotten so angry with me, always ready to defend his dad to the death. And I work so hard not to say anything negative about the man."

"Hon, do you think Michael or Gina talk to him about you?"

"I don't know. I have no control over what they tell the kids, and I'd drive myself crazy trying to go there."

"You're right, of course." Elise's voice took on a delicious tone. "But wouldn't it give you some satisfaction to tell the kids what a two-timing louse he really is?"

Sierra forced a laugh. "And it would help them to know their dad abandoned them to marry the dental hygienist who worked for him after hours?"

"Mmm, I see your point," Elise mused. "I wonder what the policy is for nominating someone to sainthood. Saint Sierra has a quaint ring to it."

That brought a genuine laugh to Sierra's throat. "You are something else, you know?"

"Have you changed your mind about the horse?"

"No!"

"What if room and board was a gift from Aunty Elise?"

"It would probably be the last gift Aunty Elise was able to give."

"Hmm. Better make it anonymous."

"I'm going to bed."

Friday afternoon, Sierra set the plate of crackers with sliced cheese on the table.

Trevor gazed up at her. "Can I have an apple?"

"We're out of apples, sweetie. Hurry up, your dad's going to be here in a few minutes."

Emory rushed into the room and grabbed a cracker. "Did you wash my blanket today?"

On her way to the counter, Sierra stroked a hand across Em's shoulders. "Yep, it's in the dryer. Is Braden upstairs?"

A relieved smile washed over her daughter's face. "Thanks! He's in his room packing." She rushed past the sink to the little alcove that housed the washer and dryer. She might have been nine, but her special "blankie" still went on overnighters with her.

Sierra hollered up the stairs. "Come on, Braden. There's a snack on the table."

Emory hurried back and stuffed the blanket into her backpack. "Is Dad here yet?"

"I haven't heard a honk."

Braden sauntered down the stairs, his overnight bag draped over his shoulder. He stopped at the table and stuffed several crackers into his mouth. "Bye." Puffs of cracker dust spewed out with the word. He gave them a wide, crumb-filled grin and headed for the front door.

Emory made a face at her mom. "That was disgusting."

Sierra grinned. "No, that was *boys!*"

Her daughter laughed, grabbed her bag, and gave her a big hug. "I'll miss you."

Sierra kissed the tip of the sweet nose. "I'll miss you, too, pumpkin, but I bet you'll have a good time."

A shadow of guilt crossed her daughter's face as if it were somehow wrong to have fun at her dad's.

"I *want* you to have a good time." Sierra rocked her daughter back and forth in a tight hug. "Got it, girl?"

Em giggled and looked up at her with a smile. "Got it!"

Sierra gave Trevor his overnight bag and followed him and Emory out the front door.

Braden gave her a funny look. "What are you doing out here?"

"I need to talk to your dad."

Defensiveness crossed his face. "Why?"

"I just need to talk to him."

Emory chimed in. "He won't call her back."

At Sierra's look, Emory explained, "I heard you talking to Elise."

A few minutes later the black Lexus pulled into their gravel driveway. The redhead in the passenger seat didn't even turn to look at them. The woman never did.

Sierra followed the kids off the porch, but sandy-haired Michael, dressed in an expensive charcoal suit, jumped out of the car. That was a first. He herded their bewildered children back toward the house. "I'm not going to be able to take the kids this weekend."

"What?" An outraged Braden, who hung close to the car, dropped his backpack to the ground.

Michael gave him a sharp look, then turned back to her. "Gina and I are headed out of town, and Emory borrowed my iPod." He turned to their daughter. "Em, I'm in a hurry, could you get it for me?"

Em darted back to the house.

Sierra crossed her arms. "It's the kids' weekend to be with you. They've been looking forward to it."

"Don't lay a guilt trip on me! Things come up."

"You've canceled the last three weekends."

"Geez, Sierra. I don't work my tail off to make a better life for my kids just to have you breathing down my neck."

Trevor moved close and wrapped an arm around her thigh.

Michael directed a stern look at their youngest. "Take your thumb out of your mouth, Trevor. Big boys don't suck their thumbs."

Trevor immediately pulled his thumb out and wiped it on his pants. Sierra laid an arm across his small shoulders. She kept her voice low and calm. "We need to talk."

Gina's voice floated across the small yard. "We're going to be late, Michael."

Sierra ignored the interruption. "When can I get a check? I can't feed or house our children without some help."

Gina's voice came again. "Michael."

Emory ran back out of the house and handed her dad the iPod.

Sierra glanced at the car, then back to her ex-husband. "Where are you going that you can't take the kids?"

His eyes shifted from her to the porch railing. "I have a business meeting."

Sierra couldn't contain the edge to her voice. "On a Friday night?"

Gina's voice grew urgent. "We only have thirty minutes to make the flight, sweetheart. We need to go right now."

He barked toward the car, "I know!"

Gina's window zipped up, and the woman faced the garage once again.

Sierra clenched her fists, but kept her voice low. "You're flying somewhere, yet you can't pay their child support?"

"It's a dental conference, okay?"

Right. Michael hated conferences. "When will I get a check?"

Annoyance hissed out with his next words. "My bookkeeper messed up. You'll get it next week."

"It's been two months. I need it tomorrow."

"Next week, okay? I gotta go." He shoved his hands into his pockets, then paused as their youngest caught his eye. "Trevor, I said, take your thumb out of your mouth!" And he was gone. No hugs for the kids, no reassuring "I'll call you guys when I get there," or "I'll see you in a few days." Just taillights fading in the distance.

Emory started to cry. Her hands hung limp at her side, misery in the slump of her shoulders. Trevor automatically raised his thumb to his mouth, then jerked it back down. And Braden … Braden was nowhere to be seen.

Sierra went to her daughter and tried to wrap her arms around the sobbing girl, but Emory stiffened, then jerked away and ran into the house.

"Mom?" Trevor's sad face looked up at her. "Why didn't Dad take us?"

She picked him up. How to be honest and yet try to keep their relationship with their dad intact? "Oh, honey, Daddy had a meeting. I'm so sorry."

"I want to go with him."

Sierra rubbed his back, anger and sadness for her children a physical ache in her heart. "I know you do, sweetie. I know."

A staccato noise sounded in the backyard.

Holding Trevor, she followed the intermittent clatter toward the open gate at the rear of the house. Braden stood in the middle of the backyard near the gravel walkway, pelting the wood fence with rocks.

"I'm so sorry, Braden. Your dad—"

"Shut up!" Another angry handful of gravel scattered across the boards.

Trevor wiggled down. "I want to go in the house."

"Okay. I'll be in soon." Trevor disappeared through the patio door into the house. Sierra walked toward her eldest. "Braden, I—"

He turned to glare at her. "Go away!"

Sierra stopped several feet from him. "Honey, I can't—"

"I hate you both!" His face contorted with anger, but there were tears in his eyes.

"I'm sorry."

He ran past her into the house, and the heavy boom of music pounded from his room the rest of the evening.

Monday morning Sierra loaded the last of the breakfast bowls into the dishwasher and shut the door. Thoughts on how to help her children, especially Braden, had spun through her mind all weekend. Her son was slipping away and becoming another person. One who was angry and at times hateful.

The doorbell rang and Trevor ran to answer it. "Grandma!"

The spunky woman, with short gray hair and round glasses, rained grandma kisses on his cheeks. "How's my favorite Trevor boy?"

"Grandma, did you know we got a horse?"

Sierra gave her mom a subtle shake of her head.

"I did hear that. Have you gone to see it yet?" Her mom sent her a mischievous look. Sierra rolled her eyes and mouthed, "Thanks a lot." She grabbed her jacket, the yellow folder stacked with crisp résumés in it, and the list of businesses she planned to approach. "I'll be back in a few hours."

"Wait a sec." Her mom moved around Trevor to set her purse on the back of the couch. She rummaged in the roomy bag for a moment, then handed Sierra a folded section of newspaper with a notepad clipped to the front. "I went through the want ads yesterday and highlighted a few things I think you should apply for. The addresses are there on that piece of paper."

Sierra took the papers. Her mom meant well. "Thanks, Mom, but I already—"

Her mom moved in next to her and started down the list. "I think you should try Harlow's Nursery first. It's closest to the house and the hours look decent. I called this morning and they haven't hired anyone yet."

Sierra clutched the paper. "Did you tell them I was coming?"

Her mom grinned with delight. "Of course."

What kind of impression would they have of a woman whose mom calls about a job for her? She forced a smile. "Thanks. I'll see you two later."

Her mom grabbed her arm and lowered her voice to a sober whisper. "What have you decided about the horse?"

Sierra whispered back. "We're not keeping it."

"But, honey, I talked to Kyle Olsen at church Sunday and his cousin Ross has acres of pasture just going to waste. I'm sure we could talk to him."

Sierra rounded her lips in a very deliberate "No." She smiled to soften the words. "I'm not budging on this one."

Chapter 3

Midafternoon Sierra pushed the glass door open and hurried through the drizzle to her van. She plopped down in her seat and pumped her fist. "Yes! Mission accomplished!" With a flourish, she tossed the empty folder on the passenger seat and started the car. Natalie Grant's beautiful voice drifted through the speakers. "I like you, Natalie, but you're just a little too tame today." She pressed a button and dc Talk's "Jesus Is Just Alright," jetted into the car. "That's more like it!"

She dialed Elise.

"Yessss, darling?"

Sierra glanced up the street, then turned out of the parking lot and toward home. "You may be speaking to the new associate manager for Garland Treasures."

Her friend squealed. "I *love* that store!"

"*And* they have full benefits. I should hear back tomorrow."

"So, who cares if Michael pays!"

Sierra laughed. "Well, I'm not *quite* there, but I'll give you points for optimism."

"I'm sure he'll pay." Her voice came out low and gravelly. "One way or another."

Sierra made a face. "Nice hit-man voice."

"I try."

Sierra's house came into view. "Oh, crud."

"What?"

"There's a repair van in my driveway." Sierra tried to read the logo, but a tree near the street obscured her view. She slowed and turned into her drive, squeezing into the space next to the large white vehicle.

"At least it's not a fire truck." Elise continued to spread her joy. "Or an ambulance."

"Let's not go there."

Sierra's phone beeped. "I'm getting another call."

"You get 'em girl!"

Sierra stared at the side of the white van. The bold logo was attention grabbing at least. "Black Knight Plumbing Service—We'll do your dirty work." *Wonderful.*

She pressed a button on her phone. "Hello?"

"Sierra? This is Ron Flannery. October's rent was due ten days ago. When can we expect payment?"

Sierra paused, at a loss. "I called on the first of the month, Mr. Flannery, and spoke with your wife." She glanced around the front seat, trying to gather a coherent thought. "I'm sorry, I thought—"

"Madge didn't tell me you called." He hollered to the background. "Madge, did Sierra Montgomery call about the rent?" Whatever Madge said seemed to annoy him; he huffed into the phone. "Next time, call me; I take care of the rentals."

"I'll be happy to. I didn't realize Mrs.—"

"Will you be paying the rent? Because we have an applicant who needs housing immediately."

She had a sense that the sympathy Mrs. Flannery had showered on her two weeks ago wouldn't be forthcoming from her husband. "I lost my job and my ex—"

A disgruntled sigh sounded in her ear. "That is unfortunate, but if I don't have the rent by Wednesday, I'll have to evict you."

The words were like a dousing of cold water. "All right. I'll do my best."

"Fine."

Sierra leaned back against the headrest and stared at the white van. Almost immediately, the phone rang again. She checked the screen. Same number. A sense of hope rose.

"Hello?"

"Sierra?" It was Madge speaking in an urgent whisper. "I'm so sorry, dear. I thought Ron wouldn't mind if you stayed a month or two until you got back on your feet, but I didn't know our grandson, Ronnie, would need the house."

Ah. "That's okay, Madge. I understand."

"Stay in touch, dear."

Sierra smiled, imagining the woman hunkered in a corner of her kitchen, nervously listening for Mr. Flannery's footsteps. "I will. Bye."

Apparently it was her lucky week. A horse she couldn't keep, her kids reeling emotionally, a plumbing issue, and now the threat of eviction. *But* she might have a job! Maybe Mr. Flannery would let her stay until her first paycheck.

Sierra found her mom and youngest son in the upstairs bathroom, crouched behind a plumber who was intent on winding a cable down into the toilet. *Ick!*

"Hi. What happened?"

Her mom started, but the plumber barely gave her a glance. Two little crow's-feet made perfect indentations between her mother's brows. They'd been there forever, even in Sierra's baby pictures. Today the furrows burrowed a few millimeters deeper. "Trevor flushed a ball down the toilet."

Sierra raised her eyebrows at her four-year-old. "You did, Trevor?"

His blond head nodded sadly. "I thought it would float."

Sierra squished through the wet towels covering the vinyl floor and wrinkled her nose. Those would need a lot of bleach. She held her arms out. "Come here."

Trevor burrowed his face against her neck when she picked him up, his body tense. She carried him out to the hall.

He raised his head. "Grandma got mad."

"She did?"

He nodded. "She said, 'That was naughty!'"

"I'm sorry, sweetie. Grown-ups get angry sometimes."

"I wanted you to come home."

She kissed him. "I'm here now."

"Got it." The male voice rang with satisfaction.

She set Trevor down and peeked into the bathroom. The toilet gurgled as the man wound the cable free.

"You know which ball it was, don't you?" The crow's-feet made an intense "V" above her mother's nose. "Montgomery Dental Office." The words were said with a flourish, as if Michael had planned on having their son plug up her toilet with one of his dental giveaway toys.

"Figures." Today nothing would surprise her.

"Call him, honey. You shouldn't have to pay for this."

The absurdity of her mom's comment struck her, but she tried not to let it show. "Michael didn't put the ball in the toilet, Mom."

Her mom's eyes snapped fire. "No, but he gave it to Trevor."

"I need to pay the plumber."

Her mom's thin lips tightened, tension bristling in her frame. Then her shoulders dropped. "I'll clean up here."

Sierra gave her a quick smile of thanks and headed downstairs for her purse. The plumber finished scribbling on the form clamped to a metal clipboard, ripped off the top copy, and gave it to her.

A fine bead of perspiration broke out across her forehead. She wrote the amount in her register and did a quick tally before writing the check. Michael had better get her a check, one that actually had funds to back it up.

Her fingers were loath to let go. The plumber gave her a funny look as he tugged the check out of her hand.

When Sierra walked back into the kitchen, her mom emerged from behind the louvered doors that housed the washer and dryer. As the rumble of the washer gyrated into action, her mom washed her hands at the sink using brisk motions and a healthy squirt of antibacterial soap, rubbing the towel with meticulous precision into the crevasses between each finger, then turned toward her.

Sierra knew that look.

"Honey, I came across something I think we need to discuss."

"Oh?" Sierra swiveled toward the fridge to pull the last package of hamburger from the freezer and popped it into the microwave. It bought her a few moments.

"I found this behind the flour canister."

Sierra knew exactly what she'd found. She'd stuck it in the cupboard behind the flour when Braden had come into the kitchen a few days ago and she'd forgotten to retrieve it.

Her mother waved the small piece of paper.

Sierra squinted. Yep, it was the check. The one that had been stamped repeatedly in black and red. Sierra nodded and walked to the cupboard. "Michael's check."

The ridges in her mother's forehead deepened. "You don't sound the least bit concerned, Sierra. This is getting ridiculous. How will you pay rent? Feed the children something besides …" She eyed the box in Sierra's hand with a grimace of distaste "… Hamburger Lickins?"

Sierra set the package of cheesy enchilada next to the stove. She'd been chewing her fingernails for days over the same questions herself, but discussing them when her mom had her cannons loaded would only feed the feral headache she felt coming on. "Wednesday is Emory's night to pick dinner." She hefted the box. "Hence the Lickins."

Her mother peered into the same cupboard Sierra had pulled the box from. "Letting a nine-year-old choose the menu isn't the wisest decision, sweetheart. You can't expect a child to understand that the nitrates and sodium in those boxed meals will eventually kill you. *Oprah* just had a segment on the damage that occurs at the cellular level when you fill your body with nitrates." She pinched her bottom lip in thought. "Or was it *The View?*" She waved her hand. "Not that it matters. Boxed meals are toxic."

Sierra smushed the raw burger into edible bites and gave in to the impulse to roll her eyes. Her mom and her penchant for touting the latest talk-show headline.

"I think you and the children should move back home."

"What?" The spatula clattered against the side of the pan, swiping a large chunk of burger onto the floor. "Back home? With you?" Sierra stared at her mom. Then she thought about the phone call from her landlord, and her stomach turned over. She retrieved the spatula with numb hands.

"Really, sweetie, you need to be more careful." Her mother calmly moved to the sink for a paper towel, ripped off a couple of squares then bent to the floor, her movements efficient and controlled as she mopped up the meat. "Of course *with me*. Surely you can see that this is too much for one person to handle. You don't have time to clean. You barely have enough decent food for the kids. I think the Lord is trying to tell you that you need help." She dropped the wad into the trash under the sink and poked the few bottles standing like sentinels next to the garbage can. "Where do you keep the bleach? With Trevor still sucking his thumb, you need to think about these things. That's all you need is to be worrying about a kidney transplant."

A kidney transplant? "What are you talking about?"

Her mother turned in exasperation. "E. coli, honey." She sprayed some Lysol on the floor and wiped it up. "If he ran one of his Matchbox cars over that spot then sucked his thumb? The least of your problems would be Michael's check bouncing."

Sierra dearly loved her mother, but there was a reason children grew up and moved *out* of the family home. If she moved home, one of them would be dead within the week, and it wouldn't be from E. coli. Her gaze roamed over the scattering of Cheerios that lurked under the edge of the stove. Better not to tell her that Trevor had stuck his hand on a raw chicken thigh last week then popped a finger in his mouth to taste.

Sierra hoped her smile showed how much she valued her mom's desire to help them. "I appreciate the offer, but I think we'd do better living in our own houses."

Hurt crossed her mom's face. "If you say so. It's your life." She washed her hands with fervor again, shaking them over the sink before grabbing a towel. "I'm just concerned that you're not looking at this rationally."

And *that's* why they couldn't live together. Her mom's "concerns" and germ phobias would drive Sierra insane within weeks. She shuddered.

"Are you cold, dear? I thought it was chilly in here." Abbey rubbed her arms. "One more thing you wouldn't need to worry about. My thermostat is set to 72 degrees."

"Things are tight at the moment." *That was an understatement.* "But I may have gotten a job today." *Please, God!* Not that she ever prayed anymore. But desperate measures and all that.

Her mom whirled from wiping down the counter, anticipation in the widening of her eyes. "Harlow's Nursery?"

"No, Garland Treasures."

The edges of her mouth flattened out. "What did Harlow's have to say?"

Sierra turned down the sizzling meat. "Nothing. I just dropped off my résumé."

A disgruntled frown formed on pinched lips. "Garland's refused to donate to the ladies' banquet auction last year."

"Well, if I'm hired …" She leaned toward her mom with a grin. "As associate *manager*, I'll be happy to donate something."

Her mom allowed a small smile. "That would be nice, honey." She rested a finger on Michael's deficient check and scooted it to the edge of the counter. "What are you going to do about this?"

Sierra stared at the check. If she didn't get a chunk of the funds Michael owed them, she and the kids would be packing their lives into boxes with nowhere to go … except her mom's. One more upheaval for them to deal with. Shoulders set, she grabbed the check and headed for the door. "I'm going to take care of it." Shrugging into her coat, she turned back. "Do you mind staying?"

Her mom crossed her arms with a satisfied look. "Oh, no. I'll take care of dinner. Give him a kick in the pants for me."

"Mother!" Sierra couldn't help but laugh as she picked up her purse.

"Oh, and I left a message for Sally to call me back with some details so I can place the ad about the horse. Just let the machine get the phone."

Her mom waved her off. "I'll handle it."

Braden hopped off the bus and stood on the sidewalk, waving back to Emmett Peterson behind the darkened window as the yellow bus rumbled away from his stop.

Emmett had loaned him a new CD by DeathTrain. It was buried in his backpack, beneath the sandwich he hadn't eaten. He hated crunchy peanut butter.

Emory ran past him toward the house. "Grandma's here!"

Braden kicked a rock off the sidewalk into the grass. His dad had told him not to do that. It could damage the lawn mower.

He walked into the house and dropped his backpack on the couch, then went over to the kitchen table and helped himself to the cookies that Emory and Trevor had already gotten into.

"Hi, Braden. Did you have a good day?"

The cookie was warm and still gooey in the middle. His grandma always put in extra chocolate chips. He shrugged. "It was okay. These are good."

She patted him on the head as she set a plate and a glass of milk in front of him.

The phone rang, and Grandma answered it. He reached for the same cookie as Emory and got to it first. She glared as he stuffed it in his mouth in one bite.

"Oh, hi, Sally. This is Abbey Lassiter, Sierra's mom. You called me for Sierra's number, remember?" Then his grandma laughed.

He took a drink of milk.

"Yes, Sierra told me she called you about the horse. Is there any chance we could go see him today?"

Braden looked at Emory. She grinned back at him. They high-fived. "Yes!"

"What?" Trevor looked at them. "Why'd you guys do that?"

Braden whispered. "We're going to see the horse."

Sierra stormed out of Michael's office and through the parking lot, her thumb pressing the *speed dial* number on her cell before she'd even unlocked the car door.

Elise answered on the second ring.

Sierra threw her purse into the passenger seat and shoved the key into the ignition. "He's in the Bahamas." The car idled while she shrugged out of her coat, transferring the phone to the other ear. "Michael can't pay his child support, but he can fly to a seminar in the tropics." And she was sure there was a dental seminar there. It made a great tax write-off. Whether Michael actually attended the sessions was between him and the IRS.

"He didn't!" Elise said.

"He did. And I lied to his bookkeeper. I told her I needed his hotel address for the kids. I *hate* dishonesty." Sierra dug between the seats to find the hands-free ear bud. "I wanted to know where he was, and the words just flowed out easy as you please. I was smug about it, Elise.

Smug." She latched her seat belt and eased the van out of the parking lot into traffic.

"How far the smug have fallen."

"Don't laugh. I'm serious. This is like a major character defect. How can I teach my kids not to lie if one shoots right out my mouth when it suits my purpose?"

"So, how did you find out Michael's in the Bahamas?"

"I asked his bookkeeper to reissue his child support check."

A note of concern entered Elise's voice. "Did she?"

"No."

A clicking noise of teeth against tongue came over the phone—Elise's nervous habit when she was thinking.

"What?"

"Hon, I don't want to add to your load."

"Spit it out."

"Okay, but don't shoot the messenger." She paused. "My sister ran into Michael's mom today at the mall. It seems he bought another dental practice last spring from a Dr. somebody-or-other who'd retired."

"Do I want to know?"

"You need to. All the patients from the new practice have jumped ship and gone scurrying to a dentist across the street."

Sierra flipped her blinker to turn onto her street. "So he has no money coming in and a big payment to Dr. somebody-or-other, plus trips to the Bahamas to pay for."

"A *whopper* of a payment, according to his mom. Have I ever told you how sorry I am that I introduced the two of you?"

"Only a zillion times."

"Well, I am sorry."

"I'm not."

A note of tenderness entered Elise's voice. "I don't blame you. Those three angels are adorable."

"They are everything." And without that money they were going to be uprooted again. How was she going to keep her family from coming apart?

"Oh, gotta run. Customers." Elise's kiss-kiss through the phone ended the call.

Sierra pulled into the driveway. Her mom's car wasn't at the curb. Had the Hamburger Lickins driven her to the store? If they lived with her mom, they'd never swallow another cell-damaging nitrate again. Full of good nutrition and helpful advice, they'd ever so slowly be loved to death.

She stepped through the side door into the kitchen as the garage ratcheted closed behind her. She set her keys and purse on the counter next to the phone and spotted her mom's note.

Horse—22 yrs. Gray gelding. Gentle. $600

No way! Six hundred bucks? She gripped the counter, a desperate hope building inside. If she could sell the horse for that much, they could stay in their home at least for a little while longer! She chewed a fingernail. Would Mr. Flannery give her an extra day or two if she could prove she owned $600 worth of horseflesh? Would he take the horse in lieu of a check?

She stared at the note's flowery script. It was just like her mom to take Sally's call and then draft the ad for her. Surprising that she hadn't added the classified number in the margin. Sierra reached for the phone book in the drawer next to the silverware. Ten minutes later her six-hundred-dollar horse was listed for sale, set to run in tomorrow's paper.

Chapter 4

Braden's hand gripped the car door handle. He wished Grandma would drive faster; he couldn't wait to tell his mom about Chance. The horse was *awesome!* As soon as the car stopped in the driveway, he flew out of the car and raced for the house. He wanted to tell Mom first.

He pounded up the porch steps, twisted the knob, and pushed his shoulder into the door. He heard the car doors slam behind him and then his brother and sister running through the gravel.

His mom sat on the couch. She looked excited to see him.

"Mom! Chance is so beautiful! Sally let us ride him and everything. He's so cool."

His mom's eyebrows pinched together, and she didn't look excited any more. "What do you mean?"

"Chance. The horse."

Her voice sounded strange, like she was scared or mad. "You rode that horse?"

Ah, man! He knew she'd ruin it. She didn't want them to have a horse, all because of her friend. That was what Grandma said.

His sister ran through the door in front of his little brother. "Mom, we saw Chance. Can we keep him, please?"

His mom didn't even answer. She looked at Grandma and her face got all funny looking and kind of red. "You took them to see that horse without me?" His mom never looked at Grandma like that. He felt kind of scared inside. Like when his dad got mad at him.

"Now, Sierra, I know you don't think it's a good idea, but it went very well."

His mom's voice was quiet. "I can't believe you wouldn't ask me first. A horse is the last animal I'd let my children around."

Braden rushed next to his grandma. "Mom, it wasn't dangerous. He—"

His mom barely looked at him. "Braden, stay out of this. Grandma and I are talking. Go play your video games."

She never listened to him. He wished he was at Emmett's house. Emmett's mom didn't make him play baby games on his Game Boy.

"I can't afford a horse. I have two days to pay October's rent before we're evicted."

They'd have to move? He looked at Emory, who stared back, her eyes wide. Maybe they could live at one of those apartments with a swimming pool. Cool. But they couldn't keep a horse there.

"Heavens, Sierra. Why didn't you say something? Do you want me to loan you the money?"

"You can't afford to do that, Mom."

"Well, you have to figure something out."

Sierra started biting a fingernail. "I'm trying to get a job. I just need more time."

"Well, unfortunately time isn't what you have. You're going to have to move home, honey. We need to start packing your things up," Grandma went on. "I'll call Paul Willan from church. He owns the hardware store and has loads of boxes. I'm sure he and his wife would love to help. They are the dearest people. We could probably get some boxes moved over to the house tonight."

His mom looked panicky. "I thought you agreed that selling the horse was the best option—I saw your note."

Grandma's face twisted like she was confused, then she laughed. "Oh honey, that's how much Sally wants to charge to stable him every quarter. I guess her husband isn't getting the sheep after all."

His mom looked at him, then back at his grandma, all nervous-like. "I'm selling the horse. I already placed the ad, and with the money from the sale, I'll be able to pay the rent until I get a job."

Braden clenched his fists. "No, you can't sell Chance!"

His mom looked at him like he wasn't old enough to understand grown-up stuff. "I'm sorry, but we can't keep him."

The words came storming out of his mouth. "You never do anything we want. I wish I lived with Dad." His mom's face got sad, and he wished he hadn't said it so mean. Sometimes he didn't mean to yell—the words just fell out of his mouth without him even trying.

"Braden, I'd like you to go upstairs. Emory, why don't you and Trevor go play Chutes and Ladders for a little bit?"

He stomped upstairs to his room and dug the new CD Emmett loaned him out of his backpack. His mom would be mad if she knew he had it. She didn't like music that used dirty words. The music made him feel weird, kind of bad, but he liked the angry music when he was mad. He flopped onto his bed, grabbed his Game Boy, and turned his headphones up loud.

"I'm calling about the horse," a voice said over the phone Tuesday morning. "Is he still for sale?"

Yes! Sierra danced around the bathroom and silently pumped the air with her fist. "Yes, he is. Would you like to see him?" She scooped the damp towels into the laundry basket, her grip tight on the phone she'd been carrying with her all morning, with the hope she would get this call.

"When would be a good time for you?"

"Actually, Sally, the lady who boards him, will show him to you."

A pause. "I'd really prefer that the owner be present."

Sierra froze, clutching one of Emory's pink hair clips she'd picked up off the floor, as a picture formed of her attempting to lead the horse out of the barn. Her voice came out slightly strangled sounding. "I don't think I can do that."

"We're flexible on the time. If you're not available for a few—"

"No, I mean I, uh, I'm not really fond of horses."

Again silence, then the puzzled voice asked. "Are you the owner?"

She cleared her throat and dropped the hair clip in the top vanity drawer. "I am."

The businesslike male voice asked, "Do you worm him regularly?"

"Um, I'm not sure."

A pause, then, "Is he shod?"

Shod? "I don't know."

His voiced sounded odd. "Do you happen to know what color your horse is?"

"No, I—" Sierra remember the ad her mom had drafted. "Gray!" She leaned back against the counter and stared at the water-stained shower door. "I've only owned him a few days, and I've never seen him. I'm not much of a horse person, sorry."

He chuckled. "The picture's getting clearer. My wife has to work, but my daughter and I would like to come look at him this afternoon about three."

"I'll let Sally know you're coming." Sierra gave him directions and hung up the phone.

Chapter 5

Ross Morgan tossed another bag of fertilizer onto the bed of his blue pickup as he heard the smooth rumble of tires flying over gravel. Kyle's red four-wheel-drive pickup followed the circular drive to the barn and parked next to Ross.

Kyle Olsen swung his door open and climbed down out of the beast. "Hey, cousin."

Ross hiked another bag into the back of his truck. "Don't you have work you need to be doing?"

Kyle eyed the pile of bags stacked in the rear of Ross's pickup. "Nothing this labor intensive. You need to get out of the landscaping business."

Ross chuckled and paused to lean against the pickup bed. "It pays the bills. What are you doing out this way?"

"Heather wanted me to deliver some of her leftover pot roast to Sid."

Ross glanced over at Sid Barrow's farm next door. "Sid does love his pot roast. So how are Heather and the girls? I haven't seen them in a while."

"The family's doin' good." Kyle rubbed the top of his mustache and cleared his throat twice. "Hey, I've got a situation."

Ross grinned at his cousin and rolled back to another time when Kyle had used those same words. "Tell your mother I am not taking Isabella to the prom."

Kyle's hearty laughter filled the air. "It's been eighteen years and she still thinks you missed out."

Ross laughed with a shudder. Isabella had been a bossy girl living next to his cousin's family and had been a constant pest to Ross. Kyle's mom thought it was a match made in heaven. "What's up this time?"

"Well, it involves Sid, but I thought I'd run it by you first."

"Sid won't like that."

"Well, you're more son than neighbor to him, and I figured you'd know best if he'd be up for this."

"He keeps his shotgun loaded, you know."

Kyle chuckled. "Sid has some boarding stalls available, doesn't he?"

Ross felt the muscles in his back tighten, like they had after his mother suggested he and his father spend some bonding time on the golf course last Father's Day. He'd spent the day digging his ball out of bunkers and listening to his dad talk about how he wished Ross had gone to law school and, like Ross's brother, joined their dad's law firm.

He gave his cousin a direct look. "The polo training is about all he can handle. He's too old to be taking on more work."

Kyle leaned back against his truck door and scuffed the tip of his shoe against the rocks. "There's really not a lot of work involved, especially as this one doesn't need to be trained to chase those balls around the field."

Ross shook his head. "Sid would skin you alive if he heard you talking about his ponies like that. And no, he doesn't need to take on one more horse. Don't ask him." He felt a smile emerge. "Though he'd skewer me good if he knew I'd told you that."

Kyle nodded. "Yeah. That's what I thought." He tilted his head at

Ross's barn, then the field behind it, and let a slow smile spread across his face. "Well, lookee here at all this fenced pasture just going to waste…."

Ross let out a long laugh. "You dog. You set me up."

Kyle's grin kept growing bigger. "Are you biting?"

"Who'd you offer it to?"

Kyle's voice took on his normal enthusiasm, and he rubbed his hands together. "Abbey Lassiter. She's looking for a place to stable her daughter Sierra's horse. Sierra has three young kids, and Abbey said they're pretty desperate to find a place for Chance."

Ross shook his head, still bemused at how his cousin had suckered him in. "The barn hasn't been used since I was a kid, and the fence is close to falling down."

"You wouldn't have to do a thing."

"Except say yes."

Kyle's smile stretched to his back molars. "Except say yes."

"And chase down that horse when he gets out."

Kyle's smile weakened. "Well, I could help with that. And I'm sure Sierra would be here in a heartbeat."

Ross challenged him with a raised eyebrow.

"Really, Ross. I've known Sierra for years. She's very capable."

Ross brushed a thumb across his jaw. "So I give her a call to let her know the horse is out. She runs over, lassoes, uh, Chance—did I get the name right?" At Kyle's cheeky nod, he continued. "She lassoes Chance and settles him back in the barn, then gets her leather gloves and wire cutters and goes out in the muddy, wet field and repairs the fence?" He paused. "Did I miss anything?"

Kyle didn't hold back the chuckle. "The rain."

"That's right, the rain. No, the *sleet*. So Miss Sierra is out in the driving sleet repairing the fence while Ross the Louse is in the house reading the newspaper and drinking his coffee in front of the fire. Is that what you're trying to tell me?"

Kyle's blue eyes crinkled with laughter. "Trade me with Sierra and you got it right. And I'd expect you to save me a cup of that coffee."

Ross shook his head and felt his lips twitch in an answering grin. "No, let me tell you what would really happen. Ready?"

Kyle stuffed his hands in his pockets. "You got the platform, buddy."

Ross scratched the back of his head and gazed around the yard. "I would come home from a long hard day of mulching Mrs. Latham's flower beds. Cold, wet, exhausted, and hungry. You with me?"

"I'm with you, man."

"I pull up my drive, and there's Chance, not a care in the world, blocking my road. I get out of the truck, and he bolts. I drive to the house and call you, but you don't answer, and your cell phone is dead. I get a lead rope and spend an hour chasing the nag down. Then, in the dark—"

"Don't forget the sleet."

He nodded. "With sleet pounding my back, I try to find the blasted hole in the fence. And when I find it, I can barely fix it because my fingers are frozen."

"Where're your gloves?"

"Forgot them in the truck because I was spittin' nails when I couldn't get a hold of you."

Kyle leaned back with a loud hoot.

Ross crossed his arms. "Glad you can see why this won't work."

His cousin clapped him on the shoulder. "When can we trailer him over?" Kyle was the type who wanted to rescue every stray that crossed his path. No doubt it was the reason *he* took Isabelle Mittingham to their prom.

"All right." Ross sighed. "Let's go look at the barn."

Ross watched the green Honda van roll to a stop near his house Tuesday afternoon. He rested his shoulder on the side of his pickup bed and watched as an older woman step from the car and then lean down to help a young boy get his foot loose from the seatbelt.

Ross crossed the circular yard between the barn and his house to greet them. "You must be Abbey Lassiter. Kyle told me you might be by today."

"Hello. And this young man is my grandson Trevor."

Ross smiled down at the child. "Hi, Trevor."

The boy kept close to his grandma. Abbey bent toward Trevor. "Say 'hi' to the man, honey."

The boy fidgeted and a shy smile emerged. "Hi."

"So you and Kyle are cousins? I don't recall ever seeing you with Kyle at church." Her smile was gracious, but a determined question was in her eyes.

He decided to appease her curiosity. "My folks and I attended across town when I was growing up. I visited a few times when I stayed the night with Kyle. I belong to Faith Community now."

"Ah." The answer seemed to satisfy, and her smile warmed. "I always hoped Kyle and my daughter—" She laughed self-consciously and glanced down at Trevor. "Well, you know how mothers can be. And now Kyle is married and Sierra is single again."

Ross slapped his gloves lightly against his leg, and he looked down at Trevor, but the boy wasn't listening. His attention had been caught by a fuzzy caterpillar that was slowly crawling over the rocks. Ross looked at Abbey. "So, do you want to see the barn? Kyle mentioned you have a horse that needed stabling."

Abbey laughed and started walking with him toward the barn. "Now there's a story. My daughter Sierra inherited it, if you can believe that. Miss Libby had no idea when she wrote her will how terrified of horses Sierra is. My daughter is really quite a level-headed person, but she went through a traumatic experience when she was young." She glanced quickly at Trevor, then gave Ross a negative shake of her head. "I can explain later."

Throughout the tour of the small barn, the woman gave him more details than he needed to know about her daughter's life. When Trevor found a black beetle climbing over some rags in the corner of the tack room, Abbey was too busy explaining about Sierra's divorce to even notice. It felt like gossip and Ross didn't like it.

He interrupted with a polite smile and brought the conversation back to the barn. "Do you think this would work?"

Abbey laughed again. "Oh, listen to me, I do go on sometimes. I just thought it'd be helpful if you understood what the poor girl has been through."

He rested his hand on top of a stall door. "That's thoughtful of you, but I prefer to let people tell their own stories."

"Oh." For the first time Abbey had nothing to say.

He hid a grin and let his hand slide off the stall. "Well, if you've seen—"

"*But* there are extenuating circumstances." A finger waved in protest. "Sierra would never say anything about what's happened to her. She has a hard time accepting help. And if I can't find someone who will board her horse, those children will have one more disappointment to deal with."

A chuckle escaped his lips. "Does she know you're here?'

She tilted her head. "When a person is under stress, do you think she always knows what's best for her?"

Ho boy. "And you do, I presume?"

"Of course, I'm her mother." She clapped her hands together. "Now, let's talk payment. I'm on a fixed income but I have a little spending money."

What kind of trouble had Kyle gotten him into?

Sierra dished macaroni and cheese with sliced hot dogs onto Trevor's plate.

"Macaroni and cheese again?" Braden stared at his plate and made no move for his fork.

"It has hot dogs." Emory scooted her chair closer to the table.

The phone rang, and Braden jumped up. "I'll get it." He reached for the phone, and Sierra's hand gripped the serving spoon that hovered over her plate. A few cheesy elbow noodles dripped onto the dish.

"Hello?" There was a pause and then his chin pulled in and his brow furrowed. "You want to buy Chance?" Clarity swept across his features, and furious brown eyes shot darts at her.

Sierra took the phone he shoved at her before he pounded up the stairs. "Hello?"

Pure delight lit Greg Adams' voice. "We love him! Can I drop the payment by in an hour or so?"

If Emory and Trevor weren't looking at her like she'd just slaughtered their best friend, she would be doing cartwheels. "Certainly. That would be fine."

A few minutes later, Sierra heard a key in the front door and her mom breezed into the house with a singsong voice. "Who wants black-berry cob-*bler?*"

Emory pushed back from the table and ran to her grandmother. "Someone bought Chance!"

Shock and dismay rushed over Abbey's features as she clutched the dessert dish. Then she marched toward the kitchen counter shaking her head with Em trailing behind.

Sierra sighed. "Mom, just say it."

"I just don't know how you can do this to them, after all they've been through."

"I'm being responsible. Ensuring they have some stability in their lives. Keeping them safe."

Abbey set the cobbler down and reached into the cupboard for plates. "It just keeps coming back to that Molly girl, doesn't it? I should have gotten you into counseling."

Sierra started clearing the half-eaten macaroni from the table. "That has nothing to do with me selling Chance." She pulled some storage containers from a drawer. "If I sell him, there's no moving in with you and no uprooting the kids again." She just wanted the day over. Mr. Flannery could get his money tomorrow and tell his poor grandson Ronnie that he'd have to live in the dorm, and she could keep looking for a job.

Her mom jerked the silverware drawer open, grabbed a knife and started cutting into the golden biscuits covering the cobbler. "Keep the horse, Sierra. Just give it a few more days."

"I don't have a few more days, Mom. I'm being evicted."

"I'll pay for Chance's expenses. I know the perfect—"

"I already sold him, and I don't want to talk about it anymore." Her mom just never stopped.

Her mom served the cobbler in silence, her back stiff. Braden slunk downstairs and ate his piece, then returned to his room.

After the dishes had been washed and the counter wiped—soap, then bleach—her mom kissed the kids, gave her a brief smile, and left.

Sierra helped the kids get ready for bed earlier than normal. The Adamses would be there any minute, probably with their beaming daughter.

Covers to his chin, Trevor reached up for a hug. "Can you read me a story?"

She kissed him. "Not tonight, sweetie."

"Pray!" Trevor said.

Sierra stifled a sigh. Her prayers had dried up to nearly nonexistent since the divorce, but she'd kept the routine for the older kids, and Trevor had adopted it too. "Keep Trevor safe, and help him to sleep well. Amen."

His eyes remained pinched shut. "And help us keep Chance. Amen."

Her heart broke at the innocent faith that, little by little, would be eroded by unanswered prayers until it would seem pointless to even ask.

Braden stalled in Trevor's doorway, both hands pressed against the frame. "Why do we have to go to bed now? It's only seven forty-five."

Sierra flipped the light off. "We have a big day tomorrow." *Delivering a check to Mr. Flannery.*

Emory stood in her pajamas behind Braden. "Excuse me."

Braden didn't move so Emory tried to squeeze past.

He pressed his hip against the door to keep her from entering.

Emory pushed harder, her face turning red.

"Braden, let her in!" Sierra said.

He moved, and Em shot into the room. She glared at her brother, then hopped onto the bunk bed above Trevor.

Sierra held Braden's angry gaze and felt her shoulders drop. "Go get ready for bed, honey."

He made a disgusted sound but turned and walked into the bathroom.

A drawer rolled open. A mere twenty seconds later the toothbrush thunked against the bottom of the drawer, then the drawer banged shut. Sierra sighed. *Pick your battles.* At least his dad could take care of the cavities.

The house finally quiet, Sierra jogged down the stairs. She breathed deep and felt some of the tension release. Disappointed kids were going to bicker, right? Some back talk had to be normal. But it was the growing disrespect that bothered her. She paused at the bottom of the stairs, her hand on the banister, her thoughts flipping back to when Braden had been happier, more like himself. Before school started, before summer began. A glimmering memory flickered—of Braden throwing her a wide smile, backpack on his shoulder, ready to go to his dad's. But he didn't go. His dad and some buddies had flown to California to go rappelling instead. It had been spring.

It had been the start of broken promises and her children's broken hearts. She moved to the kitchen and slowly pulled down a mug for cocoa. Maybe Michael needed the stress relief of kid-free weekends. But raising children wasn't a task that you could get to at your convenience. The kids needed him.

The phone rang as she stirred chocolate powder into the steaming milk, putting a halt to her thoughts.

"Sierra?" a male voice came over the line. "This is Greg Adams. Turns out my wife wasn't as keen on getting a horse as I thought. We're going to hold off for a little while." Sierra felt hope being sucked from the room.

"Oh. Okay. Thanks for letting me know." Then she hung up.

Sierra thought about her mother's offer to pay for the horse. The kids would be thrilled if they could keep the animal. A chill ran down her spine at the thought. What if something happened to them? Could she live with that possibility? Sure, not every horse was dangerous, and her kids could probably ride Chance for years and survive unscathed.

But Mr. Flannery was expecting his check in the morning—she needed a miracle. Yet she knew God—He was out of miracles when it came to her.

Sierra woke up and stared at the ceiling, a sense of foreboding pressing down on her. October thirteenth. Mr. Flannery expected to hear from her today—or better yet, hear the sound of a moving truck filled with her belongings.

She pulled on her robe and went to wake the kids.

Emory, her night owl, staggered toward the bathroom, her eyes tiny slits of sleepiness.

"Em, meet us in the kitchen in a few minutes."

Trevor bounded down the stairs. "I'm hungry." A moment later she heard a cupboard door bang and then the ping of Fruit Loops hitting the bottom of a cereal bowl.

"Come on, Braden." She peered into his room for the second time. "Time to get up, lazybones."

"I don't want to go to school."

"Sorry, not an option. And I need you in the kitchen for a family meeting in a few minutes."

He scowled but got out of bed.

A few minutes later, Sierra pulled out a chair to face them as they hunkered over their cereal bowls. "Guys, we're going to have to move."

Braden perked up. "Where?"

"Grandma's."

"Aww. I thought we'd have an apartment with a pool."

Sierra tried to smile. "No. But we shouldn't be at Grandma's more than a month or so."

Emory's head leaned against her hand, still not fully awake. "I don't want to move."

Trevor piped up. "We can make cookies every day." He grinned at his mom, and she tousled his blond hair. Just what her hips needed.

Forty-five minutes later the bus pulled away and she walked back into the house and strode straight for the kitchen, thoughts pelting her brain. Should she call Greg Adams back and offer to lower Chance's price? Talk to Greg's wife about … what? How great horses were and how badly her daughter needed one? Disgust rolled over her. How selfish to want to protect her own children but endanger another.

Braden's cereal bowl still sat on the table, messy droplets of milk surrounding it. Armed with the dishcloth, she cleared the table and swiped over the milk. On her way back to the sink, the answering machine's flashing red light caught her eyes.

The cereal bowl quickly clunked down on the counter, she reached to press the button.

"Hi, this is Melissa from Garland Treasures. I just wanted to let you know that we have filled the position."

Sierra leaned against the counter and stared into the kitchen that by tomorrow would be filled with Ronnie Flannery's Top Ramen noodles and whatever else college students ate these days. She stared down at the dusting of white crumbs and smear of peanut butter where the kids had made their lunches.

But the job was supposed to be mine.

The phone rested near her elbow, and she slowly picked it up. Her mom was going to be thrilled.

Chapter 6

A bare half ring and her mom picked up.

"Sierra!" Her mom sounded jubilant. She'd probably guessed what was coming.

Sierra took a breath. "Is your offer still open for—?"

"The spare bedrooms are aired and ready. Wal-Mart had their summer sheets on clearance, so I picked some up. I didn't figure the kids would mind the colors. Fridge and cupboards are stocked, and I was just putting together a casserole for the crew tonight."

Why am I even surprised? "The crew?"

Her mom sounded like a proud hen with all her chicks gathered under her wing. "Remember I told you about Paul Willans? He and Sylvia are just waiting for the call to come by. He kindly offered to get some boys from his youth group to help load the big items after school. You will need to put those in storage. I'm sure Jim's Lock & Key has some units available. I knew you'd want to call on that yourself, but I have a little money set aside to pay for it." Her mom paused. "Let's see. I think that's about it. Oh, did you get any boxes?"

The walls were already closing in. "I didn't know I'd be moving."

Her mom brushed the comment aside. "I'm sure Paul has plenty. I'll ask him to bring some when he comes. So, does nine o'clock sound about right?"

Sierra wanted to grab onto something. She felt like she'd mistakenly floated into the rapids and was heading straight for a drop-off. "Sure, Mom. That sounds fine."

Her mom's voice grew soft. "I'm so glad you're coming home, honey."

Sierra watched the school bus stop, red lights flashing. The doors opened, and Braden came charging out, but stopped halfway down the big steps to stare at their yard.

Two big pickups loaded with boxes dominated the driveway, and another had backed across the yard up to the porch where two football players wrestled her washer into position next to the dryer.

Braden continued down the steps and dropped his backpack onto the sidewalk. "We're moving today?"

"I hadn't planned on it being quite so soon, honey." Sierra waited for a reaction, but he was still digesting the news. She hated putting them through this. If only Mr. Adams had taken the horse or Michael's check had cleared. A slight smile lifted the corner of Braden's mouth and she shook off the frustration. Maybe his sense of adventure was kicking in. She took a step to give him a hug, but her mom was already there and got the hug and grin that Sierra longed to feel.

"Today's a perfect day to move to your grandma's!" Abbey said.

Braden turned an eager face to her. "Seriously, Mom?"

She touched his shoulder. "Yep."

"Cool!" He brushed past them to where the guys worked to strap down the appliances.

"Hey, Em," Sierra said.

Her daughter, who didn't like change, sidled next to her and tucked under the arm she held out. "Why do we have to move?"

Sierra darted a look at her mom. "Well, Grandma and I thought it would be easier while I'm looking for a job."

"What about our room?"

"Come here, sweetie." Sierra's mom held her arms out, and Emory flew into them. "How would you like your very own room at Grandma's? I brought some wallpaper books home for you to look at. You can paint and decorate it however you'd like."

A feeling of panic set in. "Oh, I don't know if we should do that, Mom. We're not going to be there that long."

Her mom frowned. "Sierra, it's not good for the kids to be moved back and forth, and there's no guarantee the next job will work out better than this last one.

Three years wasn't stable?

Her mom continued, "I think you need at least a year to build a good cushion of savings."

Sierra glanced at the pickup where the sofa leaned upright against the blanket-draped washer and dryer. What her mom said made sense, but it didn't make the jittery feeling subside. Smothered by love. It was happening already. She could take the advice over the phone and in person for short intervals. But twenty-four hours a day … she was going to be helpfully henpecked into a nervous wreck. Maybe a miracle would fall into her lap and she'd land an amazing job this week. But she had to believe in miracles for them to happen, didn't she?

Chapter 7

Blindfolded, Braden's mom laughed from the front seat. "Where are we going?"

Grandma turned and winked at him in the rear seat. "Remember the rule, no questions allowed."

It was one of his grandma's favorite games to blindfold somebody and take them out for a treat. But he *knew* where they were going. He was sure of it, because Grandma had turned right out of the driveway instead of left toward town. If they were going shopping or for ice cream they would have turned left. Instead of houses and buildings he saw fields of grass out his window. The click-clack of the blinker made him sit straighter, trying to see out the windshield around his mom's seat. Grandma slowed the car and turned.

Yes! There was a barn! He knew it!

Grandma smiled back at him and gave him another wink. She wasn't afraid of horses. Boy, was his mom going to be surprised. He hoped she didn't cry. Sometimes he heard her crying at night when she thought he was asleep, and it scared him.

His grandma stopped the car next to the barn. Braden unlatched his seat belt and shoved past Emory to grab out the van's side door handle.

The barn door opened, and a tall man carrying a tray of tools came out. Cool! Braden jumped out of the van and hurried over to the man. Braden stuck his hands in his pockets and slowed when he got closer. "Can I help?"

The man had on dark jeans like him, but he had an awesome silver belt buckle. Braden wanted one like that. Maybe he could use his dad's computer and find one on eBay.

The man smiled. "I got it covered, but thanks."

Braden dropped his eyes to stare at the ground. He shouldn't have asked. And it didn't seem like his dad wanted him to come over to the house anymore anyway. It was a stupid belt buckle.

The man shifted his feet and spoke again, "But I bet I can find another hammer."

Braden hesitated. "That's okay. We're probably not staying long once my mom knows where we are."

The man tilted his head. "Your mom doesn't know you're here?"

Braden sighed. Grown-ups didn't listen very well. "She knows I'm here. She just doesn't know she's here."

The man kind of chuckled and glanced over at the car where his grandma was hurrying around to the passenger door to help his mom out. "I think I'm missing something. Your mom doesn't know she's here?"

"Grandma blindfolded her." He shrugged. "Kind of to make it a surprise, I guess. But I don't think she's going to like it." But he hoped she did.

Years ago, Ross had been a kid who'd wanted to do man things too. That was why he finally let the boy carry the tool tray as they walked over to the green Honda. Mrs. Lassiter helped a grinning blindfolded woman out of the passenger seat.

The cute dark-haired woman in jeans and a sweatshirt raised her hands to the white strip of cloth tied around her head with a laugh. "Can I take it off now?"

Ross pulled his eyes from the excited woman and glanced at his barn, trying to figure out what the big surprise was. Abbey gave him a secretive smile, then said, "Okay, now."

The woman ripped the blindfold off, anticipation alight in the laughing brown eyes that darted as she turned in a circle to find her surprise. After a few moments, her mouth started to close, the expectancy waning. Her gaze held his for a moment, then passed on. Soon those eyes found his again and settled there, her puzzlement growing. "Mom?"

Abbey chuckled and leaned to squeeze his arm. "No, it's not *him*, Sierra."

Sierra looked away, wariness and uncertainty in her brown eyes. "What's the surprise?"

"Should be just a few more minutes, honey. In the meantime, this is Ross Morgan." Abbey nodded toward him. "Ross, these are my grandkids, Braden and Emory. Trevor you've met." She beamed with grandma pride.

Ross returned the shy smiles they gave him.

"And this is my daughter, Sierra. The one I told you about."

Sierra shot her mom an uneasy look. She turned a questioning gaze toward him and a wisp of a smile crossed her face. "Hello. I'm sure—"

"Ross recently bought this place from his parents, Sierra, and he's done all this landscaping himself. Isn't it lovely?"

Sierra looked around. "It is."

"There! Look, kids." Abbey pointed up the road, shielding her eyes from the afternoon sun.

Ross didn't need to turn to know what was coming up his driveway. Abbey had called and arranged the *surprise* yesterday. The kids were jumping and screaming, but he kept his eyes on Sierra.

Excitement brought her up on tiptoe to stare in the direction her mom pointed. Immediately the joy turned to puzzlement, and then hurt and shock drew deep lines in her forehead. She opened her mouth as if she wanted to speak but had no words. A whisper of anger swirled to the surface, and after a lingering glance at her mom she swiped a finger under her eyes, then brushed it against her shirt. Then did it again. She looked up the road, then at the children. Finally she noticed him watching.

The vulnerability and worry touched something deep inside him, and he knew in that moment that whatever her mother had done, he wouldn't be a part of it.

Sierra turned away from the man's intent stare. It was unnerving having a hunky stranger, who appeared to have stepped off an old Marlboro billboard, look at her so compassionately.

Her mom had an arm around both Emory and Braden. Trevor hopped from foot to foot beside them, each pair of eyes focused on the red pickup and horse trailer slowly making its way up the driveway, a small ribbon of dust rising behind.

Braden glanced back at her, a tuft of hair near his cowlick bobbing in his excitement. "It's Chance."

Sierra nodded and tried to smile at him, her feelings roiling in a tangled knot inside. Her mother had disregarded each of Sierra's concerns. Steamrolled them, actually. Were her feelings really so invisible, so unnecessary in her mom's world?

She sensed the man come up beside her. "You didn't know, did you?" He had a kind voice. Deep with the warmth of caring.

She shook her head but kept her eyes on the red truck.

"I'm sorry."

Those two words undid her. She felt her chin tremble and pressed her lips together.

The gravel crunched as he moved away.

What now? Tell them not to unload the horse? How could she let her children have one more letdown, and this one from her?

Kyle parked the pickup next to the barn and slammed his door shut with a wide smile. "Hey, Sierra! Ross." He walked over and gave her mom a hug, "Sorry to keep you waiting. Chance here wasn't too wild about climbing into the trailer."

Sierra gripped the blindfold in her hand tighter. "Chance" and "wild" weren't words she wanted paired in the same sentence.

Kyle bent down to greet the kids. "And you three must be the new owners of the horse tied up in that trailer."

Sierra's heart sank at the delighted way the kids nodded their heads.

Braden spread his legs and stuck his hands in his pockets. "We rode him already."

"Well, you're going to get a lot of riding out here," Kyle said, straightening.

Braden grinned at Emory. It was as if the county fair had come to them with unlimited rides. Or rather one ride. Chance.

And she was the reluctant ticket holder. Could she leave her kids lives to chance? And hope that nothing like what happened to Molly would occur? How much hope did she have left? Surely not enough.

She moved quietly over to the group surrounding Kyle. Her eyes found Ross again, who was watching her with dark eyes set in a handsome face that hinted at thoughts stirring well below the surface. His gaze held hers for a spine-tingling moment before she looked away.

Kyle clapped his hands. "Okay, let's get that horse unloaded."

Sierra's heart started pounding. Her mom followed Kyle and the kids toward the trailer. Sierra felt rooted to the spot, wanting to call them back.

Ross walked up to her, blocking her view of them. "Do you want me to ask Kyle to take the horse back?"

"Um. I don't know." He was offering her a way out! Her knight wore rugged man's clothes. A dark wool jacket, black jeans, and work-worn boots. She shivered, but more from fear of Chance than having him near her, right? Elise would be grinning and elbowing her.

He glanced behind him. "You don't have much time." Over his shoulder, Kyle was unlatching the rear doors of the trailer.

Terror lurked behind those doors. "Yes! Please ask him."

He nodded and started toward Kyle.

"Wait! No." She reached for his arm.

He turned, a half-grin on his face. "Conflicted?"

"Very. Highly anxious, in case you hadn't noticed."

A teasing laugh flickered through his eyes. "A gentleman would say he hadn't."

She looked at the kids crowded behind Kyle. He said something to them, and they obediently backed up a few feet. "They're so excited."

"Abbey said it's their first horse." Questions rode the statement.

She gave him a polite smile. "Yes. I'm sure she did."

Kyle hollered over. "Hey, Ross, you want to give me a hand?"

The man lowered his voice. "It wouldn't be the end of the world if he took the horse away."

Sierra took a deep breath and attempted a smile. "Yes. Yes, it would."

The man hesitated, a kind smile lingering, then he walked toward Kyle. She followed more slowly. Why couldn't Miss Libby have been into golden retrievers?

Sierra stopped behind the kids. She felt her mom's gaze, but couldn't look at her.

Braden grabbed her hand and started swinging it. "Can you believe it, Mom? Grandma rescued Chance."

"Mmm-hmm." She knew her mom was listening intently.

Abbey wrapped an arm around Sierra's waist. "It's for the best, honey."

"I don't want to talk about it right now, Mom."

Her mom gave her a slight squeeze and let her hand drop.

Centered in the middle of the opening above the twin doors was a large gray rump. Much larger than she'd anticipated.

The hinges groaned when Kyle pulled the rear doors wide. He marched to the front of the trailer and disappeared through a side door. His muffled, "All clear," was a signal Ross apparently understood since the man immediately unclipped the chain that draped behind the horse.

Moments later the gray rump swayed as it backed up, then slowly settled one giant rear hoof, then the other, against the terra firma.

Sierra gritted her teeth to keep from ordering Kyle to push that dangerous hind end back into the trailer and haul it away. She didn't care where. Canada might be far enough. Last week Braden had asked if he could buy a lizard. At the time she'd shuddered at the thought of a reptile in the house and had visions of the washing machine dragged from the wall as they hunted for the escaped creature. But an aquarium-full would be preferable to a thousand-pound beast of muscle and hooves.

A quick glance sideways sent that idea smoking into the discard pile. She couldn't do it. Not with Braden, Emory, and Trevor bouncing up and down, throwing glowing looks her way every few seconds.

Then Braden ran up from behind Chance and petted him on the neck.

"Braden!" His name screamed its way straight from her solar plexus. She rushed over and grabbed his jacket, jerking him away.

Ross and Kyle stared at her. Kyle's mouth sagged, while Ross seemed to assess her with a slow gaze.

Her eyes sought out the barn behind them, anything to avoid the censure that had to be staring at her from the man. Her heart pounded, she could feel the pulse of it in the palm that still gripped the back of Braden's sweatshirt. Braden shot a look up at her, the whites of his eyes stark against his face.

Ross walked steadily toward her. "You okay?"

She nodded, unwilling to look directly at him. She really wasn't a crazy woman. Maybe if she explained. "Braden ran right behind him." Ross's calm appraisal of her didn't waver, so she knelt down to focus on her son. "You are *never* to go behind that horse." Her voice carried the weight of maternal protectiveness. Only she knew how close she was to completely falling apart. "Do you understand? Chance could kick you, honey. He's not like Sparky was." Old faithful Sparky who'd barked and chased sticks and never minded Braden using her as a pillow or a wrestling partner.

Ross rested a hand on Braden's head. He spoke to her son, but his eyes held hers with a quiet look. "Sometimes we're afraid of what we don't understand." He glanced down at Braden. "How about we get to know your new horse?"

Ross sensed Braden's embarrassment in the way the boy hung his head and dug his sneaker in the dirt once they stopped at the front of the trailer where Chance waited. Kyle looked like he wanted to walk the horse to the corral, but he kept staring at Sierra as if he wasn't certain how she would react.

Keeping a steady arm around the boy's shoulders, Ross bent so they were ear to ear, facing a large velvet Roman nose. Ross pointed with his left hand. "Chance deserves your respect and your full attention at all times." He glanced sideways at the boy, whose eyes hadn't lifted from the ground. "Like your mom said, you want to be cautious about running around behind him. He doesn't have eyes back there, and if he gets startled he might kick."

Ross sensed movement at his side.

Trevor and Emory had inched up next to him, and the little guy reached up to pet the gray nose. Better do some educating before any fingers got chomped.

The girl spoke first, disappointment in her voice. "He didn't seem so old when we rode him the other day."

Ross wiped a hand down the long nose that had dropped to sniff at the newcomers. "I hear he's twenty-two years old, just getting into his golden years. But I don't think he's ready for a nursing home yet, do you?"

Emory didn't look convinced. "Maybe."

Ross caught Kyle's eye and tried not to laugh. "He's still got plenty of galloping left in him." He'd stuck a baggie of apple slices in his pocket before leaving the house, and he pulled one out now and gave it to Chance. The thick lips with grandpa whiskers tickled his hand and grabbed the chunk of apple. Chance swung his head away and the deep, crunch, crunch of the strong molars seemed to intrigue the kids.

"Can I give him one?" Braden gave him an eager smile.

"In a minute. We need to go over horse safety first."

Trevor looked at him, his young face earnest. "What's a nursing home?"

Braden answered. "It's where old people go."

A grin nudged Ross's lips. *Back to horse safety.* "Horses need—"

His cell phone rang. He checked the number and gritted his teeth, then flipped it open. "Prestige Landscape Design, Ross speaking."

The commanding voice of Alex Cranwell, who owned one of the

largest commercial landscaping businesses in the state, boomed in his ear. "Where are you, Morgan?"

The familiar irritation rose. He hated it when the man called him by his last name. "What's going on, Alex?"

"There's a problem with the water feature design. Marie doesn't like it. This job may not be a big deal to you, but being that it's my house and not one of your regular little residential jobs, I need you over here pronto."

Ross looked up at the dark clouds swirling overhead. "I'll be there in a few minutes."

"I expect you to be on-site, Morgan, when your guys build the waterfall next week." A long sigh. "Let me make it plain. You've got the makings of a first-rate commercial landscaper, but if I can't count on you for a simple job like this, then I'm not sure you're ready for the commercial side of things."

"I hear you, Alex." Every call from the man ended the same way—always dangling the carrot and threatening to jerk it away. He clicked the phone off, wishing he hadn't been home the day Alex Cranwell drove up with all his promises of commercial glory.

"I gotta go, guys." He looked over at Kyle. "Do you have time to talk to them about taking care of Chance?"

Kyle pulled his sleeve up and checked his watch with a frown. "I'd like to, but I need to get back to the shop."

Ross clapped his hands, trying to sound upbeat. "How about you guys come back after school tomorrow?" A glance at Sierra showed her doubt.

Braden kicked at a rock. "We're supposed to go to my dad's."

"But we probably won't. He doesn't like us coming over anymore." Emory sounded matter-of-fact.

Braden shot back. "He does too. He's just busy, he told me." But he saw confusion and doubt on the boy's face.

"Monday then," Ross played referee. "I'll feed him until you guys come back. Maybe your mom can swing by and check on him for you once or twice this weekend."

Sierra gave an uncertain nod. "Okay."

He started toward the barn. "Follow me, and I'll give you a quick tour and show you where we're storing his hay and grain. Your grandma had some delivered this morning."

He caught the look Sierra shot her mom.

"And then we'll feed him some more apple pieces before I have to go." His cell phone rang again. He checked the number and let it go to voice mail. Alex Cranwell would have to wait a few more minutes.

After Kyle and Ross left, it took Sierra and her mom a frantic few minutes to find the boys. Frantic for Sierra, that was. If Trevor had gotten into the field with that horse and been hurt…. But her mom found them.

Trevor was marched back to the van, her mom's hand firmly around his wrist. "They were throwing rocks into Ross's koi pond."

Sierra sighed. "Boys, get in the car."

On the drive home, the backseat held the quiet of disappointed children.

Braden asked in a sullen tone, "Why do we have to go home?"

Sierra kept her eyes on the road ahead of them. "Ross and Kyle had to leave."

"So? We could have stayed. Grandma let us ride him before."

Sierra leaned her elbow against the top of the passenger door. "Please stop, Braden."

The words were grumbled, but clearly audible. "I wish we were at Dad's."

Emory's fingers gripped the seat in front of her, her voice anxious. "Mom, what if Dad goes to our old house to pick us up tomorrow?"

"I left a message for him, honey. He knows where Grandma lives."

The car grew quiet, a ticking bomb of emotions.

Her mom broke the tense silence between them in the front seat. "I was surprised you remembered Kyle Olsen. He's changed a lot since grade school."

"I see him every time I get my oil changed."

"Oh, that's right. He took over his dad's auto shop on Franklin."

Sierra decided to take the peace offering of simple conversation. "In third grade he won a banana split in our Sunday school's contest to memorize the books of the Bible. But he got sick and threw it up. I thought God was punishing him for beating me."

Her mom's crow's-feet showed. "God wouldn't do that. He doesn't care who won."

Sierra looked out the side window. "I know."

A few minutes later they turned into her mom's driveway. The delicious aroma of chicken potpie greeted them when they trooped into the house.

Her mom placed her keys on a hook and her purse on the counter. "Emory, wash your hands and set the table, please. Braden and Trevor, wash up and get ready for dinner."

Sierra pulled the plates down and set the stack on the table. Emory gathered the silverware. "Milk or water, Em?"

Emory paused halfway to the table, gave a decided nod and said, "Milk."

Sierra opened the fridge, then shut it again. She stared at the list precisely centered on the freezer door. "What's this?"

Her mom glanced over. "Oh, I came up with those last night. I thought if we had some guidelines, everyone would know what to expect. Less friction in the coop." Her mom said it with a smile as she slipped on oven mitts.

> *Phone calls limited to ten minutes.*
> *Dirty dishes loaded promptly in dishwasher. Dishwasher emptied*
>   *when clean.*
> *Dirty clothes placed in hamper in bathroom, not on bedroom floor.*
> *No school friends over unless prearranged.*
> *No running in house.*
> *No throwing balls in house.*
> *Bedtime for children: 8:00 weeknights, 8:30 weekends.*

Oh, my word. It was like she was ten all over again. Sierra gripped the fridge handle and carefully pulled it open. She would not say anything. It was her mother's house after all. Just a temporary situation. *Very* temporary.

But she didn't have a job yet. *Lord, please give me a job.* There she went, throwing up a prayer in a moment of duress. Why did she still do that when she knew He wouldn't answer? Sierra poured the milk in the glasses and shoved the container back in the fridge.

"Oh, I just thought of another one," her mother said before going over to the list and writing something else on the sheet. Sierra felt her blood pressure build. She had to get out of there.

"I'll be back in a few minutes, Mom."

"But, honey, dinner's ready."

Sierra sped past her toward the hall. "Go ahead and start without me." She grabbed her cell phone, pressed the familiar numbers, and headed for the backyard.

Her mom called after her. "It's dark out there, honey."

Sierra kept walking. "I'm fine."

"*Hel*-lo." Elise's singsong greeting rushed over her like a spring rainfall.

"She's driving me crazy."

"Oh, hon. Unload it all."

Sierra paced the back fence, the kitchen window broadcasting a square of light onto the middle of the grass. "Where do I begin?" Sierra stopped. "She hijacked Chance."

"What?"

Sierra nodded and started pacing again. "Yep. She's paying some Ross guy to board him, and she already had his feed delivered."

"She didn't!"

"She did!"

"Married or single?"

Sierra stopped. "What? I'm having a crisis and you want to know if the guy is available?"

"Is he?"

"I don't know." She nibbled her fingernail. "He didn't have a ring on."

"Hmm … crisis, but you noticed the lack of a ring. Is he good looking?"

"Does it matter so much?"

"Only as icing. Not a requirement."

Sierra felt a small grin form. "Drop-dead gorgeous."

"No!"

Sierra switched the phone to her other ear. "Can we get back to my mother, please?"

"Moving along. Are you going to keep the horse?"

"No. *Yes!* I don't know."

"Keep him. Trust me on this. You'll thank me some day."

"I'm a hypocrite."

"You're only just realizing that? What did you do this time?"

Sierra allowed a grin. "It's not funny. I prayed."

"Hold on, I feel the earth moving."

"Elise!"

"Did you mean it?"

"Kinda. But it was pure desperation thrown out to the cosmos."

"God made the cosmos."

"I know, I guess."

Elise knew when to let silence do the talking.

Sierra leaned back against the fence and watched her family through the kitchen window. They were probably tracking her by the light of her phone.

"She has a list."

"Your mom? Of what?"

Sierra drawled the words. "Rules to live by."

"You've got to name it."

"What?"

"The list. Like, *Abbey's List of Torment*."

Sierra chuckled. "Yeah or Abbey's Alcatraz." She sighed. "She means well."

"Of course, she does. She loves you."

Sierra looked up at the zillions of pinpoints in the sky. The Milky Way gleamed like a magical road to a far-off somewhere—it spoke of freedom. She breathed in deeply and exhaled the words. "I'll call it *The Motivator*."

"There you go!"

"You're a jewel, Elise."

"Rhinestone?"

"Rare sapphire."

"Ohh! You keep calling!"

Sierra laughed. A quick glance toward the house had revealed Trevor, his face pressed against the bright kitchen window, little hands cupping his eyes. "I'd better go. The kids are hunting me."

The next evening, Sierra lifted the still-warm enchilada pan from the midst of the dirty plates waiting to be cleared from the table. She set it on the counter. "Where's the plastic wrap?"

Her mom pointed to the drawer next to the stove.

She pulled off a square and molded it to the pan, then opened the fridge and stuck the leftovers in. "I'm going to check on the kids."

Her mom waved her off with a tight smile. "I'll clean up."

They still hadn't talked about her mom's handling of the horse, and it had reduced their conversation to short, tense exchanges.

Sierra found the kids already waiting on the front steps. She sat down behind Emory, gave her a hug, and kissed the top of her damp strawberry-scented hair. "I love you, Em."

Her daughter shifted to grin up at her. "Me too."

Trevor left his backpack in the grass where he'd been collecting vibrant maple leaves and ran back with a handful to show her. "These are for you."

She pulled him close, careful to not crush his treasures. "Thank you! They're beautiful!"

Braden kicked a rock off the cement walkway with a scowl. "When's Dad going to be here?"

"Pretty soon." She read through his frustration to the fear that his dad wouldn't show.

Finally, fifteen minutes later, the Lexus pulled into the driveway and parked close to the steps. With a huge grin Michael rolled down the window. "Hi, guys. Did you miss me?"

Emory beamed and ran over to give him a hug through the window. "Yes!"

Trevor ran up behind her. "Hi, Daddy! Grandma let me help make cookies. "

He looked tanned and relaxed and reached out to rub the top of Trevor's head. "Hi, punkin."

Maple leaves crunched under Sierra's feet as she retrieved Trevor's backpack from the yard. Sierra had a weird sense that time had warped for a moment. Several years ago this was the scene that used to play nightly in their driveway. Michael pulling up tired, but contented, and smiling while they all piled out of the house to greet him with hugs and kisses. Braden and Emory had been around Trevor's age.

She handed Michael the backpack. "I see you made it back."

He avoided her eyes and focused on their daughter. "Yep. Hey, Em, you're getting too old for that. Leave it here."

Emory froze, backpack in one hand, favorite blanket in the other. "I sleep with it, Dad."

"I said you're getting too old for it. Now go put it in the house." He looked at Sierra. "I don't know why you haven't made her throw it away."

"Because she needs it, Michael. It gives her security."

He glanced away, a hint of irritation in the curl of his lip.

"I went by the office and asked Luanne to reissue your last child support check," Sierra said. "She needed your authorization but couldn't reach you."

Frustration darkened his features, and she got a glimpse of how an angry Braden would look as an adult. "I told you I would take care of it." He lowered his voice with a quick glance in his rearview mirror at the boys in the backseat. "I don't want to discuss this in front of the kids."

Emory climbed in and Sierra squatted down next to the car, one hand on the door and spoke in a whisper, "You aren't returning my calls, Michael. I want to work this out amicably, but if I don't get paid I'll have to involve the district attorney. I don't want to, but you aren't giving me a choice."

He gave a short laugh. "Great. Just great, Sierra. Thanks."

"It's up to you, Michael. Not me." She dropped her hand and stood, taking a step back. The car raced backward to the end of the driveway, then stopped, tiny motes of dust floated around the still tires. The car surged back up next to her.

Michael leaned out the window, the words blasting, "Did you buy a horse?"

She shook her head, rooted to the gravel, every muscle wanting to retreat. "No, I did not buy a horse," she said simply.

Relief drained the anger. He whipped his head toward the back seat, the car easing slowly backward again. His voice floated out the window. "Braden, you better—"

Sierra rushed up to his open window. "But I have one."

The car stopped, and Michael leaned his arm on top of the steering wheel. "What do you mean, you have one?"

"I inherited him."

He shook his head and stared out the front windshield. "I can't believe you'd let them have a horse. How can you even afford it? You're living with your mother!"

"That's not my doing, now is it?" Sierra said. "Besides, that horse is the best thing in their world right now." And in that moment, seeing their three anxious faces in the backseat, she knew it was.

Chapter 8

Sierra walked back into the house with thoughtful steps. Dishes clinked, then a cupboard closed in the kitchen. The pain of childbirth was nothing like the ripping of her soul at seeing her kids anxious and hurt, pulled between two parents. Chance would be the oasis in their lives. If she could let him.

A chair scooted in the kitchen, then another. The table would be pristine once again. White doily in the middle anchored by two yellow candles and a white ceramic sugar bowl.

She'd always lived beneath her mom's need for orderliness, yet there was something comforting about it. Sierra stopped at the living room bookcase filled with knickknacks and pictures that backed up against the outside wall of the kitchen. She paused in front of one small photo. Familiar, yet often unnoticed in the years of living. A picture of her dad a few months before he died.

What made her mom's faith so strong? God hadn't protected them, hadn't kept her dad from dying when she was young. Her mom thought Sierra's faith issues hinged on a lack of belief. But they didn't. The belief was there. It was her trust that had big chunks missing. Gaping holes from her dad's death, the death of her marriage, Molly's accident. And those were just the personal ones. When she looked beyond her small world, she saw famine, tsunamis, murder, rape…. The list was endless, and so was her lack of trust.

Sierra passed through the living room with its blue floral couch and comfortable recliners situated neatly around an oak coffee table, amid a scattering of wicker baskets. In the kitchen, yellow gloves to her elbows, her mom scrubbed the stainless-steel sink free of potentially dangerous bacteria. Dishes too large for the dishwasher rested on the drying rack next to the sink. Her mom's back was stiff and her profile set as she scrubbed away.

Sierra reached for the towel hanging from the stove handle and picked up a wet skillet. "Michael's angry about the horse."

The scouring pad kept its brisk pace at the bottom of the sink. "I heard."

Sierra noted the kitchen window was cracked open.

"Are you keeping Chance, then?" her mother asked as she slid the dry skillet into its drawer below the oven.

"Mom, it's not about keeping the horse. It's what you did. To me."

Her mom puffed the weary exhale of someone who'd been misunderstood. "I knew you'd blame me."

"I'm not blaming you, it's just that—"

Her mom twisted slightly, forearms resting on the edge of the sink, gloves dripping gray suds from the wire scouring pad. "You don't see what's best for the kids. If you'd only open your eyes, see their joy with that horse."

"I know, Mom. I saw."

"Do you realize how this divorce has torn them apart? How seeing you and Michael at odds creates such anxiety in them?"

Guilt coated her with each picture of her failure. "Yes, Mom. I do know."

With a shake of her head, her mom turned back to the sink. "I just don't understand how you can even consider selling him." In a neutral voice she asked, "What does Elise say?"

Sierra wiped every trace of water off the vegetable steamer. Whenever there was a point of contention, it was like her mom slowly, inch by inch, pulled the rug out from under her life until Sierra stumbled and doubted. Elise's agreement would give her mom one more reason to keep pulling.

Sierra set the steamer in the cupboard. "She said to keep him."

Her mom made a tsking sound. "Well that certainly surprises me. For once she shows good sense."

"I'm not selling the horse."

Her mom gave a satisfied nod and rinsed the sink. "I think that's for the best."

Sierra slipped the dishtowel back over the oven door handle to dry and spoke the words to herself. "And if it's not, I'll be crying at my children's funerals."

Saturday evening, Sierra and her mom sat alone at the kitchen table and ate broiled halibut steaks and creamed peas in near silence. It was odd how much the presence of the kids defined her relationship with her mom.

"The fish is tasty. I hadn't tried this recipe before." Her mom cut a sliver off the remaining steak and lifted it to her plate. She took a bite and looked up. "Are you going to church tomorrow?"

"I hadn't planned on it." Almost involuntarily her gaze lifted to the pink list still taped to the fridge. Would her mom add church attendance to the bottom of The Motivator?

Her mom chewed slowly, then swallowed. "When were you planning to get back into fellowship?"

"I'm not really sure." Sierra dropped her eyes to the roll she was buttering, noting the line of dirt under her fingernails from helping her mom mulch the flower beds that afternoon.

The crow's-feet appeared. "The kids need spiritual training, honey. Sunday school is vital at their age."

Her mom was tugging at the rug again. How had spiritual training helped her and her brother, Win? She was divorced, and Win was a rootless wanderer with his own trust issues.

A frown darkened her mom's face. "It's not like they're getting it over *there.*"

And what about your *unforgiveness toward Michael?* she wanted to ask. Had her mom missed that lesson in spiritual training? But Sierra kept her eyes on her plate. They'd had too many conversations regarding her exhusband. One more wouldn't help.

"I'm sure you're right, Mom."

"I'm surprised Elise doesn't ask you to go with her. I know she's quite religious."

The way her mom spoke of religion contrasted so starkly with what Sierra saw in Elise. Warmth without expectations. Joy. Respect for others to choose their path without judgment or censure. An easy acceptance of the differences between her and Sierra.

"She doesn't push." The thought floated out and Sierra cringed. She needed a lock over her mouth.

Her mom carefully set her fork down. "Because I care, now I'm pushy." She aligned her knife next to the fork and gave Sierra a small smile. "I'll back off, honey. I certainly don't want to get in your way."

"That's not what I meant."

Her mom picked up her plate and carried it to the sink. "Sometimes we say exactly what we mean."

Sierra put her elbow on the table and rubbed her forehead. And maybe she *had* said what she meant.

The covers rustled as Sierra rolled over and reached for her phone the next morning, speed-dialed the number, and settled back against her pillow.

A sleepy voice answered. "Hello?"

"Elise?"

Her friend yawned. "What time is it?"

"I don't know. I wanted to catch you before you left for church."

"Hon, I at least wait until the sun is up."

"Funny. I think it's just before eight."

"Has He answered yet?"

"Who?"

"God."

"Oh, that. It wasn't really a *prayer* prayer."

"Hon, He understands groans that words cannot express."

Sierra smiled. Holy spirit Elise, in action. "Well, no one's come knocking on the door offering me a job."

Elise yawned again. "Not yet."

"I need a favor."

"And that would be?"

"Will you go with me to check on the horse after church today?"

Energy suffused her voice. "I'd *love* to! What are we checking?"

Sierra laughed. "I don't know. But Aunty Elise, who thought it'd be so great for me to keep the horse, can check whatever it is that needs to be checked."

"I didn't say nuthin' about helping. Moral support is my sole calling."

"Well, you can 'moral support' your way through checking that horse."

At twelve thirty, an ooga horn from the driveway announced that Elise had arrived.

Sierra grabbed her purse and locked the front door. Her mom was at an after-church women's committee luncheon. She started down the front steps and laughed. Elise sat in the driver's seat, top down on the Mazda, wrapped in a fur jacket with a rich maroon scarf covering her hair.

Elise peered over her black sunglasses. "What?"

"It's October!"

"Hon, when the sun's shining, you gotta live a little."

Sierra climbed in. "Is the heater on?"

Elise started the car. "Full blast." A few minutes later, they crept slowly up the gravel drive lined with oak trees. "Now wasn't that lovely of God to stable your horse so close to home?" Elise saw God's hand in everything. Sierra chose to love her in spite of the quirk.

"Um, that would be my mother who arranged that."

Elise just smiled.

The Mazda passed the last fence post at the end of the drive, and Elise stopped the car. "Whoa! What a setting!"

Sierra took in the details of the scene she'd missed on her first shock-filled visit. The grounds surrounding the immaculate two-story farmhouse could have been lifted from a postcard. A pristine emerald lawn created the canvas for the stunning arrangement of decorative trees and shrubs artfully placed among the lattice arches, Grecian benches, and other garden décor. And not a stray weed edged the circular drive that passed in front of the house and around to the barn.

"Wow!" Elise turned a shining grin on her. "Whoever created that is an artist."

"I think that would be Chance's landlord."

Elise's eyes got big. "No!"

Sierra nodded once. "Yep. He's a landscaper."

"I'm getting chills."

Sierra gave her a dry look. "That would be because the top is down."

"Spoilsport." Elise shifted back into first gear and motored toward the barn. She parked the car and shut it off. "So, what are we doing again?"

Sierra opened the door and climbed out. She kept pace with her friend, who walked gingerly, her maroon heels sinking into the damp earth as they made their way to the wire fence.

"Checking on Chance." She hadn't thought to ask what Ross meant until after his blue truck was rolling back down the driveway last Thursday afternoon.

"Define what we're checking for. I can't do any horse chasing in these shoes."

"Lice? Ticks? To see that he doesn't have four legs straight in the air? I don't know." Other than watching the horse graze in the field, she didn't really see the point.

"Oh, there he is. What a sweetheart. Look at him, Sierra." Elise glanced at her, sunshine in her smile. "Can we pet him?"

A hundred feet away, Chance plodded with slow, steady steps toward the fence. Toward them. Sierra shuddered. "No. He looks fine. Let's go."

She cooed. "Oh, look, he's coming to visit."

"Let's go, Elise. I'm not kidding."

Her friend turned. "Hon, look at his face. There's not a mean bone in his body."

Sierra eyed the thin squares of wire that separated them from the approaching mammoth creature. Thirty feet and still coming. Her knees turned to jelly and her breathing accelerated. She backed toward the car. "Elise, he's—"

The crunch of gravel made her turn. There in denim jeans and a black T-shirt, giving her a slow smile, was her knight.

Ross didn't stop until he reached Sierra. Her eyes clung to his with a hint of panic in them. The woman at the fence in the fur jacket waved at him, looking like she was having the time of her life. He grinned and waved back, then turned to the striking woman beside him, his voice low. "You're looking highly anxious again."

She tucked a piece of hair behind her ear and looked away. "It shows?"

"It crossed my mind that if I came up behind you and neighed really loud, I might see you climb the side of the barn there." Her smile held embarrassment, and he was sorry he'd teased her.

She lifted a hand toward the pasture. "You said to check on the horse, so I thought if Elise came with me, it wouldn't be so … I mean I could actually—so anyway, we've checked on Chance and he seems to be fine." Her amber eyes caught his for a moment, then she dashed back to her friend. "We should probably go."

Her friend called to them. "You guys need to come pet him. He is absolutely delicious."

"She's not going to eat him, is she?" he asked.

Sierra wrapped her coat tighter. "If wishes were horses …"

He stared and she gave a self-conscious laugh. "The old nursery rhyme. 'If wishes were horses, then beggars would ride.' It'd solve one of my problems if she did eat him."

He wanted to ask what problems she meant, but the statement didn't sound like an offer to share her thoughts. And if Mrs. Lassiter's gossipy diatribe about Sierra's ex-husband could be trusted, her problems were pretty obvious.

"It's a good idea to check on him until I can do a thorough job of inspecting the fence. We wouldn't want him to get out."

Her countenance grew pinched, and she scanned the fence as if looking for holes. "He really could escape?"

"It's not likely, as long as we supplement him with a little hay and grain. There's some grass yet for him to graze on."

Ross tilted his head, considering her. "Do you want to go pet Chance, try to get used to him? I could help you—"

She took a step back, closer to the car. "No, thanks. I'm fine right here. In fact, I need to get home." She raised her voice. "Elise, we should go."

The woman named Elise had lowered her face to the fence and was making cooing noises to the horse.

Sierra hollered louder. "Elise, if you don't come, I'm taking the car and leaving."

The large woman waved a hand at them. "All right, all right. I'm coming."

Ross watched Elise say good-bye to Chance. Good grief, she'd kissed the horse. Shaking his head, he shifted toward Sierra. "You'd really leave her?"

She slanted him a shy smile. "No, but it's a good threat. Elise doesn't let anyone drive her car." She added with a tilt of her head, "But she's very generous with everything else."

"The best kind of friend."

She nodded. "The very best."

They were flying back along the highway. Sierra tucked her hands between her legs to try to warm them.

Elise tilted her head toward her, platinum curls whipping along the sides of the scarf. "Okay, he's *so* dreamy."

"I couldn't believe you kissed him, Elise!"

"Not the horse, silly. The *man*."

Sierra had been trying to put thoughts of the *man* out of her head.

"Well, I still can't believe you put your lips on that animal."

"Hon, it's the only thing male that's touched these lips in a long time."

Sierra shook her head. Only Elise would see that as a bonus.

Her friend flattened her palms on the steering wheel, maroon-tipped fingers straight. "Okay, I need to say something. When you take your kids out to visit their horse tomorrow, what are you going to do?"

Sierra nibbled a fingernail. "Drive by very slowly so they can throw carrots out the window?"

Her friend looked at her aghast. "You'd let them roll the windows down near that ferocious animal?"

Sierra moved to the next finger. "It's not funny."

"You're right. I'm sorry. It's just that Chance is such a teddy bear. If you'd just try to—"

Sierra gave her a piercing look.

Elise clapped a manicured hand over her mouth. "Oh, hon. I sounded just like your mother, didn't I?"

"One Abbey Lassiter in my life is enough, thank you."

"It's just—"

"No more. I already went against good sense and kept the horse."

Elise raised a hand into the rushing breeze streaming over them. "Not another word." She gave her a naughty smile. "For today, at least."

Sierra lifted her chin and let the wind plow through her hair, wishing it could lift her out of the car and away from tomorrow's ordeal. She knew Braden would never be satisfied on the safe side of the fence.

Elise dropped Sierra back at her mom's after they had spent a couple hours sipping cappuccinos in the solarium at Taco Pete's. Odd place to find good coffee, but last year over a plate of enchiladas, they'd discovered that Pete was a java aficionado and his brew showed it.

Despite bribery by way of caramel flan, Sierra had not let Elise cajole her into talking about Ross. Yes, he was handsome—okay, gorgeous—*and* kind. But what did that say? Her instincts had failed before. Until she figured out where the defect lay—with her or with them—that was one pool she wasn't eager to wade back into. Elise had just smiled.

But later that evening the image of the cute grin on his face when he'd teased her about climbing the side of the barn kept creeping back, even as Sierra placed the steaming pot of corn chowder on the table.

"Honey, I would have been happy to make dinner." Her mom fiddled with the silverware and bowls, adjusting them for the third time.

Sierra slid the rolls into the oven. "I want you to rest, Mom. You've been waiting on us since we got here."

Her mom waved an arm around the kitchen and plopped down in a chair. "It's like letting somebody else drive your car."

Sierra kept the smile to herself. Her mom would have a fit if she realized how alike she and Elise really were.

The front door rattled and the herd of kids tromped into the house just as the buzzer on the oven went off.

"Hi, guys!" Sierra didn't have to look around the corner to know the living room was strewn with overnight bags and backpacks. According to her mom, The Motivator—though the name was a secret only Elise knew—was a work in progress. The backpacks would probably be a highlighted addendum. By the time they moved out, her mom would have two full pages of rules taped to the fridge. Maybe three.

"Hey, Mom. What's for dinner?" Braden walked to the fridge and opened it. Definitely a male trait.

"Nothing." He shot her a startled look, and she grinned at him. "We're having corn chowder."

The teasing earned her a half-smile.

She set the rolls on the counter and grabbed him in a hug and danced him around the kitchen. He tolerated her antics with the hint of a smirk. "Hey, mister, where's my big 'I'm so happy to see you' smile?"

He shrugged and stepped out of the hug. "I dunno. I'm going to put my stuff away." His fingers dragged along the table as he passed it. "Hi, Grandma."

"Hello, Braden. Glad to see you noticed your old grandma sitting here." Her eyes twinkled at him over the top of the hug Trevor had climbed up for. There was no other word to describe it. She adored her grandkids. Sierra tried to recall if her mom used to twinkle at her and Win.

Trevor climbed down from his grandma's lap and ran for her hug. Sierra swung him up and pressed her head to his. "Hey, bud, I missed you."

Over Trevor's shoulder, she looked at her mom. "Do you see Em?"

Abbey glanced toward the living room. "No."

Braden called from the stairs at the far side of the living room. "She's in her bedroom."

Trevor leaned back, his face filled with the importance of a newscaster. "Dad threw away Emory's blanket."

"What?" Her eyes swung to meet her mom's gaze.

"That doesn't surprise me." Lips pressed in a thin line, her mom shook her head and got up from her chair to stalk over to the counter and throw the cooling rolls into a bowl.

Trevor picked at the collar of her shirt. "She's too old for it."

"I'll be right back, honey." Sierra set Trevor down and jogged for the stairs. She tapped once on Emory's door and stole inside. "Hey, Em."

Emory lay on her stomach, drawing on a pad, ankles swinging in the air. "Hi." She didn't look up.

Sierra sat on the bed next to her. "Trevor told me what happened. Do you want to talk about it?"

Her daughter shook her head, eyes on the paper. A gray horse stood next to three kids. A woman, with Sierra's shoulder-length dark hair, stood a few feet away. On the far side of the page was a man with Michael's hair color and eyes. A big black "X" had been crossed over him.

Sierra pointed to the man in the picture. "Is that Dad?"

Emory nodded once. "I'm not going back to his house."

"I'm so sorry, honey."

A flush started in her daughter's soft cheeks, the first hint of tears. Emory looked up, heartbreak in the blue eyes. "He was so mean." Her face crumpled and she climbed into Sierra's arms.

After consoling Emory she marched down the stairs and straight to the kitchen. Her mom picked up the phone and handed it to her without a word.

"Thanks." She pulled the back door closed behind her and dialed the number.

"Hello." A woman answered. Apparently Gina didn't recognize Abbey's number on the ID.

"Gina, this is Sierra. May I speak with Michael, please?" She walked toward the back fence, the rain-laden grass squishing under her shoes.

"Oh. Just a second."

Sierra could picture the phone in Michael's house being passed like a hot potato. She and the former dental hygienist used to be friends. A long time ago.

"Hello?"

She should have calmed down before she called. A deep breath cooled her some. "Michael, can I get Emory's blanket back, please?"

He sighed, and his voice held an edge. "Sierra, she's way too old to be sleeping with a blanket like a two-year-old."

She wished she could make him see that these crutches—Emory's blanket, Trevor's thumb—were *temporary*. Yes, they should have given up these habits long ago. But their world shifted when their family splintered and they held onto the one little thing that gave them a measure of security and comfort.

"I understand that you don't agree with it, and she won't bring it with her next time. I'd just like to get it back."

"The trash collector picked it up this morning. She needs to start growing up, Sierra. The way you coddle the kids isn't helping them."

She ground her teeth. If she did coddle the kids occasionally, it was purely to compensate for his lack of empathy.

"Okay. Bye."

She stalked back to the kitchen and the door slammed behind her harder than she intended. Her mom held out a hand for the phone.

"Well?" The phone went into its spot on the counter.

A sadness for the life her kids had swept over her. "It's gone. He threw it away." Just like he'd thrown their family away. Would the pieces of her family ever fit back together?

Chapter 9

Braden started walking up the aisle before the bus stopped. It felt strange to walk on something that was moving. Maybe that was what an airplane felt like. His dad said he'd take him on one some day.

"Please wait until the bus is stopped before getting out of your seat." The driver looked funny with only his forehead and eyes showing in the mirror.

"Okay." *Whatever.*

He jumped from the second to last step to his grandma's driveway, but kept walking when the driver spoke to him again.

Emory caught up to him and tugged on his backpack. "Braden! Mr. Hollister was talking to you."

"So?"

"Remember, Mom said you need to be respectful to this driver. She said she won't drive you to school the rest of the year."

He shoved her away. "I don't care."

"Ow! Don't push!"

"Then stay away from me." Geez! What a crybaby. No wonder Dad threw her blanket away. The thought that had ridden with him all day came galloping back. Maybe they could go see Chance!

He ran up the front steps and into the house. "Mom!"

She came toward him from the kitchen with a big smile that made him feel warm inside. But at the same time it made a part of him feel bad too, like he was still mad at her for some reason.

He swung his backpack in his hand. "Can we go see Chance?"

She looked kinda worried and her smile got smaller, but she said, "Yes, but go change out of your school clothes."

Yeah! He pounded up the stairs to his room and threw the backpack on the floor. He ripped off his shirt and threw it at the hamper in the corner. Missed. His gaze snagged on the shoe box sitting on his bed and he raced to snatch it up. No way! Cowboy boots! Cool! He ripped the top off the box. Black! And they fit!

He ran back down the stairs and hugged his mom. "Thanks! Where'd you get them?"

She squeezed him extra tight. "You better go thank Grandma. She got them for you."

He tore into the living room where his grandma was picking up Emory's school bag. "Thanks, Grandma! I love 'em!"

She hugged him back, then put her hand on top his head. "You're welcome! Now don't wear them in the mud or they won't stay nice."

He pulled away from her hand. She still told him to zip his coat when it was raining too. "I won't."

His mom called. "Come on, Braden. We need to be back for supper."

He grinned at his grandma. "We're going to go see Chance. You want to come?"

She laughed. The folds around her eyes always crinkled when she did that. "No, I'm going to fix some spareribs and baked potatoes. You go have fun, and mind your mom."

It didn't bother him too much that his mom drove slow, but he couldn't wait to see Chance. Maybe Ross would be there too. That'd be cool.

"Oh, Braden?"

He looked at the rearview mirror and could see his mom's forehead, kinda like Mr. Hollister's. "Yeah?"

"I made your eye appointment this morning. It's in a week and a half. That was the soonest they could get you in."

"Okay." He didn't want to go. Kids would laugh at him if he got glasses. Braden unbuckled before the car fully stopped. "Mom, can we ride him today?"

"I get to ride him first!" Emory tried to squeeze past Braden out the van door.

"Emory! Move!" Braden pressed against his sister and jumped out first. He ran for the section of fence close to the green metal gate next to the barn, pulling a carrot out of his pocket. Emory and Trevor ran up beside him. He searched every inch of the empty field.

"I don't see him, Mom." Braden slumped so his chest and arms hung over the top of the fence and let the carrot dangle. "Can I get some grain and go find him?"

His mom took a long time to scan the pasture. "Um, Braden, I'm not sure that's a good idea. He's not really used to us yet."

"Aw, Mom."

He could tell she wanted to leave, but she rubbed her cheek and said, "How about you get some grain and stand in the enclosed fence area next to the barn?"

"The corral?" Ross had called it that when he showed them the barn.

Emory started to follow him. "I'll get his bridle."

"No, Em!" His mom looked freaked out again, like the day they got Chance.

It was so stupid to have a horse you couldn't even ride. He found the light switch on the wall inside the barn. Cobwebs hung from the bare bulbs and wooden beams. It was like a cool haunted house.

Braden followed the stained concrete around to the small room where Ross said the grain would be. The lid was hard to pry off, but he got it. The grain smelled good. Sweet. He carefully scooped the seeds into a dented tin bucket and started for the two big doors that separated the barn from the corral. The wooden doors hung on rusty hinges way above him and didn't look like they'd been closed in a long time. He walked through them and back into the sunlight, swinging the bucket.

His mom still looked nervous and had one hand on top of the chipped green gate and the other holding Trevor, who wanted to climb between the metal bars. "Honey, you're spilling the grain."

He wanted to roll his eyes, but he was afraid she'd make them leave if he did. He stopped swinging it and started around toward the back of the barn, banging the bucket with an old spoon he'd found near the tack room.

"Stop when you see him!" his mom called out.

He didn't look back. There was another farm with horses on the other side of the fence. He didn't think Chance could have jumped the fence. But you never knew. He carefully looked at each horse, but none of them was gray.

His mom hollered, "Is he coming?"

Braden stepped back around the barn. "I don't see him."

She let go of Trevor who scrambled through the bottom rungs of the gate. His mom climbed the gate and dropped to the dirt. Emory right behind her. She looked funny, kinda hunched over, looking at each corner of the corral, as if Chance might come tearing around the barn and she'd have to run for the fence. He tried not to laugh.

Finally, she moved over to the gate that led out to the field. It took her a long time, but she got the latch open.

He waited behind her. "Come on, Mom."

She stared across the field. "I don't think this is a good idea."

Emory put an arm around Mom, but she sounded worried. "Dad said you'd sell him. He said you're scared of horses and couldn't believe you got Chance. Are you going to sell him, Mom?"

His mom looked like she wanted to say yes, but couldn't. "No, honey, we're not going to sell him."

Braden dropped the bucket to the ground, but only a little spilled out. "We might as well. It's no fun having a horse we can't do anything with."

She looked at him a long time. "You're right, Braden." She was trying to be brave. Her smile didn't look very brave, though. "Okay, let's go see if we can find him." But she still didn't move toward the gate.

He reached around her and pushed it open. "Okay, then let's go."

Sierra wavered. All she wanted to do was dump the bucket and herd the kids back to the car. Her brain apparently hadn't communicated the horrible memories to her hand, because quicker than she could think, her fingers were reaching for the pail. "He's probably hiding behind those apple trees down there."

Braden frowned toward the trees. "Wouldn't we see his legs?"

She squinted, trying to decipher between brush and long gray legs. "I don't know." She rattled the pail again and started for the far pasture. "Chaaaaaance!" The kids chimed in, then broke into a run. The tall grass separated into three distinct paths behind them.

The pail wobbled as she tried to bang the spoon against it and jog over the rutted ground to keep up. No way were the children going to get to a thousand pounds of horseflesh without her.

Braden reached the trees first. He put his hands up and turned, arms dropping. "He's not down here, Mom."

Where could a horse hide? Sierra scanned beyond the borders of the fence, toward the neighboring pasture and its herd of horses. Brown and black horses grazed peacefully from what she could see, but no dappled gray gelding with white socks milled among them. But then, who knew what was behind the other barn or down in that dip where the brush grew thick?

"Um, let's try the other end of the field, past the barn." She couldn't believe she was in the same field with a horse—and actually searching for him. Elise would call this progress.

Braden ran beside her. "What'll we do if he's not there?"

"I don't know, honey." Sierra took a panting breath. *How in the world do people on those commercials jog and talk at the same time?* "We'll have to ask Ross if he's seen him today."

"When will he be home, because—Mom! There's Chance!" Braden jerked to a halt and pointed.

Sierra looked.

Nothing but grass between them and the wire fence Braden was pointing to. She looked again at Braden's outstretched arm and followed it to the border of the field. "Where, honey?"

"There!"

A movement beyond the fence caught her eye. A dark head swiveled, sending strands of a gray stringy mane to swaying like an out-of-sync pendulum. Chance stared straight at them.

From Ross's perfectly manicured backyard. *Oh, crud.*

Emory jumped and squealed while Trevor laughed that free-spirited laugh that only four-year-olds possessed, as the kids ran for the fence. Along the wire fence line, strands of pallid field grass mingled with the sculpted rich green lawn that surrounded Ross's white farmhouse.

Chance stood in the midst of the garden paradise next to a bronze statue of a boy holding a kite. A hint of fragrance drifted in the breeze toward them.

"Wait, guys!" Sierra called out. "We don't want to frighten him." She sped up and grabbed Trevor by the back of the shirt. "Hold on, buddy." Her imagination had her youngest on his back, eyes closed, face white as death with a red hoof print on his forehead. She shuddered. "Emory, Braden! Wait for me!"

Braden was in high gear. One foot barely on the brake, while the other revved the engine. He edged through the gate that separated Ross's home from the field. "Mom, I can get him."

"Hold on, I said!" Sierra eyed the gate—one length of wire mesh fencing hung between three boards and a post, with a swivel latch at the top. "Was this open?"

Braden shrugged, his right hand curled over the rough wood at the top of the gate, his body halfway through the enclosure. "Yeah. Can I get him now?"

She gave him a look with raised brows that negated the need for words.

He shoved back from the gate. "Oh, man!"

"Ross must have left it open." Then she had another thought. "Braden, did you open this gate when you and Trevor were playing in Ross's koi pond the other day?"

Guilt shadowed his face along with frustration that said he couldn't believe she was asking him the question. "I shut it, Mom."

Uncertainty grabbed her. Should she go with disbelief and hope the guilt would induce him to tell the truth? Or give him the benefit of the doubt? She went with disbelief. She tilted her head slightly and crossed her arms.

"I *shut it!*" Sullenness pressed his lids into narrow, angry slits.

Wrong approach. These were the moments that left her wishing for a do-over. "Honey, I don't know who else would have left it open."

"Well, I didn't!" He shoved through the gate. Her lips pressed forcefully to call him back. But a tiny spark of fear stopped her. *What if he wouldn't come?* The concern lay banked in dull embers that glowed with bits of orange and red every time Braden became surly. She was afraid one day they'd ignite, and her fears would become reality. His pain and anger over the divorce would drive him from developing into the man he held promise of becoming.

Emory vacillated, eager to follow her brother, but worry clouded her features.

Sierra knew that look. She wanted to go but didn't want to get in trouble. Sierra found herself nodding. "Don't scare him."

Braden walked up slowly and stopped a good thirty feet from Chance. Emory crept quietly behind him. All that fight to keep him from getting hurt and he wasn't even within a tail's flicker away. Trevor danced and dragged against her arm, finally standing relatively still when they reached his siblings.

The four of them stared. Chance stared right back, then dipped his head and lifted fat, velvety lips to daintily bite the last quarter inch of whatever had been growing in the soft dirt.

Sierra looked at the lush flower beds. The plants were a variety of sizes but spaced evenly except for the gap where Chance stood. Whatever it was, he had razed it. Not even a nibbled leaf lay on the bare dirt.

Chance moved on to a perfectly trimmed white-veined bush next on the buffet line. Sierra took a step forward and stopped. "Didn't Chance have on one of those halter-things before?"

Braden looked away and a warning flashed in her mind.

She looked at her elder son more closely. "Braden, do you know where his halter is?"

He scuffed the grass. "When Trevor was throwing rocks at the fish, I gave Chance another carrot and took it off."

Sierra stared at him, fear pinching her cheeks tight. She imagined him all alone with Chance, wrestling the straps off the giant horse's head. A wave of nausea passed through her.

"It didn't look comfortable," he said.

"Please run to the barn and get it for me. And one of those ropes that hooks to it." She ran a shaking hand over her face. They would get through this. *Please, God!* A prayer rose of its own volition.

He nodded, a hint of relief lighting his features. "Sure, Mom."

It started to drizzle.

She turned back. Like a giant aphid, Chance worked on the white bush. Methodically he labored, his lips pulling and teeth crunching, carving a hole in the listing shrub. Sierra looked again at the indent in the ground where the other plant had been. "I hope Braden hurries, or Ross isn't going to have any plants left."

Emory watched Chance. "Can't Ross plant more?" She grabbed her mom's hand with an exuberant swing. "I know! We can buy some for him."

She gave Emory a quick smile before fastening her gaze on Chance again. "That's a great idea, sweetie."

"Here, Mom." Braden puffed as he ran up with the halter and rope.

Sierra took the twisted black nylon with its conglomeration of metal rings and buckles. She turned it three different directions, and finally guessed at the most likely spot to fit Chance's ears. She walked slowly, so slowly, toward the horse, and exhaled a quavering breath when he ignored her.

She held the halter like a noose and bent—one foot in the flower bed, the other on the lawn—and reached for his lowered head. He swung away, and she jerked up to find that she was now pinched at the edge of the flower bed between the large gray horse and a mammoth hydrangea bush.

Sierra breathed in three short gasps and stared at the gray back that was at eye level and smelled damp and horsey. The heat of its body radiated toward her. Sierra reached out and tentatively pushed against Chance's giant hip. The horse shifted his weight closer, narrowing the gap. A sparkler-like zap of panic ignited in her chest, sending bursts of light down her nerve endings. *He's only eating. He doesn't want to hurt you.*

She took a couple of hyperventilating breaths. The only exit was around the back end, and no way was she heading in that direction. Since pole vaulting wasn't an option, the only other exit was over the leggy hydrangea behind her.

"Mom?"

She couldn't see the kids, but a worrying edge of anxiety filled Emory's voice.

"It's okay, honey. I'll be right there. Don't move!" She surveyed the shoulder-high bush next to her, heavy with the remnants of faded blue-green flowers. "Braden? Stay there and hold onto Trevor. I'm going to go back over the fence to the pasture and come around." Sierra's front teeth dug into her bottom lip.

Munching the delectable ground cover, Chance took another bite and crowded a few inches closer. He took another step, ostensibly to snag a morsel on the far side of the next shrub, but he shifted his posterior toward Sierra, a large hoof missing her right tennis shoe by millimeters. Sierra leaped for the hydrangea. Three difficult steps into the thick-stemmed bush, and she knew she'd made a big mistake.

"What in the blue blazes is that woman doing?" Ross stood frozen at the picture window. The horse was grazing on his favorite begonia and Sierra looked like she was trying to swim through his hydrangea bush. The pair was wrecking all his hard work! Teeth clenched, he stormed out the back door. A pop on the rump encouraged Chance to saunter a few steps away, where he began to nibble the climbing wisteria, giving Ross room to approach Sierra.

He surveyed the mangled plant. "A machete would have been a lot easier." The hydrangea was one of the few original plants he'd kept from his mother's yard. It colored many of his childhood memories.

"I'm sorry, okay?" She sounded fearful and annoyed with a third of the bush crushed under her feet and twisted around her thighs. "I thought my safety was a little more important than a plant."

"You weren't in any danger. This horse isn't—"

And then the bare dirt caught his eye. A naked spot where an heirloom honeysuckle used to grow. His mother's *treasured* honeysuckle—he laced his fingers on top his head and tilted his chin up. *Lord, if You don't help me, I'm going to strangle someone.* Someone being a somewhat attractive—okay, amazingly attractive—woman who obviously didn't know a darned thing about horses.

He took a deep breath and prodded the dirt with the tip of his boot. He could never replace that plant. His mother was going to be devastated.

Sierra attempted to step back, but the thick stalks had twisted around her shoe. She swayed, trying to pull her foot clear. He reached to catch her, but she regained her balance, though she wasn't any closer to getting free.

"Do you need help?"

She kept her head bent to the task. "No, I think I got it." But her foot remained trapped under a crisscross of greenery.

"Here, give me your hand." He stepped toward her, the green stems crushing under his boots.

Her hand slid into his, warm and strong, and the extra stability helped her get one foot free, but her other remained stuck.

"Grab on and I'll pull you out," he said.

She looked uncertain but put a tentative hand on his shoulders. He wrapped an arm around her waist and hauled her free. He immediately let go and she hopped, one hand clutching his upper arm.

"My shoe."

He looked down at her foot encased only in a white sock. She gave him a tiny grin, and despite his irritation he felt his own lips curve. He shook his head.

"I gotcha, Mom." Braden grabbed her other hand and she leaned in to her son while Ross retrieved the buried shoe.

Sierra took the shoe. Ross's face was still dark, but less so. Like the patches of gray and light after a heavy thunderstorm.

She nodded at the bare patch of dirt. "What was it?"

"*Lonicera fragrantissima.*" Undercurrents of annoyance remained. "A honeysuckle my mother dug up from her grandparents' homestead in Kansas and has worried over and babied for the last thirty years."

Oh, crud! Then the next thought blurted before she could stop it. "If it was so important why didn't she take it with her when she moved?"

He stared at her, as if trying to comprehend the stupidity of her words. "Why didn't she—?" He blew out a breath and looked around, as if he wasn't sure if he should laugh or order her off his place.

Trevor had clung close to her since Ross made his dramatic entrance. He whispered. "Pick me up, Mommy." She leaned down to hoist him to her hip, wishing she could reel back her words.

Ross waved an annoyed hand at the bare spot. "She did! But it started dying, so I took a cutting from it and moved it from my greenhouse to here last month."

"Oh." She swallowed hard. "Can you get another cutting?"

"Her plant died. We were going to transplant this one back to her place when we were certain it was hardy enough." He rubbed the back of his neck and frowned at the horse. "I guess we should have taken our chances."

Braden whispered near her elbow. "Chances. Get it, Mom?"

"Mmmhmm." Sierra wondered about the consequences of Chance having eaten an entire bush. A thirty-year-old one at that. She couldn't afford a sick horse. "Is it poisonous?"

His lips curved in the barest of smiles, and he slid her a look. "It'd solve one of your problems, wouldn't it?"

"Not the way I'd like." She felt a blush take over her cheeks and looked away from the hint of intimacy in the secret joke.

He shrugged. "I don't think it'll make him sick. You'll know in a couple of hours." He nodded toward her arm. "Can I have that?"

She looked at her arm where she'd looped the halter. "Oh. Certainly." Relief that she wouldn't have to put it on Chance coursed through her. She handed it to him, quickly plucking a few trailing leaves before he strode off to capture their horse.

Emory and Trevor hung close to her, but Braden shadowed Ross as he led Chance back across the yard.

Ross turned to ask over his shoulder, "How'd he get out?"

"Braden left the gate open." The words were out before she could contain them.

Ross nodded once, but her son glared at her, then looked away, his body stiff.

Remorse washed through her. Great job building her son up.

Two days later, Sierra woke and stretched, a luxurious, joyful stretch, then laid there with a grin. She had a job interview today! At McMillan's Brake Shop. She pulled her robe on and sauntered into the kitchen.

"Morning, guys!"

Emory smiled and waved her fork. "Morning, Mom."

Trevor gave her a cheesy grin, a piece of toast jutting out of his mouth.

Braden barely looked up from his plate of eggs. "Are we going to Dad's tomorrow?"

Sierra hesitated pulling the peanut butter and jelly out of the cupboard. "No, honey. He said it won't work this weekend."

"That doesn't surprise me," her mom's voice sounded from the living room. Braden slouched further down in his chair.

Sierra started toward the front door with the kids' lunches, but stopped when she saw her mom ironing the black pants she'd set out last night.

"I grabbed these out of your room this morning, honey. Were you going to wear that red shirt? I really think your white blouse would be better."

"Oh." The white blouse hung from the back of the recliner, freshly pressed. "But I always wear the red one to interviews."

At 9:50 Sierra walked into her interview wearing her black slacks and the white blouse.

The woman behind the desk was kind and asked a few brief questions, but after ten short minutes she stood. "Thank you for coming by, Sierra. We'll be in touch." The polite smile told Sierra quite succinctly that there would be no job offer coming from her.

Sierra pressed her hand against the door to exit the building, and stopped, the glass cold under her hand. Why wasn't she getting anywhere in her job search? With all the résumés she'd spread around, she'd gotten hardly any return calls and only one interview.

She exited the building and pressed the button to power her phone back on. Two missed calls. One from Elise, the other from an unfamiliar number. She dialed her voice mail and opened the door to her van.

"Hello, Mrs. Montgomery. This is Celia Ward from the district attorney's office returning your call. I'll be out of the office until Monday if you'd like to try me then."

Sierra groaned and dropped her head against the steering wheel. She was going to be stuck at her mother's forever.

Chapter 10

Early Sunday morning Sierra rolled over in bed and willed her body to relax back to sleep. She'd stared at the ceiling for hours last night, shuffling through the unpaid bills in her mind. And it didn't help that her mother had harped last night about Sierra's child-support situation and what she'd do to Michael if she could lock him in a room with some twine and a pair of pliers. Mom had grown up on a cattle ranch.

Her door cracked. "Honey, are you coming to church?"

Sierra groaned. "No, Mom." But the guilt-o-meter went into full alert, in her mom's voice, no less. *Go to church. Go to church.*

She pulled the covers higher, gray morning light filtering through her window. God didn't want her there if she couldn't trust Him, did He? As it was, she and God had drifted to a state of disillusionment. Kind of like meeting someone new and gaining a certain impression of them and then finding out over time you were wrong.

Like really wrong.

But this ingrained sense of guilt clung to something deep inside her. All that childhood training that there was a God, and if she so much as glanced at her schoolmate's math test, He knew. And was it really her place to tell the kids that God wasn't overly concerned with their lives? Some things they would have to figure out on their own.

And maybe just a tiny part of her hoped ... hoped that He cared.

Her mom didn't even try to hide her pleased smile as they scooted up the steps next to her into the foyer of The Gentle Shepherd.

"Do I have to go to Sunday school?" Braden complained, all but dragging his feet.

Her mom raised her brows, as if to say, "See? You waited too long."

Was it sacrilegious for Sierra to roll her eyes in church?

Emory grabbed Abbey's hand and swung it. "Grandma, can we pray that God will let Chance live a long, long time?"

Trevor hopped next to her. "I want to pray for a Power Ranger."

"Oh, honey." Grandma laughed and gave Emory a squeeze. "Now, kids." She included Braden in the hushed address, lining them shoulder to shoulder in front of her, like little soldiers. She straightened Trevor's collar. "God is *very* busy with a lot of important things to do. We don't want to bother Him about things like horses or toys."

So where did that leave room for the faith that Elise was always talking about? Her friend praised God for answering what Sierra thought were some of the funniest prayers. Like the time she asked God to help her find a lost pearl earring. She said that the next day God led her to the fake Christmas tree in the storage closet, and there was her earring, resting on the lowest branch. Sierra didn't know what to think about that, but it didn't stop Elise from sharing.

What would her mom think about a God who cared about horses and pearl earrings? But if He cared, why didn't He make Michael listen to his children's hearts, or bring her a job when she so desperately needed one? Where was the caring God Elise talked about?

Sierra watched out the kitchen window the next day, as the school bus stopped and the kids poured out and ran up the walkway. Emory dashed into the kitchen for a quick hug.

"Where's Grandma?"

Sierra bent down and said, "Grandma got a call this morning that Great Aunt Marta broke her hip, so Grandma flew out to Florida to help her get better."

Emory's face grew worried and she looked like she might cry. "For how long?"

She wrapped her arms around her daughter. "A few weeks."

"Can we go too?" Braden looked hopeful.

"No, sweetie, you have school."

"Awww. You never let us do anything fun. Dad said he'd take us to Disney World sometime."

Like that will happen. Sierra kept the thought to herself.

The phone rang, and Braden ran to answer it. He walked back from the kitchen, holding it out for her. "It's Ross."

She turned away from the kids to answer it. "Hello?"

"It's Ross." The masculine voice sent a tingle up her spine.

"Hi." She felt a slow grin sweep over her lips.

"Sorry to call, but Chance keeps getting loose, so I'm going to put him in a stall until I find where he's getting out."

"Oh." The tingly feeling swept away.

"I can feed him in the morning, if you can get the evening shift."

"Thank you. That's very kind."

"Two flakes of hay and a cup of grain is all you have to give him until we turn him back into the field."

She realized she was nibbling her fingernail again and tucked it under the elbow holding the phone. "All right. Thanks."

A heavy silence held the line.

"I guess that's it."

Was he trying to stay on the line? She pressed her hand to her forehead, bouncing on her toes. Think! Say something intelligent to the man. "Uh huh." She dropped her hand. *Real smooth, Sierra.*

"I'll see you around."

"Okay."

"Bye." His voice held the hint of a smile. And the line clicked.

She scrunched her eyes shut and wanted to stamp her feet. Didn't she have *anything* intelligent to say? Her eyes shot open. What was she doing? She didn't *want* to date anyone. She had more pressing problems like finding a job than drooling over some hunky guy who was probably all wrong for her anyway.

Emory frowned at her. "Are you all right, Mom?"

"Hmm? Oh, I'm fine, honey." She put an arm around Em's shoulder and walked with her toward the kitchen. "Why don't you start on your homework, and I'll get dinner going."

Emory spread her books across the table, and Sierra pulled a bag of lettuce from the vegetable crisper and started rinsing it in the sink.

Braden moped in and set Sierra's cell phone on the counter.

She shook the dripping leaves over the sink. "Who were you calling, honey?"

He turned away, his face heavy with dark emotions. "Dad."

She dried her hands, followed him to the living room, and put an arm on his shoulders, hoping he'd lean in for a hug. "Did you talk to him?"

Braden stepped free of her arm. "He wasn't there."

"I'm sorry."

He shrugged and walked upstairs, and her heart grew heavier with each step he took away from her. And she knew it was *away*. They were losing their son, and Michael didn't even seem to care.

Back in the kitchen she mixed bread crumbs and egg into the ground beef. How could she reach Braden? How could she be both mother and father to her kids? Her eldest child was at a critical age in his development. He craved a father. And she was powerless to make Michael see that.

And how healthy was it for the kids to live under their grandma's continuous hovering? Sierra needed to move them into a place where they had the freedom to leave their markers and the like strewn across the table on occasion.

She opened the oven door and set the meatloaf inside, then reached for her phone to call Elise. When she flipped open the phone, her message icon popped up. Her heart beat a little faster, taking on a cadence of hope. *Please. Please. Please—be a job offer.*

Maybe God did care. The thought caught her by surprise. Maybe— a tingle of awareness lifted each hair across her arms—maybe God was trying to reach her, to show her, like Elise said. She pressed the button for her voice mail.

A brisk female voice came on. "Hello. This is Cheryl from Webberling

SHERRI SAND

Heating Systems." Anticipation shifted to despair as she heard, "We have filled the position you applied for. We'll keep your application on file for one year—"

Sierra pushed the button to delete the message. The prickle in the air evaporated. Hormones and stress could create weird feelings. She felt exposed and silly all at the same time. Was she so desperate that she'd actually thought God was working on her behalf? She wanted to brush a tough protective coating over her throbbing nerve endings. Even her mom didn't believe that God spoke like that. The strange impression that there had been a job waiting on her voice mail, that it'd been sent from God, was just that: a strange impression. Because she'd forgotten one critical detail, God was much too big to worry about a small thing like her survival.

After their bellies were full of dinner and slices of leftover peach pie her mom had made after church, Sierra loaded her excited brood in the van.

"Can we ride him tonight, Mom?" Braden hung over the front seat as she started the car.

She tried to sound upbeat. "Um, I'm not sure."

A few minutes later, wipers whipping, she turned up the familiar driveway and headed toward the barn. Seeing the empty cement apron next to Ross's house dissipated a tendril of worry that he might be home. She didn't want to see him until she figured out her weird reactions to him *and* what to do about his honeysuckle. She drove past the house and parked next to the barn.

Braden and Emory were out of the van before she shut it off. Trevor unbuckled and hurried to follow.

"Where's your coat, honey? It's raining."

He didn't even pause as he jumped out. "I'm okay." Her mother would be raising her eyes in that "See what I mean?" manner.

Sierra zipped her coat and hustled out of the van. It took major willpower to step through the darkened doorway of the barn. She flipped her hood back and walked toward the kids, who were crowded in front of the stall. The barn wasn't nearly as dark as it looked from outside the door. Yellow light cast a pall over the dusty wooden beams and old stairs that climbed up the loft on her right.

Chance looked at them from over the stall door. Braden rubbed the gray forehead, while Emory stood on one of the bales stacked against the enclosure and scratched behind a long ear. Trevor watched from a few feet back, hands in his pockets.

Then Chance swung his heavy head and Braden dodged back. Sierra leaped toward them and pulled Emory down and Braden back a step. Chance swung his head lazily around again.

Braden pulled his collar free and stepped toward the stall. "Geez, Mom." Emory stared at her with wide eyes.

"I thought—he looked like he was going to … " To what? Knock down the stall door? She closed her eyes. *Get a grip, Sierra.* She took a breath and studied the horse locked securely behind the heavy wooden gate.

Emory pointed down the aisle. "I think he just heard a noise."

Sierra attempted a smile. "You're probably right."

Her daughter took a small step toward Chance. "Is it okay—?"

Sierra nodded and Em hopped back up onto the bale. She let them pet him a few more minutes before she said, "Okay, guys. We need to feed him."

Ross had said two flakes of hay. Hay stuck out from the bale Emory stood on like a bunch of blonde bristles. Sierra grabbed two handfuls and Emory jumped down.

Braden crouched next to her, with Emory and Trevor on the other side. She grinned at the way the four of them were bent in position like sprinters at a track meet. "Okay. One, two, three … pull!"

The effort left her hands red with white lines where the straw slid through her grip. The hay was wedged in tight and she dropped the wisps she'd managed to pull free. The kids stood holding tiny bits of straw in their fists.

Braden studied the bale and then straddled it, attacking one of the twin metal bands and digging his fingers into the straw under it.

Sierra worked on the other one. The wire binding the bale together was like a taut rubber band around a ponytail. She could barely edge the tips of her fingers under it. No way they could tug it off the bale.

What now? Straddling the bale, she looked around. Braden ran for the tack room. Emory and Trevor trailed after him, searching until Trevor found a pair of rusty clippers under a workbench. The red dust ground into her palms, but after a few minutes of maniacal squeezing she managed to cut first one wire, then the other.

When the second wire sprang free, she saw what Ross meant about flakes. The hay folded over into thick files. An opening in the stall divider allowed them to drop the hay and grain Braden got from the tack room, right into the feeding trough. A few minutes later the heavy crunch-crunch of colossal molars grinding the granola-looking mixture filled the barn. Sierra leaned on the gate that separated her from the horse.

Emory stood on one of the intact bales and wrinkled her nose. "It stinks."

Sierra agreed. The stall needed to be cleaned. Chance shifted his weight, resting the tip of one back hoof on the dirt floor. The power in those hindquarters. If she got behind Chance and Chance didn't like it ... how long would it take someone to find her? What would the kids do? She didn't need Braden entering the stall attempting a rescue.

She couldn't help the terror that surged through her every time she walked near the giant gray animal. And she worried that Chance sensed her fear. Didn't that make animals more aggressive? She'd read that when training a dog, you had to show them who the alpha leader was. Well, Chance was the alpha leader of this pack.

She stood on a bale with the kids and studied the horse. Braden twisted to see her around Emory, the bale rocking beneath them. "We need to clean his stall, Mom."

Sierra chewed her lip. There was no way she was going in that stall, but she couldn't ask Ross to do the job for her either.

The sound of a vehicle crunching up the gravel drive entered the barn. Braden bolted for the door and looked out. "It's Ross." Her son disappeared. Sierra sighed. So much for avoiding the man.

Ross rolled to a stop under the carport alongside the house. With a big grin Braden opened the door of the truck.

"Hey, Braden," Ross said. "You guys feeding Chance?"

"Yeah. We might ride him today."

"That so?" The eagerness of the boy tugged at him, stirring feelings long dormant. That hunger to be noticed and to matter to a father figure reached so deep. "Well, I'm planning to work on the fence tomorrow night. Do you want to help me?"

"Yeah! Could we do it tonight?"

"No, I've still got some work to do. I just ran home to fill my growling stomach."

Braden laughed. "Yeah. We need to clean Chance's stall, but Mom's starting to look squirrelly again."

"Squirrelly, huh?"

"Yeah, like how a squirrel runs around when it's nervous."

"Gotcha." He chuckled, imagining Sierra running around the barn.

"My mom's scared of horses. Do you want to come see him?"

If he went to the barn, it wouldn't be to see just Chance. The image of the woman with hair dark like Braden's came to mind. He glanced at his watch and shook his head. "I'd like to, but I need to eat dinner and get back to work."

Braden's eyes dropped to the gravel. "Okay." He gave him a half-hearted smile and started back for the barn.

He watched Braden disappear through the doorway. The disappointment in the boy's smile wasn't the only thing that stopped Ross from heading into the house, it was the sadness behind it. He glanced up the road toward Alex Cranwell's house with a sigh, shut the pickup door, and started for the barn.

The four of them were lined on the bales of hay next to Chance's stall. "Hey."

The whole family turned, and Braden's face lit up. The boy jumped down and ran over. Sierra's gaze lingered for a long moment, but other than that Mona Lisa smile, she didn't say anything.

He tilted his chin toward the flakes of hay. "I see you managed to break the bale open."

She nodded and clenched her palms together. A hint of rust from her efforts with the baling wire stained her fingers.

"I gave him grain, too." Braden hooked a thumb through his belt loop.

Ross shifted his weight and adjusted the thumb already resting in his own belt loop. "I bet he liked that."

"He does. He's still eating it." Emory tossed a grin over her shoulder.

"He eats loud." This from the smallest guy.

Ross glanced at his watch again and took a step toward the door. "Well, I—"

"His bed stinks." The little boy balanced next to his mom on the bale and pinched his nose.

Sierra was biting her lip, but when he caught her eye a smile peeked through. She tousled the boy's hair.

Braden shifted his stance, matching Ross's cocked hip. "Could you help us?"

Consternation washed the smile from Sierra's face. "Braden." She shook her head at the boy.

Braden's head went down, and Ross caught the flash of anger in his eyes. *Lord, I don't have time to do this.* He sighed, knowing full well that he needed to help this family. But God wasn't working on his timetable. But with the way the woman had destroyed his hydrangea the other day, there was no telling what his barn would look like if he left. He put a hand on Braden's shoulder. "I'll show you where the pitchforks are."

Sierra watched them walk off, Ross's hand still on Braden's shoulder. Her son's face was clear and animated as he chatted with the man. Emory and Trevor scampered over to a stack of hay bales to play king of the mountain.

Ross and Braden reappeared a few minutes later with two pitchforks and a wheelbarrow. Man-sized gloves swam on Braden's hands.

Ross's stance seemed stiff, and he definitely wasn't smiling. He led Chance into an empty stall and bolted the door shut.

Sierra walked over to the dirty stall. "You don't have to do this, Ross."

His smile was brief. "It's not a problem."

She chewed her bottom lip. "About your mom's plant, I can't apologize enough for what happened."

Hands at his hips, Ross swung to look at Chance, who circled his new surroundings. "I can't say I would have cried if it had poisoned him."

She couldn't tell if he was joking. There was no hint of a smile anywhere on his face, just hard planes as he stared at Chance. She waved a hand toward the wheelbarrow. "Really, we can take care of cleaning the stall."

He tilted his head and watched her a moment. Then a slight smile crossed his face and his tone seemed deliberately upbeat. "You would, huh?" He grabbed the pitchfork and entered the stall. "This from the woman who parted my hydrangea bush like the Red Sea?"

She felt heat like two branding irons in her cheeks. "I'm so sorry. I just—" He stabbed a heaping load of dirty straw and carried it to the wheelbarrow and dumped it in, Braden right behind him with a smaller forkful. "I didn't know I'd mangled the bush so badly until you pulled me out of it."

Ross looked at her and grinned. "Don't worry about it. It was due for a good trimming anyway." He went back in for another scoop, then stopped, resting the pitchfork tines on the ground, and laid an arm across Braden's shoulders. He pointed to where Braden was working. "Let's leave the clean straw and just get the stuff that looks dirty."

Braden nodded. "Okay."

Ross gave his shoulder a squeeze, then moved to separate some of the straw with the tines. He glanced at Sierra, a warm glint in his eye. "You've got a hard worker here."

Braden grinned at him, a glow on his face that gave Sierra pause. How sad that her son was so hungry for a man's attention that he'd look for it in someone other than his father. Yet Michael had all but disappeared from his life in the past several months.

Sierra gave her son a teasing look. "Yes, he is. Though I'd say he'd rather scoop up horse poop than unload the dishwasher."

"This is real work, isn't it, Braden? Builds muscles on a man."

Almost of their own accord, Sierra's eyes moved to Ross's well-developed shoulders and arms to verify that it was indeed so. She made herself look away.

Braden strained to lift the huge pile of straw he'd scooped. "Yep!"

Sierra cleared her throat. "My mom said you did all the landscaping here yourself."

"That I did."

"I don't think I've seen another place quite like it."

"Thanks." A boyish grin flashed before he turned away to dump another load. "I bought this place from my folks six months ago." He shrugged. "It's been a lot of work, but I enjoy it. It's also great advertisement for my business." A slight shadow crossed his face. "My neighbor, Alex Cranwell, hired me to do his landscaping after he bought the place across the road."

Braden lifted the handles of the wheelbarrow. "You want me to dump it now?"

Ross stood his pitchfork on end. "Yeah, on that pile outside that I showed you. Thanks, Braden."

Her son disappeared through the barn door.

"You know there's a lot of value in saying a person's name," Sierra said.

He looked at her with interest. "That so?"

She felt heat rise in her face again. While they worked she'd watched Braden, watched how he relaxed around Ross. She lifted her eyes back to his. "It acknowledges a person's identity, tells him that he's noticed."

"And people want to be noticed, don't they?"

"In the worst way." She stared in the far end of the barn where Emory and Trevor were playing hide-and-seek around the small fort they'd built out of a pile of bales. *Have I ever truly felt noticed?*

"It must be tough raising kids by yourself."

She gave him a half smile. "It has its moments."

Weary after the two hours of haggling over the waterfall redesign with the
Cranwells, Ross climbed Sid's sagging front steps and rapped on the door
twice. Something he did so often, it was a wonder there was any paint left
on that spot.

"Door's open."

Ross let himself in and flopped down into the blue recliner across
from his nearest neighbor and best friend.

"What's got your pants all in a dander?"

Ross slid his gaze to Sid. "I have a boarder."

The grizzled old man muted the television and rolled the piece of fescue to the other side of his mouth in a familiar dance between lip and
grass. "Oh, you do? Now that sure does surprise me."

"Yeah, well it wasn't my idea." Ross knew he wasn't in the best
mood. When he couldn't stand his own company any longer, he'd head
for Sid's.

Sid nodded, blue eyes still sharp and clear. "Kyle." It wasn't a question
and Ross didn't need to answer. Sid's chuckle made him feel that here at
least, all was understood. "Another one from church?"

"I think that's what he said." The last wayfarer Kyle had collected had
said he was a chef. Kyle persuaded Sid that he needed a cook "just until
the unfortunate fellow gets his feet under him." Three nights later a fire
truck stood in Sid's front yard and five hundred gallons of water soaked
the kitchen.

"How long's Kyle got him livin' with you?"

"Sierra?"

Sid's forehead bunched, which had the effect of gathering his white
eyebrows into bushes over his eyes. "He's headed for the Sierra
Mountains?"

"What? No, Sierra is a woman—"

"What in tarnation? Kyle set you up with a woman?" Sid's eyes were set to ignite.

Ross exhaled. "A *horse*. I'm boarding a horse for a woman named Sierra."

After Sid settled back down to roost in his chair again, Ross explained. "And she's terrified of horses. The woman tried to cut a path through my hydrangea to get away from the thing."

Sid looked alarmed. "The horse was chasin' her?"

Ross chuckled at the picture. "No." He looked away. "Chance had just finished off Mom's honeysuckle."

A shine came over Sid's face when Ross mentioned the honeysuckle. "Now I know your ma is going to hit the high notes when you tell her, but you got to admit that horse has re-*finement*." Sid had a way of drawing the vowels out of sophisticated words. He'd find them in the daily crossword and then look for an opportunity to saddle one onto a conversation. It didn't help that Sid tended to prefer horses over people, and when one exhibited good taste it tickled him to no end. "Not just any critter'd pick honeysuckle. Not when you got that fancy stuff crawling up that cedar lattice."

"Yeah, well I don't think Mom is going be as excited as you are."

"Women and their flowers." Only it came out "wimmen and their flawrs." Sid might be one of the wealthiest polo trainers in the country, but he sure wouldn't win a grammar contest.

Ross gave him a look. "You know how much that plant meant to mom."

Sid waved a hand as if he were swatting a fly. "I know, I know. Remember, I dug the hole when your daddy was away at some lawyers' conference." Sid never said "loi-yers"; instead it came out the way it was spelled. "Woman couldn't stop talking about how her great-grandmother brought a plant over from Holland. She went on and on how each generation snipped a starter off the old homestead bush."

Ross felt a smile grow inside where Sid couldn't see it. The older man might growl and complain, but he was as softhearted as they came. When Ross's dad had been away building up his corporate practice, Sid had looked after them. Primed the pump when the electricity went out. Repaired the fence when the steer escaped the barbed-wire enclosure.

And helped raise a boy who couldn't seem to find his way in a world that routinely spit out kids who couldn't read.

"So you need to replace your mom's plant. But that wasn't what had smoke rolling out your ears when you walked in."

Ross felt the tension of the last two months climb back onto his frame.

"It's that landscaping job across the road, isn't it?" Sid pulled a pocketknife and a small piece of wood from his pocket. It was his "I've got all the time in the world to listen" invitation. And skill didn't enter into it. He couldn't whittle animals or any other kind of still life, but he could create a pile of shavings like nobody's business.

"What I'd really like to do is plant poison oak and a little hemlock in Cranwell's backyard."

Sid shook his head from side to side. "I told you from the start that Alex Cranwell would be a headache. I could tell the way he climbed out of his pickup his ego was bigger 'n he was."

"And I should have listened."

"If he hadn't filled yer head with that nonsense about breaking you into commercial landscaping, maybe ya would've. And been better off for it."

Ross gave him a tired smile. "It'll happen. Alex will keep his word. He just doesn't know when to back off and let me do my job."

"How much longer do you have at his place?"

Ross tilted his head as he considered. "If he doesn't change the plans, and it's a sure bet he will, we should have the majority of the landscaping done by February." He sighed. "It'll be worth it when it's all done. Alex has some big contracts coming up."

"I don't know why you want to start something new when what you're doin' is workin'."

Ross stared at the shavings that curled from Sid's knife. "Alex Cranwell is the best shot I have to break into commercial landscaping. It's not an easy business, Sid. If I prove myself to him, he could save me years of work getting established in the industry."

The knife stilled a moment. "Are you sure you're trying to prove yourself to him and not somebody else?"

Ross ignored the way Sid's words rubbed at old wounds. "Residential landscaping more than pays the bills. I just want to do something different. Take on a new challenge."

Sid gave him a shrewd look. "Has yer dad been out to see what you've done to the place yet?"

Ross studied the carpet that was new thirty years ago. A person wouldn't know the kind of money Sid made until he walked into his state-of-the-art barn. Ross shrugged. "Mom says he's been expanding, took on a new partner. I'm sure he'll make it out soon."

"You've been done, what? Two, three months?"

"About that. Maybe it's hard for him to see the place so different."

Sid leaned forward. "It's yer mom that put her heart and soul into that farm, and she loves what you've done."

Ross shrugged. "It doesn't matter. I'm too busy with Alex's place to give a tour anyway."

Sid rolled the strand of fescue around, then finally spoke. "How sure are you, son, that Alex'll send some of those jobs yer way?"

Ross tried to be optimistic, but he felt his dinner grow heavy in his stomach. "From what I hear, his word is gold." But late at night, he worried about the same thing.

Sid's eyes held a knowing twinkle that signaled a subject change. "Now, tell me more about this Sierra woman."

Ross shifted in his seat. "Single mom. Three kids. Deadbeat dad. Had to move in with her mom." He shrugged. "Not much to tell."

"Hard on the eyes, is she?" The twinkle was still there.

Ross chuckled. "Far from it, but I think she's a little young for you."

"So what's worryin' you, son?"

Ross rubbed the back of his neck. "It's the distraction of having that horse around. He keeps getting out, and Sierra's scared to death of him. I want to help her, but I have the biggest job of my life in front of me, and I don't have time to babysit all of them."

"Doesn't sound like the horse is the only distraction."

Ross ignored the comment and focused on the shavings that curled from Sid's knife. "I came home tonight for a quick dinner before heading back to Alex's but ended up mucking their horse's stall."

Sid shifted his brow a fraction but kept stroking his knife against the wood.

"I'm on a limited time frame," Ross went on, feeling as if he were defending himself. "I need to get this done before we get a hard freeze."

"Mmm-hmm." Somehow Ross didn't feel as if Sid was siding with him. "Where's her husband?"

Ross's eyes shifted to the floor. "Her mom said she's divorced."

"The apostle Paul says to take care of widows and orphans."

"She's not a widow and they're not orphans. They have a dad."

Sid's eyes rose with a penetrating look. "I don't think the Good Lord'd agree with you, Ross."

Ross propped his forearms on his knees. "They are *not* a part of my life. They use a corner of my barn and keep the weeds down in the pasture. I don't have the time to take care of their horse."

"Did the Lord tell you to take this Alex Cranwell job?"

He couldn't meet Sid's gaze. "God dropped it right in my lap." Yet Ross *hadn't* prayed about the decision.

Sid stopped whittling. He leaned in, his breath stirring the fine shavings on the dinner tray. "Looks like He dropped a needy family in your lap too. Better ask Him what He wants you to do afore He drops a three-legged donkey on your front porch." He tilted back in his chair. "Now that would cause you some problems."

Chapter 11

Braden looked over. "Mom, are you going to feed Chance while we're at Dad's this weekend?"

The butter knife stilled in the apricot jam. Feed Chance. By herself? She carefully spread the jam over the peanut butter. "Mmmhmm." Maybe Elise could help her. Though picturing Elise in her designer clothes cutting open a hay bale just didn't fit.

The table was silent, and she glanced over. Braden had guilt all over his face.

She looked at Emory, who shrugged. Sierra cut the sandwiches in half. "Why?"

He gave her a sheepish grin. "I think I left the pitchfork leaning in the corner of his stall."

She dropped the butter knife. "Tell me you didn't."

He nodded his head with a wince. "I'm afraid Ross won't see it. Sorry."

She attempted a funny grin. "Not as sorry as you're going to be, mister!"

Chance, nose-down in the feed trough, munched the container of grain Sierra dumped in to distract him. She perched on a hay bale and stared down at the pitchfork lying tines up in the middle of the stall floor. Nope. Ross hadn't seen it. She stepped off the bale and clutched the grain bucket and metal spoon from the tack room. It was the only protection she could find.

The sound of the horse's crunching slowed the closer she got to the stall door.

Silence.

Then the sound of thick lips chasing stray granules around the stainless steel basin. Finally, heavy breathing and soft snorts as Chance made sure the container was thoroughly empty.

And still Sierra stood in front of the wide wooden door with its small barred window and black steel latch. *I cannot do this. I cannot go in there with that ... massive animal.* Cold sweat dampened her forehead and prickled under her arms. *But is it fair to endanger Chance? The pitchfork could cripple him if he stepped on it and freaked out. Then they'd have to put him to sleep, and it'd be her fault. The kids would hate her. Come on, Sierra. Buck up!*

Sierra lifted the latch. Chance swung his head around, ears forward. That was a good sign, wasn't it? Flattened ears signaled danger, didn't they?

Sierra took a step forward, then stopped motionless. Uh-oh, one ear forward, one back. Okay, two forward. One more step, then another halt. It felt like a sick game of Simon Says. An eternity later she reached the grain bin. Chance's head was lowered somewhat, the perfect height to grip the halter and move his hind end away from the pitchfork. Sierra reached for the black halter. Up went the head. She dropped her arm slightly. Chance faced the wall, one baleful eye staring at her, left ear flat.

How do I get out of here?

Sierra started to back out, but Chance matched her turn, angling his rump toward her. Paralyzed, she glanced about the stall, looking for some kind of help. Her gaze slid over the powerful hooves mere feet from her body. A picture of Molly flashed into her mind, lying in the hospital bed, deathly still, monitors beeping as her life drained slowly away. Sierra's breath came in short gasps. Sweat welled up through her pores and flashes of heat zipped through her body. Sierra inched toward the rear of the stall. The stall door was closer, but she'd have to move farther in line with the deadly hammers attached to the ends of Chance's hind legs.

Chance tossed his head, and Sierra screamed and sank into soiled straw, covering her head with her arms, waiting for the thrashing of hooves. But all she heard was a swish of hay. Her nerves sensed a void left by the retreat of the large warm horse body. She inched her arms down and sneaked a look over the top of them. Chance was gone.

The only sound was the ring of hooves on concrete as he trotted toward the end of the barn and out toward the corral. That and the throat clearing that came from just outside the stall. "You all right, miss?"

Sierra raised her head. A white-haired gentleman stared at her in concern.

What could she say? *I thought I was being attacked by a horse that no one seems to think is dangerous?*

Then she saw the smile he was trying to hold back.

She gave a self-conscious grin. "Did you see that wild beast go tearing out of here?"

He slapped his leg and chuckled. "I haven't seen a sight like that since Starfire tossed ol' Ross onto the manure pile."

The man leaned forward and held his hand out. The skin was rough and weathered, like an old dried apple. It reminded her of a grandpa's hand. A bit of comforting cushion behind the calluses.

He was on the short side, not much taller than Sierra, but he held himself with a presence that filled the space around him. His voice boomed, resonating through the barn. "You must be the boarder Ross told me about."

"Oh?" She'd like to have been a mouse in the corner during that conversation.

He chuckled, nodding his head at her expression. "It wasn't as bad as you think."

Sierra gave him a slight grin and raised an eyebrow. "And what do I think?"

He brought his arms together, one hand gripping the other wrist. He tipped back on his heels, like he was settling in for a good conversation. The playful twinkle was her clue. "You think that Ross wants to make glue of that old horse out there."

Glue? That raised both eyebrows. Glue was made from horses? The implication lifted her hands to her hips, both of them fisted. He wanted her horse dead? She understood the loss of the plant, but to kill an animal over it—

"And sooner rather than later." He was still nodding, the twinkle deepening. "But you'd be wrong."

"I would?" *Glue wasn't made from horses?*

"Yes. Ya see, ol' Ross, he gets a little impatient at times. Downright testy at others." He shook his head sadly, as if poor old Ross needed sympathy. "In particular when things get a little out of hand."

"Like his mother's prized bush getting eaten?"

He nodded approval at her understanding. "Ex—actly." He drew the word out. "He needs a little time to adjust to having people underfoot."

"And horses."

He winked at her, the dip of his chin indicating Chance through the big doors in the corral. "They're more people than you know."

He changed posture, leaning an elbow against the stall. "Now when I got here, it looked like that horse was givin' you a lesson."

Sierra felt her forehead crease. "No, I …" She stopped. She wasn't about to tell him she'd been scared to death.

He looked at her, his eyes reading right through to the words she wasn't saying. "You were scared." Only it came out "skeered."

She waited, not admitting anything.

"Now, there's nothing wrong with being scared. You just cain't let the horse know it." He nodded toward a black rope hanging from a nail on the wall. "Now get that lead rope."

"Why?" Her throat tightened, making it hard to swallow. "What do you want me to do with it?"

"*You're* goin' to teach that horse a lesson."

She laughed. A twittering, reedy sound. Totally unlike her. She'd never had a high-pitched girlie laugh in her life.

"Um … Mr. uh—"

"You can call me Sid."

"Sid. Okay, Sid." She firmed her stance. "I'm not going out there." She punctuated the words with two short jabs toward the corral.

"Well, now. That does put you in a pur-dicament." He stretched the word out while rubbing his variegated white and gray stubble.

Sierra lifted her chin. "The only predicament I have is how I'm going to get rid of that horse."

"What's his name? Lucky?" He raised wildly long eyebrows for clarification. The strands looked like free-range caterpillars that had crawled over each other in a crazed mishmash.

"Chance."

He pursed his lips, then sucked them in as if he was about to deliver dire news. "You have kids?"

She nodded. "Three."

He shook his head and drew in a breath. "See, ol' Chance out there, he's about wore out." He leaned his whole back against the stall door. "Not good for much more than the glue factory.

There really is a horse glue factory? The kids definitely needed to wash their hands after crafts.

"But to your kids, I'm sure he's finer than old Black Beauty himself." She knew he was right. A sinking sensation started up near her shoulders and traveled down through her chest, compressing itself into a tight ball in her stomach.

"Once a kid sets his heart on a horse, you never can tear the dream out of him. You might not see it, but it's there. Not many kids get a chance to lasso those dreams and ride them. You sell that horse—" he clicked his teeth "—and you might not get that opportunity back."

A trembling started in her right leg. He probably couldn't see it, but it was there, all the nerves screaming, "*Run!*"

She swallowed. But thoughts of her kids kept her from backpedaling to the van. She stared out toward the corral and that ... horse. She *would* do this for her kids. Their hearts had been broken enough.

Sierra gave him a look to tell him she wasn't deceived by his method. "I'm surprised you haven't been snatched up by some telemarketing service. You'd be selling vacuums by the truckload."

His raspy laughter reverberated through the old barn.

A few minutes later they stood side by side, fifteen feet from Chance, who chomped through the grassy corral as if they weren't there. But Sierra knew better. Chance was already plotting his strategy to swing that hind end around. She didn't need to understand horses to know what was coming next. A swift kick to the forehead.

A tingle started in her hands. She shouldn't be out here. If she ended up permanently comatose, the kids would end up living with Michael and Gina full time.

Sid pointed to the horse as if Sierra couldn't see him. "Now, you gotta show him who's boss."

Sierra threw him a look. "He already knows."

He chuckled. "Well, that's what we're gonna change. *You* need to decide who's boss. You or that grass eater. Think of him as a large lawnmower. You don't mince words with a machine and ask it if it wants to mow the lawn. It doesn't. It wants to be left alone in the garage."

What was it with men and machines? This was not going to work.

He continued, "You gotta grab it by the handle and point it where you want to go." He waved his hand toward the horse. "It's the same with ol' Chance there. You gotta show him you mean business."

Sierra looked from the large head to the tail. "And by grabbing him you mean what?"

"Take him by the rope and lead him like you mean it."

"He won't let me put the rope on him."

The old man put both hands up the same way she'd seen Braden's baseball coach do with the boys when he was short on patience and long on exasperation. "You don't *ask* him if he wants the lead rope on. You tell him you're doing it."

A conversation with a horse?

He grabbed the rope from her limp hand. "Watch." A slight hobble emphasized his short choppy steps. If Sierra hadn't been so nervous she might have smiled.

And there he was, leading Chance back to her, grinning like all she needed was his helpful demonstration. Sierra realized she was walking backward and made herself stop, her toes digging into the soles of her shoes. Sid and Chance halted uncomfortably close. So close that when Chance turned his head and blew out a breath, Sierra got the warm moist air right in her face. It was like being pasted with wet grass.

He held out the lead rope. "Take him for a walk around the pasture."

Words failed her.

Sid, apparently not respectful of personal boundaries, grabbed Sierra's hand and wrapped her fingers around the tethered lead rope. "Walk him." He motioned with his hand toward the far fence in the opposite direction Chance was facing.

It was a standoff. Sierra stared at Chance. Big nose high, Chance stared right back.

"He won't bite."

Chance's bottom lip quivered. Sierra took a half-step in reverse. "I think he disagrees."

Sid laughed. "Now, lead the dad-blamed horse to the fence."

Sierra went. More to get away from the big teeth right behind those lips. Chance followed. It was beautiful. She was actually leading the horse. They reached the fence, turned, and Chance followed obediently at her heels. Then Chance's chin bumped her shoulder. Sierra glanced back, right at the hairy lip that hid those great big chompers. Much too close.

Nervous, Sierra picked up the tempo, preferring a taut three feet of rope between them. Chance lengthened his step and the rope slackened. She stumbled over a tight clump of grass and her knees hit the dirt. Momentum kept her stumbling and scraping forward, until she regained her footing in a fast walk, still holding the lead rope. Sierra threw another look over her shoulder. Chance trotted now, his mane frisking against his neck. Sierra bolted. Sid was waving his arms at her. She had to reach him.

Chance was an out-of-control locomotive bearing down on her.

Sierra reached Sid, threw the rope at him and slid in behind his back, crouching to her knees as she quivered. Chance thundered to a stop, snorting puffs of smoke.

"Are you okay?" The shout made her turn, and she slowly rose. Ross cleared the fence and ran through the tall grass toward them. He was actually sprinting. Like he was scared. For her? It had been ages since anyone had been afraid for her. She took a step back and bumped into Sid.

Ross stopped directly in front of her. Crowding into her personal space, his gaze darting over her as he checked for damage. He was making her nervous, and if he tried to run his hands up and down her limbs she might have to whack him. It was all she could do not to move back, but Sid and that horse were still behind her.

She wrapped her arms around her waist instead. "I'm fine." At least the distraction had steadied her legs.

He ignored her and turned on Sid. "What on earth are you doing?"

Sid patted Chance's neck. "We're just getting the pair acquainted."

Sierra rolled her eyes. She was *not* one-half of a pair with that beast, and getting acquainted was not what that near disaster had been.

Ross was still breathing hard. "By letting her loose in a field with a horse? Sid, she's terrified of them." Ross shot her a look, then stared at the older man again. "Come on, Sid." He had his hands on his hips and annoyance wore grooves deep into his cheeks beneath snapping dark eyes.

"I am not *terrified* of horses." Fearful, yes, the kind that came from firsthand experience.

Remnants of frustration lingered in his eyes. "That wasn't you high-tailing it across the field?"

She placed her hands on her hips. "Well, when a beast is charging you from behind, what would you do?"

Sid and Ross both glanced at Chance, then each other. Sid didn't even try to stop the chuckles. Ross looked at the ground, then raised his head. She couldn't tell if he was mad or laughing at her. "It's okay to be afraid, Sierra. I just don't think it's a good idea for you to be out here, pressured by him." He jerked a thumb at Sid, then rounded on the older man again. "And don't try to tell me you didn't talk her into this, Sid. You know better."

"Ross, I'm an adult. I can handle it," Sierra jumped in.

His look conveyed disbelief. "By letting yourself get talked into something you don't want to do?"

She pulled her jacket tighter around her body. "It worked out fine."

He rubbed the back of his neck. "I would feel responsible if something happened."

"Well, it's nothing you need to worry about," Sierra said and walked back toward the barn.

Ross stood in the barnyard after Sierra left. Cold air soaked into his denim jeans, making the fabric stiff and rough against his legs. But he didn't move, not even when her car was long out of sight. The question hammered him: What was he doing getting wrapped up in her problems? Sierra Montgomery was one big complication. Single mom, messy ex-husband, and three lonely kids who'd attach to anyone she got involved with. He saw her eyes again. Vulnerable. Behind the fear lay uncertainty and pain. Definitely not what he needed at this stage in his life. It wasn't hard to bring the protective shield up. He'd had plenty of practice. He walked back toward his house.

Ross stomped the mud off his shoes and let himself in through the back door. He wasn't surprised to find Sid at his kitchen table nursing a cup of coffee. Another mug sat waiting. Ross slid into the chair across from him and took a sip of the steaming brew. Strong and fortifying. Sid's coffee embodied his character.

"You certainly know how to treat a lady, Sid. I still can't believe you turned her loose with that horse."

Sid didn't laugh. Just sort of smiled, his eyes faraway. "That gal's had a lot of hurt."

"Like most of the human population." Ross wanted to change the subject.

"That girl is the 'human population' that is before us right now."

"It doesn't sound like she wants our help, Sid."

The grizzled eyebrows glowered down at him. "Some cries are harder to hear than others."

Ross knew better than to argue, but from what he could tell, Sierra didn't seem to be sending any kind of telegram, other than one that said to leave her alone.

The older man rubbed his jaw, then moved it back and forth the way he did when he was really chewing on something. "What that girl needs is some hope. You're always saying you need a real bookkeeper."

He had a sinking feeling in the pit of his stomach "I was just teasing you, Sid. I think the system we have works just fine." The words came out fast and he swallowed hard. "And how is doing my books going to give her hope?"

"I'm jist gettin' that feelin' right here, son. In the spot God speaks to." Sid poked a finger over his heart.

"I don't think it's a good idea. She—it's complicated, Sid."

Sid gave him a thoughtful look. "Have my feelin's ever been wrong?"

Ross leaned his forearms on the table, pressing his fingertips together. "What if I get saddled with her as my bookkeeper, and it's just indigestion this time?"

Sid scratched through the hair above his ear, his right cheek hitched up in a grimace of regret. "Well, I've been meaning to tell you anyway, but my niece Leorna wants me to come back for a visit and, what with getting that new pony Traitor in, I'm not going to be available to help sort the bills this month."

Ross took a breath. *And out come the thumbscrews.*

The old scoundrel continued, "Looks like you'll be *needin'* some help."

"I'll manage." Ross bought some time with another gulp of coffee.

Sid rolled the stub of hay to the other side of his mouth. "And just how will you do that?" He shook his head. "I'd hate to see where you're at in five months." The next words were directed toward the floor. "Overpaying the nursery, underbidding jobs. Be a cryin' shame after all that hard work. Especially with you working so hard on that Alex Cranwell job."

Ross shook his head, feeling a grin tickle his lips, though he tried to hide it. "Nicely done, Sid. Though I didn't know the Lord was into strong-arming people." He should have covered his ears and locked the door when he heard Sierra's screams from the field. One beautiful brunette with vulnerable brown eyes was a distraction he couldn't afford.

"Yer forgettin' Jonah and the whale. The Lord isn't afraid to use a little muscle now and then."

Ross tried one last time. "She probably isn't qualified to do the book-keeping."

Sid folded his hands across his belly. "How is Mr. Cranwell doing these days?"

Ross scowled at his friend. "Fine, I'll ask her. But all bets are off if she says no." Something Sid had said worked its way from the back of his mind. "What's this about Leorna wanting you to visit? You haven't been to Kansas since you moved here."

Sid scratched the back of his neck and wouldn't meet his eyes. "We've kept in close touch." He cleared his throat. "She thinks I ought to move back to be with family."

Ross laughed. "Well, I guess she's in for a surprise there."

Sid chuckled, but kept his eyes on the floor.

"You're not thinking about it, are you?"

Sid's fingers bounced on the table and he gave him a brief smile. "Not anytime soon, son. Say, I better get back and check on the ponies."

Chapter 12

Sierra parked the van and walked up her mom's front steps just as her cell phone rang. She fumbled, trying to hold the phone and turn the key in the deadbolt. "Hello."

"This is Celia Ward returning your call."

Sierra shoved the door open and stumbled inside. "Oh, hi." She dropped her purse and pulled off her jacket. "I, um, I have a situation. When my husband and I were divorced three years ago, I opted not to sign up for the Oregon Child Support Program."

"Mmm." The woman sounded like she'd heard this before.

Sierra hurried to explain, "It wasn't a problem until a few months ago, when he apparently had some financial difficulties. Now he's not paying at all."

"I hope you understand that if you'd opted for the OCS Program at the onset, this conversation wouldn't be necessary. Fortunately, you can still sign up for it through the Department of Justice, but it will take sixty to ninety days for the paperwork to process and for the state to start garnisheeing his wages."

Sierra sank down on the sofa. "Sixty to ninety days? So there's nothing else you can do?"

"Not until you sign up and the paperwork gets processed."

Sierra closed her eyes. "Okay, thank you," and hung up the cell phone.

The phone in the kitchen started ringing, and she pushed off the couch to grab it. "Lassiter residence, Sierra speaking."

"Honey, it's mom."

Sierra smiled. "How was your flight?"

"Oh, fine. I took some of those vitamin immune boosters before I left. I hate breathing all that recycled air. You just never know what people are coming down with."

Sierra leaned back against the counter, the familiar litany bringing a sense of comfort that was purely her mom.

"I know, Mom, it's scary. How's Aunt Marta?"

"She's in a lot of pain yet." A pause. "Honey, have you read the paper today?" Her mom's voice sounded worried but with an undertone of excitement. Like someone driving past a horrible accident who can't stop looking.

"No, I think it's still on the walkway." Sierra walked to the kitchen window and saw the paper on the grass, rolled inside its plastic bag.

"He filed for bankruptcy."

"Who?" But the sinking feeling had already started.

"Michael."

Bankruptcy. "How do you know?" What would happen to her child support now?

"Marta told me how to find our paper on the Internet."

And of course her mom would need to keep current.

"… I just think it's a blessing you moved home when you did."

Sierra couldn't muster any inflection. "Yes, Mom, a blessing."

Sierra folded a pair of pants from the pile on the couch. "Come on guys, your dad's going to be here any minute."

Braden pounded down the stairs, hair shiny wet from the comb. He flashed her an ear-to-ear grin as he bounded for the front door.

Emory rushed up and grabbed her arm. "Have you seen my pink sweater?"

"It's in the pile of clothes folded on your bed."

A relieved smile and a dash for the stairs. "Thanks!"

Sierra followed Trevor out the front door. "Go get your coat, honey."

Trevor stopped. "Oh, yeah," and dashed back in the house.

Braden sat close to her on the first step. "What movie do you think we're going to see?"

She gave him a teasing smile. "Hmm. Maybe your dad picked *Winnie the Pooh*."

Braden laughed and gave her a playful bump with his shoulder. "Mom!"

Trevor slammed the door behind them, coat tucked under his arm. "That's what I want to see."

Sierra reached behind her to where Trevor stood and tickled his ankles. "You need to put the coat *on*, Trev."

He laughed. "Oh, yeah," and pushed his arms into the sleeves. Everything was funny to him in the excitement of being with his dad.

Fifteen minutes later, they started growing restless. "Can I go call him, Mom?" Braden looked worried.

"Sure, honey." Sierra started to chew her fingernail. Maybe Michael had been delayed by a procedure. Still he could have had one of the assistants call. She moved to the next finger. Maybe he was upset by the bankruptcy notice and forgot his date with the kids. She dropped her hand. How could anyone forget their kids?

Emory stood and walked to the end of the driveway, staring up the road. "When's he supposed to get here?"

"Any minute, sweetie."

Braden stormed out of the house, phone in his hand. "He's not answering."

A long hour later, they trudged back in the house. "Guys, how about after feeding Chance, we make some popcorn and watch a movie?"

"No, thanks." Braden ran toward the van.

Emory brushed past her to follow her brother.

"I want to see *Winnie the Pooh*." Trevor had started crying when she told them it was getting too cold to keep waiting on the porch. His face wet with tears and nose running, she carried him to the bathroom for a tissue.

"I know, honey. Mommy knows."

Ross watched the blue van stop next to the barn and the kids tumble out.

Braden ran straight over to him, then stuffed his hands into his pocket, his voice dull. "Do you need help?"

Ross studied the boy, whose head was bent, kicking at the rocks in the drive. "Yep. Perfect timing, too; I just pulled up." Braden didn't respond. "You'll need gloves. I have an extra set in my pickup door if you want to grab them."

"'kay." Braden walked for the pickup, his shoulders bent as if carrying a heavy load.

Sierra walked up with the other two kids, her lips curved in a slight smile. "I wondered where Braden went, then realized he'd been sucked over here like a magnet."

He grinned back at her. "He's going to help me with the fence, if that's all right with you?"

She nodded and studied the back of her son, a slight furrow of concern forming between her eyes. Braden sauntered back, slapping the gloves against his leg.

Sierra smiled at the boy. "So you're going to fix the fence, huh?"

He shrugged, not looking at her. "Yeah."

Ross picked up the work tray. "Ready to find that hole?"

Braden shrugged again. "Sure."

He glanced over his shoulder and saw Sierra staring after them. He tried to give her a reassuring look.

"How's school going?"

Another shrug. "I dunno."

Ross opened the gate and held it for Braden. In the pasture, Ross started down the fence line and stopped at the first wooden post. "See how all the staples are holding the wire tight to the wood? That's what we want. See this wire here doesn't have a staple." Ross set the tray down, picked out a staple and pounded it into the post, fastening the wire back into position. He grabbed the tray and held the hammer out to Braden. "You want to carry this?"

Braden took it and matched his pace as they walked. After a few moments of silence, Ross said. "Want to talk about it?"

The boy looked at him. "What?"

"You seem pretty down. Something happen at school?"

Braden kicked his boots through the clumps of grass. "No."

"Mad at your mom?"

He shrugged. "I dunno."

They came to a loose section of fencing. "You want to try?"

"'kay."

"I'll do the top." Ross held the fence staple between his lips and pulled the top of the sagging fence tight against the post with a pair of wire-pullers, then set the nail. He held his hand out, and Braden passed him the hammer to pound the staple in.

Braden strained to pull the bottom portion just as tight.

"Got it?" Ross said.

Braden nodded, the only movement his tensed body could make, his face flushed red with exertion and determination. Ross pressed a staple into the wood and held the wire so Braden could hammer it in. The first blow glanced off the staple, dislodging it into the tall grass at the base of the post. Braden's gaze jumped to his.

Ross nodded toward the grass. "Find it and try again." The boy nodded and his shoulders relaxed as he bent to push the blades of grass apart to search for it.

Braden found the staple and pushed it in the same way Ross had. The next hammer swing knocked the staple sideways, but it didn't fall off. The boy set it up again, and after several attempts managed to hammer it into the wood.

Ross tried not to think about Alex Cranwell's plans waiting on his desk. Or the seedlings he needed to pick up at the nursery, or the work he needed to do in his greenhouse. A couple hours away from the job wouldn't be a deal breaker, and he knew this boy needed him.

Braden pounded a few more staples, and they moved down the fence.

"My dad was supposed to take us to a movie tonight."

"That so?" The grass swished briskly against their jeans.

Braden shrugged. "He was busy."

"Did you get to talk to him?"

One quick shake of the head.

"Probably made you pretty mad."

"I dunno."

"I know what it's like to be disappointed like that."

Brown eyes turned up toward his.

"I bought this place from my parents and invited them to come over and see all the changes I'd made. I'd worked really hard all summer on the landscaping. But my dad was too busy to come. He still hasn't seen it."

Braden nodded and his gaze clung to Ross's.

"You know what?" He squeezed Braden's shoulder. "It's not your fault."

Color washed into Braden's cheeks, and he dropped his gaze back to the ground. A few minutes later he sniffed and wiped a sleeve under his nose.

"So," Ross said, "you play any sports?"

"I might play basketball this year."

"That so?"

Braden grinned up at him. "Yeah. My friend Emmett plays, and he said I could be on his team." A small shrug with the first hint of a smile. "I have to try out first."

"I was a baseball man in high school."

Braden frowned. "I can't catch a ball very well. My dad doesn't like to play catch with me anymore. He said I don't keep my eye on the ball." He gave Ross a goofy grin. "But a basketball's a lot bigger."

Ross ruffled Braden's hair, a protective anger welling up inside. "I bet you could do it with a little practice."

Sierra watched them coming, side by side, her son talking to the man non-stop. When they stopped in front of the van they gave her big grins.

"Were you successful?" she asked.

"Well, we got about a third of it checked. I'll probably finish it up this weekend so Chance doesn't get cabin fever.

"Mom, Ross said he'd hire me to work for him."

Sierra looked to Ross, who wore a sheepish smile. "I should have probably talked to you first."

She raised her brows. "Um, probably?"

He chuckled then nodded toward the highway. "I'm just working at that house across the road." He gripped Braden's shoulder and rocked him gently side to side. "He's a good worker, and we'd love to have him help us out after school when he wants."

"You want to do this, Braden?" She took in her son's proud stance. Shoulders back, mimicking Ross's body language. When had her son grown up enough to get a job?

Braden's grin was all teeth. "Yeah!"

"I don't see why not then, on the days it fits into our schedule." She glanced at Ross, who was smiling at her son. *And where would this lead them?*

The next afternoon, Sierra grabbed her keys and the directions to Braden's vision appointment. "Guys, come on. We need to go."

Braden came in and set the cordless phone on the counter, his expression dark.

"Did you get a hold of your dad, honey?"

He shrugged away from her hand. "No. Can you take me over to work with Ross?"

"We have your eye appointment in twenty minutes."

"I don't want to go."

"I'm sorry, honey, but we need to leave right now."

Trevor's finger woodpeckered Sierra's thigh with impatience. "I can't find my shoes."

"They're right there by the door." Braden flung the words in a tone that stated Trevor was stupider than stupid.

"Nuh-uh." Trevor lowered his head like a little bull, shaking it back and forth. "Those aren't mine."

"They are too, Trevor."

"No, sir—"

Sierra picked up her purse. "Boys!"

Braden glared at her then stormed outside and slammed the door.

She stared after him. Part of her wanted to run out there and wring his neck. The other part, the part that saw through to the hurt, wanted to gather him close and tell him it was going to be okay. But nothing was okay at the moment. She hadn't gotten a return call from Michael either, and she'd left messages at his home and office.

She stuffed her keys in her pocket, found Trevor's shoes, squeezed them over his socks, then herded him and Emory out the front door.

An hour and a half later, Trevor squirmed in her lap while they waited for the ophthalmologist to return. Diplomas and medical certificates lined one office wall, while a bookcase held all sorts of medical journals and little glass knickknacks.

"Are we done?" Braden turned, and she grinned at the dime-sized black pupils that nearly swallowed the brown irises.

"She'll be here in a minute, honey, then we'll go see Chance."

With a grunt, Braden plopped on the floor and pulled out a Sudoku puzzle from the much-used wicker basket in the kids' corner. Emory sat in an armchair and read *The Little Princess*. And after repeated warnings not to touch Dr. Remina's decorative glass turtles, Trevor was spending a little jail time on her lap. She hoped the smallest turtle had already been missing one of its blue beaded eyes.

The door opened with an authoritative rush of air. With brisk steps the young doctor, her dark hair in a tight ponytail, crossed the room and settled into the leather chair behind her desk. The manila folder in her hand looked ominous. Suddenly the comfortable room felt stark, foreboding.

Dr. Remina opened the file and gave Braden a warm look before turning her attention to Sierra. "Braden has binocular dysfunction, which is a hindering of the ability to accurately aim his eyes at a target and keep it single, as well as derive meaningful cues as to spatial location and speed of movement of distant targets." She gave Sierra a patient smile, the kind that said she was used to translating doctor jargon to baffled parents. "In other words, it's inefficient eye teaming. What this signifies for Braden is that he likely has difficulty with intermittent blurring, errors when copying school work, double vision, and poor depth perception, which would create difficulties in activities such as catching a ball."

The eye doctor continued, "Of course, eye strain and headaches are common—as well as needing extra time to complete assignments."

Hot shame washed over Sierra. Braden told her he got headaches when he did his homework, but she'd thought it was an excuse.

Dr. Remina closed the folder. The woman linked her fingers and rested them across the folder. "Braden will need to wear an eye patch for a while and do some vision therapy, but unfortunately glasses will not help his condition."

Sierra felt overwhelmed by the information. She glanced at her son, who had a confused expression on his face.

Dr. Remina smiled. "The patch will be short term, until the muscles in his eyes get stronger. But without treatment children become defeated and their overall performance suffers."

"How long is the treatment?"

"At least a year."

An avalanche of questions rushed through Sierra's mind, storming from every direction. What did the therapy entail? What was the success rate? How would it affect his schooling? And what would it cost?

"And of course, it's important that he get plenty of rest and eat well. It's amazing how a lack of sleep impacts our body functions."

Sierra nodded even as her throat constricted, making it hard to swallow. And she *needed* to swallow or she'd start crying. Her mind settled on the phrase that loomed the largest. *Binocular dysfunction?* She pictured her eleven-year-old son, eye patch covering one eye, walking the halls of middle school. The spasm in her throat grew.

Sierra tried to sort all the information and asked the one question she could speak without crying. "How much will it cost?"

"The vision therapy is three thousand dollars. And, let me see," Dr. Remina flipped through Braden's file, stopping at a blue sheet. She wrinkled her nose in a grimace. "Your insurance doesn't cover this type of treatment."

It was a double-headed hammer blow. Braden's self-esteem on one side, the unexpected cost on the other. Six months ago, Michael might have been willing to help pay, but now....

Sierra parked next to Ross's barn and the kids hopped out. The slam of a pickup door made her turn toward the house.

Ross walked around the bed of his pickup and came toward her, a warm grin easing over his face. "Hey. I didn't expect to see you this early."

"We had a doctor's appointment, so we, um, decided to feed Chance now."

His brow drew together slightly. "Everything okay, I hope."

She shrugged. "Just an eye appointment for Braden."

He nodded then gestured toward the pasture. "I found another spot in the fence where it sagged pretty bad. Lucky that Chance didn't get tangled in it when he got loose. I'll fix it tonight and turn him back out."

"Thanks, that's great. I know you're busy." She pointed a thumb over her shoulder. "I better get in there before they start racing Chance around bales of hay."

He laughed, the white tan lines from countless hours of squinting in the sun, disappearing. "Yeah, you better."

She bit the corner of her lip, then smiled. "Bye." She jogged toward the barn; hopefully the kids had stayed *outside* the stall.

"Hey, Sierra," Ross called.

She turned.

Ross walked backward toward his house with the same warm look. "Could you come up to the house before you go? I need to talk to you about something."

Her heart did a little flip, and she nodded.

Chapter 13

"You kids keepin' that old horse happy?"

Sierra recognized the boom of the rough voice and turned. "Kids, this is Mr.—?" She still didn't know his last name.

"Sid." He rested a hand on the stall. "Call me Sid." He poked the ever-present stub of straw toward Chance's enclosure. "I ain't never seen a horse as handsome as that one. You kids ought to be mighty proud. He's a dandy."

The kids beamed. Trevor looked up at the older man. "You can pet him."

"I jist might do that."

"I'll get his brush." Braden raced for the tack room.

Her heart started hammering as the kids jostled each other to be nearest the opening when Sid unlatched the stall door. Emory hurried inside to pet the big gray head while Braden moved a soft brush along his neck. Trevor hung back and didn't seem to realize that he'd wrapped an arm around one of Sid's skinny legs.

After the kids "introduced" Sid to their horse, and they'd petted and brushed Chance sufficiently, the older man closed the stall door

and maneuvered over to Sierra with a keen look in his eye. "You ought
to get these kids into 4-H."

Her voice squeaked, and she tried again. "4-H? With Chance?" The
picture of her kids in a ring leading that giant horse by themselves sent a
shiver up her spine.

He leaned a wiry arm against the stall. "It'd be the best thing for them
and that horse. Ross joined 4-H when he was about Braden's age on a
horse named Rocket. "

Braden said, "Can we, Mom?" He cast his sister an excited glance.

Emory grasped her arm and tugged on it. "Please?"

"Um." She looked toward Sid for help, but he was watching Trevor
play with two of his Star Wars action figures on a bale of hay.

She swallowed hard and gave them a brave smile. "We can look into
it." *What was she saying?*

Sid rolled the piece of straw in his mouth, proud approval in the nod
he gave her. "You sure are a good mother, Sierra. Not many moms would
do what yer doin' for these kids."

She gave him a stern look, but her voice was playful. "It's going to be
your fault if 4-H pushes me over the edge, and the kids come home from
school and find me curled in the fetal position."

He laughed. "You do paint a picture, Sierra." He pulled a handkerchief from his back pocket and wiped his nose. "When I was coming
across the field, I saw you and Ross talkin'."

She gave him a teasing smile. "And you thought he was giving me
Chance's eviction notice, didn't you?"

He chuckled as Trevor sidled up beside him. "That horse eats any
more of his prized bushes and you jist might get one." He rubbed the top
of her four-year-old's head and bent toward him. "You'll need to come
over to my house and see the ponies there."

"How many do you have?" Trevor asked, his eyes curious.

"I've got eight now. Just got a new one last week. Can you see the field through those doors down there?" Sid pointed to the doors that led out to the corral, and Trevor nodded. "Well, I don't know if you can see him, but there's a black horse at the right up near the fence."

"I see him."

"Well, that there's Traitor. We have to keep him separate. He's not too keen on the other horses."

Sierra peeked through the doors. The black horse pranced in a nervous fashion back and forth along the fence line. It made her shudder just to see the pent-up energy. He made Chance look like a lap dog. She pulled her gaze away. "Sid, how long have you lived here?"

He whistled a long, low note and his eyes crinkled in thought. "Oh, I'd say about thirty-five years. Moved here from Kansas after my wife and daughter were killed in a car accident."

"Oh, I'm sorry."

He nodded. "It was tough. Couldn't eat, couldn't sleep. 'Bout killed me to be in that house, all alone except the memories. Finally sold it and came out here."

"What made you pick Oregon?"

He grinned and settled back against the stall, picking at his teeth with the piece of straw. "Well, Kyle's grandpappy, he and I grew up together till his folks moved out here when we were in high school." The white grizzle of whiskers rippled with his chuckle. "Figured I might as well move where I knew somebody."

It struck her. *Kansas. Kyle. Ross and Kyle were cousins. Could ...?* She gripped his arm. "Sid! Do you know if that honeysuckle was from the homestead where Kyle's grandparents lived? I mean, if it was the same side of the family?"

Sid scratched his chin as he considered. "Could be," he said.

"Could you find out where Ross's great-grandmother's homestead is? If it's still there, I mean." A bubble of hope swelled. "And if it is, maybe the honeysuckle is there too."

He worked his lips back and forth in a grimace that set his cheeks to moving. "I don't know. I guess it's worth a shot. Ross'll have to ask his mother—"

"No! I don't want Ross to know what I'm doing."

He nodded smugly, as if enjoying being a coconspirator. "I'll call Kyle's mom and see what I can find out. We might need to do some of that online stuff Ross is always talking about. Ross set up a computer at the house for the pony business, if you don't mind coming over."

"Sid, you're the one doing me a favor."

"Well, now that you mention it, we probably need to talk about payment."

Sierra stared at him, disappointment curling in her gut. He had seemed so helpful, even if he had pushed her with Chance. She held back the sigh. But he *was* helping her out. Maybe Elise could loan her a small amount. "How much are you thinking?"

Sid looked everywhere but at her. "It's been a long time since I've had a good home-cooked meal."

Sierra burst out laughing. "You old conniver! I would *love* to cook you a meal."

"What're you doin' tomorrow?" He rubbed his belly, a look of anticipation and hope on his leathery features.

"Five o'clock, your place?"

Delight smoothed out the creases on his face. "The door will be open."

Trevor was following Braden up to the hayloft. She lifted her voice. "Let's go, boys. Em. We're leaving." She grinned at Sid again. "I better get them out of here."

He nodded and headed for the door. "Yeah, I better git."

"Oh, Sid." He turned, anticipation still lighting his grin. "I hope you're partial to rutabagas and sauerkraut."

The startled look on his face was priceless.

Ross had been waiting for the knock. When he opened the door, Sierra turned from watching the kids explore the pasture behind her. Glimmers of a smile clung to the dimples in her cheeks, and he felt his own lips starting to turn up. He shifted his stance and looked down.

Her voice was warm and inviting. "You wanted to talk to me?"

"Uh, yeah." He scratched the back of his neck and stepped out onto the front porch. His collar chafed and he rubbed the back of his neck again. There wasn't an easy way to start a conversation he didn't want to have, so better jump right in. "I'm looking for a bookkeeper. Sid normally does it, but he doesn't have time right now." The words trailed off.

"Did you want me to place an ad for you?"

He chuckled. "No, I wanted to see if *you* had bookkeeping experience."

It took her a moment to catch up. "Really?" Then her whole face lit up and she nearly bounced on the front step. "Truly? You mean, like a job?" Then immediately she dipped her head and tucked a piece of dark hair behind her ear, seeming to try for nonchalance. "Or just some help to pay off the, um, honeysuckle."

"A job."

She laughed. "Seriously?"

He nodded, unable to hold back a grin.

"I could just hug—" She dropped her eyes as a smile of embarrassment crossed her face. She glanced back at him, cheeks pink. "When do I start?"

"So you can process accounts payable?"

She flashed a beautiful smile. "And the receivables, if you need me to."

He scratched his head. "Okay, well, I need to talk to Sid and find out where he's at with it before I can put you on it. How about Monday?"

The smile turned shy. "Thanks, Ross. You have no idea what this means to me, for my family."

As she gathered the kids and skipped back to her van, Ross shook his head, his eyes lingering on her. He had a pretty good idea what it meant to her family, but what exactly did it mean for him?

That night in her mom's quiet house, Sierra lay on her stomach in her pajamas, phone in hand, and pressed in Elise's number.

Her friend answered on the first ring. "So, has Michael called you back?"

"No. But yesterday I went downtown and signed up for the child support program. Did I tell you it will take two to three months to process? Then I drove by his office. His car was there, so I know he's alive at least."

"You need to talk to him."

"I'm going to."

"When?"

"Friday." Even if she had to camp in his driveway to do it.

Thursday evening Sierra pulled the oven door open and the delicious smell of stuffed pork chops wafted over her.

The front door slammed and Braden came tearing into the kitchen. She turned toward the window and caught a glimpse of Ross's blue pickup backing out of the driveway. Tearing her eyes from the retreating vehicle, she set the pork chops on top of the stove and turned to lean back against the counter. "How'd it go?"

"Awesome." His grin turned sheepish. "But it was hard. Ross had me stack a bunch of bricks on a trailer and then I got to drive the tractor and pull the bricks to where the guys were working."

She straightened. "You drove a tractor?"

He gave her a look. "Ross drove with me."

"Okay." *Leave out the pertinent details until after your parent has a heart attack.*

"I'm going to call Dad and tell him." He picked up the cordless phone and pressed the buttons as he wandered toward the living room.

Sierra stretched plastic wrap over the salad and tried not to listen for conversation from the other room.

Braden stomped back into the kitchen and dropped the phone on the counter.

"Dad wasn't there?"

Braden ignored her and turned to leave the room.

"Honey, we're taking dinner to Sid's. Could you wash the dirt off your hands and carry this bowl of potatoes to the van, please?"

He scowled and trudged over to the sink.

"It was nice of Ross to pick you up and bring you back. Is he planning on doing that every day?"

"I dunno." He grabbed the bowl of potatoes. "He said when it works out."

"Careful, honey." Her voice came out sharp when the bowl tilted, and she tried to soften it with a grin. "You don't want to have to tell Sid you dropped his dinner in the driveway."

Braden didn't smile.

She wanted to hunt Michael down that minute and let him see the damage on his son's face.

Sierra popped the last bit of roll into her mouth and glanced around the table brimming with the remains of the dinner she'd brought to Sid's.

The older man set down his fork with a sigh. "Now that was dee-licious! You could give Ross some lessons." He leaned close to the table with a rascally grin. "Best rutabagas I've ever had."

Sierra laughed. There hadn't been a rutabaga in sight. Sid's table had been laden with stuffed pork chops, garlic and bacon green beans, fluffy mashed potatoes and rich pork gravy, along with homemade rolls—her mother's recipe—that could make a starving man cry. Trevor ate more rolls than anything. Raspberry jam had smeared a ghastly grin around his mouth. Sierra wiped his face with her napkin and leaned down to pick his wadded one up off the floor.

"Mom, made lemon mer—" Trevor looked to her for help.

"Meringue."

"Lemon mang pie for dessert!" Her youngest beamed the news.

Braden reached across Emory and plucked another roll off the plat-ter. She pushed her brother's arm away, and Braden shot her a dirty look.

Sierra addressed him, "Braden, ask next time, and we'll pass it to you."

Sid ruffled Braden's hair. "When you've got a man-sized appetite, you don't want to wait." Her son gave him a sheepish grin. The older man leaned back and rubbed his belly. "Now, that's what I call a meal!"

The kids helped clear the table without any complaining, then moved into the living room to watch a DVD.

"Tomorrow I'll call Stella," Sid said, "and see if she has any relatives that'd be happy to go honeysuckle hunting for you." Sierra smiled at him.

He clapped his hands. "Now let's have some of that lemon mang pie!"

Friday night, after a near silent dinner of grilled cheese sandwiches and tomato soup with crackers, Sierra cleared the table and piled the dishes in the sink. Her mom would be horrified, with the empty dishwasher a mere foot away. But Sierra wanted to hurry. The children had been moody all day, and she wasn't about to sit around and do nothing about it.

She hastened into the living where the kids sat zombielike, watching a movie. "I need you guys to get in the van." Her keys jangled as she pulled on her coat.

Braden's eyes didn't leave the TV. "Where are we going?"

She hesitated. "Dad's."

Three pairs of eyes zoomed to focus on her. Excitement entered Braden's voice. "We're going to Dad's?"

Sierra flipped her hair out from under the heavy collar of her jacket. "I need to talk to him."

Emory's face grew worried. "We're not staying the weekend?"

"I don't know, honey. Please get your coat and shoes."

Braden hunched down in the couch. "I don't want to go."

Sierra squatted in front of him, placing a hand on his knee. "I don't blame you, bud. It hurts when people don't keep their word."

His scowl didn't lighten, but he got his shoes on and stalked out to the van.

When Sierra turned into the upscale neighborhood, a panicky note entered Emory's voice. "What if he wants us to stay? I don't have any of my stuff."

Sierra kept her voice even. "Your overnight bags are in the back of the van."

She glanced in her rearview mirror and saw Braden look over into the cargo space. When she pulled up and parked behind the black Lexus in Michael's driveway, he dragged his overnight bag into his lap.

The Tudor-style home had a fancy white wooden "For Sale" sign in the grass next to the sidewalk.

"You guys wait here." Sierra hurried up the flagstone walkway.

Michael opened the door before she knocked. "What are you doing here, Sierra?"

"You broke their hearts Tuesday night, Michael. They don't understand when you make promises and then don't show." She glanced toward the van. "Have you thought about how they felt, waiting on the porch, jumping every time a car went by?"

The lines in his cheeks were taut and his eyes had the bloodshot look of someone surviving on little sleep. He leaned his head back and exhaled. "Things are complicated right now. My practice isn't doing well…."

Conflicted emotions stormed through her. Part of her grieved that his business was tumbling apart. She'd been a part of the dream to open the practice so many years before. But those feelings were only a tiny sliver of emotion compared to the anger and sadness she felt at the pain he was causing their kids.

"I know things are complicated, Michael, but the kids miss you." She studied him, trying to find that connection between them that was their kids. If she reached for it, maybe he'd listen, soften. Go back to being the dad the kids adored.

He slanted a hard gaze at her. "I can't take the kids this weekend."

She crossed her arms, her voice harsher than she intended. "Why not?"

His mouth parted, but then his gaze shot over her shoulder and his brow drew together. She turned. All three kids were walking tentatively up the sidewalk, overnight bags in their hands.

Once they realized they'd been discovered, the kids ran for the entrance.

"Hi, Daddy." Trevor dropped his bag and Michael swooped him up, holding him close a moment.

Michael set him down and pulled Emory into a tight side hug, then reached for Braden, who hung back for one long second. Head down, their eldest gave his dad a lukewarm embrace.

Trevor turned toward her. "Hug, Mom." She bent down and squeezed him. His little arms snaked up around her neck, gripping tight and her heart broke. He leaned back and his thumb-bucked teeth gleamed in a giant smile. Then he ducked past Michael and ran into the house, his bag and stuffed animal forgotten on the porch.

Emory and Braden hesitated, more sensitive to the tension in Michael's stance.

"Sierra, this isn't a good time."

"Kids, run inside. Your dad and I need to talk." Emory gave her a quick look, blue eyes wide with worry, then darted into the house. Braden stuffed his hands into his pockets as he stared down in front of him.

Her fingers brushed Braden's shoulder. "Go in the house, sweetheart." He looked at her, his expression so lost, so hurt. She nodded, wanting nothing more than to shuttle him back to the van and home to safety. "It'll be okay." He turned, shoulders drooping, and moved into the house.

Michael spoke over his shoulder. "Just for a few minutes, guys."

"I know about the bankruptcy," Sierra said.

He leaned his arm up against the doorjamb, looking irritated. "It doesn't remove my child support judgment if that's what you're worried about."

"Braden needs vision therapy. It's three thousand dollars."

"Why don't we go for the whole works and get him into braces, too."
He rubbed his face with both hands. "Look, I'm sorry. I'm under a lot of
stress right now. I know I haven't been there for the kids like I need to be,
but it's just not a good time."

"He needs this therapy, Michael. The doctor said school will remain
incredibly difficult for him without it." She paused. "The divorce decree
states that you pay sixty percent of medical procedures."

His brow drew down. "I know what the decree says. There's nothing
I can do to help right now. Maybe later ... I don't know what's going to
happen."

"Can they stay?"

He straightened and stuffed a hand in his pocket. "Gina just isn't up
for it right now."

"Why not?"

His eyes steered clear of hers. His voice was lower, but gained
strength, as if he refused to feel defensive. "She's pregnant."

The sucker punch slipped past her stomach and went straight for the
heart as a whirlwind of thoughts pummeled her. She wanted to cry for her
children who would remain on the periphery. Removed. Stepchildren.
Half-siblings. The thoughts swirled and tore at her emotions.

"She's not feeling well. And the noise. It makes it hard for her to sleep."

"*All* of your children need you, Michael."

A flicker of guilt rippled across his face, and he dragged one hand
down his cheeks. A gesture so familiar to her. It was the one he used when
he knew what was right but was torn by pressure from other directions.

"Gina just isn't used to kids."

"Well, then, this will be good practice."

Chapter 14

Ross shook the newspaper open to the home-and-garden section as he did every Saturday morning. The article on "winterizing your home" didn't hold his attention. He laid the paper aside. This used to be his favorite part of the week, but now his thoughts kept drifting to the Cranwell plans on his office desk. Maria Cranwell had changed the water feature yet again.

He took another sip of rich black brew and gazed through the kitchen window out over his pasture. A movement in the adjoining field caught his eye.

"What?" In the enclosure near Sid's horse barn, an angry black horse danced around a sway-backed gray nag.

Ross growled and headed for the back porch. He jerked his work boots on, then threw an old coat over his shoulders and stomped through the grass to bring Chance back home.

Wet field grass slapped over the top of his boots, soaking his jeans up to the knee. Halfway through Sid's pasture, Ross stopped. He glanced around trying to get a feel for what was out of place.

Slowly it came to him. Sid had usually let the horses out by now. Yet only Traitor and Chance stood in the pasture. He glanced toward the house. The back porch door stood wide open. Sid surely wouldn't have left it open on such a cold morning. His pulse accelerated, pounding in his ears.

He broke into a run, his gaze sweeping the pasture as he sprinted for the barn. A bit of red off to his left snagged his attention. The stiff breeze blew it gently, fluttering just beneath the blades of grass. Probably nothing, but his heart hammered anyway, beating against the bones in his chest. He cut toward the red bit of fluff, still scanning the rest of the field. Then he saw the black boot.

"Sid!" The scream tore through him, lost in a chilly gust of wind. He raced, the air current whipping against him. Sid lay chalk white, his skin cold and pinched, as if he had shriveled into himself. Ross slid to his knees next to the older man and leaned his cheek over Sid's open mouth, but with the gust blowing between them he couldn't tell if there was breath. He gently laid his head over Sid's chest and thought he felt a soft *thump-thump*, but wasn't sure. It might have been his own pulse surging in his ear.

Was it a heart attack? Skinny as he was, Ross knew Sid's doctor had been after him to eat better or risk having it catch up to him. He grabbed for his cell phone at his waist, but clutched denim instead. He yelled, the wind snatching away the sound. His cell phone lay in the kitchen by his truck keys.

Ross scanned the rest of Sid's body and saw that dark wetness had colored much of Sid's overalls. A patch had spread under his left leg, bathing the grass with the old man's lifeblood. Ross pulled out the utility knife he slipped into his pocket every morning and slit the tough denim to Sid's thigh. It was bad—the flesh mangled and bruised from iron horseshoes. Bits of bone and muscle clung to the material Ross peeled back. Black-crusted blood told him Sid had been out here a while. He tore off his shirt and tied it around Sid's leg, trying to be gentle, but needing to dress the wound. When he was satisfied, he laid his coat over his friend, then ran for Sid's barn phone and called for help.

Sierra flipped the blinker to pull into Ross's lane but caught the flash of emergency lights ahead. An ambulance pulled onto the highway from Sid's drive. It sped past with screaming sirens. She gunned the van and headed for Sid's. Somebody had to still be there.

She circled the empty gravel yard with her van. *Ross must have ridden in the ambulance.* A flash caught her periphery, and she turned to see Ross vault the fence back to his yard. He was bare chested in the freezing weather. Sierra floored the accelerator and sped back down the driveway to Ross's.

She met him coming out of his house, the T-shirt he'd thrown on inside out, the tag hanging out in front. His eyes were frantic. "Sid's hurt bad."

She gripped the steering wheel, terror pouring over her. "Get in the van. I'll take you to the hospital."

He opened his mouth, glanced at his truck, then nodded, and rushed to the passenger side of the van.

"What happened?"

"I found him in the pasture with Traitor and Chance." He stared out the side window, his voice so low she could barely make out the words.

"Did he have a heart attack?"

Ross's turned to stare straight through the windshield, his profile tight, angry. "He'd been stomped."

"How did Traitor get in your pasture?"

His eyes flared dark. "Chance was in his."

In the hospital waiting room, Ross looked away from Sierra, guilt eating at him. She was crying, and he hadn't offered a word of comfort, not a hug, not even a cup of coffee. He paced to the far side of the room and dropped onto a couch with his forehead in his palms and elbows on his knees. An image of a gray horse in the wrong pasture flashed into his mind. Sid lay on an operating table because someone left a gate open.

A cushion moved beside him, then settled. He glanced over and saw his cousin.

"I got your message." Kyle swallowed hard. "How's he doing?"

Ross shook his head and swallowed hard.

"Mr. Morgan?" There was the soft hush of rubber soles on the carpet.

Ross raised his head and walked to meet the doctor halfway across the room.

Dr. Ho, still in scrubs, crossed his arms. "Mr. Barrows will be moved to recovery shortly. His left femur was crushed. We managed to insert a rod and remove most of the fragments." He shrugged. "It's a waiting game at this point to see how it heals and if there's infection." The doctor's gaze flashed down to his hands frequently while he talked, as if consulting a clipboard he no longer held. "His age doesn't improve his chances, nor does the fact that he was exposed to the elements for most of the night."

Sid had been out there all night? The shock hit Ross like a bucket of ice water in the face.

"We did our best, but we may still have to take the leg." Ross met Kyle's eyes, and he broke out in a cold sweat. Spots darkened his vision for a second.

The doctor's tone changed and he reached toward Ross, concern in the eyes behind the silver frames. "Sir, do you need to sit down?"

Sid with one leg? He'd die. Just waste away. Anger thrashed in Ross's gut. *All because Chance had gotten in with that black horse.*

Kyle gripped his arm. "Ross?"

Ross shook off his hand and stepped back on shaky legs. "No. I'm fine."

The doctor eyed him carefully before continuing, "We may need to perform a second surgery to clean the wound some more. We were able to irrigate and remove most of the debris, but our focus was getting the rod in." He crossed his arms. "Considering his age, we didn't want him under the anesthesia longer than necessary. Consequently he'll be on heavy doses of antibiotics for a couple of weeks."

Sierra sniffled.

Ross looked at her. Her face was blotchy, and her eyes puffed up. She addressed the doctor. "What are the risks at this point?"

The doctor nodded. "Infection always remains our number one concern. Also how his heart will react to the trauma of the wound, the exposure, and extensive surgery." The doctor consulted the nonexistent clipboard again. "His heart rate and blood pressure remained fairly stable through the surgery, but it's a wait-and-see game from here on out."

Ross turned and his gaze caught Sierra's. Her eyes were deep pools of sorrow and fear. She bent her head, but not before he caught the flash of guilt.

In that split second, satisfaction flashed through him. He was glad that she felt culpable. And the shame of that thought rode him harder for it.

On the drive back to Sid's, Ross couldn't bring himself to break the silence that filled Sierra's van like black tar. The car coasted to a halt in front of the barn, and he started to open his door.

She turned in her seat. "Ross, please say something."

He hesitated. Sid had looked so ill in the few minutes Ross had sat with him in the recovery room after the surgery. And *she* couldn't change that. With a quick glance at her, he opened the van door. "We need to get your horse back to my barn."

She caught up to him at the barn entrance, her soft touch to his arm stopping him. Her eyes were big cinnamon pools of distress.

He stepped back and her hand fell. "Sierra, nothing I say is going to turn back time."

The wind tangled the ends of her chestnut hair as she looked away, her back to the pasture. "What do you think happened?"

The weight of his own responsibility pressed into his chest. Why didn't he double-check the gates when he turned Chance loose in the pasture last night? "Traitor hasn't adjusted to the other horses for some reason." He sighed. "I imagine he got agitated having Chance in his field and Sid tried to separate them."

"How did Chance get out?"

"The gate separating my pasture from Sid's was left open."

Her eyes grew puzzled.

"Your kids were playing in the pasture yesterday after Sid left."

"Oh." Her eyes fell from his and she drew her jacket tighter around her body. "So ..." she raised her eyes slowly, "you blame us."

He jerked his gaze toward the pasture. "I'm not mad at you."

She remained quiet, the wind whipping her hair.

The words burst from him. "I'm mad at—at ..." He threw his arms up. "I don't know what I'm mad at. I'm mad that Chance got loose in Sid's pasture. I'm mad that Sid might lose his leg, might never be the same."

Sadness filled the curves of her face. "I'm so sorry, Ross."

"But that doesn't change anything, does it?"

Sierra watched Ross stride across the pasture toward Chance, a blue lead rope dangling at his side. He gave the black horse near the fence a passing glance, then jerked back, and the low words whipped to her. "Oh, Lord!"

Whatever had happened, it was bad. Ross snapped the lead on the black horse's halter and turned him so that she could see him. A large flap of his chest hung loose, the red flesh exposed and crusted with dried blood. Sierra's stomach twisted.

Ross's face was set in angry lines. "Sid doesn't need this on top of everything else!"

Sierra backed a safe distance from the horse's path as Ross led him toward the barn, the horse's metal shoes crunching in the gravel. She waited until the black horse disappeared through the entrance, then followed, staying back until Ross closed the door to the stall.

He gave her a grim look. "We'll have to call the vet."

On a small ledge near the sink, an old black rotary phone rested atop a tattered phone book. After the call he grabbed another lead. "I'll bring Chance in here to look him over. I don't have any first aid in my barn."

The sick feeling grew with visions of more gaping wounds. Sierra steeled herself and followed him to the fence.

He tossed her a brief glance as he walked Chance back through the gate. "Nothing major that I can see, just a few bites and abrasions. He's lucky."

Yet from the look on Ross's face Sierra sensed that he wished Chance had been the injured one and not Traitor.

Chapter 15

After Sierra left, Ross tried to hold Traitor steady as the vet stitched the slashed flesh together. He felt his anger cooling off and murmured softly to the black horse as it pulled against the cross ties. It made no sense to blame Sierra for the injuries Chance had caused. It wasn't any one person's fault. When the vet finished, Ross wrote down instructions for the antibiotics then jumped into his pickup to head back to the hospital.

His cousin was supposed to meet him in the small waiting room on Sid's floor, and he wasn't going to like what Ross had to say. Kyle needed to find Chance a new home. The horse had caused too many problems, and Sierra … she was becoming his biggest distraction.

Kyle walked in ten minutes after Ross and dropped into a chair. "Sid awake?"

"There's a nurse in there now. Said to give her a minute."

"Sorry I couldn't get over to help feed Sid's ponies this morning. One of my mechanics didn't show up."

"Sierra helped."

"But she's scared of horses." Kyle stared at him as if he'd beaten the woman.

"What?" Ross tossed the magazine he'd been reading back onto the table and stood up. "It was her horse that put us in this mess."

"This isn't her fault, and you know it." An accusatory tone crept into Kyle's voice. It was one that Ross hadn't heard in a long time and didn't care to hear right now. "What is it with you? Sierra is sweet. So are her kids. I've watched you, cousin. As soon as a decent woman comes onto your radar you go on a hunt."

That jolted a snort from Ross. "A hunt? Right!" He wasn't looking for a relationship and definitely not one with Sierra Montgomery. Even if he couldn't keep her off his mind.

Kyle torpedoed in on that. He poked an oil-stained finger at Ross's nose. "Yeah, you do! You pick and dig around the edges until you find some reason to back off."

"And why would I do that?" Irritation rolled out with the words.

Kyle laid one arm across the other, legs spread. "You tell me."

"There's nothing to tell, because there's nothing there."

Kyle shook his head. "You live like you've got something to prove." He dropped his arms and his voice grew softer. "Just think about it, Ross. The only person you need to prove anything to is yourself."

Ross looked away.

When they finally got to see him, Sid looked more withered than he had earlier. The white room felt boxy and small with the hospital bed devouring most of the space. "Hiya boys." Sid's voice was reed thin.

"Hi, Sid."

Kyle was the first to ask. "What's wrong with your voice?"

The gown had slid down one of Sid's thin shoulders. "Hoarse. Doctor said it'll come back in a few days."

Kyle frowned. "Why is it hoarse?"

Sid's eyes immediately fell away from them and focused on the faded yellow drapes. "From yellin' for help, I guess."

With a groan, Ross dropped his head in his hand.

"Now, Ross. Don't go blamin' yerself. I shoulda knowed better than to head into that field the way Traitor was actin'. Nothin' ornerier than a stud protecting his territory."

Kyle folded himself into the chair next to the bed. "What happened?"

Sid pressed a weak fist into the mattress to adjust his weight. "Oh, I brought the other horses in and was headed out for Traitor when I heard him squealing and carrying on. Found that horse Chance out there. I knew Traitor could hurt him bad, and I didn't want those kids to lose their horse. So, like a fool, I tried to catch Chance before Traitor did much damage. I lost my footing and fell. Don't recall much after that."

Ross closed his eyes and wiped a hand down his face.

"Doc said it was lucky you found me when you did." Sid's chin sank down toward his chest. "Mighta moved up my retirement."

Kyle gave a halfhearted chuckle. "I never thought I'd hear those words cross your lips."

Sid's eyes moved to the far wall. "The thought's been comin' now and again."

Kyle visited a few more minutes then looked at the clock. "Mom's having the family over for dinner tonight, so I better get going."

"Tell Stella and your sisters hello. Haven't had your mother's pot roast in a good while."

Kyle touched his forehead in salute. "Will do. I'm sure she can be persuaded to bring one over when you're recuperating. Oh, and Mom said she has some information for you."

As soon as the door closed, Sid seemed to shrink back into the sheets. Growing older and smaller in the space of a heartbeat.

Gone was the verve and bluster. In its place lay a shell of the old man. Ross reached deep and found a grin. "Don't keep up pretenses on my account."

Sid scowled. "Aw, you know Stella. If Kyle tells her I'm ailin', she and those girls of hers will be down here fussin' over me. I cain't stand bein' fussed over."

Ross laughed, relief enveloping the dread.

Sid sighed. "I don't know, Ross. I'm tired."

Alarm flashed through Ross's mind. He'd suggested for years that Sid sell his farm and slow down. But without the horses, what would Sid have to live for? That answer was obvious—nothing.

"Sid, you just spent a night in your pasture, thanks to me. It's going to take a while to get your strength back. You'll feel more like yourself in a couple of weeks."

Sid looked pointedly at his leg. "Maybe it's time to sell, like you're always yammering about."

The words shot out of Ross's mouth. "Well, maybe I was wrong."

Sid raised his eyebrows. A few seconds later a low chuckle rumbled through his chest. "I see. You're scared that ol' Sid is gonna roll over and kick the bucket without them horses to keep him goin'." Sid raised himself up a few inches. "Now you listen to me, son. The good Lord assigns our days, and when He says it's time to go, it'll be time to go. No sooner, no later." He relaxed back with a firm nod.

"Yes, sir."

The color was clearly back in Sid's cheeks. "Now what's on your mind?"

"Pardon me?"

Sid's whiskers jiggled as he moved his jaw. "Son, I don't have the energy to go draggin' it out of you."

Ross sank into a vinyl chair crowded between the wall and the rolling platform that held a pitcher of water. "I'm getting rid of Chance."

Sid's grizzled cheeks really started moving then. "Now, why would you go and do a stupid thing like that?"

Tension grew and radiated between Ross's shoulder blades. "Traitor had to have his chest sewn shut."

Pain spasmed across Sid's face. If Ross thought that'd be enough to get Sid on his side, he was wrong. "That's not Sierra's fault. No reason to blame that gal and her horse."

Ross ran his hand over his hair. "Sid, if she can't get those kids to keep the gates closed, then it's not safe. I still haven't told my mother about her honeysuckle. And I discovered that before he met up with Traitor, Chance apparently found a flat of daylilies I'd ordered for Alex's place."

Sid lifted his head a fraction. "Never heard of a horse that liked daylilies."

"It's gotten to where I'm afraid to come home at night. I keep expecting to find that horse standing in the kitchen raiding my refrigerator."

Sid's chuckle faded and he pursed his lips. Ross knew that look. He also knew he didn't want to hear what was coming. "Son, I've told you before, I think Sierra needs us. And more'n just spending a few hours on your bookkeeping. I'll be sorely disappointed if you send her away."

"I'm not backing down this time."

Sid's head lowered and he stared at the bed cover. "Just as well, I expect."

Ross grew wary. "I'm glad you see my point."

The old coot sent him a cagey look. "Though, I s'pose you'd still get to see her, since that old gelding would just be grazing on the other side of the fence. Heck, maybe he'd still come visit you."

Ross tightened his jaw. "Sid, you can't take care of the horses you have, let alone take on that troublemaking nag."

"Just doin' what the good Lord's tellin' me." Sid took on the innocent aura of an angel.

Ross grinned in spite of himself. "Fine. He can stay. For now."

The fight gone out of him, Sid leaned heavily back against his pillow. "I better get some shut-eye."

Ross stood and looked down at him. He felt like a little boy who didn't want to leave the only security he knew. He blew a quiet breath. He was a grown man and knew better than to look for security in someone else. Even if Sid was the closest thing he had to a father, one that cared for him anyway.

Ross strode from the hospital into the parking lot, hands deep in his pockets when his cell rang. He flipped it open, his thoughts still absorbing the words the doctor had spoken before he left. The man had said that Sid wouldn't be mobile for quite a while and even suggested putting him in a nursing home for a month or two. Ross's grip tightened around the phone as he put it to his ear. He'd find a way to care for his friend no matter what. "Ross here."

"Ross? It's Alex Cranwell. About the job, I'm going to need to move the completion date up."

Ross slowed, wary. "To when?"

"December nineteenth."

Ross stopped next to a white Toyota. "Decem—that's impossible. February twentieth was the completion date we agreed on. I need those extra two months. I can't—"

"Look, Morgan, do I need to hire another crew? Because when a man commits to a job, he sticks with it no matter how tough it gets. Either that or he cuts the line and bails. And trust me, it won't be any easier if you were working for me on the commercial side."

Ross bit back the words he felt like saying. He blew out a breath. "It's going to cost quite a bit to hire more crews."

"Whatever it takes, Morgan. Whatever it takes." He boomed out a laugh. "Think of this as cutting down your learning curve."

Ross ended the call and flipped the phone shut. He had two crazy months to finish a four-month job, and Alex still needed to finalize some of the plans. He stopped as another thought hit him: Now he had Sid's place to care for, thanks to that gray horse.

Sierra didn't sleep well that night; too many problems demanded her attention. Sid, Braden, the money crunch. Ross's bookkeeping job would take some pressure off, but how much of a dent could a part-time job make in a three-thousand-dollar medical bill? And Braden started vision therapy tomorrow.

She tossed onto her side and pulled the blankets up to her neck, curling her hands under her chin as blackness lightened to gray outside her window. A tear slid across her nose and down her cheek. She rubbed it into the blanket then slammed her fist into the bare spot where another pillow used to lie. Where was God when she needed Him?

Twenty minutes later, dressed in jeans and sweatshirt, Sierra placed a mug of hot black coffee on the console and watched her headlights illuminate the eddies of fog on the highway. She crept along the stretch of Bailey Hill Road until she found Sid's driveway. The gravel seemed to crunch louder in the stillness of the damp fog. Barn lights were burning when she stopped the car outside the large red structure. The blue numerals on the dashboard clock glowed 6:34 a.m. Her wool-gloved fingers pulled the keys from the ignition and dropped them into the spare cup holder.

The barn door squeaked and Ross glanced up, surprise in his features. He held a jug of oats in one hand and a bottle of disinfectant in the other. He seemed unsure of what to say, his lingering gaze sending a frisson of electrical sparks through her body.

"Morning." He nodded over his shoulder. "Could you grab that packet of gauze and the tape?" At least he was talking to her.

She looked in the direction he'd pointed and saw the tray of medical supplies the veterinarian must have left. Her heart started a mad thump as she collected the items and followed Ross down the row of stalls.

He stopped next to a stall door that had a shiny number 6 affixed to it, his hand on the latch. His eyes were hard to read as he studied her. "I can do this alone, but it'd be a lot easier if I had someone to help me hold Traitor."

The tray dug into her hands. *Hold the horse as Ross leans down in front of that massive chest?* "I don't know if I can."

He nodded, quiet acceptance in his gaze as he lifted the latch.

She berated herself and swallowed hard. "I—I'll try."

He swung back, brown eyes intense. "Sierra, it's okay to be afraid. If—"

"I said I'll do it." She motioned toward the stall. "Let's just get it over with. Tell me how you want me to h-hold him."

He stood inches from her, his eyes unreadable. "I appreciate your trying." Then he unhooked the latch. "We'll cross-tie his head to the corner of the stall, but I'll need you to hold his halter to keep him from trying to reach down."

"What will he be reaching down for?"

A half-smile flashed. "To bite me."

"Bite you?"

"He's not going to like the antibiotic. Keep your feet away from his hooves. He might get a little antsy." Alarm flared and she shot him a look. He continued, "Traitor won't try to hurt you, he'll just want to get away from the sting. It'll be your job to soothe him. Just pretend you're holding Braden's hand."

She snorted at that.

His face softened, compassion showing through. "I really appreciate this. I know it isn't easy for you."

She looked away. She was *way* out of her comfort zone. "Okay, I'll just pretend I'm holding Braden's hand."

He rubbed one smooth-shaved cheek. "And, um, horses can sense fear, so just try to relax."

Chapter 16

Ross pulled the bandage off Traitor's chest. The wound didn't look as angry as it had yesterday, and he dabbed it with ointment the vet had given him. Traitor tried to seesaw his body away from the pain.

"Ross?" Panic flooded Sierra's voice.

"Whoa, Traitor." Ross put a hand on Traitor's side, trying to soothe him. "I'm hurrying. Just talk to him. He can't get loose." Ross quickly set the new gauze over his knee and cut it to fit the wound. Stupid! Why hadn't he shaped it before he brought Sierra into the stall?

Sierra spoke to the horse, holding the halter despite being jerked back and forth as Traitor grew more agitated, tossing his head as much as the short rope allowed. "It's okay, boy. It's okay." The words turned to pleading. "Stop please, Traitor. It's okay."

"Almost done."

Sierra was silent. The only sound was her shoes scraping against the floor with Traitor's movements.

Ross pressed the tape to the quivering horseflesh and smoothed the fresh bandage into place. He picked up the scraps and stood.

Sierra was paper white, her eyes huge pools of terror. Ross gripped her arm and propelled her out of the stall, then stepped back in to untie Traitor. Once he'd latched the stall door shut, she bent—hands covering her face—and heaved loud sobs.

He tugged her gently to him and her face slipped right into the hollow of his shoulder, her nose pressed against his neck. She didn't hold on to him, but she wasn't slugging him either. Ross wrapped his other arm around her shoulder and rocked her softly, resting his chin in her hair that was silky soft and smelled sweeter than his mother's honeysuckle.

She relaxed into him, one hand cupping his waist right above his cell phone. Her tears stopped and still she rested against him. He didn't move. Didn't want her to leave his arms. Didn't analyze why.

A soft flutter of laughter tickled his neck. "Um, I need a tissue."

He steadied her as he grabbed the grimy roll of paper towels Sid kept beside the sink. Awkwardly he unrolled a length using both hands behind her back and handed her the wad. Cold air chilled the dampness on his neck for a moment as she raised her head before she wiped his skin dry.

She backed up, lifting her eyes to him. Amazing, brilliant eyes. And a smile bloomed beneath her red nose. "What a way to start the day." One edge of her mouth crumpled a bit.

"Do you want some coffee? I've got a full pot brewing back at the house."

She nodded with a self-conscious smile. He wrapped an arm around her shoulder and led her to his pickup.

Sierra couldn't believe she had bawled all over Ross and now was standing in his kitchen, which was filled with the rich smell of coffee, while he pulled down two mugs from the cupboard next to the stove.

She wrapped her arms around her waist and turned. "Your kitchen is lovely. Did you remodel?" Red-and-tan checkered curtains framed the window above the kitchen table. Stainless-steel appliances shone beneath creamy cupboards. A red ceramic pot held an array of spatulas on the beige tiled counter.

He handed her the steaming mug, and she settled into the wooden chair at the kitchen table.

"Yeah. Last summer." Ross opened the fridge and pulled out a carton of eggs, some mushrooms, and what looked like a package of ham while he searched for something else. He stood up and waved a small red bottle. "Like Tabasco sauce?"

She nodded. He set the food on the counter and lifted a skillet from the rack over the island. His gaze caught on hers and grew soft. "You doing okay?"

"Yes." She felt her face heat and she glanced away, picking at a string that hung at the bottom of her old sweatshirt.

The pan clattered as he set it on the stove and then cracked the eggs, liberally applied pepper, and whisked them together with a sure hand. Dots of Tabasco followed mushrooms into the bowl.

A few minutes later he set two steaming omelets on the table with glasses of orange juice. He lathered the top of his with salsa and sour cream. He caught her staring and grinned, holding out the salsa. "Wanna try it?"

She dropped her fork and grabbed the bottle. What the heck. She heaped a spoonful of it and the sour cream onto her omelet and dug in. Or started to. Her fork stilled halfway to her mouth.

That half grin of his formed a shallow dimple in his right cheek. "Mind if I pray?"

She hesitated, wanting desperately to taste the oozing bite of egg, but politely set her fork down. "Go ahead."

His prayer was brief, thanking the Lord for the food and the company, and asking a blessing on both.

His prayers were like Elise's—conversation with a friend.

The hot, cheesy confection delighted her taste buds.

"It's a Mexican omelet."

"I've never had anything like it."

His fork paused.

She grinned at him around another bite. "I love it."

Satisfaction eased the lines on his face. "Good."

She'd expected the questions to start the minute he sat down. But he acted as if it were perfectly normal to share his breakfast table with her.

"You want another one?"

Her fork paused as she cut into the last third of her meal. "I want one, but I'd probably explode."

He laughed and crossed his arms, leaning them on the table. "These are one of my mom's specialties." He tilted his head, his eyes growing soft. "That was really brave of you to help me this morning. I'm sorry I didn't realize how hard it was for you. I never would have asked if I'd known, Sierra."

She glanced down at the tablecloth. "You deserve an explanation."

"Only if you want to tell me."

Suddenly she did. She wanted him to understand, not think she was the kind of woman who would freak at the sight of a mouse.

She twirled her fork and stared at her plate. "When I was eight, my friend Molly invited me to go horseback riding with her brother and his girlfriend." She dissected a chunk of mushroom into tiny fragments. "After our trail ride, Molly's brother and his girlfriend went into the house, but Molly wanted to go to the car and play with her dog. She had a cute little Jack Russell terrier named Bandit that went everywhere with them."

She took a sip of orange juice and hazarded a look at Ross. He sat quietly, eyes focused on her. "When Molly opened the car door, her dog jumped out and took off, straight for the horses. We ran after him, but he got under the fence into the corral." Her hand curled tight around her fork. "He was barking like crazy and trying to bite at their legs. I think he was playing, but it freaked one horse especially."

The scene lived in electric clarity, igniting the nerve endings in the back of her neck. "Molly kept screaming for Bandit, but he wouldn't come, just kept chasing this horse who tried to paw and bite at him. The horse kicked him once and he rolled a couple times, but he got back up and went after the horse again. Molly jumped the fence and started chasing Bandit, trying to keep away from the horse."

"She almost caught him, but he slipped out of her hands and ran behind the horse. Molly reached for him again and the horse kicked. His hoof caught her on the temple."

She stared at her plate. "She just lay there, with Bandit dancing around her, not getting up." She rubbed her thumb against the side of the fork. "She died a week later."

"I'm sorry." The table creaked as he leaned forward. Compassion emanated from him, enfolding her in the softness of his eyes.

"I don't want that to happen to my kids. Can you understand that?"

The pause was long, but his eyes were kind. "I can understand that."

There was a *but* behind the words and it irritated her. "What?"

The tilt of his head, the steadiness of his brown eyes asked her to listen, but warned that she wouldn't like what he had to say. His voice was gentle. "It was a freak accident, Sierra. It could have just as easily been a car wreck or a fall from a bicycle that killed your friend."

Her words breathed steam. "So it was just her time to go? It wouldn't have mattered what we were doing that day, she would have died?"

He touched her hand, but she pulled away.

His voice was gentle. "Freak accidents have probability factors. People aren't killed every day because of horses. There are greater risks to driving your car and being hit by a drunk than being killed by a horse. Especially with caring adult supervision, which your children have."

"I would rather my children be in situations where I can control all the factors."

A brief smile crossed his mouth. "Is that realistic?"

"A bicycle is not unpredictable."

"But the children that ride them are."

She looked away.

"Sierra, you can't control everything. It was an accident that killed your friend. She jumped into the middle of a dangerous situation." He leaned forward, his face intent. "Let your kids experience life without trying to make every aspect of it perfectly safe."

Her eyes held his. "It's my job to keep them safe."

He took a deep breath. "I'm not saying let them throw Frisbees from the roof. But you couldn't own a safer horse than Chance. Let the kids truly experience him."

The fluttery wings of fear brushed against her. "And how am I supposed to do that?"

"What every kid wants to do with their horse. Brush him, ride him. Lay on his back while he grazes under the apple tree."

Sierra could feel the blood drain from her face, making her skin cold. "That's foolish."

"That's what your memories are telling you, Sierra. But they're lying."

"And how would I know that? Next you'll tell me that Sid's accident was just another bizarre catastrophe in the horse business? Just a freak accident that shouldn't have happened?"

His thumb stilled on the coffee mug. "Sierra—"

"Don't! I am the one who will have to live with the consequences of any tragedies." The words were strong, but fear encapsulated each one that discharged between them.

She watched him stare across the kitchen; his jaw was firm, eyes determined. "Ross—"

He swiveled his head toward her.

Her thumbnail found a drop of dried egg on the edge of her plate. "I think it would be better if Braden didn't work for you."

A puzzled frown creased his forehead. "I don't mind. He's a fun kid."

Her eyes dropped to the table as she tried to form the words.

His voice grew flat. "That's not what you meant."

She shook her head, then raised her eyes. "He's at such an impressionable age. I just think—"

The hurt showed in his face and a thread of anger laced the words. "You don't think I'm the best role model for him."

She remained silent.

"Because I think he should be able to enjoy his horse? Or is there something else."

She cleared her throat. "I don't want him pulled between us. He looks up to you so much—"

He leaned back and finished. "And you think I'm going to undermine you." His eyes were direct. "That's it, isn't it?"

She gave a small nod and clenched her hands tightly in her lap.

"Then you don't understand who I am."

Ross drove her back to Sid's. She stared out the side window until he pulled up next to her van and shut off the engine. She reached for the door, but his words stopped her. "Braden told me what's going on with his dad. He needs someone to talk to and I like being there for him. Who else does he have?"

She looked fragile and unsure, the dark snapping eyes from breakfast now deep pools of uncertainty. Her confidence had gone soft, like cardboard planter boxes after a soaking rain.

He didn't want her to misunderstand. "Sierra, he needs you, but he's trying to fill the man-sized shoes his dad left behind. His instinct is to protect you."

She looked away and quickly swiped at her nose, as if she'd had an itch instead of an urge to cry. He braced his arms across the steering wheel. "Sierra, look at me."

Those eyes nearly knocked him back. Cinnamon-tea colored, wet and lost. "You've done a great job of raising Braden. But you are only one person. You aren't designed to be everything he needs. When a boy looks to his mom for every answer, he won't learn how to be a man."

That comment straightened her back. She gave him a scowl of disagreement. "He's not a mama's boy."

"Not yet."

She started to argue but broke eye contact and looked through the windshield instead, the starch deserting her expression.

He touched her arm. "It doesn't mean he won't need you."

"I know that." She moved her arm away.

He opened the truck door and got out to check on Traitor. She shut the passenger door and walked toward her van. "What are you going to do when Sid comes home?" she asked.

The thought hadn't left him since Sid went into surgery. "I'll figure it out."

Tuesday afternoon, Sierra unlocked the front door, then grabbed two of her Mom's suitcases and pushed the door wider with her foot. Braden ran up and squeezed in past her.

He turned the TV on and flopped on the couch.

"Honey, go help Grandma with her bags.

He scowled and dragged himself off the couch. "Geez. You make me do everything."

Her mom followed her up the stairs where she set the luggage on the floor, her back to Sierra. "Braden and Emory sure don't seem very happy to see their grandma."

"I'm sorry, Mom. I don't think they had a very good weekend at their dad's." *And she hadn't let Braden work with Ross since their talk.*

Her mom held up a hand. "You don't want to hear, so I'm not going to say it."

Sierra gave her a soft smile. "Thank y—"

"But that man is going to ruin those kids if he doesn't get his act together."

The weight of her mom's words pressed down on her. "I know, but—"

"You need to do *something*, Sierra." She shook her head. "The disrespect you're getting … it wasn't like that when I was raising you and Win. It wasn't tolerated the way it is nowadays."

"Mom, please don't scold the kids. They're having a hard enough time as it is."

Her mom raised both hands, disapproval deepening the lines around her mouth. "I won't interfere. I'm just the grandma."

Sierra knew that look. Her mom's feelings were hurt. She reached over and gave her mom a small hug. "I'm glad you're back."

Her mom sniffed. "At least you and Trevor are glad."

Sid beat the odds and came home Thursday morning. Kyle stopped by just as Ross attempted to drag the wheelchair backward through the gravel to the rear porch. He'd tried pushing it, but after nearly dumping Sid on his face, he'd turned it around. Sid gripped the armrests as if he was on a terrorizing fair ride.

Kyle added his muscle to the front and they got it to the house in short order. With Sid settled on the couch and a blanket tucked around his legs, Kyle beamed his thousand-watt smile. "How's it going Sid?"

Sid scowled in Ross's direction. "Shoulda just had them put me down. Woulda saved Ross the trouble of trying to end my life in the driveway."

Ross scowled right back at the skinny old man. "Well, maybe if you'd lay off the pot roast, the tires wouldn't have dug in. It was like pushing a cement truck through mud."

Kyle laughed. "If you two can keep from killing each other for a moment, I'll be right back." He headed outside and returned with two KFC bags. Minutes later he handed Sid a steaming plate piled with chicken and mashed potatoes.

"'Bout time somebody thought of food. A man could starve around here."

Ross felt the muscles across his shoulders tighten. "We've been home five minutes, Sid."

Whatever Sid wanted to say was garbled around his next bite.

Kyle caught Ross's eye, his raised eyebrows asking the question.

Ross answered. "Sid doesn't want any more pain medication."

Sid touched his stomach protectively. "It makes me nauseous."

Ross grumbled. "I'd take nauseous over constant bellyaching."

Sid waved a drumstick at him, grease making the whiskers around his mouth shine. "Doc Evans said one of the side effects is ulcers."

Ross raised his hands. "If you take them for a *year*. He said you wouldn't have any problem taking them for the next month."

Sid shook his head, growling low in his throat, his fork digging rifts into the potatoes and white gravy. "I don't trust them doctors."

Ross headed to the kitchen for a glass of water. He loved the man dearly, but if he stayed in the same room with him much longer, Kyle would be digging his grave.

Kyle joined him. "Do you think he'll take the medicine?"

"Nope." Ross drained the glass. "He left all the prescriptions on the hospital bed."

Kyle's face twisted in a rare grimace. "How are you going to handle this?"

Ross leaned back against the sink. "If I make it through this, I'll be eligible for sainthood. If I were Catholic, that is."

Kyle chuckled. "Father Ross. Has a nice ring to it."

"Right now Calcutta sounds like a spot I'd like to send Sid."

Kyle's eyes widened the way they did when he thought he had a brilliant idea. "Hey, what about Sierra?"

Ross tried to ignore how his forearms retained the memory of holding her against his chest. The warmth of her breath on his neck. He shifted position. "What about Sierra?"

The grin grew. "She could watch Sid. Cook for him. Clean. And humor his cantankerous old self."

Ross knew Sid and he couldn't help the half-grin that slid into place.

"Right. Like that little old man out there is going to let some woman fuss over him."

Kyle sucked on his bottom lip and nodded his head with confidence. "He will. Watch."

Ross looked straight at his cousin, who was like a brother to him, and the smile left his face. "Wait!" No way would he let Sierra encroach further into his life. It was hard enough keeping her out of his thoughts with her at his barn. He didn't need her at Sid's place too.

Kyle sprang for the living room. "Hey, Sid. Have you hired a housekeeper yet?"

Ross charged after him. "Kyle—"

Sid sputtered, trying to form a cohesive sentence. "A housekeeper? That'll be the day. No woman is going to run my house. You can get that corn-fed notion out of your head."

"I mean to take care of you while you get well."

"I don't need no woman helpin' me while I convalesce." It took him a moment to get his mouth around the corners of the word. Sid skewered Kyle with a look.

"I think you should have Sierra stay with you until you're back on your feet." Kyle's statement rocked Ross's equilibrium.

Sid's eyebrows nearly reached the gray peak of his receding hairline. "What?"

Kyle held up a hand. "Sid, you're going to need a lot of help before you're out in the barn again, and I don't think Ross has much experience in caring for cantankerous old coots."

Sid nearly bellowed the words. "And what makes you think she does?"

"She has kids."

Sid shot him a grizzled look. "Now, don't you boys go aplottin' things that cain't be. I won't go for some woman cookin' in my kitchen and telling me what to do."

Ross caught the grin Kyle threw him. "You think you could survive on Ross's cooking?"

Sid blustered. "Well, I … well, you got a point there. But there's always canned food. Ross could manage that." Sid slid him a sly look. "If I walk him through it."

"But Ross works," Kyle reminded him. "And with that Cranwell job he's been complaining about he won't be around enough to help you."

But was it wise to have Sierra so close? Ross dropped onto the recliner. He didn't like how he'd started thinking about the woman at odd times. Like yesterday when he'd been planting a flowering pear. That was when he realized he was leaning on his shovel over an eighteen-inch hole wondering if Sierra ever cried in her ex-husband's arms the way she did his.

Definitely not good for business or his peace of mind.

Ross used his firmest tone. "Sid doesn't need kids underfoot when he's trying to get well."

Kyle looked at Ross in surprise. "What else are you going to do? You don't have the time." He winked at the older man. "Sid can afford it, can't you, Sid?"

"I had you boys underfoot for years. Don't think I can't handle a couple of turnips still growing in the garden."

Kyle settled back in the loveseat as if it was a done deal. "From what I've seen she's a good mom. I don't think the kids will be a problem." He gripped the arm of the sofa and straightened as if a thought had fired into his brain. "Ross, you could always ask Clorinda if she's free to stay here with Sid all day. Heck, I bet she'd do it for free."

Clorinda was an older widow who'd moved into a neighboring house a couple of years earlier. She'd been alone for years and seemed set on a course to alter that fact. And that course was aimed straight toward Sid.

Ross leaned forward with a laugh. "I think Clorinda would be just the person to get Sid up and running again."

"Runnin' for my life would be more like it." Sid shuddered deeper into the sofa. "I think maybe Sierra and I will get along tolerably well, but just during the day. I don't need her tucking me in like a baby. I got ol' Ross here to do that."

Sierra leaned her hip against her mom's kitchen counter, coffee brewing as she waited for Ross to arrive. Two mugs waited on a tray.

Her cell rang and she jumped to grab it. Elise's number showed on the screen. "Hi."

"Is he there yet?"

Sierra bit her lip. "No."

"What do you think he wants to talk about?"

Sierra laughed, but it came out nervous sounding. "I don't know."

"How'd he sound on the phone?"

"Fine. Normal."

"Warm?"

Sierra thought back to when Ross called that morning. "Mmm, kinda. More reserved."

"I still can't believe you told him to stay away from Braden."

"I told him I didn't want Braden *working* for him. I just—I don't want Braden to get attached and then hurt, like with Michael."

"And …?"

Sierra scrunched her eyes closed, and the words rushed out. "I thought he'd pull Braden away from me."

"Good girl. Now explain it just like that."

"I don't know if I can, Elise."

"Hon, he's a good man. Do you want me to come hold your hand while you talk to him?"

"No!"

Elise's tinkling laughter came through the phone.

Sierra heard the crunch of tires on gravel. "He's here. I gotta go."

Chapter 17

She heard Braden's heavy tread pound down the stairs, excitement in his voice as he called out. "Ross is here." His bedroom looked out over the driveway. He stopped at the kitchen, one bright brown eye smiling at her, every muscle in his body wired to spring for the door. "Did you know he was coming?"

Sierra nodded. He didn't wait for more, and she followed him to the living room.

Braden held the door wide. "Hi, Ross."

"Hey, buddy." Ross, in denim jeans and a dark green sweater, mussed Braden's hair with a gentle rub to the top of his head, then tipped up her son's chin and eyed the patch. "Hey, is this for Halloween?"

Braden glanced back at her, a shy grin covering his embarrassment. "It's an eye patch from the doctor. But I'm going to be a pirate." His words accelerated in speed and excitement. "Do you need me tomorrow? I can come after school."

Ross looked at Sierra and paused before capturing Braden in his dark gaze again. "Probably not tomorrow."

Braden's shoulders dropped. "Awww." But he said it with a grin. "Can I come back with you to feed Chance? Mom hasn't done it yet."

Ross gave him a sad half-smile. "Not tonight, buddy."

Sierra touched Braden's shoulder. "Honey, why don't you go work on your homework while Ross and I chat for a minute?"

Braden rolled his eyes. "I hate homework."

Ross grinned at him. "How are you going to get into college without it?"

"I know, I know. You already told me."

Ross gripped Braden's shoulders and rocked her son back and forth. The kind of affection men give boys. "I need to talk to your mom."

Braden pounded back up the stairs, and Sierra swung around to Ross. "You've talked to him about college?"

He shrugged with a glance around the living room. "Some."

This could be harder than she and Elise thought. "Would you like some coffee?"

"Please." He put his hands in his pockets.

"Sit anywhere. I'll be right back." Her heart was thudding as she entered the kitchen and assembled the tray. She took a deep breath and returned to the living room, setting the tray on the coffee table.

Ross lifted the carafe and held it over her mug with a raised brow. She nodded and he poured her a cup.

"Thank you." She settled into the recliner and took a sip of the brew, feeling her cheeks heat. She did not want to have this conversation. Maybe Elise could come in through the back door and duck behind the recliner to hold her hand.

He sank back onto the sofa with his mug. "Sierra—"

"Ross, I need—"

The slight smile was polite. "Go ahead."

She gripped the mug with both hands, her fingers cold though the room was warm. "I need to apologize."

He looked toward the window, his jawline firm. "There's nothing to apologize for."

Her words were soft but definite. "Yes, there is."

He angled his head back toward her, his eyes as unreadable as his face.

"Ross, I love my son so much and," she looked down, "I'm scared to death I'm going to lose him. He's angry and looking for someone to follow who isn't his mother or father." She let her gaze find his. "It's you. You have my son's admiration and his heart."

The warmth of the cup started to seep into her fingers. "You're right that I want to control aspects of his life that I can't. It's hard to let go."

His eyes held hers long after she was silent. One edge of his mouth curved and her heart accelerated as he said, "I know."

She caught his gaze. "Please don't hurt him." *Or me.*

He leaned forward. "I'm not perfect, Sierra. But I would never intentionally hurt anyone. Especially Braden."

She gave him a small smile. "I know. I do know that. I just freaked out."

"Moms are allowed to do that about once a month, don't you think?"

"I think I've gone through a year's quota in the last week."

He laughed and relaxed back into the cushions. His grin was soft. "I missed your smile this week."

"Thanks." She let her eyes linger on his, then said, "Braden hasn't stopped asking if he can go work with you."

He folded his hands behind his head and nodded with a slow grin. "Yeah, I'd like to have him back on the job." His eyes held hers until her cheeks grew warm and she looked down at her mug.

His voice was deep. "Sid came home today."

"That's great! When I visited him Monday, he thought he might come home this week. Sounds like he surprised the doctors."

Ross grinned. "That's Sid calling card. He doesn't fit the mold." The warm expression on his face made her stomach quiver. He sat forward, a teasing note in his voice. "I've been sent as the emissary."

She took a sip of the cooling coffee. "Oh?"

"We'd like to hire you to be Sid's nurse."

"Hire me?" *A real job?* "But I don't have any nursing skills."

He gave her a dry look. "I think raising three kids more than qualifies you. Sid just needs some meal prep, help with his meds, and some company. Nothing too complicated."

"How's he feeling?"

"Cranky, sore. Pretty much what you'd expect from a seventy-three-year old man who hates being laid up." Ross cleared his throat. "Um, I haven't been totally honest."

Her fingers tightened on the mug, and she leaned back into the recliner. "What do you mean?"

"Sid can be cantankerous at times."

She frowned at him. "And this is supposed to make me jump at the offer?"

He laughed. "What I mean is, Sid doesn't have any trouble letting the growl out with me. I'm not sure our friendship can survive his recuperation."

She cocked her head at him. "So let him take it out on tough old Sierra?"

His laugh grew deeper, his eyes crinkling at the corners. "That's not what I meant, though I'm sure you could handle it. Sid's old school. He wouldn't take it out on a lady."

Sierra curled her legs under her. "Hmm. So you are actually looking for a rescue, not a nurse."

"*Ex*-actly." He dropped his head, then tipped his chin to look at her. His eyes were a rich brown, like warm mocha. Her throat constricted. Did she want him looking at her like that? Like they were friends? How could she trust that down the road his eyes wouldn't hold something more? Or that she might wish they did?

Ross gave her a teasing smile. "Sid is adamant that it's you or no one. And if you don't, then I'll be the guy making his breakfast."

"You make a mean omelet."

"So, are you going to come to the rescue?"

She sipped her coffee, then looked at him over the mug, and felt a slight smile teasing her lips. "I think I might be able to help out."

Sierra's cell rang minutes after Ross left.

Elise's whispered. "Is he still there?"

"No, he just left."

"Well? I'm dying here."

Sierra squealed. "I have a job, Elise! Can you believe it? And I start tomorrow. Maybe I can save enough to move in a couple months." She dropped onto the couch, started chewing on her nail. "But I don't know if I should have taken it."

Elise settled into the phone call. "Tell me all."

"Well, he walked in—"

"What was he wearing?"

"Elise!"

"Did he sizzle?"

Sierra bit her lip. "Designer jeans and a green sweater." She thought they were designer jeans, anyway.

"I'm drooling."

"Stop!"

"Okay, I've wiped my chin, now go on."

"I apologized about Braden. Elise, he's talked to my son about college."

"No!"

"I know! So, Sid came home this morning and needs a caregiver. He sent Ross over to hire me."

Elise squealed. "God's talking to you, hon."

Sierra stilled. Had it been God? *How did you ever know?*

Her friend's voice dropped. "Now, why shouldn't you take it?"

Sierra started chewing on the nail again. "Elise, Ross is too nice, too kind, too...."

Elise finished for her. "Good to be true."

She drew her legs up on the couch. "What if he is? How will I know?"

"It's all on faith and common sense."

"He and Sid are close. I'll probably see him all the time. Maybe this isn't such a good idea." She sighed. "I don't want to screw up again. I like being single. Did you know that?" She stood up and paced the room. "I can come and go as I please, not answer to anyone. You know?"

"Hon, he hasn't asked you out."

She dropped back onto the couch, biting the corner of her lip. "Do you think he will?"

"Do you want him to?"

"I don't know. Yes, maybe." She drew her legs up again, thinking about how he'd looked at her on the couch and she got scared all over again. "Probably not."

"Well, there you go."

"What?"

"If he asks, just say no."

She saw his mocha eyes again, warm on hers. "I don't think I can."

Friday morning Sierra slid the key Ross gave her into the lock and slowly turned it. She tiptoed through the small foyer and into the living room.

"Mornin'." Sid lay on the couch, a cheerful twinkle in his eye. The warmth of his smile gave her a momentary impression of coming home.

"Good morning! I thought you might be sleeping."

"Nope." She caught the slight grimace as he adjusted himself on the couch. Then his eyes lit. "So Ross badgered you into it?"

She gave him a cheeky grin. "Nearly made him beg."

Sid slapped his good leg. "Bet he liked that."

She chuckled and set her purse near the door. "And why do you say that?"

"Oh, Ross's never been one to let anyone else steer the boat. If the idea don't come from him, he tends to sour up."

"I heard you can be pretty ornery yourself."

"Tellin' stories, was he?"

She zipped her finger across her lips. "None that I can repeat."

He chuckled.

"Ross said he's taking care of your horses and staying nights with you."

Sid rubbed his whiskers. "Yeah, I haven't found anybody else to feed the ponies, so he's stuck with that job for the time being. And, o' course there's no one to keep up their training."

She held up her hands. "That was *not* in my job description."

That brought out a bark of laughter from him. "Well, it shoulda been."

"All I know is that I'm to feed you and make sure you take your pain medicine."

A mulish look dragged Sid's cheeks down. "I don't need no pain medicine. Besides, I don't have any."

Sierra held up a small sack. "Ross called the doctor and set you up with a new prescription since you *forgot* yours at the hospital. I picked it up from the pharmacy this morning." And she'd need to get repaid today or her checking account would go into crash-and-sizzle mode.

Sid's expression turned tetchy. "People get hooked on those narcotics. Ross needs to honor an old man's predilection against drugs. They can damage yer liver, ya know."

Predilection? Sierra bit her lip against the smile. Sid must be on the road to self-education. Yep, there on the couch next to him lay a book of crossword puzzles and a dog-eared thesaurus.

"If you can handle the pain without snapping at the cook, I'd be happy to forget I have them," Sierra said.

Sid relaxed back into the country blue cushions. "I think we'll get along tolerable well." A definite twinkle lit his eyes. "Just don't tell Ross. He's liable to get snappy."

Sierra felt her lips twitch into a grin. "I think you two like snapping at each other."

"Now, I can see why Ross cottons to you so much."

Heat gravitated to her cheeks in less time than it took to breathe. "No matchmaking. I think I'll have my hands full enough with you, anyway."

That delighted him. "It ain't matchmaking to report the truth. Now where's the little fellah?"

"Trevor? My mom offered to watch him."

He gave her a sly look. "Didn't want the little guy to see you get fired on your first day?"

"You'll be lucky if I don't quit!"

Sid heaved himself into a more comfortable position again. He pointed in the direction of what looked to be the kitchen. "There's two checks on the counter in there. One for groceries and one for you."

"You don't have to prepay me. If I could just get reimbursed for the prescription that would be great."

"We might need to get something straight here, missy. I don't cotton to anyone arguing except me. That check is for you and your younguns. Take it, and I don't want to hear another word about it."

Sierra murmured an assent and picked up the tray of empty dinnerware from beside the couch. "I'll clean up a little and fix you some breakfast."

Sierra set the tray on the kitchen counter and picked up two envelopes. She slit the one with her name on it and peeked at the check. Shocked, she took firm steps back into the living room. "Sid, this is too much. Are you paying me to take care of you for the next decade or what?"

Sid smiled. "Now don't go a quibblin' on me, but just so you know, I have high expectations." His jowls nearly quivered in anticipation. "What's your pot roast like?"

Sierra spent the first day doing some menu planning and tidying. Plastic gloves and cleaning supplies were a priority. But mainly she kept Sid company. They watched *The Price Is Right* later in the morning. When she realized there was nothing but scrambled eggs or more oatmeal to feed him for lunch, she made a quick trip to the grocery store for wheat bread, sliced turkey breast, and some tangerines, as well as a few dinner ingredients. In the late afternoon she caught *Oprah* with him. Who would have guessed?

At five-thirty a chicken-and-rice casserole bubbled as she placed it on the hot pad in the center of the kitchen table. Canned beans and french bread rounded out the meal.

Sid searched the table. "Where's the salad?"

"Well, I thought beans might be easier."

"Easier to digest?"

"No. I meant easier on your teeth." Her mom suggested she stay away from salad. Lettuce and dentures were a difficult combination.

"Never heard of lettuce being hard on your teeth."

Sierra bit her lip. "I thought maybe you had dentures."

He looked at her wide eyed, like she was crazy, then burst out laughing. "Missy, I've had these teeth over seventy years. And I like salad with my dinner."

"Yes, sir."

He poked suspiciously at the dark glass of juice by his plate. "What's that?"

"Prune juice." Another of her mother's helpful suggestions.

His eyebrows hunkered down. "That's what I thought." He spoke to the glass. "Sierra, I think we need to get a few things straight. I might look old but my plumbing works fine, and I got all my body parts including these here chompers." He pushed the glass away. "So you go ahead and make my food just like you would for your family." His eyes caught hers. "With salad."

She nodded, warm humor budding at his serious expression. "You like salad."

His nod was succinct. "I like salad. Didn't have much lettuce growing up. Lived on beans mostly." He eyed the green vegetable on the corner of his plate with distaste.

Two quick raps on the back door announced Ross's arrival. "Hi. How did it go today?"

Sid gave a mournful look at the table. "Well, other than the prune juice and the beans, we got along tolerably well."

Sierra swiped the dishtowel at him and turned to Ross. "I see what you mean by cantankerous."

Sid laughed. "Now see here, missy. You've got cantankerous pointed in the wrong direction. *That* one's standing right over there by the sink."

Sierra grinned at Sid. "No, what I'm seeing is two peas in a pod."

Sid herded his rice and chicken into a neat pile far from the beans. "Ross, sit down. There's plenty of vittles."

Ross walked to the sink and washed his hands while Sierra pulled down another plate for him. As she grabbed the utensils, she glanced at him with a straight face. "Prune juice?"

Ross laughed. "No, thanks." After she set a fork and knife on the table, he glanced at Sid, then handed her a sheaf of papers. "I picked these up today when I was in town."

She glanced at him "What … oh, 4-H." The men were watching her, and she wasn't sure how to react. "Um, I'm not sure if we're going to do that."

Ross gently took her arm and moved her to a chair at the table. He pulled his chair in front of her. "Sierra, your kids need this. Braden needs this."

His eyes were kind, and she locked onto them. "Ross, you know why I can't." *Please understand.*

He gripped her hands gently. "You're going to lose Braden if you don't start letting go."

She pulled her hands free and leaned back. He rested his elbows on his knees and locked his fingers loosely between them. "I'm not trying to hurt you. You see, I understand what Braden's going through." He seemed to hesitate, then looked toward Sid.

Sid waved his fork at him. "You're doing good. Keep talkin'."

He glanced toward the side. "Growing up, my dad tried to mold me into what he thought I should be. He wanted his boys to make something of themselves, be different than the regular crowd who graduated and then went to work using their hands. I got pretty angry in high school and hated him for a while." His eyes found hers. "And I see your fear pushing Braden down that same road."

Sierra turned to Sid. "You think I should do this? Even after what happened to you?"

Sid nodded, setting down his glass. "I do. It'd be the best thing for them. What happened to me isn't going to happen to yer kids."

She stood, the papers wrinkling in her grasp. "I need to think about it."

Ross rose and pushed his chair in. "I'll walk with you outside."

"Now don't feel like you have to leave. Why don't you get another plate, Sierra?" Sid raised his fork toward her.

"Thanks, but my mom probably has dinner ready for me, and I have to feed Chance." She needed to get out of there to think without all the pressure.

"Well, part of the job is for you and those little ones to eat dinner here anytime. You got that?"

"You might regret that invitation after a couple of meals with the chatterboxes."

Sid gave Ross a grizzly look, though his mouth twitched. "Might be a nice change around here."

Ross shook his head with a shrug. "A man's lucky to get a word in around your opinions, old man."

Sid waved them toward the door. "You'll be fortunate if I let you have any of this chicken." He pointed his fork at Ross. "And don't go running her off."

Ross walked with her toward the door. "Not a chance." Outside, he covered a jaw-popping yawn.

"You look exhausted." She hadn't meant to voice the thought, but fatigue clung to his face, sharpening the planes.

He rubbed his face. "I was up pretty early. This job is going to be the end of me."

She walked toward the van. "Why don't you hire someone to help with the horses? No one expects you to do it all."

"Sid doesn't trust anyone else with his ponies." He shrugged and looked away as they reached her car. "It's not a big deal."

She dug her keys out of her purse. "You don't want to find anyone, do you?"

He shifted his stance, his eyes on the barn.

She crossed her arms. "Ross, do you think you have to prove how much you love him by running yourself into the ground?"

He stared down at her. "Of course not. Why would I do that?"

"Guilt."

"Guilt for what?"

"That you didn't hear him out in the field. That Chance escaped from the pasture and got in with Traitor. You feel responsible."

Ross looked away, anger tightening his features. "Look, I don't want to talk about that, okay? I just wanted to ask if you could start on my books soon. With Sid getting hurt, things have gotten crazy and I need to get some bills paid."

She unlocked the van. "Just tell me when."

"I'll let you know tomorrow." And he stalked back to the house.

Her mom's kitchen smelled wonderful when Sierra walked in. The pot of chili sat in the middle of the table, the two bowls across from each other. Michael had actually agreed to take the kids for another weekend to make up some lost time.

"Hi, honey. How'd it go?"

"Fine." Sierra dropped her purse onto the counter and shoved her keys in the cubby next to it.

The buzzer went off and her mom pulled the corn bread from the oven. "Doesn't *sound* fine."

Sierra opened the fridge and got the butter. "I don't want to talk about it right now."

"Did your dinner turn out?"

"Yep. He loved it, except for the prune juice." A small chuckle emerged when she remembered his face. "I think he was offended."

Her mom covered her mouth. "Oh, dear."

"Yeah, and the no-lettuce-denture-thing didn't go over so well either. He has all his teeth."

Her mom pressed a hand to her chest with a laugh. "I'm so sorry, honey."

Sierra let the grin come out. "Yeah, last time I take advice from you!"

Her mom cut the corn bread, her eyes focused and sharp. "So what happened?"

Sierra sighed. Why couldn't mom let it go when she didn't want to talk? She set the salt and pepper on the table, and pulled the ladle from the drawer. "They think I should put the kids in 4-H."

"What a marvelous idea!"

"*I* don't think it's so marvelous."

"Well, I think it would be the best thing for the kids. Especially Braden. You need to think this through, honey."

Sierra didn't want to think it through. She wanted to be left alone and not pulled and prodded in directions she didn't want to go. Her cell phone rang and Sierra jumped up and checked the number on the screen.

She bit her lip and headed for the living room. "Hello?"

"What numbskull doctor put an eye patch on Braden?"

Sierra hoped Braden was playing in another room and not hovering near his dad. "I talked to you about this last weekend. Dr. Remina should have sent you a copy of the paperwork."

"I got it. But my son's not going to wear some ridiculous patch like he's cross-eyed."

Sierra spoke in slow, measured breaths. "I'd be happy to go over the report with you. Dr. Remina said—"

"Gina tested his eyesight—"

"What?"

"She used to work in a pediatric office."

"Doing what? Taking appointments? She is not an optometrist."

"Oh, and you are?"

"Michael, I took him to an expert. His teacher recommended—"

"We have an appointment to have him tested with our optometrist. I researched binocular dysfunction and I'm not convinced that's what's going on. I think he needs to straighten up and give a little more effort than he does."

"Have you considered that he's worn out and frustrated with school because of his vision issues?"

"I'm not going to argue with you."

Sierra ground her teeth. "Okay, please let me know what *your* optometrist finds." After Michael said good-bye, she stormed into the kitchen and shoved the phone into its receiver.

"I dished up your chili." Her mom wiped a few crumbs of corn bread into the sink. "Was that Michael?"

"Yes." She leaned against the counter and crossed her arms.

"He doesn't want Braden to wear his eye patch and thinks the diagnosis is ridiculous." She glanced at her mom. "He had *Gina* give him an eye test."

Her mom stated calmly. "I knew the day Elise brought him over that he was no good."

Ah! Sierra turned slowly toward her mom and pointed her finger. "That's why you don't like Elise, isn't it? She introduced me to Michael." She put her hands on her hips. "Mom, that is not fair to Elise. *I* married the man."

Her mom's movements were brisk as she wiped down a cupboard. "If you'd never met him, all this heartbreak would never have taken place."

Sierra stared at her mom, who pushed too much but did it because her heart was so big. She walked over and gave her mom a hug. "I could have married anyone who made Michael's choices. You need to let it go."

Her words echoed back to her. *I need to let go too of the fear that keeps me from living.*

Chapter 18

In her pajamas, Sierra rolled onto her back, phone to her ear, and dug a hand into the bowl of popcorn next to her. Her mom never let them eat in bed as kids, but she had brought this in to her tonight with a sweet smile, and an admonition not to get crumbs on her sheets.

Elise answered on the first ring. "What happened?"

Sierra rolled over onto her stomach. "Ross and Sid have decided that I need to put the kids into 4-H. And my *mother* thinks they're right."

There was a long pause, and Sierra groaned and let her face drop into her pillow, muffling the words. "Not you too."

"What?"

Sierra raised her head. "Elise, I would die if something happened to my kids and it was my fault for letting them do it."

"Hon, your fear is talking here. Let's just send it to the parlor room for a little time out and shut the door on it. Okay, take a deep breath. Now pretend you're Braden and tell me about Chance from his perspective."

Sierra rolled on her back and covered her eyes. "I don't want to do this."

"Okay, *I'll* pretend I'm Braden reciting a poem I—he just wrote."
Elise cleared her throat and lowered it. "*Chance.* By Braden Montgomery."

Sierra groaned.

"I've got this horse named Chance,

But I never see him dance.

Cuz my mom freaks out

Whenever he's about.

I wish I could be lucky

And watch him go bucky.

But I guess I never will

'Cuz she locks me to the grill."

Sierra leaned up on her elbow. "Locks me to the grill?"

"It rhymed." Elise paused. "How ya doin'?"

"I think Self-Pity is serving tea to his friend Fear in the parlor."

Laughter burst over the line. "You'll get there, hon. Hey, if my mom
had been given a horse, she would have sold it the next day for two quarts
of whiskey, so I think you're doing pretty good."

Sierra flopped back on the bed. "I wish I'd never met Miss Libby."

Michael dropped the kids off Sunday night and was gone before their feet
hit the front porch. Emory and Trevor clambered over each other to reach
her hug first. She wrapped them each in an arm, smiling an invitation for
Braden to join in, but he walked past them. Sierra gave the pair one more
squeeze. "Okay, guys. Go put your backpacks away."

Emory grinned, her dimples growing. "Sure, Mom." She leaned in and gave Sierra a quick peck on her cheek then bounced toward the stairs.

Her mom walked into the living room. "Hi kids."

"Grandma!"

Sierra's heart swelled as Emory and Trevor rushed for her mom, who swooped them into a big hug.

"Grandma, look at the shirt Gina gave me."

Her mom's eyes shot to her before she painstakingly examined Emory's light blue treasure. "That's lovely, honey."

Sierra felt the knot begin in her stomach. *No money for child support, but you can afford gifts?*

Emory grinned at them. "It used to be hers, but now it's too small."

Oh.

Her mom herded Emory and Trevor toward the stairs. "Let's go unpack and put your things away."

Braden ambled to the refrigerator and opened the door. "Don't we have anything to drink? Dad and Gina let us have pop."

I'm sure they do. Glad to see Michael took his dentistry seriously. "Where's your eye patch?"

A quick shrug. "It's stupid."

"Did your dad make you take it off?"

Braden glared at her. "I don't want to wear it."

She leaned against the counter. "I'm sorry you feel that way, but it's not an option."

"You're stupid!" Braden slammed the refrigerator door and raced past her for the stairs, his feet pounding up to his room.

Sierra stared after him, her heart as empty as the echo of his feet.

Braden walked into the kitchen the next morning and yawned. He dropped into a chair at the table.

"Hi, honey. Did you sleep well?" His grandma smiled and poured batter on the waffle iron. It closed with a hiss, creamy batter oozing out the edges.

"Yeah."

She put a plate in front of him and scooted the syrup closer. "Did you get your homework done?"

"Yeah." But he hadn't. He squirted syrup on the waffle.

"Not too much, sweetie." His grandma moved the syrup to the middle of the table.

His mom wandered in, in her robe, her hair messed up. She rubbed his head when she walked by.

"Hi, sweetie."

"Hi, Mom." He liked it when she touched him. But he was still mad at her. She tried to make him do everything. Like wear that stupid patch. His dad said not to wear it until he went to Gina's doctor.

A few minutes later, he stuffed the last bite into his mouth. There were three giant waffles in his stomach and he patted it.

"Boy, you were hungry." His mom bumped his arm with a smile.

He grinned at her and burped.

She made a face and rolled her eyes. He could tell when she realized he wasn't wearing the patch. The lines on her forehead squished. "Braden, honey— "

He scooted back from the table and took his plate to the counter. He tilted the plate up until the fork slid off and clattered into the sink, then let the plate flop back to the counter. "What, Mom?"

She shook her head at him, but her lips were all flat, like she wanted to say something, but knew it wouldn't do any good. It made him feel bad, like he should be wearing the patch. But Dad told him not to. Pressure built in his chest.

Grandma gave him a firm look. "Put your plate and fork in the dishwasher, honey."

He jerked the dishwasher door open and grabbed his plate. A piece of paper stuck to the bottom and he pulled it off, shoved the plate on the bottom rack, and slammed the door shut.

He dropped the paper toward the counter, but it slid to the floor. He turned to go back upstairs. His grandma frowned at him. "Braden, pick that paper up and put it in the garbage, please."

He rolled his eyes and reached for the yellow paper with the ring of syrup in the middle. "Geez." He opened the cupboard door where the garbage was and stopped. The word *4-H* caught his eye and he read it. The meeting was tonight! For kids and horses!

He shook the paper toward the table. "Mom! Are we doing 4-H with Chance?"

Sierra's eyes shot to her mom who shrugged, as if to say, "I didn't leave the paper there." Her heart felt pulled under by the joy and excitement shining from Braden's face. "Um, I was thinking about it."

He dropped into the chair beside her, his grin wide. "The meeting's tonight. Can we go? Please?"

Was she wrong to keep him from it? Emory wandered in, dressed in jeans and Gina's blue T-shirt.

Braden shot out of his chair toward her holding the paper in the air. "Look! Mom might let us go."

Emory looked up at her brother, her voice catching some of his excitement. "What is it?"

"4-H. Remember at the barn? Sid told us about it."

Emory whirled around to face Sierra. "Are we going?"

Sierra pressed her lips together, then released a breath. "We'll go to one meeting."

"Yeah!" Emory and Braden hugged each other and danced in a silly circle around the kitchen.

Her mom started laughing, as Trevor walked in rubbing sleepy eyes. "Why are they doing that?"

Sierra pulled him onto her lap. "They're just happy."

The bus pulled away, and Sierra grabbed her purse. "Trevor, get your coat. We need to get to Sid's."

"Honey, why don't you just leave him here today? Trevor, you want to make cookies with Grandma?"

"Yeah!"

Sierra sighed. She wished her mom would let her answer before steamrolling ahead and getting the kids excited. "Thanks, Mom."

Her mom folded her arms. "What about the meeting?"

Sierra groaned and set her purse down and ran back for the flyer on the table. She read it as she headed toward her mom in the living room. "It starts at five. I don't think I'll be able to leave Sid's that early." Guilt and relief flowed through her.

"Don't worry about it. I'll take them."

"Really?" Sierra let herself be pulled toward the door. "Maybe this isn't such a good idea, Mom."

"Go feed that man. Maybe dried prunes would go over better than the juice, do you think?"

Sierra gave a weak laugh and pulled the door closed behind her.

Her phone rang when she pulled up to Sid's house. "Hello?"

"Hi." Ross's rich voice came through the line, and she tried to ignore the way her blood pumped a little faster. She was still irritated with him for getting her mixed up in the 4-H deal. "When you fed Chance last night, did you open any gates?"

"No." A chill worked its way over her skin. "Why?"

"Alex Cranwell called me at five this morning when he saw Chance in his backyard."

Sierra slumped in the seat, then gathered her purse and opened the door. "I'm so sorry, Ross. What did he do?"

"He walked over fresh sod and newly blown bark, and took a potty break on the stone path next to Alex's water feature. Nothing too damaging." He sighed and his voice sounded weary. "Could you talk to the kids about the gates? I don't think they're getting them closed."

Sierra stopped on Sid's walkway. "Ross, they rarely have a reason to open—"

"Someone's not getting them latched. Then the wind pushes against it or Chance bumps it. He's probably learning to test them. He got out twice last week."

"Why didn't you tell me?"

"What cou—it's not a big deal. I put him back. I just need them to be more careful."

"Okay." The kids were *not* leaving the gates open—Sierra knew that much.

"I'll bring my bills over this morning to Sid's if that works for you."

"That would be fine." When he hung up, Sierra took a breath and shoved the phone back into her purse and opened the front door.

Sid was on the couch, the remote in his hand. "Did you know that global warming is melting the Arctic so fast it's predicted to swamp the U.S. coasts by 2099?"

"You are watching way too much TV, my friend."

He muted the educational program.

"How'd your weekend go?" Sierra asked.

Sid's look turned mulish. "Stella sat with me. Wouldn't feed me until I took my medicine."

"Drill sergeant, was she?"

"Makes a nursing home look downright appealing."

There was *rap-rap* on the door, then Ross walked in looking just as attractive in work jeans and a jacket as he did in the green sweater.

He set a large box on the living room floor and looked at Sierra. "Everything you need is in there; checkbook's on top. I think we have a few days to get it sorted before the vendors start calling for their money."

She stared at it and then at him. "Um, is there a system you want me to follow?"

"There's a ledger with a record of all my past billings. Just enter the receipts and then write the checks." He gripped the edge of the front door in his hand on his way out. "Call if you need me."

Sierra caught him as he started up the walkway. "Hey."

He turned, and she jogged down the steps to him. "Ross, I don't mind doing the books, but your system seems pretty straightforward. Are you sure you want to pay me to just write out the checks? You could probably do it faster yourself."

His eyes shifted to the horse barn and she sensed a barrier go up. "I'm dyslexic. I can't pay bills or process payroll by myself."

"Oh," was all she could manage.

"I sent out a couple of urgent payments last week. Friday I had two messages waiting." He sent her a sheepish grin. "I underpaid the nursery and overpaid the quarry."

She laughed, then covered her mouth. "I'm so sorry. It's not funny."

He grinned at her, then started back up the walk. "Yeah, I can tell."

Ross looked good from the backside, too. Her heart stuttered and she turned toward the house. Life didn't stay in its designated cubbies when Ross crossed her radar.

Sierra came back through the door, and Sid quickly stuffed some papers between his leg and the sofa pillow. He flipped the TV back on and focused an intent gaze on it.

She gave him a dry look. "If you'd start whistling, I'd be thrown off the trail even more."

He gave a self-conscious chuckle, then rubbed his thumb along the edge of the paper sticking out. "Just something I'm thinking about. I don't want Ross knowing about it jist yet."

She zipped her fingers along her lips.

He let out a chuckle and dug the real estate flyer out from behind his leg. "I have this yearnin' to be close to my roots again. Then my niece, Leorna, keeps asking me to move back home." His chin dropped toward his chest. "So, I've been thinking about it, but didn't figure it'd happen for a few years yet. And now with this bum leg, there's nothing to keep me here."

She sat in the chair across from the couch. "Except Ross."

He nodded once, a sad smile playing beneath his white whiskers.

"So what now?" Sierra asked.

"Leorna's been keeping her eye out for a place for me." His eyes pierced hers from under heavy white brows. "Just looking, mind you." He chuckled. "Though Leorna calls every couple days to see if I've packed yet."

"Sounds like you're more than halfway there."

He looked out the window. "I miss being home. Miss seeing all the nieces and nephews growing up."

"Why don't you want Ross to know?"

Sid sighed. "He's got a lot going on with that Cranwell job. He don't need more distractions."

Her horse was one of those distractions. An arrow of guilt hit.

He poked a finger at a picture on the real estate page. "I was thinking about callin' this fellow, Dick Reynolds, and seein' what he thinks I can get for the place."

"Might be interesting to find out."

"Get me the phone, will ya?"

Two hours later with Ross's bills spread across the table and Sid napping on the couch, the phone rang. "Sid Barrows' residence, Sierra Montgomery speaking." She tucked the phone to her shoulder and matched a mud-encrusted packing list to a statement.

"Oh, Sierra! This is Leorna. Sid's told me all about you. I think it's just wonderful how you're taking such good care of him for us."

"He is a delight."

"How is he healing up? We are just tickled that he's planning on coming home. I've been on him for *years* to move back."

"He told me about the plans you two are cooking up."

Leorna lowered her voice. "I know. Isn't it just tremendous? He doesn't have any grandchildren, you know, so I think it's on his mind to get to know his great-nieces and nephews. And my, if there aren't a slew of them."

"It sounds like a perfect opportunity for him."

"That it is. Is he available, by chance?"

"I'm afraid he's napping at the moment."

"Oh, dear."

"Is it anything I could help you with?"

"Well, Ned, that's my husband, just spotted the snuggest little place for sale just a few blocks from us. I have the realtor's number if Sid wants to call on it."

"Why don't I get the number from you and give it to Sid when he wakes up?"

When Leorna had given her the number and finished chatting about her grandkids, Sierra hung up the phone and wandered back to the living room.

Sid was awake and watching a documentary on the Cold War.

"Leorna called." She handed him the information and sat down. "I really think you need to talk to Ross about this."

He fingered the paper but didn't look up. "I will when the timing's right."

"The longer you put it off, the harder it will be on both of you."

Ross closed the front door and plopped into a chair as Sid adjusted himself on the couch. "Well, lookee what the cat drug in." Sid glanced at the clock above the TV. "Dinnertime, isn't it? Thought you might show yerself around this hour. How's the job going?"

Ross yawned. "Tiring. I've got extra crews working the swing shift. Did I wake you up when I left this morning?"

"Nope. Didn't hear you come in last night, neither." A blaring commercial for detergent came on and he muted the TV. "Will you finish on schedule?"

"I don't know. It's going to be tight."

"Must be tough with the new deadline."

"Yeah." Ross nodded with a chuckle, his gaze drifting toward the kitchen where a pair of long feminine legs captured his attention.

Sierra came to the doorway and caught his eye with a smile. "Dinner's ready."

"Now don't that smell good?" Sid exclaimed as Ross wheeled him to the table, then sat down. "Ross, will you say the grace?"

Ross looked at Sierra, but she'd closed her eyes. "Dear Lord, thank You for this meal and Sierra's skill in making it. Continue to heal Sid's body and let his recovery be fast. Bless and protect Sierra and her family. Watch over her kids and guide them as they grow. Amen."

He peeked to his right. Sierra opened her eyes slowly and picked up her fork. Then set it down. She picked up the lettuce bowl and passed it to the right. "Salad?"

Sid took it from her and placed a mound of it on his plate.

Ross spoke the words before he had a chance to think them through. "Do you believe in God, Sierra?" And when he saw the look on her face, he wished he hadn't.

She held the tray with the sliced french bread suspended above her plate, her eyes wide on his. She turned and passed the bread to Sid, then adjusted her napkin in her lap. "Even the demons believe, isn't that what the Bible says?"

Sid piped up. "Yessir, it does."

Ross caught her gaze again. "I shouldn't have asked something so personal."

"No, it's fine." She reached for the salt and pepper, held them a moment, then set them beside her plate. Her next words seemed carefully measured. "I believe in God."

Sid tipped his head. "Now there's a difference between believing and *believing*."

She didn't look at either of them, just made tiny divots in her pasta with the fork tines. "I would be the first one."

Sid patted her arm. "Nothin' wrong with that, Sierra. Nothin' wrong at all."

She gave Sid a tiny smile, though Ross thought her eyes glistened.

Chapter 19

Sierra closed her mom's front door and heard feet pounding down the stairs.

Braden flew toward her, his mop of brown hair bouncing. "Mom, you should have come to 4-H tonight! We learned the different parts of a horse, and Mrs. Vaughn said she'd teach me pole bending with Chance!"

Emory ran from the kitchen. "I want to do barrel racing, but Grandma thinks Braden should train with Chance, and she and I can save for my own horse."

Sierra kept her expression bland. "Really?"

Braden rested a hand on her arm, his smile growing wider by the minute. "There's a 4-H clinic in four weeks. Mrs. Vaughn said I could enter some of the games."

Her chest tightened. "Games?" She regretted not taking the kids to the meeting herself. *One* meeting was all she'd promised.

Braden beamed. "Yeah! With Chance! Mrs. Vaughn said she has room in her horse trailer for him."

Abbey followed from the kitchen, wiping her hands on a dishtowel and wearing a proud smile.

Sierra tried to smile back but felt it list toward dread. "Wow. You've been busy."

Her mom patted Emory and Braden on their backs. "You would have been proud of them, Sierra. They were so well mannered and listened attentively when Mrs. Vaughn was talking."

Of course, her mother would focus on the behavior. Did she *know* about the 4-H clinic and the games? Sierra said, "In four weeks, they're, um—?"

"Mrs. Vaughn is the sweetest thing. Offered to trailer Chance to the clinic with her horse."

"Mom—"

Her mom gave her a squeeze. "The kids are going to be just fine."

"Games on horseback, Elise. With Chance." Sierra sat on her bedroom floor, arms draped over her knees, and stared at the mahogany bureau.

"Take a deep breath, hon, and blow it out." Elise exhaled. "There. Now remember how scared you were of childbirth when you were pregnant with Braden? You got through it and nothing could wipe the smile off your face."

"You're comparing childbirth to *this?*"

"Picture it this way. It's like you're pregnant with the kids' expectations, and the fear that's freaking you out is just the labor. You need to breathe through it and keep pushing."

Sierra rolled her eyes and leaned back against the bed. "Elise, that's gross!"

"Hon, you gotta do this for them." She switched tactics. "What'd the kids think of 4-H?"

Sierra picked at the blue carpet. "They're on top of the world."

"When's the last time you saw them this excited, not counting when you got Chance?"

"I don't know. Before the divorce maybe."

"Mmmhmm. You gotta keep pushing, baby."

Sierra chuckled. "Do you keep a scorecard for every time you're right?"

"Top drawer of my desk! Bye, hon."

Sierra clicked off the phone, crawled into bed, and turned on her side to stare into the darkness. Her mind went back to the thoughts of Ross that had lingered all evening. He'd prayed for protection for her kids. She pulled the blankets up under her chin. The way he said it, as if releasing all fear and worry into God's hands, bewildered her. No begging or pleading, but a simple trust, as if he knew God would do it. She flopped on her back. But that's what it came down to. Trust. And she didn't have much.

Ross tossed and turned in Sid's upstairs guest room but couldn't get a pair of big cinnamon eyes out of his head. She believed but didn't *believe.* What did that mean? And what did it mean to him. *Lord?* The Bible was clear on many things, and this was one of them. He finally drifted off, seeing the shadow of shame in her eyes when he asked about her faith.

Five o'clock came early. Ross crept down the stairs and tiptoed past his snoring friend on the way to the kitchen. At the counter he grabbed the last apple from the basket of fruit Sierra usually kept stocked. Must be grocery-shopping day.

He headed toward the mudroom for his work boots but noticed Sid's Bible on the table. Better set it by the couch so the older man didn't have to wait for Sierra to arrive.

He picked it up, but the apple slipped and he lost his grip on the book, which slid back to the table. A paper poked out from under the cover. He started to push it back in but stopped. It looked like … he pulled the glossy real estate flyer from the book. He slowly raised it, his eyes drawn to the smiling circled face of a realtor named Dick Reynolds.

Ross's truck rumbled down Alex's driveway on his way to pick up more rock from the quarry. He glanced right, toward Sid's. It hadn't been the greatest afternoon with his thoughts ping-ponging between Sid and Sierra. Especially having seen that paper stuck in Sid's Bible. At the end of the paved drive his foot held the brake while the blinker flashed left, as he considered. Maybe he should go visit his friend and have that conversation that had been playing through his mind all morning. He flipped the blinker right and drove the twenty yards to Sid's driveway.

Sid was watching The Discovery Channel when Ross stepped through the front door. "You're here early."

Ross rubbed his hands to get some of the cold out of them. "Yeah, I need to talk to you." He glanced around, not wanting an audience. "Where's Sierra?"

"Grocery shopping." Sid muted the television. "What's on your mind, son?"

"What have you decided to do about your farm?"

Where Ross had expected Sid to sour up and complain about his leg keeping him from the ponies, a look settled into the crags of Sid's wrinkled mug, causing Ross's stomach to knot.

A look of peace.

"The Lord and I have been having some long chats about that."

He waited, but Sid had apparently gone to the arena where those conversations took place, leaving Ross to sit and wonder in the stretching silence.

Just when Ross was going to ask what he and the Lord had decided, Sid spoke. "I have a niece who's been wanting a visit."

"Well, let her come, then Sierra wouldn't need to stay here every day."

Sid cleared his throat. "She's actually been wanting me to visit since before the accident."

"You've mentioned that. She's in Kansas, isn't she?

Sid nodded, but a nervous pinching of his lips signaled that Ross was missing something important.

"She wants me to move out there, actually."

"Move." The word echoed in his mind. Sid had that look on his face. Like he knew something about Ross that Ross didn't even know. It unsettled him. He felt as if he were fourteen again and Sid was about to render a decision. Mucking stalls for two summers had made him the richest boy in Eugene, without being paid a dime—it had brought Sid into his world.

"Son, life isn't about keeping things comfortable."

"Sid—" He couldn't be serious, could he?

"We've got to listen with our hearts. Let the Lord lead in all the pastures of our lives. I've been holding the reins too long as it is, or I'd have done this years ago."

"Then why didn't you?" Ross didn't mean for the words to sound so harsh, but hurt and—if he were honest—a large portion of panic had set in.

Sid just looked at him, that knowing gleam in his eye.

"Don't blame this on me, Sid. I didn't keep you here."

Sid sighed. "Ross, you're like a son to me. I've done all I could to fill a father's role in your life." His head dropped a little lower, as though the weight of something heavy pulled it down. "I don't know that I did right by doing that."

"Of course you did. Dad was never there."

Sid looked up, his blue eyes sure and steady. "But maybe he would have been if I hadn't let you run to me with all your troubles."

Ross got up and paced to the window. "Is that why you'd move? So Dad and I can make up?"

"Ross, I don't have any business telling you what to do. You're a grown man, and a fine one at that." That look of peace settled back over his face. "I miss my family. I got great-nieces and nephews that I've never seen. It's time to go back. To be near Rose and Caroline." His wife and daughter who had been killed so many years before. Then a new thought struck Ross. Did he—was Sid dying?

"Do you have cancer?"

Sid erupted with a laugh. "No, I'll be around for a good while yet."

"You don't think it would be hard, being back where it happened?"

Sid's smile grew soft. "I'm homesick for them. I want to be close to where they're laid." He chuckled. "It'll save you the cost of shipping me back there after the Lord's chariot swings through to capture my soul."

"Sid—"

"Sierra thinks it's a fine idea." Sid leveled bright blue eyes at him, utter sincerity in the gaze.

Ross clenched his fists. "What does Sierra know? She's hasn't even worked here a week! I've never seen you to capitulate to a half-baked idea like this before."

Sid mouthed the word as if tasting it. "Capitulate." He dragged his pad from under the crossword puzzle and sounded the word again as he wrote.

"Come on, Sid." He sat down in the easy chair across from him and leaned forward. "You've said yourself you'd never go back. Why now?

Because *Sierra's* convinced it's the best thing for you? I can't believe you'd let her and your niece pressure you into moving. Sierra doesn't—"

That was when the back door slammed.

Ross and Sid jumped. Framed in the middle of the kitchen doorway stood Sierra, looking as if she'd been there long enough. A grocery sack sagged in each arm.

She set the grocery sacks on the table and gave Ross a fierce look through the living room archway. He braced himself as she marched into the room. Ignoring Sid, she made straight for his chair.

Her head jerked as she repeated the words, "Pressuring Sid into doing something he doesn't want to do?"

Ross stood. "Sierra—"

She leaned forward. "Have you ever seen that man get pressured into *anything*? I couldn't even get him to drink *prune* juice."

Ross gently grasped her arm and turned her back toward the kitchen. "Let's discuss this outside."

She pulled her arm free and marched ahead of him to the back door. Sid's chuckle resonated through the small living room, and Ross felt the tips of his ears burn as he shut the door behind him.

Sierra clomped down the cement steps and turned to face him, her stance rigid in the ankle-deep grass. He really needed to bring his mower over. He dragged his eyes from the unkempt yard back to her face, where her eyes were shooting sparks at him.

She crossed her arms in a protective manner. "I can't believe you think I would try to persuade him to move."

He sighed and looked toward the barn roof. "Sid's vulnerable right now. He's cooped up in this house, feeling hopeless about his ponies. I'm sure Kansas looks pretty tempting. So when you and Leorna jump in and fill his head with ideas about moving—"

Her eyes narrowed. "What do you mean 'fill his head'?" She drilled an outstretched arm toward the house. "That contrary old man is the one who's been spouting all those ideas. Maybe if you weren't so set on keeping him here, you'd pay better attention to what *his* needs are."

That brought his hands to his hips. "Listen, I didn't bring you out here to make judgments about me."

"Of course, saying *I* pressured *Sid* isn't making a judgment?"

He dropped his arms. "Sierra, I'm sorry. Okay? I didn't know you would be eavesdropping from the kitchen."

She angled her head, her face tense. "Next time I'll be sure to stomp my feet through the mudroom so you can stop slandering me before I get there."

"Never mind." He marched past her toward the barn.

The staccato crunch of gravel broke into his thoughts and Sierra caught up to him and grabbed his arm. She tugged as if to spin him around. He stopped but didn't turn, so she stepped in front of him, toe to toe. Her finger was dangerously close to clearing his sinuses.

Sierra sucked in a breath, hurt driving each frustrated word. "I don't know what your problem is, but you cannot just walk off like that."

Ross didn't say a word. Not a hint of what he was thinking showed in his face. He stared at her as if she were a weed in his flower bed.

"I thought we were friends, Ross. But for you to assume that I would hurt you by persuading Sid to move—" Sierra felt a sting in her nose, and her eyes started to blur. That made her angrier. "You don't have any right—"

Then he kissed her. Hard. One arm holding her tight around the shoulders and the other pinning her waist to his. The cold zipper of his Carhartt jacket pressed against her collarbone as his mouth moved against hers.

She gripped his shoulders to stay balanced as the warmth of his kiss filled all of her senses.

He released her and took a step back, his gaze unfathomable.

Her fingers touched her lips, a part of her wishing he would do it again. What was she thinking? She didn't even *like* him right now. Except she did. Very much. "Why did you do that?" She wished for a post to lean against to keep the world upright.

His breath was tantalizing. Spicy and something more. Something very male. The words were definite. "I've wanted to do that for a long time." He shifted his feet and his eyes dropped away, his face taking on a harder edge.

She waited, but he wouldn't look at her. She spoke quietly, "You're still mad."

He sighed and raised a hand. "It's not that simple. Sierra, I—" He dropped his arm, his eyes catching hers briefly. "I need to get back to work." He turned and strode toward his pickup.

Sierra wanted to walk back to the house with dignity, show him he hadn't hurt her, but her legs were unable to manage more than shaky steps as she tried to walk up the back steps into the kitchen.

Sid coughed. He was sitting in his wheelchair at a perfect angle to the large window overlooking the yard and barn behind it. A weathered hand stroked the bristle of whiskers on his cheek, not bothering to hide a wide grin.

She turned her back on him and marched to the sink, snatched a mug from the cupboard, and filled it with water. Her voice sounded strained even to her own ears. "Front row seat, huh? I thought the doctor told you not to get into the wheelchair without help."

She took two small sips and dumped the water into the sink. She wasn't thirsty, but agitation demanded she do *something* with her hands now that she had an attentive audience.

Why had Ross walked away like that? He'd kissed her, then … left. She picked up the towel and wiped the mug. But it wasn't like *she* had initiated the kiss. Maybe he'd seen something in her eyes and realized that he'd stirred emotions a little too strong for his taste.

"You plan on rubbing the handle right off that mug?" Amusement glinted in the squint of his blue eyes, and she looked down at her hands.

The damp dishtowel was twisted and tight in her hands. Heat washed over her as she set the mug down carefully on the counter.

"It's been a long time since Ross has shown interest in a woman."

Heat crept up her neck. "I think we have different definitions of *interest*, Sid."

"Sometimes it takes Ross a little time to get the hang of things."

She gave him a small smile. "I'm sure he knows what he's doing."

"Well, now, you could be wrong there. Like how he walked away out there, leaving you as forlorn as a foal without its mama. I bet he's kicking himself over it right now."

She did not want to be discussing this with him. She reached for the bags of groceries on the table and walked past the box of Ross's bills with their checks neatly written out. "I think I'll start dinner."

A speculative look settled over Sid's face. "Maybe you're going about this wrong."

She set the package of pork ribs next to the stove. The sigh flowed out with the words. "And how's that?"

"It's an easy habit to get into, doing things yer own way."

She interrupted. "Sid, I—"

He held up a hand. "You don't ask for help, just plow through, doing the best you can."

He adjusted himself in the wheelchair, easing his leg out onto a kitchen chair. "I've seen it in your eyes, how you struggle to do it all with those kids of yours. How do you think I got through the loss of my wife and daughter? There was many a night the shotgun in my closet called my name. But something kept beckoning me to live. To get me through that moment to the next one. And it weren't natural."

A part of her was intrigued, wanting to hear how God got him through such a tough time. But she'd tried that and God hadn't gotten her through. He hadn't comforted her in the middle of the night when she was crying alone in bed, knowing her husband was across town in someone else's. And where was He when her dad had driven to the coast, full of his own despair and anxiety.

Sid continued, "God had other plans."

She ripped the plastic off the package of meat. "Don't you ever think God is just too big to get caught up in the minuscule details of our lives? I mean there's war, Sid. And famine. Big things for Him to worry about." She shrugged. "Or ignore. I don't think He's too concerned about me and my kids."

Sid leaned forward, an intent look on his face, tufts of hair sticking up on end. But the words were gentle, kind. "That's where you'd be wrong. Who do you think brought you into this world? Your mother? You think you and your husband could just form those three little kids on your own? You don't think a Creator was involved in that? And that if He was involved enough to create your life, He'd be pretty invested in its outcome?"

Sierra bit her lip, a part of her longing to believe that what he said was true. But there was too much evidence against it. She arranged the ribs in a pan, keeping her back to him. "I believe in God. I did the whole 'asking Jesus into my heart' thing when I was thirteen." A pang struck as the flash of remembrance slid over her like a wool blanket that had grown too scratchy. The easy relationship she thought she had with God, comfort and security wrapped in a loving heavenly Father, had died along with her dad. She brushed the past aside. She'd grown up since then. Gotten married, had kids, been betrayed … God hadn't seemed to care enough to keep up with her, just kind of drifted back to His heavenly places.

"He lost interest in me long ago." She gave him a quick smile over her shoulder. "But I'm glad your faith helped you through a tough time."

"So what are you going to do about Ross?"

"There's nothing to *do* about Ross."

Humor deepened the lines around his mouth. "You were just hanging on to make him feel better?"

Embarrassment burned her skin from the inside. Sierra shoved the ribs into the oven and set the timer. "I'm going to make some biscuits. Do you need help getting back to the couch?"

Sid's laugh loosened the knot between her shoulders, and she gave him a wry grin. "Sid Barrows, you'd better hightail it, or I'll short-sheet your bed."

His laugh deepened. "Wouldn't surprise me if you did. Wouldn't surprise me at all."

Chapter 20

Ross tossed a sack of mortar next to where one of the retaining walls would go. Why had he been such an idiot and kissed her? Because he wanted to, that was why. And it was the stupidest thing he'd done in a long time. Especially when he was still mad at her. He tried to ignore the memory of her pressed close to him, holding on and kissing him in return.

He grabbed another sack and lobbed it on top of the first, and the guilt he'd been trying to avoid hit him. He'd no business kissing her in the first place, not knowing if her heart belonged to God or not. He paused, the heavy sack resting against his thigh. But he didn't know that for sure. She'd prayed with them at dinner.

Stop it, Ross. Things may not always be clearly black and white, but he wasn't going to start blurring the lines.

Abbey's green Honda pulled up and parked. Braden jumped out and ran over to him with a big grin. "Need any help?"

He sure loved the boy, but that only complicated things with Sierra.

"I believe I do. You want to start offloading those rocks from the trailer and stack them right here?"

"Sure." Braden headed for Ross's pickup cab where his gloves were stored. "Hi, Big Red." The boy waved to the tall redheaded crew boss, who was orchestrating the planting of some shrubs.

Dusk set in a couple hours later, and Ross wiped his sleeve across his forehead.

Braden stood next to the rocks he'd stacked, one shoulder slumped lower than the other. Dirt and dust covered his dark jeans, and he wore a tired smile.

"You ready to quit yet?" Ross asked.

"Yeah."

"Hop in and I'll take you home."

In the cab, Braden stuffed his gloves back in the pocket on the bottom of the passenger door. "Ross?"

"Yeah?" He looked over. Braden was staring down at his feet.

"We're doing 4-H and there's a clinic coming up.… I don't know how to do any of the games."

"What games are you talking about?" Ross wished he had the time to teach him, but until this job was done, he just couldn't.

The boy's white teeth flashed in a grin. "I think the keyhole and the flag race sound the funnest."

"Those were my two favorites."

"Yeah, Sid told me." He looked out the side window. "I asked my dad, but he doesn't know anything about them and he's too busy right now anyway." He turned toward Ross. "You're busy too, so if you can't teach me, that's okay."

Ross stared out the windshield—Alex Cranwell pulling from one side and a pair of vulnerable brown eyes in the face of a lost boy pulling him from the other. "I won't have much time, but we can probably fit some training in right before dinner every day and after church. What do you think?"

"Cool! Thanks, Ross."

Ross pulled into the driveway behind Sierra's van and idled the truck.

Braden grabbed the door handle. "You want to come in?"

Part of him was tempted and his hand reached to shut off the ignition, but he saw Sierra glance out the window and then walk away. He sighed. "Not tonight."

Probably not for many nights.

At eight-thirty, working under floodlights he'd rented a week ago, Ross watched the gold Mercedes pull up to the garage. Alex got out and sauntered over, resting his foot on a bag of grass seed next to the shipment of arborvitaes and rhododendrons. He rubbed his chin in a way that didn't bode well for the crisp evening.

Ross nodded. "I see you made it back."

Alex twisted to look out over the valley. "Yeah, flew in this afternoon. Got another contract lined out with a Seattle retailer that bought some property on the west side of town."

The dangling carrot was meant to make Ross salivate, and it did.

He surveyed the yard. "Frankly, I was disappointed when I pulled up. I thought you'd be a lot further along."

Ross felt the muscle in his jaw flex, and he shifted his stance.

"You see," Alex went on, "when you've got the potential to get some lucrative contracts, you want to make sure those contracts don't go away. And to do that you need to make sure everyone is happy. And right now, Ross, I'm not happy. What do you think? Do you think I'm going to be happy come Christmas?"

"I'm certain you will be." The words came out flat.

"I sure hope so." Alex straightened, flashing porcelain caps. He clapped Ross on the shoulder on his way back toward the house. "I'm glad we had this talk."

Ross seethed. Alex knew why he wasn't further along. In the past few weeks, Marie Cranwell had created six change orders, all with Alex's okay. The last one required them to rip out a mortared flagstone border that curved along the south side of the new English garden. The border had taken three weeks to install, but Marie decided she would prefer a powder-coated wrought iron fence instead.

"Alex." The man turned and Ross walked to meet him. "I've mailed a couple invoices for the change orders, but haven't received payment."

Alex shook his head, as if he'd figured all along it'd head in this direction. "Ross, let me be straight with you. You bid this job, and I expect you to complete it based on the price you gave me." He placed an arm across Ross's shoulders, walking him back toward the arborvitaes. "When I bid a job I do everything in my power to make my customer happy. And my customer is happy when he gets what he asked for, and pays what we'd agreed on."

Ross stopped and Alex's arm slid off his shoulders. "You agreed to pay the change orders out of pocket."

Alex looked at him hard, like a father who was disappointed when his son just didn't comprehend something. After a five-beat pause, a grin wiped the look away. "Ross, I like you. I think you'll go far in commercial landscaping." He shook his head, his eyes boring into Ross's. "Don't let anything get in your way."

"You're awfully quiet tonight, honey."

Sierra gave her mom a smile. "Long day, I guess." The kiss and the way Ross had walked away from her today were too much on her mind. And the conversation with Sid kept creeping back. Were people like Sid and Elise deluded, or had they discovered the key to trusting God that seemed to evade her? Her hand faltered as she reached to pick up one of Trevor's LEGO toys. Or did God just have an easier time loving them?

Sierra tucked the kids in bed then headed to the kitchen. The warm, buttery smell of popcorn wafted to her. "Yum."

Her mom turned. "I thought you looked like you could use some popcorn." She pulled a mug from the microwave. "And hot chocolate."

A soft laugh pressed through. "You take such good care of us, Mom."

Her mom waved a hand, but her smile was pleased. "Oh, honey. That's what moms are for."

Sierra plopped at the table and dug a handful of popcorn out. "Mom, how do you know that God cares?"

"The Bible tells us He does. What else do we have if we don't have God?"

"I don't mean the nebulous knowledge that there is a God out there in the universe somewhere that *loves* you. I mean in the day-to-day. When Dad died, when Michael left. When Braden started getting so angry. Where was God's love then?"

Her mom wiped her napkin in a tiny circle and gave her a tight smile. "You just know it's there, honey. I'll get us some waters."

In bed, Sierra held her cell phone, the silver case slick under her thumb. She paused, then pressed Elise's number.

"Hi, hon. See anymore of Mr. Sizzle?"

"Um, a little too much." She knew Elise's eyebrows were rising. "But I don't want to talk about it yet."

She ran her thumbnail down the side of the silk piping on the creamy antique comforter. "Elise, you said God was talking to me when I got the job with Sid. What did you mean?"

"I meant that He's showing you that He cares."

"He seems pretty unreliable. I mean, how can you trust a God that helps you sometimes, but not others, especially when it comes to the big stuff?"

"Hon, He doesn't say that nothing bad will happen if you trust Him. Just that you will never be alone again."

Sierra drew her knees up to her chin and smoothed a finger over a shiny maroon toenail. "But I've felt pretty alone."

Elise sighed. "Yeah. Feelings can be the toughest roadblock. Hon, look at it like this. If your world is a paperback, God's truth is always on the same page. You can open the book, shut it, flip the pages, turn it upside down, but the truth remains right where it always was. Feelings, they'll jump all over. You're never going to find the same one anywhere. Feelings change, truth doesn't. You have to decide which you are going to trust."

"You and your analogies."

"I know; it's a gift." Elise paused. "I'm going to church tomorrow if you want to check it out."

"Church leaves me feeling dry."

"Hon, nothing against your mom's church, but mine doesn't have the yawn factor hers does."

Sierra laughed. "Shouldn't you be worried about a lightning bolt or something?"

"I'll let you in on a little secret. God adores my sense of humor." Elise laughed, but Sierra could tell she meant it. Sierra's mom would be running for cover if she'd heard Elise.

"Thanks, but I don't think I'm there yet."

"Just so you know, God isn't a destination. He's the transportation."

The next evening Sierra had just put Sid's plate on the table when she heard knocking on his front door. She hurried from the kitchen. It'd be just like Sid to try to get up and answer it.

Trevor's cupped face peered into the living room window to the right of the front door. Emory's joined his.

Sid chuckled. "I think the herd has arrived."

Sierra opened the door. "Hi guys!"

Her mom ushered the kids in and looked toward the couch with a smile. "We were passing by and wanted to stop in and meet you."

"Sid, this is my mom, Abbey. Mom, this is Sid."

Her mom shook his outstretched hand. "It's good to meet you. I hear you're partial to prune juice and rutabagas."

He slapped his good leg with a chuckle. "That girl of yours sure knows how to fix a meal, and I hear she learned it from the best."

Her mom beamed, Emory at her side. "Oh, I don't know about that," Abbey said, "but I do love to cook."

Sierra heard Ross's pickup come rumbling toward the house, and she glanced out the window to see Braden fling open the passenger door and run up the steps and into the house. After a quick hug, he said, "Ross needs to talk to you."

"About what?" Her heart started to beat harder. She hadn't seen him since the kiss yesterday. Not that she thought about it much. Except, of course, when she was cooking, eating, trying to sleep, or breathing.

Braden's eyes slid toward his grandma. "About helping me work with Chance for my 4-H clinic."

Panic zinged up her spine and her heart started pounding. "I don't think—"

A spark in his eye, Sid leaned toward Braden. "What is he gonna teach you?"

Braden brightened. "The keyhole and the flag race."

Sid slapped his leg. "His best events. He'll teach you all the tricks."

Braden's grin grew wider, then he turned for the front door. "I'm going to wait in the pickup."

"Wait, I—" Sierra said.

Braden's shoulders sagged and he looked at her, the old sullenness shadowed in his eyes. "What, Mom?"

"I just—" She looked at her mom, who'd tilted her head as if to say, *Let him do this, honey*. Sierra rubbed a hand over his shoulder. "Be careful, please."

A radiant grin emerged, and he turned and bounded out the front door. She watched him run over to the pickup and climb in. The driver's door opened and Ross climbed out. Sierra met him on the front porch.

His eyes held hers for a long moment before his gaze moved toward the barn. "Braden said you okayed my working with him and Chance."

"Not totally, but everyone seems to think it'll be okay."

He gave her a half-smile, his eyes soft. "I understand, Sierra. He'll be fine. Trust me."

Her heart lurched and she looked at him. "I'd like to."

He glanced away, started to say something, then stopped. He stuck his hands in his pockets and turned, heading back down the steps. "We'll be about an hour or so," he said over his shoulder.

Sierra wrapped her arms around her waist against the chill and went into the house and closed the door, her eyes straying toward the living room window where she could see Ross's pickup roll down the driveway.

Her mom chuckled. "It's not like it's Trevor out there. Braden's eleven, honey."

The same age Molly had been.

Braden felt his heart speed up. He was going to ride Chance. He looked over at Ross, who grinned back. "You look tired," Braden said.

"Not too tired to go riding."

Braden leaned forward, wishing Ross would drive faster. At the barn, he jumped out and waited for Ross to climb out of the pickup. *Come on!* Ross rounded the front of the pickup and laid a hand across his back. It made Braden's chest feel warm, like when his mom gave him a hug.

Inside the barn, Ross nodded toward the wall. "Get the lead rope and bring him in. While I set up the course, you can give him a good brushing."

Braden stopped. "By myself?"

Ross turned. "You comb your own hair by yourself, don't you?"

"Cool!" Braden grabbed the lead and walked out to the pasture, the grass making the front of his tennis shoes wet. Chance let him walk right up, his big nose sniffing Braden's hand and shoulder. Braden clipped the lead to the metal ring of his halter, and they turned for the barn. Chance plodded right behind him. *Yes!* Braden's heart beat so hard.

Once inside, Ross showed him how to cross-tie Chance. "Now, when you curry him, you need to be careful over his back and shoulders. His bones are right below the skin, and you can hurt him." Braden nodded, making sure to be extra careful.

When Ross left to go get the saddle, Braden ran the rubber currycomb over the big body, and Chance nickered. A warm feeling swelled inside.

Ross walked toward him, carrying Chance's large saddle in his arms. "Looking good. How about we saddle him up?"

He showed Braden where to place the blanket and saddle so it didn't pull Chance's hair, then he cinched the belly strap and adjusted the buckles. "Now after we walk him a bit, we'll tighten the cinch again. Wouldn't want it to roll out from under you when you're rounding the barrel, would we?"

"No!" That'd really freak his mom. She'd probably never let him on Chance again.

Ross untied Chance's halter and looped it around the horse's neck then lifted the bridle. "This is a snaffle. We ask Chance to open his mouth by putting our fingers right here." Ross held the bridle up by Chance's nose and slipped his thumb into the side of the horse's mouth. "When he opens, we put the bit in his mouth like that, then lift this part up and tuck his ears in." The bridle slid into place.

Braden itched to get on Chance "Can I ride him now?"

"Let's lead him outside, and I'll take him around the first time." He leaned closer and nodded toward Sid's. "In case your mom is watching with binoculars."

Braden laughed. "Okay. Then can I try?"

"You bet."

Outside, they led Chance through the gate and into the pasture. Ross held the reins. "I'm going to jog him a little to warm him up. See what he can do." Ross pointed to where a barrel sat with a flag sticking out of a can on top. "That's for the flag race."

Cool!

Ross put his foot in the stirrup, and the saddle creaked as he passed his leg over Chance's back. He made a clicking noise and Chance started into a trot toward the barrel.

Braden wished he'd hurry up.

Ross went up and down the field a few times and rode the horse in some patterns. He trotted back to Braden with a smile. "He knows his stuff. I'm going to take him around the barrel and see how he does."

"Okay."

Ross took off straight for the flagged barrel. As Chance rounded the barrel, Ross grabbed the old rag tied to a stick, and they galloped back across the starting line. He raised the flag toward Braden in a victory sign, then turned and trotted to the barrel and stuck the flag back in the can.

Ross rode him over to Braden with a huge grin. "I'd say old Chance here has done this before."

That was way cool!

He got off and handed the reins to Braden. "Now before we can start you on the flag race, we need to teach you how to ride."

"I rode him at Sally's." Braden reached for the reins, but Ross didn't hand them over.

"That's good, but I need to know that you can handle Chance before I let you up on him. Okay?"

Braden nodded. He wished Ross would hurry up.

"A horse isn't like a car. You can't steer him with the reins."

Huh? That's what they always did in those Westerns he saw on TV.

"You want your hands to be as still as possible. A horse will always move away from pressure. So instead of pulling his head where you want him to you, you're going to guide him with your legs."

Braden sighed. This sounded hard.

"Mount him and I'll show you what I mean."

Finally! Braden climbed on and sat way up there, his feet dangling above the stirrups. Ross adjusted them, and he slipped his feet in. Chance looked a lot different from up here with that narrow neck straight out in front of him.

"Now, when you want Chance to go, you squeeze both of your legs."

Braden squeezed, then he lurched as Chance moved forward. "Hey, it worked."

Ross walked beside him and nodded with a smile. "Yep. Now when you want him to turn left, you're going to press your right leg into his side and he'll move away from it to the left."

Braden tried, but Chance kept going straight. "It's not working."

"Try it again, you're probably using both legs. It can be tricky to move just one leg."

Chance turned to the left. "Hey! He did it!"

"If you want to go right—"

Braden pressed his left leg and Chance moved to the right. "It works, Ross! This is so cool!" Braden practiced turning him a few more times.

"I should have told you this first, but when you need to stop him, you pull gently back on the reins."

Braden pulled Chance to a stop. "Can I do the flag now?"

"Let's practice walking him around some more. Then I'll have you trot him a bit before we test you out on the flag."

Braden squeezed his legs and Chance lurched forward again. He wished his dad could see him.

Saturday night, Braden sat across the coffee table from his dad, a marble checkerboard between them. "It's your turn, Dad."

"Hmm?" His dad raised his eyes from the dental magazine he was reading.

"I said, it's your turn."

"Oh." He didn't even study the board, just moved one of his pieces.

Braden jumped it. "It's your turn, Dad."

"Oh!" Gina sat up straight in the black leather recliner. She looked at his dad, her eyes excited. "Mike, I felt the baby move."

"You did!" His dad jumped up from the leather couch and knelt next to her, his hand on her stomach. "What'd it feel like?"

Gina pressed her hand over his. "Like little bubbles."

Emory and Trevor ran over, and his sister asked, "Can I feel?"

Gina smiled at her. "Sure, honey, but I think she's too small still for you to feel her."

His dad laughed. "*Her*, my foot. That's a boy in there." His dad leaned his mouth closer to speak to her belly. "Aren't you my little green-eyed man?"

Braden slowly put the checkers away. He wished he had green eyes like his dad. None of them did.

His dad grinned at him. "Hey, Braden, do you want to see if you can feel the baby?"

Braden stacked the checkers—red, black, red, black. "No."

His dad frowned. "What's wrong?"

"Don't you think you're a little old to have more kids?"

"He'll be your brother."

"I don't want another brother. I hate him already."

Gina and his father stared at him. His dad's mouth hung open before he snapped it shut. Then he yelled. "You apologize right now!"

Braden stood up. "No."

His dad jerked to his feet and put a finger in his face. "I don't want you talking like that in this house, young man."

"Well, I don't want to be here."

"Go to your room."

"Fine!"

Sunday morning, Sierra rolled over in bed, enjoying the snuggly warmth without the pressure of getting up to fulfill little-people demands. She'd been surprised when Michael asked to have the kids again. He really was trying with the kids. She closed her eyes and burrowed deeper. A horrible howling made her jerk, then she realized it was the coffee bean grinder in the kitchen. She closed her eyes again. *Clack-clack-clack. Clack-clack-clack.* Her mother in her Sunday morning heels. Sierra flopped onto her back. *Clack-clack-clack.*

Her mom had asked her last night, as she did every Saturday evening, if Sierra would come to church. But why bother, when she didn't feel any different after the service than before?

Her thoughts drifted to Elise. Elise had something her mom didn't. Would it help to know what that something was?

She threw back the covers and got up.

Sierra wandered into the kitchen threading her dressy black belt through the loops of her dark slacks.

Her mom assessed her appearance with arched brows. "Are you going to church, honey?"

She nodded. "With Elise."

Her mom's lips pressed into a tight line. "Well, that's nice, dear. If you don't mind all those hands in the air."

Sierra gave a nervous laugh. "And a few deacons rolling down the aisles?"

Her mom gave her a sharp look. "It's not how I raised you, but you're old enough to decide where you want to fellowship. I'm just glad you're finally going. As long as you don't go overboard, Sierra.

Some people in that church can't speak a sentence without a 'halleluiah, praise God.'"

"Mom, it's one visit."

"Well, I'm just saying." Her mom left the kitchen.

Sierra called Elise from the van. "I'm coming today."

"I'll pick up the coffee. Meet you in front in fifteen."

"They're not going to make me dance in the aisles or anything, are they?" At the pause she said, "Sorry, my mom made me a little nervous."

"Relax, hon. It'll be fine."

Elise was waiting on the front steps of the church with two Starbucks coffees.

Sierra took a sip and followed Elise into the foyer. An elderly gentleman with dentures too big for his gums reached for her hand with both of his. "Hello. So glad to have you with us today."

Elise turned. "Harold, this is my dear friend Sierra."

"Lord bless you, Sierra." Such love in those faded blue eyes.

Elise leaned close as they entered the sanctuary. "Harold loves God more than any person I know. It's like touching elbows with the Holy Spirit to be near that man."

Hmm.

Elise introduced her to more of her friends, and they all seemed normal. Sierra listened hard, but didn't hear one "halleluiah, praise God."

The worship was a little out of her comfort zone with guitars and drums and a few raised hands, but nobody rolled around foaming at the mouth. Partway through the worship, Harold shuffled his way in and took his seat in the aisle across from her, next to a white-haired woman who turned to him with the sweetest smile.

When the pastor started his sermon, Sierra's eyes kept straying to the old gentleman. The sharp angles of his shoulders poked through the dark plaid Sunday sweater. Oversized ears cupped forward as if they'd grown toward the pulpit like a flower seeking sunlight. What gave Harold that kind of joy? Sierra's mom didn't radiate that kind of joy and she practically lived at the church.

Sierra felt as though she'd stumbled across something profound, but she didn't know how to tether it to words she could grasp and get a hold of.

What made Harold different?

Sierra found herself listening to the sermon intently, with occasional glances toward Harold. Yes, he was focused on the sermon. But there was nothing earth-shattering in Pastor Darnell's talk about the woman at the well. Of course, Jesus knew she was living with a man. He was God. Omniscient and all that.

She leaned forward to see Harold's face better. Quiet peace radiated, as if the pastor were recounting a story Harold knew intimately, having gotten it firsthand from its source.

Sierra turned slightly to observe Elise. Her friend had the same kind of look on her face, a peace and contentment that all was well in her world. Sierra glanced back at Harold. His serenity seemed to come from within. Deep from some central point of who the man was. It was like he knew who he was, or rather to whom he belonged.

Hmm. After church, she stepped into her van with more questions than answers.

Chapter 21

Ross's cell phone rang. "Prestige Landscape Design."

"Hey, Ross, it's Carl over at Grainger's. Nancy in accounting said we hadn't gotten a payment from you, so I told her I'd give you a call."

Ross set the vine maple down and rubbed his forehead. "Completely spaced it. Sorry, Carl. I'll get a check out today."

"No problem. I heard you were under the gun on that Cranwell job. I'll let Nancy know she can expect a check in the next day or so."

Ross left the maple next to the hole and headed for the pickup. He turned the truck around and started back down the driveway toward Sid's. He hadn't had time to sort things out in his mind with Sierra, and now he needed her help. She must think he was a total jerk. He deserved it if she ripped his checks to shreds.

He parked in front of the house and walked quickly up the sidewalk, the engine ticking in the cool air. *Dig deep, Ross.* He rapped on the door and entered.

Sid's eyes lit up. "Ross! I've missed you, son. Know you've been busy across the road."

Ross's eyes strayed toward the kitchen.

Sid followed his gaze with a knowing nod. "Wondered how long it would take you to come around."

Ross rubbed the back of his neck and headed for the kitchen.

"I'd tread lightly." Sid chuckled. "At least the kitchen knives haven't been sharpened in a while."

Ross threw him a look over his shoulder.

Sierra had her back to him as she cut up vegetables. Ross cleared his throat and she whirled. A ripple of pleasure was there and gone. Guardedness slid into its place. He eyed the knife pointed toward him. "You, uh, making dinner?"

"Yes." She turned back to the counter, a carrot taking the full brunt of the knife.

"I, uh, Braden's been doing great with Chance."

"Thanks for taking the time. I know you're busy. I hear my mom has brought Emory and Trevor over to enjoy the show."

"Yeah. They help Braden brush him down when we're done."

"Hmm." She reached for a stalk of celery.

Ross winced at the damage she did to it. Better get out of there fast. He rubbed the back of his neck again. "Did you, uh, have a chance to write out the checks?"

She pointed the knife toward a corner of the kitchen, her attention never leaving the vegetables.

He stared, trying to figure out—did she expect him to go stand in the corner? "Listen, Sierra, I'm sorry. I've acted like a jerk. I just haven't had time—"

"They've been sitting by the door for the last week, waiting for you to sign them."

Ross wiped a hand over his face. "Sorry. It's been a rough day." She stared at the counter, and he walked over and gently tugged her outside so they could have a private conversation.

She bit her lip, then looked past him toward the barn, shivering in her thin blouse. "Ross, why have you been avoiding me?"

His heart clenched at the hurt in her voice. He'd caused that pain, yet she was brave enough to ask. He was the coward. He led her to his pickup, where it'd be warmer.

He opened the driver's door and she scooted in and over to the passenger's side. She seemed smaller, sitting so still with her hands pressed to her thighs, brown eyes watchful.

He shifted in the seat. *Honesty always.* Sid had taught him that. He leaned his arms against the steering wheel and turned his head, catching her gaze, his voice soft. "I like you a lot, Sierra."

Color entered her pale cheeks, but she didn't look away.

"Yet I shouldn't have kissed you."

Confusion rolled across her features.

"There are certain convictions I live by. But I was upset and not thinking clearly. I'm sorry."

Sierra's arms went around her waist. "So you weren't thinking clearly."

He sighed. *Great start, Ross.* How could he explain that he was drawn to her in a way that turned his world around, yet he didn't know where she stood with God? "Sierra, you haven't done anything wrong. I—"

"So by these *convictions,* you mean God, don't you?"

Ross hesitated. If he said yes, he'd lose her. He could see it in her eyes. Slowly he nodded. "I should have—"

Her hands clenched in her lap. "So if I was a Bible thumper, then you could kiss me all you wanted, is that what you're saying?" Her gaze skewered him.

He took another breath. "It's not—"

"You don't need to explain anything."

When Sierra finally stepped into her mom's living room that night, the kids ran to greet her. Braden reached her first and gave her a tight squeeze, then leaned back. He still wasn't wearing his eye patch; he hadn't worn it since Michael told him not to.

"Did you see me and Ross in the field today? Chance is doing so awesome. Ross showed me how to back him up and turn him and everything. He set up the obstacles for the trail course and Chance can do them *all*. Ross said he was probably a 4-H horse in his younger years. Isn't that cool?"

Sierra attempted a bright smile. "That is so awesome, honey." *God, keep my kid safe.* She'd tossed up quite a few of those prayers lately when she watched Braden from Sid's living room window. Sid finally told her to pull the blinds, that she was making him nervous with all that hovering.

She ran a hand over Braden's silky mop. "How'd it go with your dad this weekend?"

His eyes slid from hers and a sullen note crept into his voice. "I dunno."

"What happened, honey?"

He pulled away from her hand. "I don't want to talk about it." He flopped on the couch and clicked on the TV.

"Mom?" Emory's voice was soft. "Can we pray for Daddy?"

Where did that come from?

"Um, sure Sweetie. What would you like to say?"

"Can you do it? He's been really crabby and his work isn't going good." Emory waited, trust innocently riding the silence, certain her mom would have the words.

Sierra's chest dropped in a deep exhale. *Pray for Michael?* What could she say? She cleared her throat. "Dear God. Could you please help Daddy feel happier and please help his business do better. Amen."

When Emory squeezed her waist before trotting off toward the kitchen, she knew she'd passed. *Why did Emory want to pray?* It wasn't like they were a praying family, other than the bedtime ritual, and that was done by rote. "Dear God, protect Emory and keep her safe. Amen." It was just part of the routine, like reading a bedtime story or making sure the same stuffed animal was tucked under the covers.

Of course, the kids occasionally expanded the prayer to include protecting Grandma or helping them get a new bike or a special toy. But they never prayed in the middle of the day, like Someone would actually be waiting and listening. *Were Michael and Gina talking about the bankruptcy in front of the kids? Adding more pressure to their lives to the point that Emory was driven to prayer?*

She followed her daughter. "Em? What made you want to pray?"

Emory peeled a banana, a delighted smile showing the fractional space between her two front teeth. "Mrs. Adair told us that Jesus wants to help us all the time. We just have to ask."

"Who's Mrs. Adair?" Sierra mentally ran through the teachers at Emory's school, but the name didn't pop up. An aide or parent volunteer?

"My Sunday school teacher."

The pieces fell into place. "I think you mean Mrs. Duncan, honey." That was the name Sierra recalled in the time or two she'd taken the kids to Sunday school at her mom's church.

Emory shook her head, her bangs dancing until they settled back just below her eyebrows. Sierra needed to get the scissors out before school tomorrow. "No, my Sunday school at Gina's church."

Gina's church? Sierra felt her blood begin to boil. What was the woman thinking? Steal her husband and lure her children into thinking Michael, Gina, and kids were one big happy family because they went to church? *The hypocrites!*

"Daddy didn't go. Gina wanted him to, but he said he was too tired." She took another bite, her eyes excited. "Gina let me try to feel the baby move. Daddy wants a boy, but Gina wants a girl."

Sierra asked the question slowly. "Honey, does Daddy talk about the baby much?"

Emory's eyes lit and she nodded emphatically. "We talk about the baby all the time. I can't wait to see if I get a little sister!"

Trevor had followed them in and wasn't about to let his opinion go unrecognized. "I want a boy!"

"What does Braden want?" Sierra carefully watched the reaction of her two kids.

Trevor walked over and opened the lower cupboard door where her mom kept the kids' cups. "I'm thirsty."

Emory remained silent and lowered her face to stare at the floor.

"Em? What does Braden say about the baby?"

Emory lifted one shoulder in a halfhearted shrug, her expression fragile. "He and Daddy fight all the time."

Sierra kept her voice calm. "What do you mean, they fight?"

"Well, Braden was rude to Gina and said he hated the baby, which made Gina cry." She looked up, a shadow in her blue eyes. "Daddy yelled at him and told him to apologize."

Sierra sensed this moment was pivotal for her daughter. She sifted the words from a minefield of choices. "Braden should apologize. What he said was wrong." She bit her bottom lip. "We can't always change how we feel, but have a responsibility to keep those thoughts to ourselves if they are disrespectful or unkind."

Emory looked down at her lap and whispered, "So it's okay for Braden to hate the baby?"

I could use some help here. Sierra sent the plea as if God were actually listening. She waited.... Nothing drifted down from the heavenlies bearing gold-wrapped wisdom.

"I don't think Braden hates the baby as much as he hates the hurt he has inside."

Emory looked up, her nose wrinkled in confusion.

"Remember how mad you were when Brenda Steeples pushed one of the kindergarteners at recess and then called you a tattletale for telling the teacher? Did you hate her, or did you hate how it made you feel?"

Another shrug. "I guess the way it made me feel. But Brenda Steeples doesn't like anybody. And today Mrs. Miller gave her two pink slips for hitting Tommy Stevens."

"So do you see that Braden isn't mad at the baby as much as he's hurt that Daddy doesn't live with us anymore?"

"I guess." She tossed the banana peel in the garbage. "Can I go watch a video?"

Sierra walked over and gave her a quick hug and kiss. "For a few minutes. Then you need to brush your teeth."

Now to corral a boy who needed some loving.

Ross stepped through the door of his dark house, flipped on the lights, and headed straight for the office. A sigh of relief and a good portion of frustration whooshed from his chest. That afternoon, he'd called every vendor he could think of and asked them to fax over his outstanding bills.

His fax machine was loaded with them. His stomach growled. Food first. He stormed out to the kitchen and dug through the fridge for sandwich fixings. Armed with a pastrami sandwich and a Pepsi, Ross dropped the mayonnaise knife in the sink and started back toward his office, but not before he turned the coffee maker on, pouring in extra grounds. It was going to be a long night, and he needed to attack this mess with double-strength java.

Braden was no longer in the living room, so Sierra went up the stairs and nudged his door open, not sure what to expect but certain he wouldn't be tackling his homework. He lay against his pillows, a Game Boy propped on his knees, tinny noise from the headphones that were pressed to his ears leaking into the room.

"Hey," she said the word gently.

He grunted, the scowl on his face darkening. His fingers pressed the buttons rapidly.

"Can we talk?"

His voice was flat and loud. "I don't want to talk."

Sierra stepped over his backpack and navigated a mound of clothes to pull the desk chair closer. She would have liked to sit on the bed next to him but gave him his space.

"How are things at your dad's, honey?"

He shrugged. "Not that great." He flipped the headphones down but didn't turn them off. The game rested next to him on the bed. He stared at his knees, one hand picking at the fringe of his thermal blanket.

She said the words carefully, "Emory said you're having a hard time with Gina's pregnancy."

He wound the blanket tighter around his finger. A tear ran down his face and he wiped it with a quick movement of his wrist.

"I know it's hard that your dad and Gina are having a baby. But it doesn't change how your father feels about you."

Braden lifted his head. His eyes were filled with misery. "You don't know that, Mom."

"I know your dad, honey. He loves you very much. Daddy's just been going through a rough time. I'm sorry he's not been very dependable for you lately. Grown-ups make terrible mistakes sometimes. But that doesn't change the love he has for you."

Braden picked up his Game Boy. "Thanks."

Sierra hesitated. She wanted to wrap him in her arms, pour some of the love he so desperately needed from her own heart into his. "Do you want a hug?"

He shook his head.

She squeezed his shoulder. "I love you, bud."

He didn't lift his eyes from the Game Boy. "Love you too, Mom."

In the backyard, under the stars, Sierra's thumb hovered over the cell phone's keypad. She needed to tell Michael how much their son was hurting. But what if Michael yelled at Braden for talking to her? Her son would feel betrayed. She flipped the phone shut and walked slowly back to the house. Near the door, she paused and looked up at the inky sky with its brilliant sprinkling of cosmic lights. Her mom used to say there were holes in the pavement of heaven and the stars were God's light shining through. She aimed the thought toward those lights. *Please protect my boy's heart.*

The next afternoon Sid lay napping on the couch when the light rap on the front door came. Sierra peeked through the living room window and saw Ross on the front porch. Good. At least he knew better than to walk in like usual. She grabbed the doorknob and swung it open.

He stood looking at her for a moment, then grasped her arm and pulled her gently outside and shut the door behind them.

She pulled her arm free and wrapped both of them around her waist. "What could you possibly have to say now?"

His face was weary and he ran a hand over the back of his head, his gaze gliding over the porch before reaching her. "I did a lousy job explaining myself in the pickup yesterday. You haven't done anything wrong, Sierra. What I was trying to do was ask—"

"It's over with, Ross. Don't worry about it." She gave him a tight smile. If only her emotions would get over it as easily as the words that flowed from her mouth seemed to imply.

He pressed his lips into a tight line and looked down, nodding. When he raised his head, his eyes were warm, and she backed up, her heart pounding. Didn't he need to get back to work?

He stepped forward and looked into her eyes. "I don't think it's that simple."

She looked away.

He touched her cheek with a gentle finger. "I'm sorry I hurt you. I was upset the day I kissed you, then with the job … and Sid. I just needed some time to sort things out."

She moved her head away from his hand and slowly took in his disheveled appearance. Whiskers that hadn't been shaved, hair that needed a brush to mind the damp curls back into place. At least he'd taken a shower.

That was what started the whole mess, his frustration over Sid moving. "Isn't that what your backing off was really about? You're upset that Sid might do something for himself for a change, instead of staying here and keeping you company?"

He crossed his arms, and the fire banked in his eyes started to smolder. "I want what's best for Sid. And trust me, Kansas isn't best."

"Really. And what is?"

"Staying here. Where friends who are closer than family can look after him. Help him get around. Keep him from getting lonely."

She studied this man and felt a wave of compassion for him, and it irritated her.

"I'm sorry, Ross." Maybe she understood him because she saw the same pain in Braden's eyes. She wanted to touch Ross's arm, tell him it was going to be okay.

There was a fragile honesty to his words. "I don't want him to go."

"I know."

His gaze caught hers and held for a moment, rousing all her earlier feelings for him—and doubts too. An apologetic smile tugged at his lips. "I'm sorry for not talking to you sooner."

She wasn't that ready to forgive him, not when his kiss had opened her heart to hope and then rejection. "That's what *friends* do."

The lines around his eyes sharpened and his gaze swerved to her mouth. His eyes rose slowly to hers, and his voice was grave. "I guess I didn't have friendship on my mind at the time."

She fidgeted and looked away. "Is that all you wanted to tell me? Because I need to get dinner started…."

"I know you worked your tail off balancing my books, and then I acted like a jerk and didn't come get the checks." He gave her an endearing grin. She folded her arms and his grin lessened. "Will you keep doing my bookkeeping?"

He stood, looking like a lost boy, his face gloomy, but with the faintest flicker of hope. The tiniest breath would blow it out. "I would deserve it if you said you wouldn't help me, Sierra."

She dropped her arms. "Okay. I'll do it, but you're on probation."

The synapses must have fired slowly, because it was a long moment before her words seemed to register. A tired but grateful smile thanked her. "I had a few more bills arrive this morning. I thought maybe you could take a look at them when Braden and I are putting Chance through his paces."

Hearing her son's name paired with the horse still gave her a chill, but she was doing better. God seemed to be holding up His end of the bargain, at least. "That'll be fine, I'm sure my mom can get Emory and Trevor ready for bed."

"I appreciate this more than you know." And his grin caused all sorts of butterflies to take off in her stomach.

Chapter 22

Ross and Braden were working with Chance in the barn while Emory and Trevor watched cartoons in Ross's living room. With her mom visiting a friend in the hospital, it was the best she could do and still help Ross get the rest of his bills paid on time.

Sierra sat on the floor of Ross's office finishing his checks. A neat stack of newly arrived invoices, sorted by vendor sat in front of her. She clipped the last unsigned check to a bill and set it with the others, then shut the adding machine off.

Feet pounded down the hall toward her. "Mom!" Emory's face was white, her eyes huge and filled with terror and tears. "Braden's hurt. Chance fell—"

"What?" Sierra scrambled up, horror clutching at her chest and throat in waves. She tore past Emory, her breath coming in hiccupping gasps. *Braden!* Was he all right? Where was Ross?

Emory ran at her heels crying. "I was watching out the window. Chance fell, and—" She cried harder.

Sierra shouted the word that ended in a wail. "What?" *Oh, God. Keep him safe! You were supposed to keep him safe.*

"Braden didn't get up." Emory sobbed as Sierra ran outside into the dusky evening.

Sierra ran around the house and saw Chance in the pasture, grazing off to one side and Ross's dark shape crouched over—

"Nooooo!" The wail burst from her as she climbed the fence, dropped to the other side and fell to her knees. Getting up, she staggered forward and with stumbling steps made it over to her son.

Blood covered Braden's face and his eyes were closed. Ross had stripped his shirt off and held it pressed to Braden's cheek.

"Is he breathing?" The high-pitched shriek sounded like someone else's voice.

Ross nodded. "Yes. I called an ambulance."

"Is he okay, Ross?" She couldn't stop the flood of panic. Braden's arm was warm. But Molly's had been warm for a week, until technology could no longer thwart the ebbing of life.

"He'll be fine." But his voice held worry, and he wouldn't look at her.

She rubbed her son's arm gently, but the words were fearful, harsh sounding. "Braden! Wake up!"

"Sierra, stop!" Ross was breathing hard. "Look at me."

She panted, short gasps that made spots dance in front of the still form of her son.

"Look at me!" He barked.

She wrenched her eyes up and started to cry, great heaving sobs that came from her chest.

"He. Will. Be. Fine." He nodded once, his eyes locked on hers. "Okay?"

She heard an ambulance in the distance, gradually growing louder. After an eternity the flashing vehicle turned up Ross's drive. She jumped up and opened the gate, then motioned them straight to her boy.

Sierra sat by the hospital bed and watched her son's face. If she looked away she might miss something. A grimace, a flutter of eyelashes. That sweet, sleepy smile he always gave her when she woke him up for school.

She felt the air stir as the large wooden door pushed open, but still Braden didn't move.

"Oh, honey. Is Braden okay?" Tears quavered in her mom's voice.

Sierra nodded, wiping a finger under her eye. "Uh-huh. He's fine." She brushed the hair off Braden's forehead, careful to avoid the bandage covering the ten stitches on his cheek. "He's going to be fine. Aren't you, baby?"

"Is he sleeping?" Her mom moved around to the other side of the bed and laid a hand on Braden's arm above the IV.

"Mmmhmm. Just sleeping." Sierra kept smoothing his hair back.

The door moved the air again. Sierra dashed another tear away and wiped her wrist under her nose. A masculine hand settled on her shoulder. She reached up and it clasped hers, its warmth encircling her palm. She felt the gentle kiss on top her head and Ross's whispered words of apology and comfort. She leaned forward and rested her chin on the rail, her eyes never leaving Braden's face.

Ross watched the unconscious boy lying in the big hospital bed. Sierra's heart had been hammered to smithereens, and he could have prevented it. He'd known it was getting too dark to keep practicing, but Braden was so eager, so determined to cut his time down.

"What happened?" Sierra's voice sounded strained.

Ross cleared his throat. "He leaned too soon for the flag and his foot slipped out of the stirrup. The track around the barrel was slick and Chance lost his footing and nearly fell. Braden came down on the barrel. I think the coffee can sliced his cheek." Her shudder came up through his hand on her shoulder. "I'm sorry, Sierra. I knew it was getting too late to keep practicing. Next time—"

She slipped her hand from his, her voice hollow. "There won't be a next time."

He squeezed the muscles in her shoulder gently. "Okay."

The door shushed open, and her fur-coated friend Elise bustled into the room, eyes only for Sierra and the boy in the bed. "Oh, hon. How is he?"

Sierra dropped her head in her hands and wept for the first time since they'd left the pasture. Her shoulders convulsed under Ross's hand, but the sobs were gut wrenching despite their quietness. Ross tightened his grip on her shoulder, willing her pain into his own body. *Lord, heal that little boy.*

Elise's shoulder brushed his and a swirl of something floral and exotic drifted to his nose. The words were so low he could barely hear them. "Is he going to be okay?"

He leaned toward her ear. "The tests didn't show any bleeding on his brain, and he has some stitches on his cheek. But the doctors can't figure out why he hasn't woken up yet."

Sierra went to a place deep inside where blackness closed in around her. She spoke into the darkness. *You were supposed to keep him safe. I entrusted him to You.*

No warm assurances drifted to her, no heavenly arms offered comfort. She heard the cracking of her heart and the pouring out of hope. But nothing else.

Elise rubbed her arm, her soft prayers flowing nonstop. Sierra wanted to tell her to shut up, to stop putting her son before a God who didn't care. She held Braden's hand, her fingertips stroking the inside of his palm, moving over the callused bumps on the fleshy pad at the base of each finger. She leaned closer and pressed his hand tight between hers. He was her son. If only she could will her strength, her health into this young body that had once received all its nourishment from her.

Michael! She half-rose in her chair. "I forgot to call Michael."

Abbey gave her a teary look and patted Braden's arm. "I'll go call him, honey."

Sierra turned to Ross, her brain starting to process other important details. "Where are Emory and Trevor?"

"I took them to Sid's and called my mom. She'll stay with them as long as we need."

She nodded as she sank back into the chair and continued to watch her son. He appeared to be resting so peacefully. *Please, wake up, honey.*

Fifteen minutes later, the door sprang open and Michael rushed in, Gina right behind him in a tan raincoat that made her look bigger than her five months. Michael's eyes were frantic as he filled the space next to Abbey. "Is he okay?"

Sierra nodded, then looked back at Braden. She wanted to explain, tell him everything the doctor said. That their boy *should* wake up. But her throat closed and another sob built in her chest.

Ross's fingers moved minutely on her shoulder as he shifted behind her. "The doctors said there's no bleeding on his brain."

Michael's hands relaxed their grip on the bed rail, and his voice softened. "When will he wake up?"

No one spoke, so Ross said, "They don't know."

At midnight it was just Michael and Gina in the room with her. Sierra's mom had left earlier to take the kids home and put them to bed. Ross had gotten her a sandwich at around ten before he left, but it sat on the tray next to the window.

Gina had fallen asleep in a chair, so Sierra and Michael waited ... and waited.

He sat with his knuckles under his chin, then reached a hand to straighten Braden's blanket where it wrinkled over his chest. "You hope and pray nothing like this ever happens to your kids."

Sierra sat silently, her mind empty of words. Then the thought came and it filled her body with its intensity. "I'm selling that horse."

Michael gave her a fierce look. "Good."

An hour later when the nurse checked on him, Braden stirred, then opened his eyes. He rolled his head toward his mother and gave her a sleepy grin. "Why are you crying, Mom?"

Sierra gripped his hand tighter, her thumb rubbing the top of it. "They're happy tears, sweetie."

Braden reclined on the sofa in his grandma's living room, the remote in one hand and a half-eaten cookie in the other.

Sierra sat down on the couch near his feet, the only part of him she could reach with the coffee table blocking the way. Her mom had pushed it closer so he could reach the tray of cookies, finger sandwiches, and pitcher of icy apple juice she'd arranged for him.

Braden weaved his head back and forth trying to see around her to the TV. "Mom, could you move?"

Sierra twisted her fingers together and took a breath. "Honey, I need to talk to you."

"What?" His eyes didn't leave the video of *Superman* his grandma had rented.

"I placed an ad to sell Chance."

He stopped chewing and his eyes locked on hers, confusion and a growing anger in them. "Why? Mom, you can't do that!"

"I know it's hard for you to understand, but I can't keep him when—"

His eyes grew desperate. "Mom, please don't sell him. I'll do anything. I'll keep my room clean. I won't fight with Emory anymore."

She squeezed his leg beneath the blue quilt, her hand trembling. Why did it have to hurt so much to keep her son safe? She swallowed and played the coward card. "Your dad agrees that it's best."

The flesh around his mouth pulled and twisted in the way it did when he was trying not to cry. "Mom, the clinic is only two weeks away. You *said* I could do it."

"Honey, I didn't know it was going to be so dangerous."

He flopped his hands against the quilt. "It's *not* dangerous. I just leaned in too early. It wasn't Chance's *fault*."

"I'm sorry, honey." When he pressed the heels of his hands against his eyes, she touched his arm, the need to comfort him a physical ache, but he jerked his arm away.

She drew a deep breath and closed her eyes. *We will get through this, won't we?*

Late in the morning, the doorbell rang and Sierra's mom twisted from the sink, dishwater up to her elbows. "Can you get that, honey?"

Sierra walked through the living room where Braden still hunkered on the couch, scowling at the TV.

Ross glanced up when she opened the door.

She swallowed. "Hi." His lazy half-smile got her heart beating faster again. "I, uh, appreciate your staying with me at the hospital. It helped."

"My pleasure." He raised two brown paper bags. "Is Braden up for company?"

She stepped back to let him in, feeling a wry grin twist into place. "I think he's always available for you."

Ross moved past her and squatted next to the coffee table. "Hey, buddy. How're the stitches?"

The comment pulled a near-smile from Braden and he raised his hand to touch the bandage. "Okay."

Ross handed him the sacks. Braden reached his hand into the smaller one first and pulled out a LEGO Transformer. A lukewarm smile touched his face. The second bag held a helmet. "What's this for?"

Ross reached for it. "It's a riding helmet. I should have gotten you one when we first started working with Chance. It probably would have kept you from staying the night at the hospital." He adjusted the straps. "Try it on."

Sierra pressed her lips together and stuck her hands in her pockets.

Braden wouldn't take it from him. He stared down at the blanket. "Mom's selling Chance."

Ross twisted on his heels to look up at her, an argument in his eyes, but he didn't say anything. He turned back to Braden and stood. "Your mom loves you a lot, Braden."

Braden looked back at the TV.

Ross jangled his keys. "I better get back to work."

He walked past Sierra and took her arm, pulling her outside.

She sighed. "Thanks for supporting me with Braden—"

Gone was his smile. His eyes pierced right to her core. "You're making a mistake. A big one."

Her throat tightened.

His voice grew firm. "You can't just—"

She held up a hand. "Yes, I can. You were supposed to keep him safe. You and God. You promised me it wasn't dangerous."

He jammed his hands to his waist. "All life holds risks, Sierra. You either minimize them the best you can or you stop living."

She crossed her arms again. "I think selling Chance is minimizing things greatly."

His voice rose. "But at what cost?" He leaned closer. "You say you're doing this to protect your son, but I see a woman who has been completely blinded by fear and is destroying her son because of it."

She felt as if he'd slapped her.

He turned and headed down the steps to his pickup.

Sierra wanted to slam the front door against his words. How could he possibly understand? He didn't know the gut-wrenching terror of a parent whose child has been gravely injured. She bit her lip and watched him drive away.

But what if he was right?

The first call came early the next morning when Braden and Emory were at school and Trevor was curled next to Sid on the couch watching *Barney and Friends*. She answered her cell as she flipped Sid's over-medium eggs onto a plate.

"Hello?"

"Sierra? This is Greg Adams. My daughter and I looked at a horse of yours about a month ago. Is it still Chance that's for sale?"

Sierra set the spatula next to the plate and leaned forward against the counter. "Yes, but I need to tell you that my son was injured a couple of days ago riding him."

"What happened?" Alarm entered the man's voice.

"The horse slipped rounding a barrel in a game they were practicing, and my son fell off and was unconscious for several hours."

His voice settled. "Oh, I thought you meant the horse kicked him or something."

How could the man still want a horse knowing the danger?

"We'll take him. I have a friend with a horse trailer who said he's free to pick him up about three this afternoon." A smile entered his voice. "My daughter finally convinced her mom she's ready for a horse."

"Oh, well, that's wonderful." Sierra's hands started to sweat, Ross's question, *But at what cost?* slipping into her mind. *Could this hurt stay with Braden longer than any physical injury would? What would it do to their relationship?*

Sierra swallowed the sigh. "We've moved him, so let me give you directions."

She set the phone down and stared at the counter. Would Braden be able to forgive her?

Chapter 23

Sierra slid the plate of eggs in front of Sid. She cracked two more into the hot pan and scrambled them with the spatula.

"Can I do it?" Trevor scooted the kitchen chair over until it banged into the stove. Sid hobbled into the kitchen on the crutches the daily in-home physical therapist had taught him to use. A walker would be next, and then he'd be back on his own. Sierra didn't even want to think about how much she'd miss him.

"Okay, but I'll hold the pan."

Her son looked up, apparently catching something in her tone. The toast popped and she set two pieces on a plate to the right of Sid, next to the butter and jam. "More juice?"

"I'm capable of pouring my own juice," Sid said as he leaned his crutches against the table.

"Never thought you weren't, Mr. Ornery."

Sid grinned and wiped his whiskers with his handkerchief. She couldn't get him to use a napkin. Said paper didn't clean his face nearly as well.

"So you and Ross on speaking terms again?" Sid's bright eyes danced with some secret knowledge.

She avoided direct eye contact by pouring herself a mug of coffee. "Did you and Leorna have a good visit this morning?" He'd been on the phone when she and Trevor walked through the front door.

"Ross is a fine catch. He's a little slow on the uptake at times, but some things can be overlooked." He dragged his toast across the plate, sopping up the last bit of yolk.

"Did that realtor ever call you back?"

"I've no doubt Ross'd make a good husband, just needs a little fine-tuning."

"Too bad we couldn't stuff you in a box and send you out to Leorna for a nice, long visit." She gave him a sweet smile.

His toast paused midscrape. "You want me to drop the topic?"

"Please. It's not open for discussion."

"Too soon? Need to let your feelings mature a little more?"

"No." She gave him a look. "None of your business."

His deep laugh crinkled the lines around his eyes, making him look like Santa Claus with a little yolk on his chin. He bobbed his head knowingly. "Some day you'll thank me for nudging you in Ross's direction."

She gave him a look. "Could be dangerous if someone tripped and knocked one of your crutches out from under you."

He laughed and raised his hands. "All right. All right."

She lifted the mug and took a sip. "Back to Leorna. Are you moving, Sid?"

He sighed and set his fork on his plate with deliberation. "Yes, I believe I am. I'm getting too old to train the ponies." His eyes clung to hers as if begging for confirmation.

She smiled her understanding.

He nodded once, as if laying that final piece to rest. "I want to go home. Be near my family again." His smile grew nostalgic. "It's funny, you know. When my wife and daughter died, I couldn't stand being there. Too much pain, too much death for me to handle all at once. But as I get ready to meet the Lord, I yearn for the comfort of being close to them."

He drummed his fingers on the table. "Being young, you might not understand that. Now, don't go telling Ross." His fingers had stilled and his look grew gruff.

"There's no chance of that," Sierra said. "But you need to talk to him, Sid. And soon."

Trevor slid off his chair and ambled through the doorway toward the living room. A soft click and the muted sounds of *Sesame Street* came into the room.

"That reminds me." Sid licked his lips as if he had succulent news to impart, and his eyes held that leprechaun sparkle, like when he was about to pull a good one over on Ross. "Stella called this morning, said her niece went out to the old homestead on Monday, but couldn't find the honeysuckle. They had a bad winter and the plant hadn't been doing too well the last few years, so they think the cold did it in."

Sierra sank back against the counter. "So Ross's heirloom plant can't be replaced." And she had no chance to make amends for it, not that she had a real desire to at the moment.

"Now hold yer horses girl, I'm not done. Tracy, Stella's niece, brought her husband back the next day, and they looked under every weed and bush there was." Eyes dancing, he waited for her to ask.

His mood was contagious. "And?"

He clapped his hands and leaned forward like he was about to award the jackpot. "They found it, nearly dead under blackberry briars. Tracy clipped off the only living branch on it and mailed it that day. Stella thought it shoulda showed up yesterday, but Tracy packed it good and wet. You'll just need to stick it in a vase until it roots, then put 'er in the ground come spring."

She went straight over and gave him a hug. His ears turned pink, but he didn't complain. "Sid, thank you so much. And thank Stella for me."

She helped him back into the living room, but a light blanket tucked around his legs brought about his bleating at her to quit fussin' over him. She adjusted the pillow under his knee and he sighed and sank deeper into the couch. Trevor scooted closer and perched on the few inches of open couch near Sid's chest. The old man drew an arm around him and anchored him in place.

"Now, you get back to whatever you need to do in the kitchen. Me and Trevor here are gonna watch *Sesame Street.*"

Sierra glanced out the living room window and saw Chance grazing in Ross's pasture, and her thoughts spun back to Braden. A dark cloud passed over her heart. She didn't seem capable of making two of the important males in her life happy.

Ross jammed the shovel into the ground and worked it deeper into the hard soil, mad at himself for losing his temper with Sierra. When he'd calmed down, he admitted to himself that it was love for her kids that drove her to sell Chance, even if it was motivated by fear.

But what was really bothering him was why he couldn't let her go. In spite of everything, she filled his thoughts. She drew his heart in a way no one ever had. It was the look in her eye when her boy was hurting. The determination she'd shown to try to overcome her terror so her kids could keep an old horse, and the way she teased and cajoled an old man who missed a daughter and a wife buried back in Kansas. Everything in him wanted to protect her, love her, to wrap her in his arms when she was weary, to bring the sparkle back into her eyes.

And yet he'd hurt her. But what made him jam the shovel hard into the ground was the knowledge that she couldn't be his.

At ten to three, Sierra gripped Sid's front doorknob. She couldn't look at him, didn't want him to know the terrible thing she was doing. "I need to run an errand."

He frowned. "Why're you all fidgety?"

She stilled the keys. "I, um …"

He pointed to the recliner. "Sit down and let 'er out."

She sat on the edge of the chair, her keys digging into her palm. "I sold Chance."

The muscles in his face contracted as shock morphed into a kind of pain, then the wisdom of his age seemed to smooth out the crevasses. "Sierra," her name came out on a sigh, "you can only run from fear so long." He waved toward the door. "You better go run your errand."

She stood near Ross's barn as a shiny aluminum horse trailer pulled up his drive. A part of her wanted to wave her arms and tell them they had the wrong address, the wrong horse. This one wasn't for sale.

But she didn't. Greg Adams and his friend first loaded the tack, as they called Chance's gear, then led the big gray horse into the trailer. The shiny metal door shut the old horse from her gaze.

Greg Adams handed her the check. Slowly she reached for it, gripped it tight in her hands, and never said a word.

That night her mom met her at the front door, her arms crossed tight over her chest. "Braden told me you're selling Chance, honey." Disapproval pressed her lips into a tight line.

Sierra shut the door and walked past her to the kitchen. She dropped her keys on the counter. "It's been a rough day, Mom."

"How can you just sell him like that? The kids *finally* have something they look forward to—"

"I don't want to talk about it."

"Well, let me tell you, the joy just whooshed out of this house when you placed that ad." Her mom drilled her with one good look then turned to the sink.

Her mom's words pounded the doubts deeper. But then she thought about Braden lying so still and white in the hospital bed. The cupboard door squeaked in her hand, and she set the glass on the counter with a hard thunk. She *was* doing the right thing. She opened the fridge and poured a glass of apple juice and drank it down. What would they be telling her if she was preparing for Braden's funeral today? *I'm so sorry. He was such a sweet boy. It's too bad you inherited that horse.*

Emory rushed into the kitchen, questions in her eyes. "Mom, are you really selling Chance?"

Sierra knelt down and reached for Emory's hand. "Yes, honey. I don't want to, but he's too dangerous. Braden could have died."

Emory pulled her hand free. "But he didn't. And Ross got him a helmet."

Sierra stood. "I know, sweetie, but it's still not safe."

Big tears formed in her daughter's eyes, and she jerked away when Sierra touched her shoulder, then ran from the kitchen.

Her mom leaned back against the sink with a sigh.

"Don't say anything, Mom."

Abbey shook her head. "I warned you. Braden's worse. He wouldn't come down for dinner." The beep of the microwave interrupted her, and Abbey opened the black door and brought out a plate covered with a paper towel. "I was just warming his food up. Put his fork on the table and I'll go call him."

Braden wandered into the kitchen a few minutes later. Apparently a growling stomach was able to move him from his exile.

"How was school, honey?"

He wouldn't look at her. "Did anyone buy Chance?"

She looked to her mom, but her mother turned away. *God, please!* she prayed, but then she remembered she wasn't talking to Him. *He* was the reason she was in this mess. If He'd kept Braden from getting hurt, she wouldn't have had to sell that horse.

She crossed her arms, but her voice was gentle, "Yes, someone did."

He looked at her, his mouth open, fork in midair. Then a darkness crumpled his features and he dropped the fork onto his plate and stood up.

"You need to eat, sweetie."

"I'm not hungry."

"Then we'll put it back in the fridge."

He got up, carried his plate to the sink and dumped it, using his fork to poke it down the disposal.

"Braden, that's not okay!"

"I don't care! I hate you!" Braden stomped up the stairs and bounced his door against its frame.

Abbey went over and switched the water on, ran the disposal, then walked out of the kitchen.

Sierra stood in the vacuum they left behind.

Braden's attitude got worse over the weekend. By Monday morning guilt rode in the car with her all the way to Sid's. And that evening her mom left to visit Alma Thayer in the nursing home, but most likely she'd left to escape the bedlam in her house.

Braden was in his room *not* doing his homework. A casual after-dinner inquiry about school assignments for him and Emory had triggered a Mt. St. Helens'–sized eruption from her son. More ugly words. Fortunately the majority of the blast had been contained to his room after he slammed his door. Rumblings continued to filter through the thin floor, the most frequent one being the shouted, "I hate you, Mom."

Emory and Trevor had gone to bed quietly. Actually Trevor had asked to sleep with Emory. Sierra couldn't bring herself to say no, even on a school night.

Alone in the stillness, she reached for her cell on the kitchen table and made the call she'd been avoiding.

"Hi, hon. How's Braden?" Elise's warm voice answered.

"Elise, I, um, I sold Chance."

"Oh, hon, you are having it rough, aren't you?"

Her nose stung, but Sierra laughed and wiped her eyes. "How come you always love me, even when no one else does?"

Elise's voice grew gentle. "How could I not? You're a precious child of the King."

Sierra slumped down in the kitchen chair. "How can you trust Him so easily? I mean, I prayed and went to church, Elise, and He still let Braden get hurt."

"You can't please Him into doing something you want. He's not conditional like that. But He always has your good in mind."

"I don't buy that."

"That's because you can't see through the Creator's eyes. Your good and His good may seem very different, but His good is always better. His good is about eternity, not just the here and now."

Sierra snorted. "I don't think I'm wild about His rules."

"Sweetie, I say this with all the love in my heart. If you and God disagree on something, He's not the one who's wrong."

"If you weren't my best friend, I don't think I'd like you very much right now." Sierra teased her.

Elise gave a dramatic sigh. "I know. It's up to best friends to say the hard stuff." Her voice turned serious. "Sierra, we either trust God with what we don't understand, or we do our best to plow our own path, but it will always take us farther from Him and what's best for us."

Sierra laid her head on the table. "How can you know that?"

Elise's words were simple. "Because I know Him."

There was a rumble of a pickup pulling into the driveway. She hissed into the phone. "I think Ross is here."

"No!"

There was a *rap-rap* at the door. "What do I do?"

"Answer the door, silly."

"No! I'm in my pajamas, and we're not really speaking right now."

"Pajamas at eight o'clock, girl? Well, you can't leave him out there. Are you sure it's him?"

Sierra crept to the kitchen window and peeked out. Ross's truck was parked behind her van. She crouched beneath the counter and whispered, "It's him."

"Well, let him in."

"I'm not going to let him in. Maybe he'll go—"

"Mom, Ross is here." Sierra craned to look up into her daughter's face. Ross stood right behind her. He rubbed the back of his neck and stared everywhere in the kitchen but at her crouched on the peach vinyl.

"I gotta go." She shut the phone and stared up at Ross and her daughter. *Wonderful.*

Laughter played around his lips. "Maybe this isn't such a good time."

Sierra stood and straightened her pajamas, running a hand through her hair. "Now is fine."

Ross rubbed the top of Emory's head. "Thanks for rescuing me."

Her daughter gave him a grin that Sierra hadn't seen in days. "No prob." Her eyes skittered away from her mom's and she ran back up the stairs.

Sierra looked at the counter next to him. "About not answering the door, I'm not really dressed for company, and—"

There was a smile in his voice. "I deserved it. I was a jerk for talking to you the way I did. If it matters at all, I understand why you're selling Chance."

She looked away. "Thanks." She needed to get him out of there. She was still mad at him for not wanting her to sell Chance, wasn't she? And why did he have to look so darn appealing?

He drew a hand down his face. That was when she noticed the drawn features that had hidden behind his smile. "The bank called today, and I have checks bouncing all over town."

"Hmm."

"I can't figure it out." He leaned back against the counter. "If you didn't double any payments, I should have had enough in there to cover everything."

"Are you sure? I mean I know you can't ... you know, see numbers well."

His lips twitched. "I see them, just in the wrong order." He glanced toward the window and crossed his arms. "I know roughly what my jobs will run me, so I keep enough funds in my account to cover them." His gaze drifted back to her. "I have all the statements, everything from the bank, and every packing list I could find that the guys had laying around."

He rested his hands on the counter and looked at her. "Do you think you could help me? I can hire someone else if you don't think you're up for it. It's just you already have a handle on the bills."

Why not? It wasn't like the day could get worse. A son upstairs who hated her at the moment and a landscaper who couldn't date her, but still needed her help. She waved her arm in a grand arc toward the dinette. "Sure, bring 'em in. I can add a leaf to the kitchen table."

He narrowed his eyes in a perplexed way and started to open his mouth, then shook his head with a slight grin. "Are you okay?"

At that moment Braden must have switched stations *and* raised the volume, because the walls started thrumming with a heavy beat.

He tilted his head to look at the ceiling. "Aren't your kids in bed?"

"Yep. My mom escaped to a nursing home tonight."

He gave her another odd look.

"To visit a friend, but she may see if they have any rooms available."

"I can come back if this isn't a good time."

"No, no. This is great, if you don't mind a little rebel pounding of the floor above us. It'll help me keep the adding machine in sync." She snapped her fingers in unison to the heavy music. "Just bring everything in and set it there and we'll crank 'er out."

He gave a slight chuckle. "Have you been drinking?"

"Nope, just another facet of my lovely self coming out." Elise would be either proud or mortified.

Braden chose that moment to pound on the floor and scream. "I hate you, Mom! I want my horse!"

Ross nodded slowly, understanding in the heat of his gaze. "Do you want me to talk to him?"

Promises like so many flecks of amber burned in his eyes. He straightened from the counter and she saw him as a dad, a man not afraid to be the heavy hand.

But he'd already made it clear that friendship was all he had to offer, hadn't he? "No, thanks. You want to bring everything in?" She risked one quick glance.

He leaned toward her. "You don't have to do this alone."

She knew her smile was brittle, felt it in the way it cracked into her cheeks. "We wouldn't want to confuse things again, would we?"

His face turned somber and his eyes slid from hers. A heartbeat, then, "Okay, I'll go get the paperwork."

Two hours later, they'd covered it all.

He leaned back in his chair with a heavy sigh. "It just doesn't make sense. I haven't spent this much money. I know I haven't."

She set her pencil down on the spreadsheet they'd created. He wiped both hands down his face. "The guys don't get everything turned in, but they're not usually that bad." He narrowed his eyes and stared down at the floor to his right, the words more for himself. "If Alex Cranwell doesn't pay for all the extras he's pushed on me, I'm going to take a huge hit, but not this much."

The thump of an angry boy demanding to be noticed sounded on each of the twenty-two stairs. Braden stomped into the kitchen and jerked the refrigerator door open. "I'm hungry."

Sierra looked him. "It's bedtime, Braden. Grab a banana and head back up, please."

Her son grabbed the half-gallon of milk and reached into the cupboard for the Cheerios.

"No breakfast cereal," Sierra said, keeping her voice level. "If you want something, take a banana."

The ping of Cheerios hitting the bottom of the bowl filled the kitchen. Braden opened the milk and would have poured it if it hadn't been suddenly removed from his hand.

Ross held the milk and stated in a mild voice. "Would you like a banana, or would you like some help back to your room?"

The defiant look slipped. A boy gaped up at his idol with hurt in his eyes. Ross must have seen it too because he laid a hand on Braden's shoulder. "Braden, I—"

The shrug and scathing look dislodged Ross's hand. Braden whipped around and ran up the stairs. His door slammed, and the blare of hard rock music rained through the ceiling like dripping acid.

Ross put the milk away and gave her an uncertain smile. "That went well."

Sierra dropped her head into her hands. The tears came, slowly at first, filling the wells and then running down the bridge of her nose and onto her notes. She had mastered the art of a silent torrent.

She was losing her son. A chair creaked and a warm hand rested on her shoulder, then slid down to rub circles over her back. Slow circles of comfort. Sierra cried harder. The chair skidded closer and he tugged her into his arms and pressed her head to his chest. The rich smell of loam mixed with the sweet scent of hard work filled her nostrils. His embrace was more than comfort, it pledged character and stability. Tantalizing but elusive elements in her experience with men. That unreliable organ palpitating in her chest told her Ross's convictions were weakening again.

She ducked out of his arms, her hair catching against his watch with a tug. Sierra kept her face lowered as she stood and headed for the sink to snag a dishtowel. She wiped the tears and blew her nose into the towel.

She sneaked a look over the fringe of the towel. The tenderness on his face made her tears well up again. "You better go. I have to go talk to Braden."

"Sierra—"

"Could you lock the door on your way out?" She ran up the stairs, her mind hollering *coward* as she passed Braden's door. When the front door closed quietly, she slipped down to her room and crawled under the covers. She didn't move until morning light crept over the window sash and inched across the floor.

Sid was waiting when they walked through the front door. Trevor settled in his usual spot under Sid's protective arm. "Hello, there, young fella."

"Morning. I'll get oatmeal and eggs going." Sierra patted Sid's arm on her way to the kitchen. Soon a small bowl's worth of oatmeal bubbled in a saucepan as she pulled the eggs from the fridge.

Sierra hollered toward the living room. "Oatmeal's ready, Sid."

A few minutes later he hobbled in and settled himself at the table.

She set the salt and pepper in front of him along with the small bowl of brown sugar.

The doorbell rang just then. Their eyes met and Sierra raced to the front door and opened it in time to see a man hustle back inside his white delivery truck and raise dust on his race back down the driveway. A small package sat on the front porch. She snatched it up like it was a newborn abandoned to the elements and took it to the kitchen table. She grabbed a pair of scissors from the drawer and sat down at the table to cut the box open.

A wad of newspapers stuck to the packing tape and she peeled them down to the bundle wrapped in paper towels and plastic. The plastic was quickly discarded and the paper towels unrolled on the Formica table to reveal the honeysuckle, withered and dry.

Sid eyed it doubtfully. "I guess you could put it in some water."

Sierra shook her head and stuck it in her water glass. "It'd take a miracle."

Sid gave her one of his wily grins. "God's in the business of them. He brought Lazarus back from the dead."

Sierra turned away from the table to crack his eggs into the skillet. She wasn't in the mood for any more sermonizing. She scrambled them with a spatula and glanced at the older man. "What?"

Sid had that look in his eye.

The speculative gleam turned to a grin. "Tell you what, you pray and ask God to give that plant life."

"Then what?"

He picked up one of the wadded Kansas news pages and smoothed it out next to his bowl of oatmeal. "Then it'd be a miracle."

She snorted.

He eyed her, spoon halfway to his mouth, a drop of milk clinging to its underside. "Then you couldn't deny Him."

"I don't deny Him, Sid."

"You deny that He cares."

"True."

A piece of oatmeal clinging to the corner of his mouth, he chewed then swallowed. "You wouldn't be able to deny the sovereign love of Almighty God."

She opened her mouth, but could think of no rebuttal.

"So are you gonna do it?"

Sierra didn't want to ask God to give the plant life. She'd feel silly and hypocritical. She wanted to say no, but he looked so eager, like he'd stumbled onto the very thing to make a believer out of her again. She smiled. She could humor the old gentleman. Maybe *he'd* learn something from the experiment. She sure wasn't going to.

"Yes, Sid, I'll ask God to give the plant life."

"Every day."

She agreed. "Yes, every day."

Satisfied, he nodded, took another bite, and motioned toward the stove. "Don't forget my eggs."

The discussion was over when Ross plowed through Sid's back door. "Sierra, can you come over? I have my crew bosses' ledgers that we can compare the bills to."

In answer, Sierra lifted the spatula dripping half-cooked eggs.

Ross sighed, then grabbed another plate out of the cupboard and plopped onto the kitchen chair across from Sid. "Is this going to take long?" He stared at the middle of the table where the dead honeysuckle sat in Sid's water glass. "Nice flower. Like how you're sprucing up the place."

She saw the sly look he slid over to Sid.

Sierra dumped a heap of runny eggs on his plate and slapped a bowl of oatmeal next to them. She crossed her arms with the dripping spatula hovering near his head. "I'm ready to go," she said.

He laughed and Sid joined him. Ross stood, pried the spatula from her grip, and guided her into his chair. "Methinks the lady needs a break."

Sid laughed harder. "You always were a swift one. Got that from your mother."

Ross scraped the raw eggs back into the skillet and with little effort served up eggs for them. Sid chased his last egg around his plate with a corner of his jellied toast. "Leorna called again last night." He darted a glance toward Ross "Said she's found a couple of places that wouldn't need much upkeep."

"To buy? You're looking for a house already? What about the ponies?" Ross pointed a hand toward the barn.

"Now, don't get fired up on me, son." Sid might have thought anger drove Ross's words, but Sierra saw the bewilderment in his expression.

"Sid, those ponies are your life. How can you abandon them?" *Abandon me?* Sierra heard in the echo.

Chapter 24

"That was not right, Sid." Sierra let the sentence hang and waited for him to bite.

"What does that mean?" The scowl had simmered into an outright glower in the minutes since Ross had excused himself on the pretext of getting the office ready for her.

"You took the coward's way to tell Ross you're moving." She set the leftover orange juice in the fridge. "And mumbling into your plate isn't going to make anyone feel sorry for you, except maybe yourself." She cleared the dishes from the table and patted his shoulder on the way to the sink. "I know this is as hard on you as it is him, but he deserves an honest conversation with you, not some off-handed comments about a house you're buying."

He stuffed the last of the toast in his mouth, his words rounded by the food. "Has anyone told you you're the bossiest little thing?"

"You and Ross could probably write a book on it."

"You pray for that plant yet?"

He just couldn't let her have the last word. Sierra grinned at his cantankerous expression. "Yes, Sid, I prayed." Not that her prayer felt like it went any farther than the ceiling. But hey, if it made him feel better.

He harrumphed. "Well, good."

Sierra glanced over at the brown twig she'd moved to the windowsill and prayed again. She couldn't help herself.

An hour later, Sierra checked the last ledger entry against its match on the statement. "We're still missing half the paperwork, Ross. Mostly for Grainger's."

Ross ran a hand through his hair, adding more rumpled furrows. "I don't get it." His hand stilled, tufts of hair sticking up between his fingers. His voice held a hint of wonder. "Could you add up all the bills that are checked off? Just the ones we show packing lists for?"

Sierra eyed the mound and pulled the adding machine closer. "You want to read them to—never mind. Sorry."

"It's okay, Sierra." His chocolate brown eyes were firm and flowed with melt-in-your-mouth kindness. "You don't have to tiptoe around my dyslexia."

She pried her gaze away and got busy flipping pages and working up steam on the adding machine. She gave him a total.

He frowned and rubbed his brow, slowly turning to look at her. "That's the amount I had budgeted up to this point. Could you call Grainger's this morning and have them fax all the copies of the packing lists they have for us that cover their statement?"

"Sure." Sierra fingered a paper clip, trying to decide how to approach Ross without setting off an earthquake. He made as if to rise, but the softest brush of her fingers to his arm stilled him.

"Ross, can we talk about Sid?"

"What is there to talk about? Sounds like he's made up his mind."

"Would it be the end of the world if he didn't go back to training?"

"It's what he does." His voice was unyielding.

"Maybe it's what he *did*. Sid is a seventy-three-year-old man. Have you considered that maybe his age is what got him injured?"

Ross looked away and she wondered if he was blaming her, too. She laid a cautious hand on his arm. "I'm not here to tell you how to feel, Ross. But don't let your needs keep an old man from following his heart back home."

"I thought his home was here." *With me.* It wasn't hard to hear the unspoken words.

She leaned in, forcing him to meet her eyes. "You are like a son to him. He loves you more than life. Do you think it's easy for him to go back? Ross, he needs your permission to leave."

He stared at her as if she'd just said Chance had requested steak for dinner, medium rare.

"He doesn't need my permission."

"He needs it more than you realize. You should know better than to let his belligerent act fool you."

The look on his face was unreadable. "If we're finished here, I'm going to check on the job." Then he left.

Sierra stared at the closed office door. Did he realize how much Sid loved him? *How much I love him?* Confused by the thought, Sierra pushed it away. How could she fall in love with a man who didn't want her?

Ross lay on his back and stared at the ceiling. He turned his head to check the blue numerals of his clock. 3:08 a.m. Sid was moving and there was nothing he could do to change it. He shut his eyes and rolled over, trying not to think about the touch of Sierra's hand on his arm, the sincerity of her voice as she tried to convince him that Kansas was best for Sid. If he'd never hired her for Sid, Kansas wouldn't be a thought in his friend's head. Or would it?

His mind drifted to the scene of Sid lying in the pasture, broken. He had never been old and frail in Ross's eyes until that moment. Had Ross chosen to ignore what was so obvious to everyone else?

Sid was done with the ponies. Despite his amazing recovery, there would be no going back to them.

The Lord hit him with his selfishness pretty hard.

He wanted his life to slide back into comfortable. Sid right next door, always ready with a cup of coffee and a listening ear. Not to mention a well-oiled jaw.

Like a dad.

Like the relationship he wanted with his own father.

Behind those realizations were the questions Sid had alluded to. Had Sid's place in his life prevented him from discovering a relationship with his dad?

The next evening, after he knew Sierra would be gone for the day, Ross headed his pickup toward Sid's. He let himself in through the back door, calling a hello.

An answering holler came from the living room. Sid reclined on the couch, afghan over his legs. He shut off the TV and sat with the remote on his lap.

The older man worked his mouth as though he had something of import to say, his blue eyes looking everywhere but at Ross. He finally cleared his throat. "Ross. Son, I—"

Ross held up a gentle hand. "Sid, there's something I need to say."

Sid waited.

"I've been doing a lot of thinking. About you, about this farm."

Sid shifted on the couch, his eyes focused on the orange afghan.

Ross took a breath. "I've been pretty selfish."

Sid waved a hand. "Now, don't start blamin' yer—"

"I have, Sid. I wanted what was best for me. You've been the rock in my life, listening and supporting, and I've depended on that." He scratched the back of his neck. "I've been thinking about what you said about Dad. I think I found offenses where maybe there weren't any, at least not intended, and I shut him out a long time ago."

Sid's cheeks sagged, regret in the sad blue eyes. "A lot of that was my fault. If I'd—"

"You can go to Kansas."

"Well, of course I can move to Kansas. Ain't nobody telling me I can't." Bluster coated the words.

"Sid, you can move to Kansas."

The bluster lost steam as the words poured out. "You sound like a danged parrot repeating yourself. Of course, I know that, Ross. I can move to Kansas. Who's saying I can't?" Sid hunkered forward to dig a handkerchief out of his back pocket and went to wiping his nose. "You don't just make these kind of decisions on the spur of the moment. I know what I'm doing." He wiped his nose again, then blew. "Dang allergies."

"It's hard for me too, but I want you to know that I think it's a great idea."

"Were you at the nursery? I think you dragged some of that pollen in here." Sid's eyes watered, but Ross let him have his dignity.

"Yeah, I probably have some pollen on my clothes. I love you, Sid."

"Oh, for crying out loud, you'd think it was the middle of spring the way my allergies are acting up."

Ross smiled.

Chapter 25

Beaming, Sid met Sierra at the front door. Excitement sparked off the older man until Sierra thought he might have a stroke before he could get the words out.

"Mornin', Sierra. Thanks for coming on the weekend. Stella was feeling poorly." His eyes shone brighter than the chrome on his new walker.

"My mom must have gotten the same bug, so I hope you don't mind that I had to bring the whole gang with me. Their dad's going to pick them up before dinner."

"Don't mind at all." The kids dropped their shoes in a jumbled pile near the door and each gave Sid a quick squeeze, except Braden, who muttered *hello*, then scampered up the stairs with his Game Boy.

Trevor clutched the leg of the walker. "Can I push it, Sid?"

Sid laughed. "Maybe later, after I've sat down."

"'kay." Trevor climbed onto the couch next to his sister, who was already curled in the afghan and glued to the TV.

Sid's health had improved so much that Sierra now stuck his dinners in the fridge and was home by the time the kids got off the bus. The physical therapist said Sid would never play hopscotch, but he should be able to function without a walker in six months. When the therapist had suggested that Sid donate his walker to the Windy River Nursing Home, Sid had mumbled that the next home for the darn-fangled metal contraption would be the nearest ditch.

Sierra dropped her purse by the door and laid her coat on the back of the recliner. Sid nearly ran the walker into the backs of her legs in his haste to follow her into the kitchen.

His lips were clamped tight, but his aging teeth peeked through in a smile he couldn't shake.

"Okay, Sid, spill it." Sierra pulled the daily ration of oatmeal out of the cupboard and glanced at him over her shoulder. "Just what do you have up your sleeve?"

Finally, he couldn't contain himself. "Well, aren't you going to do it?"

She turned, a blue measuring cup in hand. "Do what?"

"Pray for that plant." He jabbed a pointy finger at it.

She rolled her eyes in mock exasperation. "Dear God, please give that plant life."

He shook his head, his grin wide. "Not there, girl. You need to go pray *over* it."

"So it feels the vibes?" She walked obediently to the windowsill.

Sid didn't answer. He'd changed the water at least. Poor thing wasn't soaking in brown gunk anymore.

"Closer."

She snorted. "Do you want me to lay hands on it too?"

His grin grew expectant, like he was waiting for her to stumble across some amazing discovery.

"What, Sid?"

He just stared at the plant.

Then she saw it.

Mold.

Round balls of green mold grew on the stick. Disgusting, and probably a health hazard. If Trevor got his hands on that thing, her mother would be racing for the disinfectant.

"Do you see it?"

She gave him a sad smile. Ross needed to get the man's glasses updated. Sierra gingerly picked up the honeysuckle and tossed it in the trash, then dumped the water in the sink.

Sid huffed, his face red. "What are you doing, girlie?"

"What? It was moldy."

This time Sid rolled his eyes. "That weren't no mold, Sierra."

She snatched it out of the garbage and pulled it close to her face. Miniscule white roots protruded from the bottom of the plant and what she thought was mold were tiny green buds. "Holy cow!"

Sid shook his head reverently. "No. Holy God."

"Wow." Apparently a few prayers *had* leaked out into the cosmos. Sierra stared at the bits of life showing in an otherwise dead branch. *Or* the plant hadn't been dead after all. Sierra wrestled with those thoughts the rest of the day and finally decided there had to have been a few live cells lying dormant inside the branch. But a shiver of hope resided.

What if it *had* been dead?

Sierra set three peanut-butter-and-jelly sandwiches on napkins and carried them to Sid's kitchen table. Her cell phone rang and she swiped a few crumbs into her hand and tossed them in the sink, then reached for her phone. "Hello?"

"Hi, this is Greg Adams again. We have a problem here."

Had his daughter gotten hurt? Sierra placed a palm on the counter and leaned into it. "What happened?"

He sighed. "We rented the neighbor's pasture next to us, but he has some horses that are picking on Chance."

"What?"

"They're being mean. Like bullies on a playground."

"Could you move him to another pasture?"

"That's the thing. We really like the convenience of having our horse next door."

"It's only been a few days. Maybe …"

"I don't think it's fair to Chance. The vet says he's starting to get depressed."

A horse could get depressed?

"I'd like to bring him back today."

"Bring him back? Can't you sell him? I mean, he's *your* horse now."

"That could take weeks, and we have no way of separating him from the other horses. Look, I know it's a hassle. If you want a hundred bucks or so—"

"No, that's fine. Bring him back. And, I, uh, I never cashed the check. I'll just mail it to you."

Sierra got off the phone and stared at the ceiling. *What are You doing?*

Two hours later, Braden came pounding down the stairs, his voice thrumming with excitement. "Mom! Mom! Chance is back."

Emory and Trevor flew off the couch and ran to the window. She caught a flash of teeth in a huge grin as Braden shot out the door. She followed him to the fence where, a pasture away, Chance grazed. "Can we go over there?" His eyes were so hopeful, so excited.

She bit her lip. "Honey, we're not keeping him. Mr. Adams brought him back because some horses were being mean to him."

A confused frown grew between his eyes. "We're not keeping him?"

She touched his shoulder, but he jerked away. "No, honey, we're not. I'm sorry."

"You ruin everything!" And he ran back toward the house.

Sierra stared across the field at the old gray horse. She was doing the right thing, wasn't she?

Braden stormed back up the stairs. *Mom is so stupid.* Chance wouldn't hurt him. Just because her friend died, she thought everyone was going to get killed by a horse. He grabbed his headphones off the bed where he'd tossed them and jammed them on his head then flopped on the bed next to his Game Boy. He turned up the volume. He wished his mom had never inherited the stupid horse in the first place.

He'd just pushed play to start his DeathTrain CD over for the fourth time, when a movement made him turn his head.

His mom stood in the doorway. "Didn't you hear me calling, honey? Your dad's here to take you guys to dinner." He turned his head away, so she wouldn't think he cared. He could see her out of the corner of his eye. She took a step into the room, then she turned around and left. He was glad she thought he was mad at her, but a part of him was sad, like when his dad first left. He'd tried so hard to do things right, to not fight with Emory, so his mom wouldn't get sadder. It felt like it was his fault when she did.

Braden hurried down the stairs after her, to tell her he was sorry, but his dad was waiting. He put a hand on his neck. "We've been waiting for you, son."

"Sorry. Bye, Mom."

"Bye, honey." She smiled, but her eyes looked sad and he felt the badness in his chest get bigger.

"Dad, that's our horse." Emory pointed out the window as they passed Ross's place. Braden didn't want to look, but he did anyway.

He saw his dad turn to Gina, his voice low and angry, but Braden heard every word. "I thought she was going to sell that horse."

Braden put his headphones on. Nobody understood. The heaviness in his heart got bigger on the drive across town.

In the restaurant Braden drummed his fingers on the table.

"Braden, I said to take those headphones off." His dad glared at him.

"Sor-*ry*. I didn't hear you."

His dad leaned low across the table at the Italian restaurant. "I want you to mind your manners, young man. This is family time and I want you to be a participant, not sit there and listen to your music." He saw the moment his dad had the thought. "Can I see the CD, Braden?"

"I'll put it away." He started to set it under his seat, but his dad had that look in his eye and held his hand out for it.

"Give it to me, son."

"But I won't listen—"

"Stop arguing. I don't know what your mother tolerates, but if I tell you to do something I don't want any back talk. Got it?" His dad's eyes were narrowed, like when he was really frustrated. "Now give me the CD."

"Fine." Braden pulled it out of the player and slapped it into his dad's palm.

His dad's expression lightened. "Thank you. Braden. I'm sorry I got mad, son, I just want—" His gaze dropped to the black and red disc. "DeathTrain?" His forehead pinched tight and he swung his head toward

Gina. "Did you see this?" He swung back to Braden and bounced the CD in his hand. "Does your mother know you listen—"

Gina touched his dad's arm. "Honey, maybe we can talk about this—"

Braden glared at her. "You're not my mom, so stay out of it."

A vein stuck out on his dad's neck, and he gritted his teeth together. "Don't you talk to Gina like that! I want you to apologize."

Braden looked at his plate.

His dad's voice was quiet but really mad. "Now!"

Braden stared right at his dad. He didn't care how mad he was. "It's true. She's not my mom."

His dad pointed a finger at him. "I don't know what's going on with you, Braden. But if you don't get an attitude adjustment pretty fast, you're going to find yourself in military school. And trust me, you won't be able to get away with this there."

The front door slammed shut and Sierra set the teapot down and went to greet the kids. She picked Trevor's coat off the floor and gave him a quick hug. "Shh. Grandma's not feeling well."

Emory threw her coat on the sofa. "I could draw her a picture."

"That'd be great, sweetie." She touched Braden on the shoulder. "How'd it go?"

"I don't want to talk about it." He ducked away from her hand and stomped up the stairs toward his room.

Emory's face took on the lofty expression that had tattletale attached to it. "Dad said if he doesn't shape up, he'll send him to military school."

Hot defense rose in Sierra's throat. Braden was just a kid. A good kid who'd had his most precious possession ripped away. *You can only run from fear so long.* Sid's words taunted her. How long would Braden carry this hurt and sense of betrayal with him?

Sierra followed him up the stairs. He flopped onto the bed and grabbed his Game Boy. His face was shadowed, but the hurt didn't show anymore. Maybe if she could find the hurt, she'd find her son.

"Braden, can we talk?"

His eyes flicked to her face and then back to the game. No expression. "About what?"

"I heard it didn't go very well with your dad tonight."

"So!" The word was defensive and angry.

Her son's brown eyes glared at her and she swallowed a sigh. "Has your dad taken you to the eye doctor yet?"

"No." He glanced in disgust at his wall. "Dad doesn't think there's anything wrong with my eyes."

Anger built in her chest like the bulge of a building volcano. "Well, it doesn't matter what your dad says; I want you to start wearing your eye patch."

"I don't care!"

She saw the hurt then. The resentment of putting him at odds with his dad. Sierra reached to stroke his arm, but he drew away from her.

"How are you doing with Gina's baby?"

"Fine. Can you go now?"

Emory peeked in the door, holding her cell. "It's Elise."

It was with guilty relief Sierra left his room. She lifted the phone to her ear. "Hi."

"Hey there. Just wanted to see if you were dodging all the shrapnel."

Sierra walked down the stairs to her room and sank back onto the bed. "I was just up trying to talk to Braden. He hates me right now."

"Oh, hon."

The pressure that had been building leaked. "Yeah, it's been a lovely day. Mom's sick, so I took all the kids with me to Sid's. Then Chance's new owner returned him."

Elise sounded puzzled. "Did he go with a warranty?"

"No! But some other horses were picking on him and he was getting depressed."

Elise snickered. "Couldn't they put some Prozac in his grain?"

"Funny. So Braden saw Chance in Ross's field and is devastated that we're not keeping him. But does he cry? No, he lashes out at everyone."

"Are you sure you're supposed to sell him? Maybe God brought—"

"Elise." She nibbled her fingernail. But the thought had been crossing her mind too. She dropped her hand and sighed. "And I guess Michael threatened him with military school tonight if he doesn't get his act together."

"Seriously?"

"Well, I can understand Michael's reaction. Braden's been a miserable pain in the rear. And some of his attitude bleeds off on Emory. It's been a lot of fun around here." And the thought pursued—maybe if she hadn't sold Chance...

"Right now, military school sounds pretty good. We'd at least get some peace and quiet. Did you know that you can make out every word of a hard rock song through the ceiling?"

"Oh, Sierra."

"Maybe it'd help him learn to respect his parents a little more. The toilets in his dorm would be sparkling, I'm sure."

A movement caught her eye.

She raised up and there stood Braden in her doorway, his face white except for his brown eyes wide with shock and fear ... and hatred.

"Elise, I need to go." Sierra dropped the phone on the bed.

Chapter 26

Braden sprinted through the living room. The front door ricocheted into the wall with a bang. The soles of his tennis shoes flashed as he darted down the front steps.

"Braden!"

He was a blur in the dusky evening, arms churning as he ran from Sierra across the road and into the walnut orchard.

Sierra followed into the trees, but she couldn't see him. Damp brown leaves covered the ground. Symmetrical gray trunks stood in straight lines for a great distance in every direction. She paused next to a tree, her hand pressed to the bark and listened. But the silence was still, watchful.

"Braden!" She ran farther in, darting around the trees, thankful the leaves had fallen to let in the meager light. *Please come out, baby. I'm so sorry.*

She jogged through the grove until a hurried look at her watch showed that a half hour had gone by. Maybe he'd circled back to the house.

Sierra ran out of the trees and back across the road. The front door was still open, and her heart sank. But she still checked every room of the house.

Her mom raised up when Sierra darted into her bedroom, checked the closet, and glanced under bed. "What's the matter, honey?"

"I can't find Braden."

"You think he's under the bed?"

"I need to make sure before I call the police."

"Oh, dear. I didn't realize he was that upset."

Sierra, still kneeling on the floor, clutched the bed skirt in her fists. "He thinks his dad and I are going to send him to military school." Her throat tightened and her nose burned. "I think he ran away."

Her mom threw the covers back and put her legs over the side. "He'll be home shortly. Once he gets hungry he'll show up."

Sierra nodded, grasping for the hope in her mom's words, but her gut told her Braden didn't want to come back.

Rushing back to the living room she grabbed her cell and dialed the number, watching out the window for a glimpse of Braden's blue sweatshirt along the edge of the trees.

Nothing but empty road and silent trees stared back at her.

"Hey, hon."

"Elise, I can't find Braden. I think he ran away. Please pray."

"I will, hon. I'll be praying for you, too."

Sierra's breath caught and she whispered the words. "Thank you. I need to call Michael."

Sierra pressed in the number, and he picked up on the second ring.

"Michael, it's Sierra. Braden ran away about forty-five minutes ago."

"Why? What happened?" Panic edged the blame in his voice.

She sank to the edge of the couch, her gaze still intently focused on the walnut orchard. "Emory told me what you said about sending Braden to military school. Then he heard me on the phone saying I thought it would be good for him."

"I was *threatening* him, Sierra. I wouldn't have done it."

"I know, and I was being sarcastic. But *he* doesn't know that."

Michael sighed, and she could imagine his knuckles rubbing along his jaw the way they did when he was worried. "What is going on with him?"

"His world is crashing in on him. You're having a new baby and I sold his horse."

"What does my baby have to do with this?"

"I think he feels that he's lost his place in your world. Plans you've made with him haven't worked out and he feels threatened by everyone's excitement over Gina's pregnancy. I don't think he feels needed by you anymore." Sierra tightened her grip on the phone. "And he gets pulled between us when I want him to wear the eye patch and you tell him not to. It's not been easy for him." Her nails dug into her palm. "He finally seemed to be finding himself again before I sold Chance."

"Have you called the police?"

"No. I wanted to call you first."

"Call them right now. I'll start driving around. Call me if he comes back."

"I will." But would he come back?

The knock on the door was firm. Sierra opened it to two police officers.

"Mom, there's a police car in the drive—" Emory stopped on the bottom step, her eyes huge.

"Honey, go put a movie on for you and Trevor. I'll talk to you in a few minutes."

Her daughter gave a ghost of a nod, her eyes never leaving the uniforms as she slowly backed out of sight.

The officers stepped into the living room, the crispness of the evening air following them in. The men sat on the edge of the couch, and Sierra took the recliner with her mom perched on its wide arm. The bald officer with the penetrating eyes held his pen still. "Why do you think he ran away?"

Sierra leaned forward. "He was angry. Hurt. He overheard me tell a friend I might send him to military school."

The officer gave her an assessing look before jotting on his notepad. "Ma'am, do you think he'd harm himself?"

"No. No, I don't think so. There have been some hard adjustments for him. I just sold his horse and his stepmother is pregnant." *Why don't they grab his picture and start searching?*

The blond officer interjected. "Has he run away before?"

"No."

"Could we get your ex-husband's information? We'd like to talk with him also."

Abbey patted her back. "I'll get the address book, honey." She hurried toward the kitchen.

"Ma'am, do you mind if we search your house and vehicles? Sometimes children will hide close by." The men offered comfort with their authoritative presence, but she also felt the weight of their scrutiny.

"I already looked, but that's fine if you need to. Please hurry." She glanced out the front window, where dusk was swiftly passing to inky night.

Ten minutes later the door closed behind the men. Her mom covered her mouth with a hand, her eyes sparkling with tears and she whispered, "He'll be fine, honey. I'll go check on the kids."

All security and hope had walked out the door with the officers. Where was her son? Then it dawned on her. *Chance!*

She ran to the kitchen for her cell phone and dialed Ross's number.

"Hello?"

"Are you home? Could you check the pasture for Chance?"

"Actually, I'm just about to pass your house."

"Braden ran away. I think he may have gone to Chance."

Within minutes, she opened the door and Ross enveloped her in his arms. The comfort she expected didn't come. There was a bleeding hole in her heart that couldn't be filled until she found her son.

Sierra swallowed. "I'm going to run up to your house and see if Chance is there."

He nodded. "I'll go through the orchard. He might have gotten turned around."

"Thanks." She brushed her sleeve against her nose and sniffed.

"I'll get you an extra flashlight from my truck." He wiped a tear from her cheek. "Call me when you get there."

Sierra drove the highway toward Ross's. *Please be there. Please be there.* Her eyes tried to penetrate the blackness of the fields and ditches, desperate to land on a figure in a blue sweatshirt and jeans. Could he have walked this far? Had someone grabbed him? Was he to Portland by now, trapped and scared in the passenger seat of a stranger's car?

Her breath came in gasps and she blinked back the tears that distorted her vision.

She turned up Ross's drive and sped toward the edge of the pasture, the headlights aimed straight out toward empty field. She raced to the fence and climbed it next to a wooden post, the wire bending under her weight. She landed with a thud in the grass and ran through the field shouting, "Braden! Braden! Braden!"

After ten minutes she stumbled, panting hard. Ross's house was a dim light far across the field. It started to rain. Not a solid downpour that drenched icy against the skin but a steady misting, like raining fog that clung, feeling light at first but steadily weighing down her clothes, until her sweater sagged against her body.

Sierra fell against a tree, crying. Crying for herself, crying for Braden. She straightened, rain running down her hair and into her eyes. Sierra fisted her hands tight at her sides and yelled at the dark sky. "Where are You, God?"

Had God turned His back on her as a twelve-year-old girl, when her dad died? Would a loving God abandon His child? Would He abandon Braden? Ragged breaths clawed at her chest. She needed to find out or she wasn't going to make it. "Please, take me to Braden."

She ran back through the wet field, climbed the gate to the driveway, and headed directly for the barn. She flipped on the light and the dim yellow bulbs lit the way to the tack room. She brushed her hand over the saddle, and her eyes went immediately to the empty hooks on the wall.

Sierra ran back outside and slipped into the van. She grabbed the phone and dialed Ross's number, steam rising from her dampness in the warmth of the car. Phone to her ear, she started the car and backed it around.

He answered immediately. "Is he there?"

"No, but Chance is gone and so is his bridle."

"Okay, then we need to scour the fields around my place."

"I'm going left out of your driveway."

"Good. I'll head—"

"Ross?" Sierra pressed the phone tighter to her ear. "Ross?" She pressed her thumb to redial, but nothing happened. A quick glance showed that the screen was black. She tossed it on the seat next to her. *I need help, Lord. Please help me find him.*

She slowly followed the winding road toward the country, the flashlight's beam aimed out the driver's window reflecting off the passing bushes and trees.

Turn.

Sierra looked left and saw a slight opening ahead in the brush. Not really wide enough for a vehicle. She shone the light on the pasture to the right of the car.

Turn!

The urgency caught her and she pulled the wheel left, just making the opening between the trees. Branches screeched against the side of the van, and her headlights bounced crazy patterns against the brush. What was she doing? The road was barely a dirt path. Braden would never have ventured into such dense growth.

Why had she turned? The word hadn't been audible, but it had been unmistakable. *God?*

She saw the headlights reflect off the massive puddle too late. Sierra slammed the brake, but the van sprayed water and the front end pitched deep to the right. She put the vehicle in reverse, but the tires whirred against the mud. She jammed the gearshift into *park,* the engine still running.

She flipped on the overhead light grabbed her cell phone and pressed the button to turn it on, her thumbnail turning white. *Please, God. Please. Braden needs me.*

The screen remained black. Her heart was going to explode. Terror pressed against her making it difficult to breathe. Sierra wailed. "God, help me! Please, help me." Sobbing, she pounded the steering wheel with her fists.

Finally, she shut the car off, grabbed the flashlight and opened the driver's door. How long would it take to jog back to Sid's and borrow his car? She stepped into water that came midway up her calf and slogged to the edge of the trail.

Sierra took a couple of stumbling steps toward the highway and stopped. It was as if she could hear an urgent whisper just beyond her ears.

A sense that she needed to turn toward the other end of the lane where the night grew a shade lighter.

She took another step toward the highway, but the urgency grew stronger.

The slow building of hope in her heart urged her to turn around. A long dormant flame had whispered to life. *Was God leading her?*

She barely dared to breathe as she loped, the unsteady bounce of the flashlight warning her of rocks and branches. She reached the end of the path and paused, then clicked the light off with her finger.

Her eyes slowly adjusted to the small meadow, shadowed by the hazy moon far beyond the clouds and drizzle. Sierra scanned the far reaches of the field, her eyes straining to see into the darkness.

Her breath caught.

They stood motionless under a bare oak tree, vaguely outlined against the sky. Braden sat hunched over Chance's neck, defeat and exhaustion in the slump of his shoulders.

I am Father to the fatherless.

The words plunged deep within her heart and anchored. God was her Father. She'd found Him, though He'd never left her.

Sierra started across the field. Relief flowed through every pore, calm where there'd been fear. She gazed at Chance, his head hanging. That beautiful horse and her son were safe.

Sierra stopped next to the pair and touched her son's leg. "Braden, honey?"

Braden startled, then slid off the horse. She wrapped her arms around him, and he grabbed her sweater and burrowed his face in her chest as he sobbed.

She realized fear was not a fence to guard her children; it had become a prison they'd fight to be free from. The crying stopped, but still he sagged into her arms. She rocked him slowly. "I love you, Braden."

His voice was muffled. "I love you, too."

"Do you want to talk about it?"

He shook his head.

She couldn't stop the tears that kept streaming down her cheeks. She stroked his hair. "Then how about I talk. Okay?"

He nodded his face against her sweater.

"I'm sorry your dad and I divorced. I know it's been hard on you guys. Sometimes grown-ups make decisions that are difficult to understand."

He sniffled.

"Your dad isn't trying to hurt you by having a baby with Gina. He loves you and Emory and Trevor very much. A new baby doesn't squeeze that love out. Hearts have plenty of room to grow and love more people."

Braden leaned back to look at her. "But what if it's a boy?"

She smiled through the tears. "Then he'll have a wonderful big brother to teach him all sorts of cool things."

"Dad's going to send me to military school."

She cupped his cold cheeks. "Braden, your father loves you. He sees how angry you are, and he doesn't know how to talk to you about it, so he tried to scare you into obeying. He didn't mean it."

Sierra watched him process that information.

He nodded once, shivering. "'kay. But you said you were going to send me there too."

She breathed in the frigid air. "I was frustrated and let words come out of my mouth that shouldn't have. I'll never send you to military school." She bent so their faces were inches a part. "Sweetheart, I love you. But I'm not a perfect mom." She touched his nose. "Just like you're not a perfect boy. But I love you that way."

Braden nodded while Sierra straightened to stare at the horse beside them, wiping away the remaining tears with her wrist. "We need to get to a phone, honey. Everyone's out looking for you."

Braden reached out and stroked Chance's neck. "Can we ride him back, Mom?" His voice held the limp defeat of a boy who already knew the answer.

A heartbeat of a pause. Chance turned his head, as if waiting for Sierra's response. Would she let fear continue to confine her kids? Braden was freezing. They needed to get back soon. She blew out an unsteady breath. "Okay."

Braden's head jerked up. "Awesome! Will you ride with me, Mom?" Eagerness tilted his head.

Her legs trembled. Could she do this? Would she trust her Father to keep them safe? "I'll try, Braden."

Braden grabbed Chance's mane and braced himself. Sierra lifted him around the waist and he scrambled until his leg crossed the horse's bare back. She shone the flashlight around and illuminated a large, malformed boulder sticking out of the grass.

Holding the wet reins, she led Chance to the rock, each nudge of the horse's hairy lips at her back sending a spark of anxiety up her spine. After two attempts, she managed to climb from the rock onto the wet animal. Chance's hide quivered beneath her legs, and Sierra reached around Braden to clutch the horse's mane. A sob escaped from her lungs into a gust of wind.

Braden clucked his tongue and Chance lurched forward. "This is so cool, Mom!"

Sierra's teeth chattered.

"Mom, you're squeezing me too tight."

"Sor-ry." Sierra closed her eyes and held onto her son.

It took Sierra and Braden a bone-jarring fifteen minutes to ride back to the barn. Sierra slid from Chance's back on numb legs. Braden looked drained but lighter. She made the first call from the barn to Michael.

Relief sagged in his voice. "Braden's all right? Can I talk to him?"

Sierra held the phone to her chest and called Braden from Chance's stall. "Your dad wants to talk to you."

He looked scared, but he took the phone. "Hello?" He listened quietly for a long time.

Braden's voice was low, but Sierra caught the words. "I'm sorry too, Dad." Another long pause. "Okay. I love you, too. Bye."

Braden handed her the phone. "Dad wants to talk to you."

"Hello."

Michael's voice was quiet. "I did a lot of thinking tonight as I drove around, not knowing if I'd get another chance to tell him I loved him—that I was sorry. Can I come get him, Sierra? Tonight? Right now?"

Her heart clenched. She'd just found Braden. She wanted to rush home and hold him close as he fell asleep. How could Michael ask?

Braden danced next to her, his upturned face hopeful.

"Sure, Michael. It's one driveway east of where you picked the kids up this afternoon."

"I'll be there in ten minutes."

Braden beamed. "Dad wants me and him and Gina to sit down and talk. He said he was sorry about disappointing me so much. And he won't ever send me to military school."

Sierra leaned and pulled him close, resting her cheek against his cold, damp face. "Your dad loves you a lot."

"Mom?" He leaned back, his arms still around her waist, eyes sad but accepting. "Are you still selling Chance?"

She glanced toward the stall where Braden had stabled Chance and smiled. "No, honey, I'm not."

Sierra sat on the ground next to the barn after Michael had driven away and she'd made the calls to let everyone know Braden was safe. Michael had offered to take her home, but it didn't feel right to climb in with the three of them. They needed to start their journey together without dragging the past along even a few short miles.

Twin lights turned off the highway and headed up Ross's drive. She rose and walked toward the house, the headlights sweeping across her as Ross turned toward his carport. The pickup stopped and the driver's door rocketed open. "Sierra?"

She walked toward him, the steady ding-ding of his open door pricking the silent night. "Hi."

Ross was next to her in three long steps. He wrapped her close in a tight squeeze. "Braden's okay?" He released her and looked toward the barn. "Is he in with Chance?"

"He's good. He's with his dad."

Ross walked alongside Sierra to the house. She seemed peaceful and fragile at the same time. He guided her toward his guest bathroom and grabbed a clean shirt and sweatpants for her to put on, then left her alone to go make coffee. When he carried two steaming cups to the family room, he found her tucked into the corner of the couch, her feet under her.

He sat at the other end. "Are Emory and Trevor okay?"

She looked down at her hands. "Yes. Mom just put them to bed."

He let the silence stretch. She shifted positions and attempted a smile, but it wobbled a bit. He reached for her foot and encased her icy toes with his palms. He rubbed the arch, trying to warm her up. "Are you okay, Sierra?"

She sniffed and brushed a knuckle to her nose. "I just realized some things tonight. Like that God never left me like I thought He did. And Braden's found his dad." She nodded to herself. "I think they're going to be fine."

"And the tears?"

The words came out softly. "Talking to God tonight, I caught a glimpse of the security of a father's love. And then seeing Michael finally catch onto what Braden needs?" She smiled through the tears. "It was wonderful. It just made me think about my dad." Her face crumpled. "I never got to say good-bye."

He held her to his chest and let her cry.

Chapter 27

Sierra rolled up to Ross's house and stopped next to his pickup. He leaned against its side, waiting. Braden jumped out of the van first and went up to Ross. The man wrapped an arm around his shoulders, but his eyes stayed on Sierra, a certain expectancy in their depths.

Her face heated from their warmth.

Ross spoke first, "Glad to see you washed all that mud off the van."

Braden grinned. "Trevor and I did it."

Sierra smiled. Ross and Kyle had rescued her filthy van from the brushy trail the morning after Braden's adventure. A few uneven streaks of dirt attested to the helpful wash job. Sierra had never been prouder.

Braden beamed up at Ross, the tie-dyed eye patch that Gina had made looked trendy on his smiling face. "Ross, guess what? My dad and I are going to a Blazer game this weekend, and we got to see a picture of the baby yesterday. It's a girl. Dad and Gina are going to let us help name her."

Ross brushed Braden's hair with his hand. "That's great, buddy."

Emory waited patiently beside him. "And Gina's going to let me baby-sit." She qualified her statement: "When I'm older."

Sierra held a package out to Ross.

A pleased smile lit his face. "What's this?"

The kids clamored closer and Braden said, "Open it."

Emory grinned at him. "You're gonna be so surprised."

"It's 'cause of Chance." Trevor stated.

His smile grew puzzled, but he tore the gift paper away from the box, then gently lifted the small pink pot dotted with red flowers from the box. Emory had picked it out. A brown branch with tiny green leaves was planted in rich loam. "What's this?"

Braden couldn't contain himself. "The honeysuckle."

Ross smiled at Sierra. "You didn't need to get me another one." But she could tell he was pleased.

"It's from the heirloom plant."

He tilted his head.

"From Kansas," Sierra went on. "Sid helped me get it."

"You got this all the way from Kansas? *How* ...? Lady, my mother is going to love you." He whooped and caught her up in a big hug. When he stopped spinning her, his eyes sparkled into hers for one long moment, then he planted a kiss on her mouth. Fast, but long enough to leave an impression.

Braden covered his eyes and pretended to gag. Emory giggled.

The kids were soon loaded in the van, but Sierra lingered by her door. "What was with the look when I drove up?"

The confident grin came back.

"What?"

He took her hand and pulled her against his chest. "Isn't there something you wanted to tell me?"

Sid and the phone call he promised to make to lure Ross home came to mind. Apprehension crept up her spine with little tingles. "Tell you what?"

"Sid told me what you said."

Her voice grew faint. "What was that?"

He brushed his knuckles under her chin and his thumb stroked her cheek, his eyes fathomless. "How you feel about me."

The horn honked. "Mom, come on!"

Chapter 28

Sierra called him when she got home, unable to keep the laughter from her voice. "Sid Barrows! You matchmaking hooligan! I can't believe you told Ross I had feelings for him."

His chuckle rasped over the phone line. "Did it work?"

"Sid, I never told you any of that."

"But it's true."

She paused a beat. "That's for him to figure out, not get pushed into it by a meddling old varmint like you."

His laughter bellowed through the phone. "You'll be thanking me some day."

"You're incorrigible, you know that?" But she could hardly wait to see Ross again.

Wednesday evening Ross rubbed his jaw as he headed toward Sid's for a man-to-man, the day-old whiskers rasping against his fingers. Maybe his friend *thought* Sierra had feelings for him, but Sid hadn't seen the shock on Sierra's face when Ross'd made a fool of himself repeating his friend's words. She'd jumped in her van and hightailed it away from him, just as fast as she could go.

He climbed into his pickup, exhausted as much from spending the afternoon working at Alex's as from trying to avoid thoughts of Sierra. His cell phone rang and he snatched it off the dash, hoping it might be her. "Ross here."

A pause. "Hi, Ross. It's Dad."

Ross's stomach turned over. "Hi, Dad. What's up?"

"Are you free this evening? I'd like to come over."

Ross's chest started to pound. He turned the key in the ignition and glanced toward Sid's where the living room light glowed. He thought again about his friend's concern that he'd come between Ross and his dad. "Sure, that would be fine. I'll be home in a few minutes."

"Do you want to clean up first?"

That was the kind of comment that used to send Ross into a slow burn. He assumed his dad was rubbing in how dirty Ross got on the job, contrasting with how he and Craig could go straight from the law office to the finest dining in town. But he let the comment settle. He turned it over and realized he couldn't find anything to it other than courteousness.

"Yeah, let me take a shower. See you in about thirty?"

Ross swallowed the last bite of his omelet as his dad pulled up. Bachelor dinner, breakfast style. He dumped the plate into the sink and walked barefoot to the front door.

His dad stood on the porch, hands in his pockets, his face pinched and nervous. He nodded once. "Ross."

Ross stepped back for his dad to enter. He led him into the family room. "I've made some changes to the place."

His dad assessed the room, approval in his gaze. "Looks nice."

Ross accepted the compliment. "How's Mom?"

His dad gave the barest grin. "You should know, you talk to her every day."

"Not quite. I think she just likes calling the old house."

"No, it's you she misses, not the house." A pause, then, "I need to talk to you."

"Have a seat." Ross picked the recliner, his dad the couch.

His dad leaned forward, his forearms on his knees. "You're doing a job for Alex Cranwell." It wasn't a question.

Ross felt his back stiffen. *Here it comes.* "Yes, I am."

"There are some rumors going around town about how he runs his business. Some of my clients are saying he takes advantage of his contractors. I can't go into detail, but I just wanted you to be careful."

The words resounded. *"I can't go into detail."* His dad cared enough to bend the rules of attorney-client confidentiality to warn him. No wonder the man was nervous. A week ago, Ross would have bit his head off for dampening some of the glory when his dreams were finally in reach.

And yet his dad still came.

Ross leaned forward and clasped his hands loosely. "I've been having some trouble getting him to pay on some substantial change orders. He's promised me a few commercial contracts when this job is done, and I don't want to mess that up."

His dad relaxed into the couch, a finger pressing into the armrest. "There's no guarantee when you're working with someone like him. Some things just aren't worth it."

Ross absorbed the words. If he quit working for Alex, he'd be right back where he started, except for the loss of all the time and money he'd put into the job. But everything his dad said lined up with the nagging voice he'd been ignoring at the back of his mind the past few weeks. Was he really getting ahead by working for Alex? "You're right, Dad." He glanced at the clock to the left of his big screen. "The Sonics are playing right now. I can make the popcorn."

His dad smiled and reached for his cell. "Let me call your mom."

Ross went to the kitchen and pulled out the old aluminum bowl.

The next morning, Ross called Grainger's and asked about the receipts he'd never received. They assured him they'd try faxing them again.

He was waiting by the machine when it started cranking out the paperwork. He picked up the first one, then the second. He sorted through the whole batch. Only half the signatures for receipts were from his crew.

Ross headed for his truck.

He roared up the driveway and caught Alex Cranwell as he backed from the garage. Ross parked behind the Mercedes, blocking the way.

Alex leaned out the window with a puzzled look. "Morning, Ross."

Ross nodded. "How's Clive Roberts these days?"

Alex smiled, a hard glint in his eye. "Clive's doing just fine, Ross. He's breaking ground for me on the Fern Ridge development. Speaking of, I need you to stop by the office and sign those papers."

"Clive's stealing from me, and I'd guess you wouldn't be too surprised to hear about that."

Alex licked his lips like the wolf he was. "Now, Ross old boy, you're learning the ropes of working in the big time. I'll call Clive and tell him that you've been generous enough. And we'll call it square. Don't forget to come by and sign those papers."

"I'm done." Ross started walking back to his pickup.

He heard the click of Alex's door opening. "You're making a big mistake, Ross. You won't get another opportunity like this. I'll make sure of it. Contractors are a small family, and if one of them starts to smell, no one will touch him."

Ross whipped around and strode back to the car. "I won't work for a thief."

"You're a little wet behind the ears, boy."

Ross smiled, then, "You'll pay me for Grainger's and for the work on this job."

"Or what?"

He just stared at the ugly sneer on Alex's face. "You'll hear from my attorney." He tossed one of his dad's business cards into the gold car.

Ross climbed in his truck and backed it around, feeling lighter with each telephone pole he passed on the way back down the gravel driveway. He didn't need Alex. He'd build his business the old-fashioned way. Hard work and integrity never gave anyone a sleepless night.

That afternoon Sierra swung into the parking lot at the Shadow Hills Stable. Ross pulled Sid's dark green pickup and silver horse trailer into a spot near the arena. As she parked, her mom twisted to look over her shoulder to the rear seats. "Now kids, I want you to—"

Sierra interrupted. "Mom, I'll take care of it."

"I know you will, honey." Her mom slid her hands into brown leather gloves. "Emory don't forget your coat. It's cold out there."

Sierra laid a hand on her mom's arm and waited for eye contact. "I want you to do what you do best, which is loving my kids more than any grandma can. But I'll be the mom." She gave her a gentle smile. "Okay?"

Her mom's expression was one of surprise, but she nodded. "That's fine, honey."

Standing up for herself hadn't been hard at all and it actually felt … wonderful. "Great. Now, kids, grab your coats. We're going to go watch Braden rock this arena." She attributed the pounding of her heart to excitement for Braden and not the fact that she was about to see Ross for the first time since their kiss.

Across the lot, Ross unlatched the rear door of Sid's trailer and swung it wide. Her son climbed inside and the gleaming gray body of Chance soon emerged, Braden at his head. She caught Ross's glance and waved at him, but he turned away without a trace of acknowledgment to swing the door closed and relatch it.

Had Ross really ignored her? Sierra no longer felt the chill of the air as she walked up to stand beside him. "Hi."

He barely cut her a glance. "Hi." Then he moved toward her son. "Hey, Braden do you see your 4-H leader anywhere?"

Braden glanced around. "No, not yet."

Ross nodded then spoke to him again. "I'm going to help Sid out of the truck." He disappeared around the other side of the trailer.

Her mom whispered near her shoulder. "Didn't he like the honey-suckle?"

Sierra nodded slowly, replaying the scene of yesterday's kiss and then her abrupt exit after Braden started honking the horn. When Ross reemerged, her eyes followed him, broad shoulders encased in a black jacket, helping Sid maneuver his walker toward them. She felt a tiny grin form as the realization hit. He really didn't know how she felt. She took a deep breath and squared her shoulders.

She'd just have to do something about that.

Chapter 29

"Hi, Sid." Sierra said, watching Ross hurry back toward the trailer after delivering the older man over to her mom and kids.

"Ross is in a foul mood and I don't think it has anything to do with the realtor sign in my front lawn." He gave her a meaningful look.

"Don't look at me. I'm not the one who meddled."

"Well, what're you gonna do about it?"

Sierra watched Ross busy himself around the trailer, then glance around the yard, looking everywhere but at the group of them off to his side. "I'm not sure yet," she said and started toward the trailer.

"How's it going?" She moved next to Ross and her shoulder grazed his.

He stepped away from her and checked the trailer latch. "Just finishing up here."

"Need any help?" She studied his profile, set in hard lines.

"Nope." He walked over to where Braden was adjusting Chance's saddle and placed a hand on her son's shoulder. "How're you doing?"

Braden shrugged. He was wearing the new Western shirt his grandma had given him, trying so hard to look like a man, but with a self-conscious nonchalance that told her he was checking to see if anyone noticed.

Ross spoke quietly to Braden. "I'm proud of you. You've worked hard to be here."

"And you've worked even harder to get him here." Sierra moved close and touched Ross's arm. "You've done so much for us. 'Thanks' doesn't come close to covering it."

Ross crossed his arms and Sierra had to drop her hand. "Braden's a great kid." He did look at her this time, but there was none of the warmth from yesterday.

Braden moved around to the other side of Chance, and they were alone. Sierra whispered, "What's wrong, Ross? Yesterday—"

His face hardened. "Yesterday you made it pretty clear—"

"Braden. I'm glad you made it." A woman bustled over, papers in hand, her breath blowing little puffs in the air. "Here's the schedule of events and the patterns for showmanship and the trail course that you'll need to look over." The bun at the back of her head bounced as she talked, her eyes scouring the busy yard. "You're entered in the flag race, the trail course, and of course, showmanship." Her gaze moved back to Braden, and she gave his shoulder a friendly pat and nodded to a tall girl with a dark ponytail beside her. "Nissa's horse is lame, so she's going to stick with you and show you where to go." Her glance took in the rest of them. "Nice to see you, folks."

Sierra crossed her arms tight against the chill and looked at Ross, but he'd already turned away. *If he wanted clear, she'd make certain her feelings were clear.*

Ross helped Sid into the arena and up the stairs into the cold stands. He maneuvered so Sid sat on one side of him and Emory on the other, with

Sierra's mom on the other side of Sid, but somehow Sierra ended up in the tiny spot between him and Emory, her thigh pressed to his. He tried to shift his weight away from her, but Sid gave him a look and said, "Yer crowding me. Scoot down a hair." He leaned around Ross and gave Sierra a sly grin. "You don't mind if ol' Ross here crowds up against you, do you now?"

"No, he can scoot all he wants." The smile she gave Ross was warm and teasing.

He can scoot all he wants? Women had a reputation for being hard to figure out and now he knew why.

Sierra glanced away. "Oh, Em. There's your dad and Gina." Three rows ahead of them, the couple he met at the hospital found their way to an empty spot.

"Can I go sit with them?" Emory gave her mom a pleading look.

"Sure, honey." Sierra held her daughter's hand as Emory stepped across the benches, then she sat back down and caught Ross's gaze on her again. A smile budded on her lips. "You look incredibly handsome, Ross. Black does great things for you."

"Thanks." He held her stare and the pink in her cold cheeks brightened.

A shy smile crept over her lips, but she kept her eyes on his. "It's so cold in here. Could you, um, would you warm up my hands?"

"Excuse me?"

"Never mind." The color in her cheeks grew darker and she looked down, her dark hair swinging forward, shielding her face from him.

He heard Sid snort beside him, but when he glanced at the man, his face was carefully neutral.

She did look cold. Ross held out his hand and she placed one icy hand in it. He slowly rubbed it between his hands, and she seemed to relax some. "Better?"

"Mmm. You could toast bread in your hands."

He chuckled and reached for her other hand. When it seemed as toasty as the first one, her fingers curled over to entwine with his. He darted a glance at her, but she was still staring into the arena. Her thumb started to rub over his in a gentle circle. *A day ago, she hadn't wanted to kiss him, but now she wanted to hold his hand?* He needed some fresh air.

"I'm going to check on Braden." He stood, letting her hand slide from his, and stepped over Sid's outstretched leg. At the bottom of the arena, he stuck his hands in his pockets and walked over to lean against the wall.

What was going on? Yesterday, Sierra had made it clear he'd crossed a line. But today he was getting a whole different vibe. Maybe he was reading into it too much. Nervous as she was with horses, maybe she wanted to be near him for comfort. As a friend. Someone who cared for her son as she did.

Ross didn't do more than study Braden waiting for his turn, and when the horses started filing for the ring, he climbed back into the stands. The space between Sierra and Sid seemed narrower than when he left. He sat down, pinched between the two of them. Funny how Sid's thigh wasn't nearly as warm against his as Sierra's.

The horses lined up across the arena, Braden's third from the end. The first girl in line walked her horse halfway across the ring toward a waiting man.

The stands grew quiet and Sierra leaned close, her breath warm on his cheek. "What are they doing?"

Ross turned, but she hadn't moved and her face was tantalizingly close, her eyes warm pools that focused intently on his. He cleared his throat. "This is showmanship. Each exhibitor will take a turn walking out to the judge there in the center and stand the horse square for inspection. The judge will ask some questions and then the exhibitor will have his horse do a 180-degree haunch turn and then jog him back to the lineup."

When the fourth exhibitor had jogged back to his starting position, Sierra put her hand on his arm and leaned against his shoulder to whisper. "Why is Chance standing like that?"

Ross leaned forward as if studying the horse and put some breathing distance between him and Sierra. The old horse's head was lowered and a back leg cocked, with the tip of the hoof resting on the ring floor. "He's sleeping."

Sierra swung her head toward him. "Will Braden lose points?"

He pulled his eyes from hers and focused on the horses below them. "No. Older horses do that sometimes. The judges don't penalize them."

When Braden walked Chance to the center of the ring, Sierra started chewing on a fingernail. She leaned into Ross, her eyes never leaving her son. "Is he doing okay?"

"Yeah, he's doing fine," he said, feeling the soft weight of her arm pressing against his. And Braden was. The haunch turn wasn't the prettiest, but it worked.

Sierra had a million questions as they waited through the Western equitation and other events before the flag race. And the questions came with sparkling eyes, soft touches, and a smile that could knock a man off his feet. He needed to get out of there.

Finally the barrel and its flag mounted in a coffee can were arranged at the far end of the arena.

Her hand touched his and she pointed to Braden waiting for his turn. "He looks nervous."

Braden held Chance's reins too tight, and the horse started backing toward a bay gelding behind him. The girl, Nissa, laid a hand on Braden's leg and spoke to him. Chance stopped and Braden leaned forward and relaxed his hands.

Finally, Braden and Chance jogged to the starting line. Sierra leaned forward, rigid, her fingers finding Ross's and tightening around them.

Braden and Chance made a few warm-up circles to gain speed, then took off between the starting poles and flew toward the barrel. Braden rounded it perfectly, grabbed the flag, and kicked back toward the finish line and across, flag held high. He nodded toward the judge and jogged toward the edge of the arena.

Sierra ripped her hand from Ross's and started clapping. She stood and gave an ear splitting whistle, shocking the daylights out of Ross, but it caught Braden's attention and he looked toward the stand, his face proud as he exited the building.

Sierra sat down, her face animated. "Did you see that?" She leaned past his chest, one hand on his knee. "Mom! Wasn't he great?"

Abbey was clapping with a proud-grandma smile on her face. "Oh, honey. He was just wonderful."

Sierra squeezed Ross's knee and grinned at him, her eyes sparkling, her face way too close to his. "Do you think he was fast enough to place?"

Ross nodded and tried to look away, but he couldn't seem to tear his eyes from hers. He managed to say, "I'd be surprised if he didn't get at least a red ribbon."

Sid dipped his head toward them. "That boy could join a rodeo."

Sierra leaned across him again. "I haven't served you a rutabaga yet, Sid Barrows, but if you mention rodeo to Braden, you'll have them coming out your ears."

That got a guffaw from the old man.

Ross cleared his throat as Sierra settled back into her seat and glanced at his watch. Only one more event to get through, and the coordinators were finally starting to set it up.

Sierra turned to him, her hand burning into his knee, her smile warm. "What are they doing now?"

Ross cleared his throat again and shifted on the seat, but her hand didn't budge. "This is the trail course. The rider has to show that his horse will remain calm at each of the obstacles he comes to. They get points for how well they do."

She nodded, her eyes never leaving his. "Oh."

He broke eye contact and turned back to the ring, watching the setup, something he'd seen hundreds of times.

Braden was the fifth exhibitor. He walked Chance across the bridge and up to the mailbox. Chance stood quietly as Braden opened the box, removed the mail, waved it at the judge, and then returned it to the box. He jogged the horse over several poles, then tried to back Chance between four poles positioned in a difficult "L" shape, but Braden couldn't get him to back right and the gray horse stepped over a pole.

Sierra started chewing her fingernail, a worried frown in her profile.

Braden zigzagged him beautifully between four cones. The only obstacle left was a freestanding gate.

Ross bent toward Sierra. "He'll do a side pass, which will get Chance to stand still next to the gate so Braden can open it."

But Chance wasn't cooperating. The horse wanted to stop in front of the gate. When Braden clucked him forward, the horse kept going past it. Braden took him in a circle back to the gate. Again Chance stopped in front of it. Braden looked like he was squeezing his legs, but Chance wouldn't move. Instead, he just reached his head forward, lifted his big hairy lips, and took the bolt between his teeth and slid it to the side, then nudged the gate open with his nose and walked through.

"No way!" Ross raised from his seat. *Chance opened the gate?* He swung toward Sierra, who stood next to him, hands over her mouth.

Sierra's eyes laughed up at him over her hands. She socked him in the shoulder, then ran her knuckles down his sleeve. "And all this time, you blamed us!"

The crowd erupted in laughter as Braden looked toward the judge and shrugged his shoulders.

Sierra wrapped one arm around Ross's waist and leaned into him, laughing. "Can you believe that, Ross?"

There were several things he couldn't believe at that moment. But as a pair of big brown eyes slid from his, he decided he was going to find out why.

Sierra chewed her nail and followed the broad black-clad shoulders out of the stands. Ross had barely looked at her during the events. Maybe she'd misread *him* yesterday and the kiss was just an impulsive thank-you.

Ross stopped, his back solid and set as he spoke abruptly to her mother. "Can you watch the kids for a second, Abbey?"

"Sure. We'll just walk Sid to the pickup."

Ross took Sierra's arm and rushed her ahead of her family, then outdoors around the side of the arena.

He stopped by a secluded corner of the building under an overhang, confusion and a hint of anger in his face. "What were you doing in there?"

"What do you mean?" She couldn't look at him.

His voice was intense. "You know what I mean. It was like you were flirting."

"I made a huge mistake, okay?" She felt like an utter fool. "I'm sorry, Ross. Can we just go—"

He looked perplexed. "*Were* you flirting with me?

"It was a lame attempt, but you don't have to worry about it happening again."

He took a step closer, his voice low. "Why, Sierra?"

She looked over his shoulder at a stand of trees, limbs bare and naked, exposed to the elements. Pretty much how she felt right at that minute.

She cleared her throat and moved back a step, tucking a strand of hair behind her ear. "I thought …"

He took a step closer. She was having a difficult time breathing. She stared down at the silver zipper of his jacket inches from her face. A gentle finger touched her cheekbone and moved down along her jaw. His thumb brushed back and forth across her chin. "Because when a woman flirts it usually means something."

She kept staring at his coat zipper. "And what does it mean?"

"It means she's interested." A heartbeat of a pause. "Are you interested in me, Sierra?"

She lifted her gaze. His eyes were warm pools of chocolate that she wanted to melt into. "Very much."

"Then I'm asking, Sierra."

She tilted her face toward his. "Asking for what?"

"This." He bent and his lips traced hers, whisper light, then stilled. "May I?"

She breathed the words into his mouth. "Yes."

His lips moved gently over hers, then his arms drew her closer as he deepened the kiss.

He raised his head slightly. "That was the *longest* 4-H clinic I have ever sat through." He gave her another quick kiss and wrapped an arm around her shoulder as they started back for the parking lot.

"It wasn't easy for me, either!" She reached up and linked her fingers through his. "But worth it?"

He pulled her close against his side. "What do you think?"

She looked up, her eyes catching on his warm gaze. "Definitely." She looked toward her family, who stood near the trailer where Braden was loading Chance, and smiled.

Sometimes you have to let the fear catch up to let it go.

... a little more ...

When a delightful concert comes to an end,

the orchestra might offer an encore.

When a fine meal comes to an end,

it's always nice to savor a bit of dessert.

When a great story comes to an end,

we think you may want to linger.

And so, we offer ...

AfterWords—just a little something more after you

have finished a David C. Cook novel.

We invite you to stay awhile in the story.

Thanks for reading!

Turn the page for ...

• A Conversation with Sherri Sand

A Conversation with Sherri Sand

How did you come up with the characters in your book?

They came to me. When I saw Sierra, I knew she was a mom who deeply loved her kids and wanted the best for them. Elise was so fun to write with her over-the-top ways. When she drove up to Sierra's and pushed her ooga horn, I knew I was going to love her. And Sid is such a dear and reminds me so much of my father-in-law, Art. And Ross, how could you not love him?

Do you have a horse?

No, but I love horses and desperately wanted one as a child. I did end up with a little Shetland pony named Sundance that I would gallop through the mint fields around our house. I spent countless hours sprawled across him backwards reading books. One time he'd apparently had enough of the dead weight on his back and he lay down. It was a shocking end to my reading time.

What do you do when you're not writing?

I love spending time with my family. We go camping as many weekends as we can in the summer. I also love to run. My husband recently got into running and we were asked to be on a team that participates in a race from Mt. Hood to the coast of Oregon. It generally takes about twenty-two hours, so our idea of fun may be a little warped.

What would you suggest to someone who wants to become an author?

Start attending writers' conferences. And if cost is an issue, order tapes or CDs of the various workshops. Also join a critique group and really listen to the feedback. When I get input from my critiquing partners, I make a point to set aside any defensiveness and adopt a thicker skin. It's not fun to find out that every word you write isn't brilliant, but if you take the comments constructively you'll become a stronger writer.

How do you find time to write? Any tips for someone who is working full time?

Set a word count goal. I try to write 1,000 words a day, five days a week. If finding the extra time is difficult, start with 300 words a day. At that pace, you'd complete a full-length novel (80,000 words) in one year. But the most important factor in writing is to turn the editor in your head off. Writer's block comes from trying to create and edit at the same time. Don't wait for the perfect idea to come floating along. Start writing now. Write anything. You want to create the habit so the ideas will come. The fear of failure keeps us from giving feet to our dreams—true failure comes from not trying at all.

Did the theme of forgiveness/unforgiveness that Sierra deals with come from your own life?

In a way it did, though I didn't consciously implement it into the novel. Like most of us living in this fallen world, there were a couple significant events in my life that I had difficulty forgiving. I finally realized that if I waited until I felt like forgiving, it would never happen. And I desperately needed to forgive. The bitterness was choking the life out of me. So with God's help and through His grace I made the choice to forgive and forgive and forgive. I wish I could say that there was instant peace and joy. Though I think that can happen for people, I'd lived in unforgiveness for so long that I had to continually make a choice to forgive until the freedom came. And when that freedom came, it was a wow moment for me!

In the story, Sierra has three young kids. You have four children. How successful are you at trusting God with their lives?

It's been an ongoing process for me. Maybe because I'm a writer and have such a vivid imagination, I can always come up with the most gut-wrenching conclusions to the most innocuous circumstances involving my kids. That makes it hard to let go and trust. But how much control do we actually have over everyday life? I had to learn that before we can trust God with ourselves or our children, we have to truly know Him. It's only in knowing God and His character that trust can develop. And when we truly know the God of the universe, we can trust Him with everything.

Ross worked hard in his landscaping business in an attempt to prove his value. Do you struggle with that?

It's difficult not to get caught up in that. Our world is performance driven. Our praise of others is usually tied to something they've accomplished. Even with our children, we praise how well they unload the dishwasher or draw a picture or mind us. It's difficult to find the words to value people for who they are, apart from anything they do. For most of my life, performance colored my relationship with God. I could not wrap my mind around the concept that He loved me despite less-than-perfect behaviors. Recently I glimpsed His grace from a new angle. Sin does create a righteous anger, but God's anger was satisfied at the cross. So rather than His anger at our sinfulness, we have His pleasure in us. That has done wonders with my ability to be myself with Him, to honestly let His light shine on all parts of me—the good and the unsightly. When you bring your faults to God and discover He isn't displeased, you can fully experience His compassion and love.

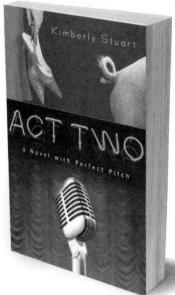